TORTURED
BY HER TOUCH

BY
DIANNE DRAKE

IT HAPPENED
IN VEGAS

BY
AMY RUTTAN

ARMY DOCS

Two brothers, divided by conflict,
meet the women who will change their lives...for ever!

Army medics Marc and Nick Rousseau
were at the top of their field when they were
caught in an IED explosion in Afghanistan that left
Marc paralysed and Nick unscathed. Now out of the
army, the estranged brothers are on opposite sides of the
country and struggling to put the past behind them...
until they each meet a woman
who challenges them in unimaginable ways.

Now, as these generous and caring women
open the brothers' eyes to new worlds of possibility,
can Marc and Nick finally forgive the past
and reclaim the bond they once shared?

Don't miss the *Army Docs* duet
by Mills & Boon® Medical Romance™ authors
Dianne Drake and Amy Ruttan

Read Marc and Anne's story in
Tortured by Her Touch

Read Nick and Jennifer's story in
It Happened in Vegas

Available from March 2015!

TORTURED BY HER TOUCH

BY
DIANNE DRAKE

First published in Great Britain 2015
by Mills & Boon, an imprint of Harlequin (UK) Limited,
Eton House, 18-24 Paradise Road, Richmond, Surrey, TW9 1SR

© 2015 Dianne Despain

ISBN: 978-0-263-24694-0

Printed and bound in Spain
by CPI, Barcelona

Dear Reader,

Back in the day, when I was actively pursuing a nursing career, I worked at the Veterans' Hospital. The patients I was fortunate enough to serve were a wholly amazing and heroic group of men and women. It always amazed me to watch them fight their battles with such courage.

When I was asked to write this book I knew immediately where my setting had to be. It was an honour to pay tribute to the brave soldiers who had once been under my care. Especially in the persona of Marc Rousseau, a doctor who comes home from the war badly damaged. My story is inspired by two people I know—people who fell in love despite great obstacles. David is a paraplegic who married his nurse—an inspiring story because the disability was never part of their relationship. True love sees no boundaries.

My heroine, Anne, never sees the disability in the man she loves. All she wants to do is encourage him—the way all people in love want to encourage each other. It's a story of two people coming to terms with *love*, not disability.

I'd like to thank Mills and Boon for giving me the opportunity to show that love can shine through adversity.

Wishing you health and happiness…

Dianne

PS Please feel free to email me at DianneDrake@earthlink.net or connect to my Facebook page or Twitter account through links posted to my website at dianne-drake.com

Now that her children have left home, **Dianne Drake** is finally finding the time to do some of the things she adores—gardening, cooking, reading, shopping for antiques. Her absolute passion in life, however, is adopting abandoned and abused animals. Right now Dianne and her husband, Joel, have a little menagerie of three dogs and two cats, but that's always subject to change. A former symphony orchestra member, Dianne now attends the symphony as a spectator several times a month and, when time permits, takes in an occasional football, basketball or hockey game.

Books by Dianne Drake

A Home for the Hot-Shot Doc
A Doctor's Confession
A Child to Heal Their Hearts
PS You're a Daddy
Revealing the Real Dr Robinson
The Doctor's Lost-and-Found Heart
No. 1 Dad in Texas
The Runaway Nurse

**Visit the author profile page
at millsandboon.co.uk for more titles**

CHAPTER ONE

"AT FIRST THERE was nothing. I was running across the field, going after my brother Nick, who'd been given direct orders not to be out there, but had recklessly gone to rescue someone, and the next thing…"

Dr. Marc Rousseau swallowed hard and closed his eyes, as if trying to remember the day that had forever changed his life. Or destroyed it, depending upon which point of view you preferred. "He'd gone to rescue a buddy, and in the end he rescued me. Nick, the irresponsible one, could have gotten us both killed. He shouldn't have done it."

It was always there, always on his mind, if not on the edges, then running straight into it. That fateful day, as some might call it. He called it that day from hell. "It didn't trip immediately, so I wasn't directly on it. Thank God for that. But in the blink of an eye I was cold and hot at the same time. With these weird sensations. I mean, I knew right away there was pain, but I was so distanced from my body at that exact second I wasn't even relating that the injury had happened to me. And in my mind all I could do was think, *I need to help someone. I'm a doctor. I've got to go help someone.*

"It probably took me a good two minutes of lying out there on the battlefield before I realized I was the one who needed help. That I was the one who'd sustained the injury. The one who was screaming."

He picked up the glass of iced water sitting on the desk of the chief of staff and took a drink. "The hell of it was, even after I knew I'd been hit, I still had to be told. My body may have known it, but my mind wouldn't accept that my body gave in so easily. All I wanted to do was get back out there in the field and do what I was supposed to do, but I couldn't move, except for wiggling around in the dirt. And the blood…there was so much of it, but it couldn't have been mine. There was nothing inside me that allowed for the possibility that I was wounded. After all, I was the medic, a healer who'd volunteered to be there, not a soldier in the real sense of the word.

"Sure, I'd had my combat training, but my job was to put bodies back together, not to become one of those bodies. But I was, and I think I realized it for the first time—really realized it—when they brought the stretcher out for me. The people who worked for me were there to carry me off the battlefield."

"And how did that make you feel?" Dr. Jason Lewis asked. Jason was a kind man, about Marc's age—thirty-six—with thinning blond hair and wire-rimmed glasses. Whereas Marc was bulky and dark. Dark hair, dark eyes, dark expression that belied nothing but torture.

"How did I feel? I felt angry as hell at first. Like, how dare they do that to me! Don't they know that I fix everybody, including the people we're fighting?"

"But IEDs are impersonal. They're just meant to destroy whatever gets in their way."

"Tell me about it," Marc muttered.

"I don't suppose I really have to," the doctor replied. "So what happened after they came to rescue you?"

"They gave me a phone, told me to call anybody I liked. Girlfriend, parent, my brother, who was out there on that battlefield somewhere, trying to save lives."

"What for?"

"That's a protocol when they think you're going to die. I had a back full of shrapnel, nails, God only knows what else sticking in my spine. It's a bad sign, with so much bleeding, and I was bleeding out. My body was trying to die. There was so much trauma to my spine they didn't see how I'd survive it."

"But you obviously didn't die."

"Too much self-righteous indignation, I suppose. You go through these stages like after a death—denial, anger, all that crap. And I went straight to anger…"

"And stayed there?"

"A lot of the time, yes." He shrugged. "Don't like it, don't want to be there, but it happens, and that's something you need to know if you hire me."

"Do you really think that's the right attitude for someone who's applying to head one of the veteran outreach rehab programs?"

"Do you really think it's not?" he challenged the doctor. "Anger turned inward can be harmful, I suppose. But when you turn it outward on your situation, you can make it work for you. The angrier I got, the harder I worked. The harder I worked, the better I healed."

"Did it *really* work for you, Dr. Rousseau? I know you were a top-notch surgeon, and those days are now behind you. You'll never operate again, no matter how angry you get. How does that make you feel?"

"Mad as hell that someone had so much control over me as to change my life the way they did. I had a plan that got wasted, a life that got altered, and none of it was of my doing, so I'm angry, but I have that right. And like

I said, I fight it like I fight all my other battles. It's just one of the many, I suppose. And I won't even deny that I'd rather be a surgeon, but that's not going to happen."

"See, the thing is, I'm concerned that your bitterness will be a detriment to our patients—the ones who want to make it back all the way or the ones who are fighting to get back as much as they can. I don't want your anger or your personal preference in being a surgeon as opposed to a rehab doc influencing them. I don't even want them seeing it."

"It won't and they won't."

"How can I be sure of that?"

"I don't suppose you can when all you have is my word. But you do have my word. The thing is, I've made it back as far as I can go. Granted, I'm a paraplegic now, but who better to work with the men and women like me than me? I mean, I understand what it's like to have your life taken away from you and in its place you're given something that's going to fight you every day of your life. I know how hard you have to work just to keep your head above water. And that's where I'm coming from."

"But will your internal struggles prevent you from recognizing someone who's in such great depths of despair he or she might be contemplating suicide? Because we run into those patients every now and then."

"I contemplated it myself for a while, so I know the symptoms."

"What's 'a while'? Define that in terms of duration, if you will."

"Weeks, maybe. I wouldn't work at improving, and all I wanted to do was die. I mean, what was the point? I couldn't have what I wanted—my girlfriend had walked out on me because I was suddenly not what she wanted, my friends shunned me for fear they'd say or do the wrong thing. My family couldn't be around me without crying. My brother was so consumed with survivor's guilt he couldn't stand to look at me—he was an army doc who escaped the field in one piece and he was also the one who convinced me to join up. He blames himself for my condition because he disobeyed orders and ran out onto the battlefield. Finds it very difficult being around me now, even though I understand that's just the way my brother is. He blames himself for my condition because of it."

"Because of your disability or your attitude?"

"I'm not deluding myself, Doctor. It was my attitude, but my attitude was precipitated by my disability. So I turned my back on the people who still cared—so much so they couldn't stand to be around me any longer. They tried and I pushed them away."

Marc shifted positions in his wheelchair, raised himself up with massive arms, then lowered himself again. "There were questions about how much ability I'd regain, whether or not I'd be able to take care of myself, find a new life, function as a man… It's overwhelming, and it scared me, and the more frightened I was, the more I just wanted it all to end. But I'm not a quitter and that quitting attitude just made me angry, which pushed me harder to prove I was OK. It's been a vicious circle, as you can see. Was then, still is. But I get through it."

"Then you're not over it?"

"I can cope with it now. But I do need to stay busy and find something other than myself to focus on, which is why I retrained, served a second residency at Boston Mercy Hospital, and why I'm sitting here, applying for this job."

"Meaning you're going to take all that pent-up frustration and turn yourself into a first-class rehab doctor."

"Amazing what a healthy dose of anger can do, isn't it? You know what they say…" Marc's eyes went distant for a second, but for only a second. "What doesn't kill you makes you stronger. Well, it hasn't killed me so far."

"I saw your records, talked to your chief resident at Boston Mercy General. You did a good job there, but what makes you think you can translate that into doing a good job here, where you're a full staff member with staff responsibilities as well as administrative duties?"

"I know how to lead, and people do listen to me. And as they say, I've got street cred now. If you came into your clinic, who would you rather listen to—someone like you who's never experienced anything more than a shaving cut, or me?"

"You've got a good point, Dr. Rousseau."

The man was trying to get his goat. He knew that. But he also knew Jason Lewis had the right to prod as hard as he wanted since what he was going to get was basically a brand-new doctor in the field. "Good enough to offer me the position?" They'd been talking back and forth for weeks—by phone, on the internet, texting. This whole interview process was dragging him down. He knew he was a liability—a great big one. But he also knew he was a good doctor. So which one outweighed the other?

Lewis laughed. "I will say you've got guts to go along with your attitude."

"And that's all I'll need to get through to some of these guys and gals. So offer me a job on the spot, and I'll see what I can do to curb my attitude."

"On the spot? You want me to offer you a job on the

spot without going to the board first, or talking to the people who will be working closest with you?"

Marc arched his eyebrows. "You've got the power, haven't you? And it's not like this interview process hasn't been going on in some form for quite a while."

"Oh, I've got the power, but I'm still not sure you're the right candidate."

"Let's see. I've got administrative experience, I'm a good doctor, I have practical experience… What more do you need?"

Dr. Lewis shook his head. "On paper you're the perfect candidate."

"But?"

"But I don't want this clinic turning out a whole battalion of *you*. And I'm afraid that's what you're going to do."

"In other words, you don't believe I have the ability to separate my personal from my professional life. So tell me, are you able to do that? Do you never take your work home with you or bring your personal life to work?"

"Most days I'm good," Lewis said.

"And most days, I will be, too. All I've got is my word. I know I've got some attitude adjustments to make still, but that could also be a strength in helping my patients, in making them understand how they're not the only ones. So, on the spot?" He held out a confident hand to shake with Dr. Lewis.

Lewis took in a deep breath, let it out slowly, and extended his hand to Marc. "On the spot, but it's a probationary spot. Three months to start with, then a reevaluation."

"That's all I can ask for," Marc said. "Thank you."

"I'm warning you, Rousseau, when you're on my

time you're a rehab doctor, nothing more, nothing less. Do you understand me?"

Marc nodded. "So I'm assuming my office is more accessible than yours because this one is too small for good maneuverability?" Inwardly, he was pleased by the offer. Now all he had to do was see if it was a match made in heaven or hell.

Anne Sebastian looked out her window at the gardens stretching as far as she could see. But it wasn't the garden she was seeing. In fact, she was seeing red! "Seriously, you hired him to head physical rehab?"

Jason Lewis shrugged. "He has the qualifications we need."

"And an attitude that precedes him. I have a friend at Mercy who said—"

"He'll adjust," Jason interrupted. "In spite of what you've heard, he'll fall into our routine nicely."

"And if he doesn't?" she asked, too perplexed to turn around to confront her brother-in-law.

"Then I'll fire him, the way I would any other staff member who becomes a detriment to the facility or its patients."

She spun around. "No, you won't. It's not in you to do something like that. Especially since he's a wounded soldier."

"Then we'll just have to keep our fingers crossed he works out, won't we?"

Anne heaved a dubious sigh. "Hannah married a real softie. You know that, don't you?"

Jason blushed. "You do know that no one else on my staff talks to me the way you do?"

"Family prerogative. Besides, she's confined to bed until she delivers, so, as your wife's twin sister, older by eight minutes, might I remind you, it's up to me to make sure things are running the way they should."

Anne was an internist who'd earned an additional PhD in psychology, and turned her medical practice into one that specialized in post-traumatic stress disorder. Her sister, an ear specialist, worked with combat vets who'd suffered hearing loss due to trauma. And Jason was also a radiologist who oversaw all the X-rays generated in his clinic.

Jason overexaggerated a wince. "A daughter. Between you two and her, I'll never be able to win an argument."

"Poor Jason," Anne teased.

"Poor Jason is right. Speaking of which, our new hire, Marc Rousseau…"

"Do we have to talk about the man?"

"Not if you don't want to. But since your office is going to be close to his, I was hoping you'd show him some consideration."

"Consideration?" she asked. "If you mean taking him on as a case…"

"Not as a case. As a colleague who, like you, started over. It wasn't easy for you. Remember? Anyway, he comes with glowing references as a doctor and miserable mentions as a human being. He admits his anger. Almost embraces it. But to get his skills, we take the whole package. That's all there is. Promise. No underhanded scheme to try and fix him or anything like that. Just be his friend. Make him aware that he's welcome here."

"Why *did* you hire him, Jason, when you've got so many doubts?"

"Because he can unquestionably do the job. That's my first consideration. And I'm also thinking that he's one of the soldiers who got overlooked in the process. It happens every day, Anne, and you know that better than anybody else. We get the worst ones, the ones who can't function, for whatever reason. With one in every eight soldiers suffering from PTSD and only about thirty percent of those ever getting help, the rest are living in a personal hell.

"They could benefit from what we do here, and I happen to think Marc Rousseau might be great at spotting troubling issues others have missed. He's perceptive." He raised teasing eyebrows. "And who better to put a man in his place if he needs it than you?"

She winced. "All it takes is a bad marriage. Want to hear my opinions on that?"

Jason smiled sympathetically. "Ah, Bill. The vanquished husband. I could go beat him up if that makes you feel any better."

"I'm sounding like the one with the rotten attitude, aren't I?"

"You've been through your share of misery."

"And come through it wiser than I was."

"Look, I know the divorce was tough, but you never let it affect your work when you were going through the various aspects of it. I gave you the benefit of the doubt and hired you pretty much untested in PTSD because I believed in you, and I'd hope you'd do the same for Marc. Give him the same chance I gave you."

"Tough divorce is an understatement. It was devastating, discovering how many times Bill cheated on me when I was overseas."

"And you're better off being rid of him."

"I am, but still…" She shrugged. "Look, I know Rousseau by the reputation that precedes him, but I wouldn't recognize him if he walked right by me, and I'm still a little on edge."

"Then you don't know?" Jason frowned. "I'd assumed since you knew he was a returning wounded soldier…"

"Know what?"

"Marc Rousseau is a paraplegic. Incomplete, lower injury. Full sensation, but not enough muscle recovery to get his legs back under him."

Anne's eyes widened. "Bad attitude and disabled?"

"Well, for sure, if you can survive working with him, you'll regain some of the self-confidence you lost in the divorce mess. But the man is worth saving because he's a damned good doctor and I want him to work out here, Anne. We need him as much as he needs us. So, besides your self-confidence, I'll give you a trophy or something for enduring him."

"Damn the disability…"

Jason laughed. "It gets you in the soft spot every time, doesn't it?"

"How did it happen?"

"He was a medic, got hit by shrapnel…nails, wire, that kind of stuff…from an IED. Was a pretty bad injury, touch and go for a while. But luckily—if you can call anything about it lucky—his injury could have been worse. He's pretty independent. In fact, the only thing he can't do is walk."

"And that's not going to happen?"

Jason shook his head. "He's in the chair for the count."

"With a lot of anger issues you're attributing to PTSD."

"He worked through the physical end of it like a man possessed, but he neglected…himself. Lost himself in the whole affair. Which is a damn shame because he saved lives, was commended as a battlefield surgeon."

Anne walked over to her desk and sat down. "OK, I'll cut him some slack, but only some. That's the best I can offer you right now."

"He's going to be spotting a lot of your patients and referring them to you. You do realize that, don't you?"

She nodded.

"And I'm not going to soft-pedal this. He'll be a challenge, Anne, but, unlike Bill and all his affairs, it won't be directed at you."

All Bill's affairs. She'd been overseas in one medical capacity or another for three tours, while the husband who'd vowed to be true had been tracked to nine different affairs. Even Bill's attorney hadn't tried too hard to help him during nearly a year of divorce proceedings. "I can take on a challenge as long as it's not personal," Anne replied. "And apart from a husband having all those affairs while his wife was off, serving her country, I don't think anything could be much more challenging than that."

"I really want Marc stable enough to stay with us," Jason said. "We need someone who's been through it so he can get to others who are going through what he did."

"I know. And you're right. So I'll be on my good behavior with him."

"And you'll help him get acclimated to the way we do things here?"

"Yes," she answered. "But he's got to meet me halfway."

"That takes believing in himself. And what better way to do that than being involved in his job?"

"When does he start?"

"He's started. I couldn't see any reason to put him off. I hired him on the spot and sent him down to his office."

"Then there was no point to this discussion."

Jason smiled. "You're my other volatile physician, so I thought I'd give you fair warning. Let's just call it a family courtesy."

"Speaking of which, tell Hannah I'll be by soon," Anne said as Jason headed to her door, leaving her to study her surroundings. She loved this place, loved the contemporary chrome look. Most of all, she loved the Gallahue Rehabilitation Center for Veterans for the good work it did. It was small, limited in the cases it could take. But the services it offered, thanks largely to Maynard and Lois Gallahue in memory of their fallen son, were amazing and much more extensive than one might expect from a relatively small clinic. And waiting lists for admittance were long.

Rumors had it the Gallahue Foundation for returning wounded soldiers would be upping its contribution, and she'd heard other notable companies were making funds available. So, as far as Anne was concerned, the sky here was the limit. She hoped so, anyway, because she saw the work being done every day. Witnessed firsthand the miracles.

"Got a minute?" she asked a little while later, poking her head through the semi-open door that read "John Hemmings" in gold letters and would soon read "Marc Rousseau".

"Depends on what you want to do with that minute. If you've come to gawk, then, no, I don't have a minute." Marc looked up at her. "If you've come to be sociable, I'm not sociable. And if you've come about a patient, I haven't even figured out how to fill out all my employment forms, so patients are a no-go as well for the next day or so."

His office was sparse—a desk with a chair shoved

into the corner, empty shelves, no diplomas. It was as if the man didn't exist. But he did, and she couldn't help but admire his massive, muscular arms, and the way his reading glasses slid to the end of his nose, revealing clear, dark brown eyes. And his hair cut…longish, over the collar, dark brown as well. He was goose-bumps-up-the-arm handsome, but the attitude…wow, was it bad!

"So, have you had enough time to get what you came for?" he asked her.

"What do you mean?"

"Your first glimpse of a doctor in a wheelchair."

Truth was, she hadn't even noticed the wheelchair.

"That's why I didn't stand to greet you. Can't." He shrugged indifferent shoulders. "Don't particularly want to, either."

"You are a piece of work, Dr. Rousseau."

He stared at her over the top of his glasses for a moment. Appraising her. Taking in every last little bit. "So how would you like it if someone came to your office just to look at your blond hair…?" Shoulder length with a slight wave. "Or your green eyes. How would you like that, Miss…?"

"*Dr.* Anne Sebastian."

"How would you like that, *Dr.* Sebastian?"

"Actually, if a man wants to look, it's not a big deal."

"If you were in a wheelchair, it would be."

"Then that's who you are? Who you want to be known as? The doctor in the wheelchair?"

"Your minute's up," he said, pushing his glasses back up his nose and turning his attention to the mountains of employment paperwork on his desk.

"Then give me another minute."

"And the reason for that would be?"

"Lunch?" She heard herself say the words, and

couldn't believe they'd come out of her mouth. What in the world had possessed her?

"Seriously? You want to have lunch with me? Or did you draw the short straw and you're the one elected to be nice to the disabled guy?"

"Believe me, if that was the reason, I'd be the first one backing out of it and running away. And I do mean running because I'm not about to give in to your poor-me-in-a-wheelchair attitude and cop some wary attitude when I'm forced to be around you."

Marc actually laughed. "My reputation really has preceded me, hasn't it?"

"Let's just say that one of your former colleagues at Mercy wished me luck and said something to the effect that it was better me than her."

"If I were insulted, I'd try to guess which one, but I really don't give a damn because this is a job and I'm not here to win a popularity contest."

"Trust me, you'd come in last place."

He actually gave her a genuinely nice smile. "Is your motive really just to ask me to lunch?"

Her heart fluttered just a bit all because of a single smile. "Someone has to."

"I can carry my own tray."

"In our doctors' dining room we have table service. Otherwise, by the end of the week, I'm sure someone would have already dumped their tray on your head."

"Lucky for me," he said as he wheeled out from behind his desk. "And just so you'll know, I'm an incomplete, I have full sensation, full function, except for walking."

"And just so you'll know, I don't give a damn about your sensation or your function or any other *man* things you might wish to confide."

"Man hater, are you? Or do you prefer the ladies?"

"Oh, I prefer men. Just not right now and not for the foreseeable future."

"I'm assuming it's a long, sad story," he said as he followed Anne to the hall.

"Longest and saddest. And the rest of it's none of your business."

"You know how hospital staff talks," he said, shutting the door behind him.

"Let 'em talk. Better them than me." Surprisingly, he picked up a brisk pace, one she found quite difficult to keep up with. Was he testing her or trying to prove something? Admittedly, he did have a lot of strength, and the way he wheeled was something to behold, something athletic.

"Keep up," he said, slowing his pace a little. "I don't know where the dining room is, and I'm trusting that you're going to show me sometime this afternoon. But at that slow pace…"

"Just shut up and wheel," she said as a smile crept to her face. Yes, he was going to be a challenge. Maybe her biggest one ever. But he did have a grudge to work out, and a whole lot of anger he was going to have to learn to curb. Without therapy! Now, that was the part that was going to be difficult for her—just as Jason had anticipated—not getting involved in such a way as to help him solve his issues.

"By the way, since you asked me to lunch, you are paying for it, aren't you?"

"Seriously?" she said, fighting back a laugh. If she did get through to this hulk of a man, Jason was going to owe her big time. Big, big time!

CHAPTER TWO

"I UNDERSTAND YOU met him," Jason said to Anne.

"He sat at one end of a table for eight, I sat at the other. Nobody sat between us. And we didn't talk. Not one word. I paid for his lunch and when he was through eating, he left. Thanked me for my hospitality and simply left."

"But other than that, how was he?"

"Rude, arrogant, obnoxious, fixed on his work to the point of not even noticing anybody else there." Her office was adjacent to her treatment room, and both were very relaxed and cozy. An immediate warm feeling drifted down over most of her patients when they came in, and that was done on purpose. Her walls were medium blue, her furniture a lighter blue accented in white, and the music piped in was a soothing Vivaldi or Bach. Atmosphere made a difference in so many of her cases, and she tried hard to achieve that comfort, as comfort equated to trust.

"But workable?"

"That, I don't know. He's as resistant a person as I've ever met. So this one is going to be the flip of a coin."

"But you'll try, since the majority of your referrals will come from him?"

"For a while. But if I see that he's not working out,

you'll hear from me, Jason. And probably not just me."
Just as that threat rolled off her tongue, she received
a text. When she checked it, it said: "See. I don't bite.
Lunch tomorrow?"

Anne sighed.

"What?" Jason asked.

"Nothing. Just an invite to lunch tomorrow," she said,
forcing a smile. "Lucky me."

Jason headed for the door. "Just be careful, Anne,
and you'll be fine."

"Don't worry. I can handle him." *How* was the question, though, especially since Jason seemed to have
made her the one-person welcome committee, probably owing to her background in psychiatry. If the shrink
couldn't handle him, no one else could, either. What an
assumption!

It was going on to seven that evening when Anne finally
decided to call it quits. Long days were her norm, especially since she had nothing or no one to go home to. But
that was OK because the last time she'd had someone
to go home to, he'd been going to other homes. A lot
of them. And it made her wonder how she could have
been so truly wrong about the man.

Had she expected him to stay faithful while she was
overseas? Of course she had. She would have. In fact,
she'd been faithful when he'd been the one overseas,
fighting, and she'd been stateside, working in a military
hospital. It would have never occurred to her to cheat
on him, and now she went home to a big, empty house
every night, fixed herself a microwave dinner, caught
up on some reading, showered and went to bed.

Big night. And nights were the worst, which was why

she put in at least a dozen hours a day at the hospital. It was better than going home.

Flipping off the lights, she opened up the door and nearly tripped over Marc, who was merely sitting outside her office door. "What do you want?" she snapped.

"You bought me lunch, so I owe you a meal. Dinner?"

"You don't owe me anything." Her heart skipped a beat as she did like the idea of eating with him but she didn't want to sound too anxious.

"Maybe an apology for being such a jerk today."

"Apology accepted. Now, if you'll excuse me…"

"Married, divorced from a lousy cheater, work longer hours than any other doc at Gallahue. I'm betting your evening consists of a microwave dinner and reading medical journals until you fall asleep."

"I do watch the eleven o'clock news."

"The epitome of a boring life. Which is why I thought dinner with me is better than dinner with the microwave. Besides, I have some questions to ask you."

"If they pertain to the hospital, ask Jason."

"Don't you find him a little boring?" Marc asked.

"As a chief of staff or as my brother-in-law? Because I'm actually quite fine with him in both capacities."

"Ah, a family tie."

"He's married to my twin sister, so that makes him family."

"And you spend all the holidays with them, right?"

"How did you know about my divorce?" she asked.

"People talk."

"But you haven't even started to practice here yet."

"And like I said, people talk."

"They talk to people who give them a warm and

fuzzy feeling, and you haven't got a warm or fuzzy feeling in you."

"Then it has to be the other thing."

"What other thing?"

"People don't see you when you're in a wheelchair. For some reason, you're invisible to them, so they talk around you."

"And people are talking about me?"

"About how your divorce became final recently. Apparently, he's been fighting you for everything, but you won. Left the man practically destitute."

"People know too much," she snapped. "It was an ugly divorce. But since he's the one who deserted the marriage and left me holding a whole lot of hard feelings, and debt, what can I say other than I'm glad he got everything that's coming to him?"

"And you're going to get…"

"First, sell my house. Then buy a nice little cottage, maybe take up gardening. I'd like a cat, too."

"A cat?"

She smiled. "Everything that makes life nice."

"No man?"

"Absolutely not! Been there, don't want to go back."

"Good, then I'm not taking out another man's woman to dinner tonight."

"I didn't accept your invitation, and I don't intend to."

"Because we're not compatible?" That was an understatement.

"Because I don't particularly like you."

Rather than being angry, Marc smiled. "Do you realize how many people actually put up with me and my attitude just because I'm in a wheelchair? They find that if they deny me or do something other than what I want, they're doing something deeply wrong or offensive. The man's a wounded war veteran and it's important to appease him."

"Appease you? Let me tell you, your wheelchair's not off-putting, Marc. But your attitude is. So thanks for the invitation but I'd rather curl up with a good medical journal than suffer another meal with you." With that, she strode away, the sound of angry heels clicking on the floor tile. Rather than frowning, though, a slight smile actually turned up the corners of her lips. This was going to be interesting.

"Well, then, we'll stick to the plan. I'll see you at lunch tomorrow."

She turned back to give him a stiff glare, but what came off was more confused than anything, and she hated wearing her emotions on her sleeve, as they always sent out the wrong impression. "Not if your life depended on it, Marc Rousseau," she said, trying to remain rigid, although her insides were quivering. "Not if your life depended on it!"

Anne snuggled down on her sofa with a glass of white grape juice and a medical journal and a soft Schubert quintet playing in the background. She wasn't really so physically tired as she was mentally stressed. Nothing had gone well today. Two of her patients had had emotional breaks—big ones. One had tried to jump out her window until he remembered her office was on the first floor, and then he'd simply smashed furniture. After which he'd apologized and offered to pay for the damages. The other had sat in her office and wept uncontrollably for over an hour, until she'd finally had him sedated and checked in for a night of observation. Shutting her eyes, she rotated her ankles for a moment, then sank further back into the sofa pillows, not sure if, when the time came, she'd be able to get up and make it all the way upstairs to the bedroom.

She really did hate this house. Hated everything in it because it stood for a happier time—a time when love had been fresh and exciting and she'd known it would last forever. And it wasn't like Bill hadn't known she'd be serving overseas when he'd asked her to marry him. He'd be good with it, he'd claimed. There was nothing for her to worry about.

Stupid her, she'd believed him. And on her first leave, she'd come back to a marriage she'd believed was as stable as it had ever been in their three years. But on her second trip stateside he'd seemed more remote. He'd claimed he was tired, too much work, just getting over a cold…there'd been a whole string of excuses, but by the end of her leave, things had been normal again, and she'd returned overseas happy to know that the next time she came home it would be for good.

But when that day came, she'd found earrings in a drawer on her side of the bed. And a bra. And panties. It had seemed, as the days had gone by, there had been more and more excuses for Bill to invent. None of them plausible. Then her neighbor, an older lady, had commented on the succession of housekeepers who'd come and gone at odd hours of the day and night. "Sometimes two, three times a week!" Mrs. Gentry had exclaimed.

One check with the cleaning service confirmed her suspicion. The cleaning service cleaned every Friday morning. Once a week. No more, no less. Her accountant had verified that with the checks that had been written. He'd also recommended the best lawyer in Port Duncan, New York.

"Protect your assets, Anne. Bill's been doing a lot

of spending while you were gone, and if you want to keep anything for yourself, it's time to lawyer up." Said by James Callahan, the attorney she'd hired that day.

Through it all, though, Anne had been numb. She had been unable to function. Betrayal. Fragments of memories left over from Afghanistan. Things she hadn't been able to forget…or fix. No, it hadn't made sense, but it had seemed like her world had been closing in around her. She'd been unable to breathe half the time. The other half of the time, she hadn't been able to quit crying. Vicious circle. Every day. Sucking the life out of her every day. Little pieces of it just falling away, one at a time.

She'd almost been at the point of complete breakdown when she'd realized she couldn't control what was happening to her, so she'd sought counseling. Her condition hadn't been diagnosed as PTSD, but the emotional conflict had given her a deep understanding of those who did suffer through it—the confusion, the anger, the pain. After seeing it on the field and coming up to the edge of it herself, before she'd realized it, she'd been in a PhD program, coupling what she knew as an MD with learning about stress disorders. It had seemed a logical place for her to be. Where she'd wanted to be.

For that part of her life, she'd put her divorce on hold and concentrated only on herself. Fixing herself first, retraining herself second. Of course, her intention had been to restart divorce proceedings once the rest of it was behind her. One trauma at a time was what she'd learned. Deal with one at a time. And while Bill had been a problem, he hadn't been a trauma. In fact, getting rid of him would be her easiest fix.

So then, a whole year after she'd decided to take that fix, he'd come after her, claiming that her being gone had caused him PTSD. Of all the low, miserable things to do…

"But he learned," she said as she shut her book and decided she was comfortable right where she was. "When I got through with him, he'd learned to pick his women dumb and dependent. God forbid he should ever get a fighter again or she might do worse to him than I did."

Sighing, she shut her eyes, and while she expected to go to sleep with visions of Bill in her choke hold filling her dreams, the person there tonight was…Marc. And he was smiling.

"Nice smile," she whispered as she dozed off. Yes, it was a very nice smile to go to sleep with.

He'd been in bed two hours now, alternately staring at the ceiling, then watching the green numbers on the digital clock. The harder he tried to sleep, the more he couldn't. Marc's first thought was a nice cup of hot herbal tea—something soothing. Then in his mind he added brandy to it, just a sip, but the problem with that was he wasn't a drinker. Never had been. No booze, no pills. Just a bad attitude to get him through.

So what got Anne through? he wondered. She seemed pretty straightforward. Even functional, considering her divorce.

"Some people are made to be more functional," he told his orange-striped tomcat named Sarge, who was stretched out on the bed, snoozing quite contentedly. Sarge was huge, a Maine Coon weighing in at twenty-five pounds. He'd been cowering on Marc's doorstep one day, all beaten and bloody, and there hadn't been a muscle or sinew in Marc's body that could have shut the door on him because he'd known exactly how the cat had felt—defeated. So he'd taken him in, nursed him back to health, yet hadn't named him, as his intention had been to turn him over to a no-kill rescue shelter for adoption.

Except the damned cat had these soulful big green eyes that Marc had been unable to resist. So he'd eventually called him Sarge, mostly because his huge size reminded him of an overwhelmingly large and tender-hearted sergeant he'd had working for him in Afghanistan, and he and the cat had become best buddies.

"She's something, Sarge," he told the cat as he pulled a can of cat tuna off the shelf. "And so damn obvious it's laughable. The lady's in charge of the PTSD program, and I'm sure I'm supposed to be her secret conquest." He chuckled as he filled the cat bowl and laid it on the floor at the back door to his apartment—a door never used, due to the six steps down. Management had offered to ramp it for him, but he'd told them, no, that one door was plenty. He lived a Spartan life, didn't need people fawning all over him. Especially his family. He wondered where Nick was right now. Maybe living it up somewhere and doing every dumb thing in the book just to prove he could. He shuddered, thinking about his brother's lifestyle. Wild. Carefree. Nothing mattered. Most of all, he wondered if Nick even appreciated the freedom he had to do so many stupid things.

Whatever the case, his parents, Jane and Henry, had been ready to drop everything to take care of him, but that was too clingy. No phone calls or texts, he'd said. He was fine. No sad faces, no mother's tears, no over-compensation from his dad. A cat was good, though. You fed him, watered him, changed his pan, and he didn't give a hang whether or not all that came from a paraplegic or someone who could walk.

And he never should have asked Anne Sebastian out, not even for a make-good on a very miserable lunch. What had he expected? That she'd actually want to go with him after he'd been so obnoxious? "I deserved it," he told the cat, who was busy gulping down his food. "I'm not exactly dating material and, God knows, I don't have friends." But for one brief moment, he'd actually thought a couple hours with Anne might be nice.

So much for thinking. So much for anything that resembled a normal life. This was it. A tiny apartment, a cat and an SUV that had been fixed for him to drive. Yep, that was his life. Except he did have a job to add to that mix now. Admittedly, he was looking forward to the work, to having the chance to help others like himself. "Time to go do the weights," he said to his cat as he spun his chair around and went to the second bedroom, which had been turned into a workout room. "Wanna come spot me, Sarge?" he called out. The cat's response was to simply stop in the hall outside the workout room and wash his face.

"Some friend you are!"

"He's interesting," Anne said to Hannah, her twin sister, the next evening. Hannah was now confined to bed as much as possible as she was nearing her due date and she'd been diagnosed with gestational diabetes. Anne perched herself on the side of the bed with a carton of ice cream and two spoons, ready to eat their favorite— vanilla fudge. Even at the age of thirty-five, they were still identical in every way that counted, right down to the clothes they picked out and the food they liked and disliked.

"Jason said he's pretty bitter."

"I suppose I would be, too, if that had happened to

me. I mean, I deal with returning soldiers every day who come back just like Dr. Rousseau...like him and worse. I was lucky. All I had to come back to was..."

"How is Bill, by the way?"

"Even though the divorce is final, he's still fighting me just as hard as ever." Anne wrung her hands nervously, then continued on in a shaky voice, "For two cents, I'd just hand it all over to him and walk away, but my attorney believes I'm entitled to my share since I was the one off fighting for my country while Bill was spending his time on the golf course and in our bed, so he's not going to let Bill go back and amend the settlement."

She shrugged, then patted her sister's enormous belly. "Glad we never had children to enter into the mix. Don't know how I would have handled having to have interaction with him because of a child. This way, I don't ever have to deal with him again. I just refer him to my lawyer." She let out a ragged sigh. "It's better that way."

"But children are going to be nice."

"For you. And I predict I'm going to make a great aunt. Spoil the baby rotten, then send her home to her mother."

"Instead of dating? You know, going out, having fun. Have a life. It's been a long time coming."

"But I'm not really going to do the dating thing for a while, if ever."

"You may change your mind," Hannah said as she scooped a spoon of ice cream from the container. "When you meet the right man, or realize you've already met him."

"Who? Marc?"

Hannah shrugged.

"Ha! Those pregnancy hormones have gone to your brain and left you with an imagination as big as your belly."

Hannah shrugged again. "Maybe you're right, maybe you're not."

"You're the acquiescent one, Hannah, and I'm—"

"The stubborn one," Hannah supplied. "I know. But relationships don't always make sense. Don't follow a logical pattern."

"Tell me about it. Look what I fell for the first time around." Anne winced. She'd fallen head over heels in days, maybe in minutes. Had married in mere weeks. "Yeah, well, next time, if there is a next time, I won't be looking for perfection as much as compatibility. Too bad Jason is taken, because I think you got the last good man. He doesn't happen to have a secret brother hidden somewhere, does he?"

Hannah laughed. "Men like that don't stay available too long, sis. I'm lucky I got Jason when I did because it was only a matter of time until some other fortunate woman would have plucked him off the market."

Anne couldn't help but wonder if Marc had been married or engaged or near the plucking stage prior to his accident. "Well, right now I have a nemesis who's going to fight me every step of the way and that's the only man I want to contend with for a while. And, trust me, that's enough for anyone."

"He'll come round," Hannah said, taking another bite of ice cream. "Once he gets settled into the routine, you'll persuade him. Or let's say out-stubborn him. Poor man doesn't even know what's headed his direction."

Anne jabbed her spoon into the ice cream. "I think he's equal to it. And I think he's going to be lots of fun," she said with a sarcastic grimace on her face to Hannah. "About as much fun as a sticker bush with large stickers."

CHAPTER THREE

His apartment wasn't much in the way of square footage, but it didn't matter because there wasn't much that he needed in this world and that included space. But he did have to admit that his office was everything he could have wanted, and more. It was spacious, accessible. Larger than his apartment, actually.

"You like it?" Anne asked as she followed him in through the door.

"Are you my appointed keeper now?"

"In a way, I suppose you could say that. We're the only two with offices and treatment rooms at this end of the building, and physical rehab has enough space it's practically a wing unto itself, so I'm appointed by proximity."

"Don't need a keeper, don't need the proximity either."

"Not your choice, Marc. This is the way the hospital is laid out and, as it stands, our offices are back to back. If you don't like it, well…" She shrugged her shoulders. "Too bad. Because I don't think they're going to rearrange an entire hospital wing to suit your needs. It is what it is, so get used to it."

"Look, Doctor, I know you're probably only following orders, but I'm perfectly capable of managing this department on my own. Tell your brother-in-law that if he believes I need a keeper, he can have my keys back." He fished his set of keys from his pocket and held them out for her. "Take them. I don't want this job after all."

Rather than taking the keys, she merely stood back and laughed at him. "You really are full of yourself, aren't you?"

He looked like he'd been stung by a bee, the words shocked him that much. "I came here to do a specific job, and I'm good at it."

"When you don't let yourself get in the way. Which probably is too often," she quipped.

"And you know what it's like?"

"To be you? No, I don't. I can't even imagine. But I do know what it's like to be the new person in the door where everybody's watching you and waiting for you to mess up. I was there not that long ago, and it was as if every time I turned around someone was staring at me or whispering. Probably because I'm Jason's sister-in-law who came in here with her own set of problems. The difference between you and me was that I wasn't so thin-skinned on my way in the door. Nor was I so defensive. I just came to do a job and so far that's what I've done."

"You're calling me thin-skinned?"

She shrugged. "Maybe not thin-skinned so much as overly sensitive. You're adjusting to a new life, where everything is different, and it seems like every little thing bothers you."

"So I'm either thin-skinned or overly sensitive?"

"Maybe a little. I mean, I had my divorce going on when I got here and it was a struggle not to let it follow me in the door. But I succeeded."

Marc spun in his chair to see her. "I don't think you can compare yours to mine."

"No. I got out in one piece."

"Out of what?"

"The war. Afghanistan. Three tours. I was a major in the army, which outranks you as a captain." She smiled. "Just in case you're interested."

"You served?" he asked, totally stunned.

"Three times overseas, would have gone back for four. I ran a field hospital."

"Sorry, I had no idea."

"Because I don't wear it as some sort of badge. I just come to work, recognize PTSD when I see it, and go to work trying to fix it."

"And you think you're seeing it in me."

"The bigger question is, do you think you're seeing it in yourself? See, the thing is, you won't get fixed, or even helped, if you don't want to. That's the deal with PTSD. You have to be willing to accept treatment in order to get past it, or at least know how to deal with it."

"Well, my injuries are all on the outside," he snapped, slapping his leg. "Something counseling isn't going to fix, if that's what you were going to ask. I healed fine, and I live fine. Better than a lot of the men and women coming back. So save your healing touch for them, Major..." he gave her a mock salute "...because I don't need it and I don't need you."

"But some of your patients will, and I'm wondering if you'll be objective enough to know which ones. Because they usually don't ask, Doctor. In fact, part of your responsibility will be to make referrals to me and that, quite frankly, worries me."

"Why? Don't you think I can do my job?"

"Honestly, no, I don't. When Jason brought your name to the board as someone to investigate, I voted against you because everything I'd heard, not to mention everything I'd read, indicated you were still fighting your own demons. But he out-talked me, swayed the voting members over to his side to give you an interview, and I lost. So here you are on a trial basis being exactly the way I predicted you'd be."

"It's nice to know who your enemies are." He arched skeptical eyebrows. "Especially when they make no effort to hide themselves."

"You're not my enemy, Marc, and I'm not yours. But I'm not sure you're capable of being a responsible colleague, either. At least, nothing you've shown me so far gives me the impression that you are."

"Maybe that's because you haven't seen me work as a doctor."

"And maybe that's because you've never worked in physical rehab. According to your résumé this is your first job in that specialty. You're here straight from your residency."

"So tell me, how long had you worked in your specialty when your sister's husband hired you to work here?"

"That's different. He knew me."

"But no experience means no experience. Isn't it all the same?"

"You're trying to twist my words," she said, struggling to stay calm.

"What I said was that you got hired based on who you'd been and not who you were. In my opinion, if that's good enough for you, it's good enough for me. Unless nepotism carries more weight than skills do."

"I'm not debating your skill as a doctor. You come with a lot of commendations, including a Medal of Honor."

"Then what are you debating?"

"Your past, your attitude. A couple of people in rehab with you said you were the worst case in the bunch. Your therapist agreed, and said you fought everything and everybody. She said when someone crossed you, you simply shut them out, and that went for the whole team assigned to you. Yet the people who worked with you on the battlefield gave you glowing praises. Which tells me that the *before* version of you is the real you and you're keeping it hidden. Or, in other words, you're afraid to let it back out."

"So you *have* done your homework." Laughing derisively, he simply shook his head.

"To be honest, Marc, I've done a ton of homework on you, starting with your trip back to med school to do a physical rehab residency. Couldn't have been easy."

He winced. "It was…fine. I mean, what were my choices? Take a desk job somewhere, teach? I wanted to practice, and this gave me an opportunity. Who better to teach someone like me than me?"

"Maybe someone with more compassion?" Anne snapped.

"You haven't seen my level of compassion, so it's not fair of you to judge me. And, no, this isn't PTSD talking. It's one angry-as-hell former army medic talking—one who lost the use of his legs and had to change his whole life plan. So I'm not like you, Anne, who had emotional difficulties because I couldn't cope. If a hysterical outbreak was all it took to get me out of the chair, I'd be happy to become hysterical in a heartbeat."

She drew in a bracing breath. She was used to being

challenged by patients. Happened every day. Their trag-
edies were greater than hers, their suffering more—
something she couldn't possibly understand, so many
of them told her. But she'd been to the very depths of
hell, too, and she knew what that felt like. Maybe not
in the same way others experienced it, because no two
people went through it the same way. But like Marc,
she'd had to fight hard to come back. And who knew?
Maybe one day he'd finally understand that suffering
was suffering, no matter the form in which it came.

"Look, we have a meet-and-greet tomorrow to give
you a chance to meet all your new colleagues. I was
wondering, since you're new in town, if you'd like to
grab a quick dinner afterward."

"You're asking me on a date?"

"Not a date, but I thought that since these meet-and-
greets are usually pretty boring, you might appreciate
the opportunity to get out of there a little early without looking like some pathetic loser who leaves there
alone."

"Aren't you the picture of compassion?" he said, his
voice perfectly even.

"Just trying to be friendly. That is, if *you're* capable
of being friendly."

"I can be as friendly as the next guy when I have
to be."

"I have a degree in psychology as well as medicine,
Doctor. Want me to tell you in how many ways that
sounded antisocial?"

"You are stubborn, aren't you?" He actually laughed
out loud. "And you think I don't know?"

"Go ahead, call it what it is…stubborn. I am stubborn, I like it and I own it."

A hint of a smile crinkled his eyes. "Well, you've

met your match. My stubbornness is going to put yours to shame."

"And you're proud of it?"

"About as much as you are."

She studied him for a moment and noticed that he'd visibly relaxed in his chair. Was he all bark, no bite? She doubted that. But she also doubted that his bite was worse than his bark. Marc Rousseau was hiding behind his disability, and doing so by lashing out. It was a typical scenario for an atypical man. Somehow, she looked forward to the challenge. No, he wasn't her patient, but when had that ever stopped her? "OK, then. Tomorrow after the meet-and-greet. Would you prefer Greek or Chinese?"

"I would prefer a bowl of cold cereal, alone."

"I didn't hear that as an option, Doctor. So Chinese it is."

"Chinese," he muttered as he rolled away from her. "I hate Chinese."

"Then Greek it is."

"Hate Greek."

"Then there's an all-night diner down the street and I'm sure they serve cold cereal." She smiled. "See you then, if not sooner."

What had she just done? Actually, she didn't have time to think about it on her way to her group session. Every morning was reserved for private patients who were not yet ready to face others, and every afternoon was much the same, except she blocked out two hours after lunch for her group session where anybody was welcome to sit in and talk.

Talking was cathartic. Too bad she hadn't talked more. If she had, she might not have found herself in the depths of despair after she'd learned about Bill. But that's where she'd ended up. Too much trauma, too much death, too many patch jobs that just hadn't been good enough. She'd held up in the field just fine because she'd had a real purpose there, but when she'd come home to face all the things a family practitioner had to face—coughs and sore throats and gallstones—she'd broken in half. That, plus a failing marriage and her whole life had started to decompose.

And it wasn't like her patients back home had needed her any less than her patients in the field. But what she hadn't felt was…vital. The divorce had robbed her. So had her medical practice, as she hadn't felt like she'd made a difference at the end of the day since she'd come back.

Sure, she could have re-upped, but she'd have been assigned stateside this time, doing exactly what she'd been doing when she'd parted ways with the army. So on those evenings when she'd been alone and she'd thought about the direction her life was taking, she'd let her depression out, fretted a little, cried a lot. Until her hands had started to shake and her mind had started to get muddled. Then there'd been missed work and missed days, and weeks that had gone by in a blur because she'd been unable to force herself to get out of bed in the morning.

Oh, she'd known it had been depression. But she'd never attributed it to PTSD. That was for other soldiers, the ones on the battlefield who came home battered either physically or emotionally. No, Anne Sebastian just felt tired and irritable, and she hadn't wanted to face her days head-on. With family swooping in, trying to get her to do one thing or another. "Get help," they'd kept telling her. "It's not an embarrassment to admit you need help."

Then one day a dear friend from her army days had come to visit, thanks to Anne's parents. Her friend, Belinda McCall, also an army doc, had admitted she'd had trouble. Hers had been temper, and outbreaks, and crying jags. Her diagnosis—severe depression.

"I'm just going through a bad divorce," Anne had replied. "And I can control my moods whenever I want to."

"Can you?" Belinda had asked. "Are you sure?"

Had she been sure? Of course she'd been sure. She wasn't a weak person. Only a person going through a bad patch.

"Must be a pretty damned bad patch for you to miss work," Belinda had taunted her as she'd handed her a brochure for a program in Oregon for returning soldiers suffering from stress-related disorders and depression.

Long story short, she'd seen herself in the description— sleeping on the job, listless. Then one day she'd curled up on an exam table and just dozed off in the middle of the day. After the fire rescue squad had knocked her door in, she'd made the phone call. Two years later, with counseling for depression behind her, she'd had her PhD in hand and had reemerged into the world ready to treat soldiers with PTSD like she'd seen in the clinic. So many of them so often misdiagnosed or forgotten. And as luck would have it, she'd landed the job at a little veterans' rehab clinic in Chicago. One run by her brother-in-law.

It had been a fresh start. What a perfect place to start over!

But was it a good place for Marc to start over? Her demons had been put to bed before she'd got here, but she had a hunch his biggest demons were still in front of him. He'd faced his disability and dealt with it as much as he could on his own. Or as much as he would allow. And he had great credentials as a doctor. So maybe he intended to spend his time behind his work, the way she'd tried doing.

Whatever the case, they were a tight-knit little medical community and she wanted to see him succeed. But if his bitterness prevailed, it wasn't going to happen. Gallahue Rehab was about the patient, not the doctor. Still, from where she watched, the doctor needed fixing almost as much, maybe in some cases more, than the patients.

"Cold cereal? Really?" she asked as she scooted into the booth across from him. His chair was folded neatly at the side and she wondered just how easily he moved from place to place. He seemed agile, with a lot of upper-body strength. Someone who spent a great deal of time working out. And maybe that was his physical rehab philosophy, to compensate for the areas that were lacking.

"Makes a decent meal."

"So does a hamburger or a salad. Makes me glad you didn't order for me. I'm all for cold cereal as much as the next person, but for my dinner I like something a little more substantial, like spaghetti or maybe the home-made lasagna with garlic bread or a big chef's salad."

"You don't have to justify it to me, just like I don't have to justify it to you. Besides, I'm having toast and coffee, as well."

Anne shook her head and smiled. "Without standing on formalities, such as waiting for me to arrive before you ordered."

"You were late."

"Ten minutes."

"Ten minutes, ten hours. How am I supposed to know if I'm being stood up?"

Anne ended up ordering the chef's salad along with garlic bread. "Why would I stand you up?"

"It's happened before," he replied. "Someone takes pity on me, asks me out and has a change of heart. Or shows up and has a miserable time."

"Are those my only two choices?" she asked.

"In my life, yes."

"But suppose I want to have a nice time with you? I mean, I did show up, and I'm in a pretty good mood. So wouldn't that allow me a third choice?"

"For about five minutes, then you'll discover how I don't talk much, or how I don't relate very well to normal conversation, and you'll be miserable."

"So, were you like this before you were a paraplegic, or did all this come about after your injury?"

"My, aren't you blunt?" he snapped.

Rather than feeling hurt or angry, Anne simply smiled at him. "Sometimes you have to be if you want to know the answer to your question. And with all the people I've questioned, the best I can come up with is, you're a mixed bag. Nice, grumpy. Compassionate, rude. Conscientious, bitter."

"That's right, you're a shrink, aren't you? All out to analyze the problems of the world and cure them."

"I'm an internal medicine doctor with a PhD in psychology. Which has nothing at all to do with my question. Which, by the way, you're trying to put off answering or maybe you're just trying to make me angry. Either way, if I'm going to sit here with you for the next hour or two and try to make pleasant conversation, I think I have a right to know what's stopping me. So,

I'll ask you again—were you always this grumpy or is it a result of your war injury? Something you held inside until you decided, *What the hell, why not let it fly?*"

"You're assuming I would want to tell you, if it were any of your business. Which it's not."

"That's not going to dissuade me, Marc. I've got a question for every bite of that cold cereal you're eating. One question per bite."

"No, you won't be dissuaded at first, but eventually you'll get tired of asking the questions and give up." He smiled. "That's human nature. And whether or not you like it, you're subject to it, like the rest of us."

She laughed. "Maybe I am, but you don't know me. By the end of the meal I'll have it figured out."

"Not if I don't talk to you, you won't."

"You don't scare me, Dr. Rousseau. I work with people like you every day and I always win." She shot him a devious smile across the table. *"Always!"*

"Don't overestimate yourself, Dr. Sebastian. You've never worked with someone like me and, as far as I know, I'm not one of your patients anyway, so none of this conversation matters, does it?"

"This hospital really wants your work. So much so they're willing to bet their rehab department that you'll be just as good as you appear on paper. We're a small facility, though, and we can't let an attitude get in the way because funding is tight, meaning one false step and it can be yanked away from us. We do good work there, Marc, because our patients get more individualized care than they do in most facilities, and we're not about to let one grumpy doctor ruin a good thing. Jason's risking a lot by hiring you, and I'm not going to let you bring him down. That's a promise, by the way.

A double-edged promise, because you've got Jason to contend with and I've got my brother-in-law's back."

"That's a lot of family loyalty," he said, downing the last of his cereal.

"It's not just family loyalty. I love working at Gallahue Rehab. Love it more than any place I've worked, and I sure as heck don't want you and your sour attitude to do anything to disrupt that."

The look in his eyes softened. "I admire your loyalty. I bet you were a good doc out there on the battlefield."

"I'd like to think I was. It was a tough job, but it's what I wanted to do. It's why I do what I do now, because of everything I saw in the field. And what I saw when I got back—the way people treated soldiers with disabilities, even disabilities like post-traumatic stress disorder that can't often be seen." She shrugged. "Too many casualties out there, and I vowed to continue the work when I got home."

"It's easy to look the other way."

"It is, but that's not me. I suffered my own difficulties and I know what it's like to need to reach out to someone who understands. I got counseling because of my divorce and that made me realize just how important it is to build a person back up from the inside. So, how about your brother?"

"He served two hitches, but he's out now. He was supposed to come back to Chicago but never did. I don't know where he is now or what he's doing. I guess he's living a…different kind of life from me. Not settled down. Maybe never will. Who knows?"

"You sound bitter."

"Not bitter, just disappointed by the way he's turned his back on the people who love him most."

"We all have our ways of coping."

"We sure as hell do," he said as he spread grape jam on his toast.

"Well, however it played out, I'm sorry it didn't work out for you."

"You and me both," he said as the server brought Anne's salad to the table.

"Want to share?" she asked. "This is too large for a single meal."

He stared at it for a minute, then smiled. "Did you order the large size because you were convinced cold cereal wasn't enough?"

"Maybe," she answered. "Or maybe I always take some back for lunch."

"Good, because I really do like cold cereal."

"Because it's easy to fix?"

"Because it tastes good."

"So does this salad, Marc."

"Are you going to nag me until I share it with you?"

"Maybe."

He laughed and asked the server to bring him another plate. "If there's one thing I hate more than someone talking when I'm trying to eat, it's someone nagging me while I'm eating."

A smile of victory crossed Anne's face as she scraped half the salad onto Marc's plate.

"Don't look so smug, Anne. You might have won the battle, but you sure as hell haven't won the war."

That didn't dissuade her, though. In fact, she handed him a big, buttery slice of garlic bread as soon as he'd finished his toast. *That's what you think*, she thought to herself. *That, Marc Rousseau, is what you think.*

CHAPTER FOUR

MARC SAT OFF, almost in the corner, and simply watched the physical therapists and others work while he made detailed notes of everything going on in the busy room.

The room had a crazy mishmash of disabilities—some curable, some not. And everything seemed to be going rather well, all things considered. But the one thing he didn't like was the mix-up of medical types. It seemed confusing to him, having one disability type working right alongside a different disability. And men and women in various forms of physical therapy together. Apples and oranges, he supposed. But he didn't want fruit salad. That's the thing.

He wanted order in his department, and maybe one way to do that was to divide the one large room into two rooms. He also wanted private therapy rooms because not every patient needed to suffer their woes in public, no matter how supportive everyone else in the room might be.

He remembered his early days, how angry he'd been. He'd thrown literal tantrums, which was something no one needed to witness. A private room would have done him better. Maybe helped him progress faster or at the very least spared his dignity when he'd gone off in one of his fits. Private rooms were a priority. Not negotiable.

Maybe no one here saw harm in the gang philosophy, and the camaraderie seemed high enough, in spite of all the many different cases, and maybe each patient could get to the point where the group thing would be good. But right now it put him in mind of the field hospital where only thin curtains had separated each surgery, leaving essentially one large room where any number of different types of procedures had been taking place at the same time. He'd hated the impersonality of it then and he hated it now.

"Note to self," he jotted, "change the system. Keep the various modalities consistent with one another."

Easier said than done, he supposed. But they may as well get used to him and his causes right from the start. Because once he fixed on an idea…

"So, what do you think of our main PT room?" Jason asked, stepping up behind Marc.

"Do you want me to lie and tell you how nice it is or do you want my honest opinion?"

"That bad?"

"Worse! I don't like the idea of mixing my therapies. I know you've got a lot of patients who need use of this space, but having hand trauma working right next to a quadriplegic doesn't serve any purpose. In fact, I can see how it might be a disincentive for the quad to do his best work."

"So you see the work as competition?" Jason asked.

"Not competition, more motivational. Or as a way to relate to each other. Right now, it doesn't serve its fullest purpose."

"And you want to change the system?"

"Of course I want to change the system. Nothing drastic. Just something to afford more continuity and privacy. And I'm thinking that'll be my first priority."

"Are you up to that big of a task to start off with, or wouldn't you rather get to know the therapists, see the various sessions in progress, get a sense for what we do here that you might consider right?"

"I'm not insulting your results here, Jason. You have a good reputation. But as for my part of it, I want it better and I believe in hitting the ground running. How much board interference am I going to have to put up with to get what I want?"

"Trust me, Marc. The further away from our board of directors I can keep you, the better. They approved your interview based on what they read in your résumé, and, as far as I'm concerned, I'd like to keep you on paper for them. The less they have to deal with you, the better. But if change is what you want, show me what, including a budget, and I'll take it to them and probably get their vote. But I'm not promising you anything other than I'll try."

Marc actually laughed. "Smart decisions, since I don't always rub people the right way."

"And why is that?"

Shrugging, Marc started to roll away from Jason, but Jason caught up to him for his answer. "I'm serious, Marc. As your boss, I'd like to know why you put people off the way you do."

"Because I'm faster at it than they are," he said as he exited the room. "It's a dog-eat-dog world, Jason, and I'm not about to put myself out there as the first one to be gnawed on."

"I'm beginning to think I made a big mistake," Jason said to Anne, who was passing through the hall a few moments later.

"You mean in hiring him?"

"In hiring him, in not having fired him already."

Anne gave her brother-in-law a pat on the back. "I think he'll work out once he knows his world here is secure."

"The problem is it's not secure until he comes off his trial basis. If any of the board members get to see the real Marc Rousseau, I don't think he'll be around too long. And I may be following him right out the door if that becomes the case."

"He's a good doctor, Jason. If that's what you get from him, nobody should complain."

"If that's all I get." He turned and gave her a hard, appraising stare. "So why are you so squarely in his corner all of a sudden?"

"Maybe a little empathy. I know what it's like to think the world has turned against you, and I especially know what it's like not knowing how to fight back. He's got his intellect and his abilities intact, but the rest of it hasn't caught up with him yet. So give him some time to prove himself to himself, and I think you'll be happy with the outcome."

"You really are a staunch supporter."

"Because I'm a true believer that you can overcome. I mean, look at me." She gave Jason's arm a squeeze. "And I'll be there about six tonight to cook dinner… Spaghetti is what she's requesting."

"Well, she's eating for two, and she does eat a lot. But she's still having false labor off and on, so I can't guarantee how she'll be."

"She'll be fine." Anne laughed. "Can you believe that in the next couple of weeks you're going to be a family of three?" A C-section was set for the end of next week, owing to the baby's large size.

Jason's face blanched. "Sometimes it's still hard for me to believe we're a family of two. You do know how nervous this is making me, don't you?"

"You're going to be a great father. Just calm down. Enjoy the process, and that includes the pregnancy."

Jason rolled his eyes at her, then scurried down the hall in one direction while Anne went to a group PTSD session in another. Today was her light day—no personal appointments. All group appointments. Too bad she couldn't get Marc to sit in on one, but she doubted he'd ever do that. Doubted he'd ever agree to a private session, either. Well, his loss, she decided as she entered the door to greet seven women, all with a diagnosis. Early on, she'd separated the genders as their traumas were rarely similar, and so far it was working out splendidly. "Hello, ladies. Glad you could all make it this afternoon."

"Any news on the baby?" one of them asked her.

"Not yet, but my sister is getting bigger every day. She's ready to get this thing over with." For the next several minutes they all talked about babies and childbirth. It was Anne's practice never to go straight to therapy as that seemed mighty harsh, so lately talk had turned to Hannah's upcoming blessed event.

For the men's group, she usually started with sports as a means to calm the general attitude as the group progressed in therapy, not so much in grand gestures but in the little things that added up. Like with Marc. If he were her patient as well as her colleague, maybe the little thing would be to ask him to come along to dinner tonight. Then refuse to accept his rejection. Talk about putting herself out there on a ledge.

"I know it's not your usual cold cereal, but I am a pretty good cook."

"And I'm pretty good company when I keep to myself."

"Do you ever budge an inch?" she asked him.

"Not unless I'm forced to. And then I force back even harder."

"It's a spaghetti dinner. That's all. I try to cook for my sister a couple times a week. She's pregnant and confined to bed, and while Jason tries hard, his best dish is a grilled cheese sandwich with canned tomato soup, and she gets pretty tired of it."

"So why drag me into what's clearly a family matter?"

"I'm not dragging you. Just extending you a cordial invitation since I don't think you get too many home-cooked meals."

"Which doesn't bother me, so it's got no reason to bother you."

"Do you have horrible table manners?"

"Not particularly."

"Food allergies?"

"None of which I'm aware."

"Then there's no reason not to say yes and come to dinner. It might put you in better stead with your boss."

"Are you implying I'm in bad stead?"

"You know yourself better than anybody else. You tell me."

"Well, if I am, that's a new record for me. Normally people start taking offense after three days, and this is only my second."

"It's not funny, Marc."

"But it is what it is."

Anne huffed an impatient sigh. "And it doesn't have to be unless that's the way you want to spend your life."

"I wanted to spend my life being a general surgeon. But we don't necessarily get what we want, do we?"

Anne bit her tongue to keep her from blurting out her next retort. Why was she taking this personally?

She had any number of patients in the very same spot as Marc, yet they didn't rile her the way he did. What was it about him that got to her? What was it about him that actually made her feel angry and defensive? Was it because her patients were trying hard at recovery and he seemed to be happy to wallow in his stagnation? Or that she found him attractive and this was only an emotional response?

Maybe it was because some other therapist somewhere had simply given up on him, which made her wonder under what circumstances she might have to give up on one of her patients. So far, she was still optimistic about that; had the idea that all patients with PTSD could be helped with enough time and energy. But Marc was practically throwing it in her face that she was wrong. That she couldn't win them all. And she didn't like that, not one little bit.

"Dinner's at six. Can you get yourself there, or shall I pick you up somewhere?"

"You still on that kick?"

"It's not a kick. It's an invitation." She scribbled an address and stuffed it in his hand. "Be there, or not." Then she left. Left Marc, left the building and left the bad mood behind. Tonight she'd get to spend the evening with her sister and she surely didn't need to drag that attitude along.

It was nearly six thirty when Anne quit peeking out the window for him. Marc wasn't coming and Jason had told her as much an hour before. Still, she'd expected him to do the polite thing—to call with his refusal, even though he'd declined her invitation in the hall that afternoon. OK, so she expected too much. Marc wasn't like anybody else she'd ever known and she was hoping he would be. But that wasn't going to be the case.

"Sorry he disappointed you," Jason said, stepping up to the front window behind Anne, "but Marc Rousseau isn't very sociable."

"Very? That bush out by the front porch is more sociable than he is."

"Don't turn him into one of your causes, Anne. It won't work."

"I don't know what you mean by that," she snapped.

"Sure you do. Hannah told me you always had a cause...whether it was the least popular kid in the neighborhood to the kid who was getting picked on in school. You brought home abandoned puppies and kittens and spent two afternoons a week having tea with a couple of the octogenarian ladies in your neighborhood to keep them company. If that's not having causes..."

"But Marc isn't a cause. I was just trying to make him feel welcome at the rehab center."

"He doesn't want to feel welcome. In fact, I doubt he wants to feel anything. He comes to us with a strong background both as a patient and as a doctor, and the truth of the matter is I hired him as a doctor, not as a patient."

"And I invited him to dinner as a colleague, not as a patient."

"Look, why don't you go upstairs and help Hannah get ready to come down to dinner? I'll set the table."

Anne nodded. It was time to forget about Marc and enjoy the rest of the evening with her family. She headed upstairs and tapped gently on Hannah's bedroom door before going in. "Hey, sis. You know Mom's coming for the first two or three weeks, don't you? And she's dragging Daddy with her. They won't be separated now that he's retired."

Hannah smiled. "First grandchild, so I'm betting they'll stay six weeks."

"Or move in." Anne laughed. "She keeps asking me if there are any prospects in my future."

Hannah scooted to the edge of the bed and let her swollen feet dangle over. "And are there? Jason said you asked someone to dinner tonight, but he was betting he wouldn't show."

"Jason was right. I did, and he didn't. Marc shows antisocial tendencies."

"You've fallen for someone who's antisocial?"

"No!" Anne shook her head adamantly. "Not fallen. I just feel…he's not adjusting well to his new situation, and I thought a night out might do him good."

"What's his new situation?"

"He's a paraplegic. Took a lot of shrapnel to the spine during the war, and it left him in a wheelchair."

"That's right. Jason mentioned the wheelchair. That he's highly functional."

Anne widened her eyes. "What do you mean, *highly functional*?"

"In everyday functions. He can get around. Do his job. Otherwise Jason wouldn't have hired him as head of the physical rehab department. Meaning he doesn't need to be one of your pet projects, Anne."

"That's exactly what Jason said to me. The thing is, he scares me a little bit."

"Physically? As in threatening?"

"No, nothing like that. More like love-hate, and I never know which one's going to pop out."

"You love him!"

"Not like that. More as a friend, I think."

"You think?"

"Well, certainly not *in* love, the way you mean it."

"Oh, like when you jumped right in with Bill?"

"Nothing like that. I'm too wise to get caught up in a mess like that again."

"You're assuming that Marc would be like Bill if you did fall in love with him."

"I'm not assuming anything. It's just that... I don't know what!" Anne bent to slide a pair of slippers on her sister's feet, then helped her out of bed. "I'm trying to be a friend," she insisted.

"How good of a friend remains to be seen. Now, be a friend to me and point me in the direction of the door. I can't see past my belly anymore."

"Are you sure there's only one in there?"

Hanna laughed. "Sometimes it feels like five or six, but I'm confident it's just one little girl." She stretched. "Do you know how nice it is to actually get to leave this room and go downstairs and feel somewhat human again? I'm so tired of being bedridden." She reached for her back. "And stiff and sore."

"You're not in labor, are you?"

"Same twinges I've been having for weeks. No big deal. Doc's going to deliver me either next week or, if we can hold out longer, the week after. He wants to wait as long as he can to make sure her lungs are fully formed and she'll be able to hold her blood sugar steady. Big preemies tend to have blood-sugar crashes."

"But it could be sooner?"

"And it could be my craving for spaghetti, too, that's causing the twinges."

"You're hopeless," Anne said, laughing. "And I guarantee in a few weeks you're going to wish you'd had more time in bed. If your baby is anything like what

Mom said we both were…" She grinned. "Better you than me. So, have you picked out a name yet?" Anne slid her arm around Hannah's waist and escorted her to the bedroom door, where she grabbed her back again.

"Well, last time Jason and I talked about it, he was leaning toward Chloe or Zoe. Mother wants Rose Mary or Mary Rose." Hannah gasped slightly. "Jason's mother has her vote in for Abigail or Gabrielle. And me? I think we should let her name herself when she's old enough."

When they got to the stairs, Anne glanced down, only to see Marc sitting at the bottom of the stairs, looking up. "Sorry I'm late," he said, "but I had to go to a couple of places to find non-alcoholic wine to go with dinner."

"Wow, he's certainly handsome," Hannah whispered in Anne's ear. "I can see why you were so grumpy about him not being here."

"It's not like that," Anne whispered back.

"Well, it should be." She smiled generously at Marc, who actually greeted her smile with a pleasant one of his own, all the while avoiding Anne's eyes.

"It's a pleasant evening, so I thought we'd eat out on the back patio," Jason cut in as he came up the stairs to take hold of his wife's arm. Anne followed them down, took the two bottles of sparkling grape juice from Marc without saying a word and continued into the kitchen.

"Personally, I don't think Hannah should eat right now because I'm betting the baby will arrive tonight," Anne whispered to Marc. "She's miscarried twice and had some false labor and she doesn't want to get her hopes up, so she's denying it, but I think it's a good thing she's surrounded by doctors tonight, because I'm betting there's a trip to the hospital in her very near future."

"Too soon," Hannah said, coming through the

kitchen door and grabbing her belly. "Doctor says not for at least another week or more."

"And doctors have been known to be wrong, so any wagers?" Anne asked, cringing in sympathy as her sister's next labor pain struck.

"No way. You're not wagering on my baby. It's not coming tonight, I tell you!"

"Maybe just a little bet?" Anne asked, smiling. "Twenty says the next two hours sees some action."

"I'm not going to the hospital in two hours!" Hannah snapped.

Anne knew her sister was scared to death, especially after the loss of her first two, but in her opinion, there was almost no denying the fact that the baby was getting ready to make her grand entrance.

"I'll take twenty on that for tomorrow," Jason added.

"One hour and I'm in." Marc tossed in his wager.

"One week," Hannah said good-naturedly, before she grabbed her belly and gasped again. "Like my doctor says, one week or two."

"Three against one. I think we'd better call an ambulance," Marc suggested.

"No!" Hannah snapped. "You eat your dinner and I'll lie down here and rest while you do. And think happy thoughts for one to two weeks in the future."

The other three doctors eyed each other dubiously.

Marc smiled. "Well, you've got a house full of doctors, so if you should need any one of them, just ask."

They decided to eat inside to stay near Hannah, and as it turned out, Marc won the wager.

"Would someone mind calling an ambulance?" she asked thirty minutes later. "I don't think it's false labor this time."

"Ambulance called," Jason shouted on his way upstairs to grab his wife's overnight bag.

"Sorry, everyone," Hannah managed to say between contractions. "Didn't mean to ruin your dinner, but this time I think it's the real thing. Finally!" She gasped as another labor pain hit. "Could somebody see if they're coming, and how dilated I am?"

Anne helped Hannah lay down on the sofa, while Marc lined up behind her, in case she needed help. "All I know is that this baby isn't going to wait much longer," Anne said as she took a peek to see the baby's positioning. "Looks good," she said, almost under her breath. She glanced at Marc. "And she's coming fast. Hannah's got gestational diabetes, so we need to be doing this in the hospital."

"If it can wait that long," Hannah gasped as Jason raced back to her side.

"Well, if we do wait that long, I win the bet," Anne said, taking hold of the hand that Jason wasn't holding.

"So what do we do?" her sister asked.

"We wait for the ambulance and hope it gets here before the baby does."

"It's a girl," Hannah panted as the next roll of labor pains washed over her. "And she's not waiting. I want to push."

Anne took another look and, sure enough, the baby was crowning. "Jason, get behind her and support her. Help keep her breathing steady. And, Marc, you take over for me while I run upstairs and get some clean bed sheets just in case the medics don't arrive in time."

Marc rolled in closer while Anne ran up the stairs, and by the time she was back down, Marc was in full delivery mode. "Push," he said as the baby's head started to appear. He looked up at Anne, whose hands were pressing into his shoulders. "Care to take over?" he asked her.

"Looks like you're doing a good job, so I'll just assist." In the distance she heard the wail of a siren, but by the time it got there it was going to be too late.

"Now relax," Marc said. Hannah was twisted slightly to accommodate his angle from the wheelchair while Anne helped her get situated.

"I need to push," Hannah screamed, then pushed again. This time the baby's head appeared, and within another minute, Marc was sitting in his chair with a squirming, rather large newborn in his lap. He handed the baby up to Anne, who did the preliminary exam, then the paramedics, who'd now arrived, took the baby, cleaned it up and laid her on Hannah's belly for a minute, while Marc backed away. From there it was off to the hospital for mom and baby, followed by Jason, who was too nervous to drive, Marc, and Anne, who actually did the driving.

"We did it!" Anne cried as they climbed into the car. "Or shall I say you did it!" She was so excited that before Marc was all the way inside, she grabbed him and kissed him on the lips, then hugged him before she realized what she was doing and pulled away. "We delivered the baby!" she said breathlessly, as much from the hug and kiss as from the excitement of the moment. "I can't believe it!"

Marc flinched as if he'd been stung. "It wasn't a big deal. We've all rotated through maternity, assisted in birthing. But," he admitted, "it was nice to get to do that again."

"This was my sister, though. That makes it different." Suddenly, the full reality of her kiss sank in. What had she been thinking? Anne attributed it to a heat-of-the-moment kind of thing and quickly changed the subject to the first time she'd assisted in a delivery back in med school. "It was like a miracle, bringing that new life into the world."

She babbled on until they reached the hospital because she didn't want to address the obvious elephant in the room—the kiss. When they had finally arrived, she changed the subject to her sister. "She had a lot of trouble conceiving," she told Marc on their way to the hospital waiting area. "They've been trying for years and were just about ready to give up on the idea, but the last round of fertility drugs took. But it's been a rough pregnancy."

"With a happy ending," he added.

"I'm glad because I don't think she'll go through this again. I'm not even sure she can. But she's been such a good patient because she knew this might be her only chance."

"You two have a strong bond," Marc commented as they took their seats in a room that was half full of others waiting for babies to arrive. In a hushed voice, Marc said, "My brother and I used to be close when we were young."

"Judging from what you said the other day, I'd already guessed that you two aren't close now."

"Not for quite a while. And as for our parents, I do see them occasionally, but it's…awkward. But, hell, I'm there for only a couple days, so I can make do."

"You don't see your parents any other time?"

He shook his head. "It's always a pity party with my mother. And my old man isn't convinced I can't just get up and walk because I look so damn good. 'Come on, boy. Just try.' That's what he's saying while my mother's hovering in the corner, weeping. It's…"

"Tough. After I found out what Bill had done, I had a breakdown. Mostly I just slept and didn't function at all. Consequently, my mother cried all the time, on the verge of her own breakdown over me, and my father told me to just quit. Like I could." She shrugged. "They meant well, but it's not easy watching someone you love suffer. For my family, that went both ways. So what's the story with your brother, if you don't mind my asking?"

"Damn good doctor, damn careless lifestyle. We don't talk anymore."

"You weren't stationed together, were you?"

"Yes. Nick always was the one who was hard to control. Still is." Marc shrugged. "I wish it was different. But it's not, and it won't be fixed until he's ready to fix it."

"Did you blame him?"

"At first, yes. And I told him so. But I got over that as he was just doing what Nick would do. You can't expect the man to be different than who he is."

"But you never had the chance to tell him you'd forgiven him?"

"I don't even know where the hell he is, and if my folks know, they're not saying."

"You've asked them?"

"Not in so many words. But I think they're trying to do what's best for both their boys."

"Is it right, Marc?"

Marc shrugged. "Time will tell, I suppose."

"Well, I'm lucky that Hannah and I get along so well."

"Damned lucky," Marc said. "Pretty damned lucky."

"Did we wear you out?" Anne asked her sister.

"Something like that." Hannah shut her eyes and

sighed. "Baby's got to stay in the NICU for a while until they get her blood sugar regulated."

"How long?"

"Maybe a week."

"That'll give you time to rest up and get ready for her," Anne said sympathetically. She knew her sister would be devastated to go home without her baby. It was going to break her heart, which broke Anne's heart. "And it's better to have her here where she can be watched for a little while."

"Marc did a good job," Hannah told Anne as she nodded off to sleep.

Ten minutes later, Anne said the very same thing to him. "You did a good job." He was in the process of pulling off his soiled street clothes, cleaning himself up and pulling on some fresh hospital scrubs.

She couldn't help but admire his body. It was beautiful. Well muscled. Nice definition in all the right places. Except the scars on his back. They were everywhere, going in every direction—some long and wide, others short and jagged. Automatically she empathized with the pain he must have felt. "Do they still hurt?" she asked him, as she ran her finger down the nastiest of all, the one that started along his spine and traveled a good length of it.

"Occasionally. Which is why I keep myself busy, to keep my mind off it."

"Are you sensitive or embarrassed to be seen?" she asked as she ran her finger across a zig-zag pattern on his right shoulder.

"Not really. It's all a part of me now, part of what causes me to do the things I do. So my attitude is, if you don't like it, or if you take offense to my back or legs, don't look." He actually smiled. "And don't go get all teary-eyed over me, because I hate pity worse than just about anything else."

"It's not pity. It's just that…that you had such a pretty back."

"What the hell did you say?" he sputtered.

"That you had such a pretty back."

"Well, that's one for the record books. Nobody's ever said anything like that to me before. Mind you, I've had other compliments. But my back?" He laughed out loud. "I never know what to expect from you, Anne."

She sniffed. "I like backs. I'm sorry. Sue me."

"I'd rather stay on your good side, I think."

"Well, your good side saved my sister's life and got her baby into the world safely. Thank you, Marc."

"For what?" he asked.

"For being there, for doing what you did… It was all pretty amazing."

"It's been a while since I've done anything like that. Actually, I've never done anything *exactly* like that out in the field, delivering a baby without medical equipment, and it *was* good, wasn't it?"

"Thank you," Anne said again, bending slightly to give him a shoulder massage.

"You can thank me like that anytime," he said, sighing as her fingers kneaded the corded muscles of his shoulders and neck.

Suddenly, she hugged him from behind in what was meant to be a casual gesture, yet it shot through her like a bolt of lightning, nearly causing her to lose her balance, her feelings toward Marc turning so strong so quickly.

"You OK?" he asked, reaching out to steady her.

"I, um…I'm just tired. And a little frazzled emotionally. It's been a big night, but I'm good." She could still feel the heat of him lingering on her fingertips and on her lips from earlier. "And about that kiss earlier..."

"Nicest one I've had all day." He smiled. "All year, actually. But let's just agree to agree that we were caught up in the excitement of what had just happened and let it go."

"Agreed," she said, even though it still caused her knees to wobble when she thought about what she'd done. "I can't even imagine how this would have gone if you hadn't been there."

"You and Jason are both good doctors..."

"Neither of us deliver babies as parts of our practice. I did during my residency, but never in the field, and I'm sure he did, too, when he rotated through maternity, but to do it in those circumstances..."

"Neither had I, not like that, until I went to Afghanistan, and ended up in charge of a medical unit where every medical procedure was fair game. We didn't turn people away, and a few of the women came to me even though I was a man. They bucked the system to get good medical help." He shrugged. "No big deal."

"Very big deal," she said. Pride swelled inside her for the things he'd accomplished.

"Look, the wheels and armrests on your chair are messy. Can I clean them for you?"

"I'm capable," he said, his voice betraying genuine gratitude.

"I know you're capable. But you're also exhausted, and I was just trying to be nice."

"Sorry. Sure, I appreciate the help. I am pretty tired. It's been quite a while since I've done anything that strenuous."

With that, Marc transferred himself to the bench

seat in the locker room while Anne took the chair and swabbed it down. When she was finished, she pushed the chair back to him and watched him make the transfer back with such strength and agility it raised goosebumps on her arms. "So, what's to say we go home? It's almost time to go to work and I'd like to grab a shower and a couple of hours' sleep, if I can."

"Since we came in Jason's car, I've already called a cab," he said as he opened the locker-room door for her. "Oh, and in case I didn't mention it before, you did a good job for a shrink."

"I was scared to death. Probably more scared than usual since it was my sister."

"Scared becomes you. It adds a nice flush to your cheeks."

They wandered down to the hospital's circular drive and Anne sat down on a bench, nearly falling asleep as they waited for the cab. In fact, she was so out of it she vaguely remembered her head on Marc's shoulder and his arm around her, supporting her. But the cab pulled up and whatever may or may not have happened ended.

Marc entered the taxi first, then folded his chair and pulled it in behind him, leaving Anne to sit in the front seat next to the cabby, a young Hispanic man who said he was working his way through college by driving a cab. Ten minutes later, Anne was dropped off at her sister's house to pick up her own car, while Marc grabbed his own car and sped on down the road.

Had she been resting on his shoulder, or had that only been a dream? Too tired to think about it, she climbed the stairs in Hannah's house and slid between the sheets in the guest room. Sleep would arrive soon, she was sure. But on the edges of that sleep, she kept seeing Marc. And he kept jolting her awake again.

He was an interesting man, to say the least. *Maybe even more than interesting*, she thought as she finally drifted off, thinking about the kiss.

CHAPTER FIVE

THE DAY STARTED much too early and, admittedly, Marc felt stiff and sore when he climbed out of bed and headed for the shower. What he needed was extra shower time followed by an extra half hour in his makeshift gym, but what he was going to get was five minutes in the shower and no workout whatsoever if he wanted to make it to work on time.

Sure, he had a good excuse, but in his life, excuses didn't matter. He got up every day and went to work just like everybody else did. No exceptions like morning stiffness because people would talk. And he hated talk and innuendo and speculation and rumors almost as much as he hated the changes he'd been forced to make to get along in this world.

Last night, for instance. He'd delivered a baby from his wheelchair! It had left him exhausted and exhilarated because for a little while he'd just been a doctor, pure and simple. It had made him feel…great, like the way he used to after a successful surgery. They'd needed him, relied on him and his wheelchair hadn't stood in the way!

Pulling the shaving mirror out from the wall, Marc took one look at the tired lines on his face and decided to forgo the shave. Who would care that he had a five o'clock shadow? And even if somebody did care, he or she wouldn't mention it. People were like that with him, let him get away with egregious things because what, after all, could you or would you say to a doctor in a wheelchair?

Nothing, he'd discovered early on. Not a damned thing.

He hated those eggshells everybody stepped on where he was concerned. Hated them to hell.

The physical rehab room was quiet when he arrived. There was only one therapist in the far corner, working on the mat bed, trying to teach a new above-knee amputee how to stand. Balancing on one leg couldn't be all that easy, and his heart did go out to the young man for the future he'd have to face. But he'd made that adjustment himself, had put in the hard work and discovered that life would go on.

"Excuse me," he said as the therapist wrestled to stand the man up and keep him upright, "but I think more emphasis placed on upper-body strength will help compensate for what he's lost down below. Upper-body strength can be invaluable, so I'm going to evaluate his treatment schedule and make the necessary arrangements to get him into the weight room more often. Maybe twice a day and as needed."

"Yes, Doctor," the therapist said, showing clear irritation that her therapy was being called into question.

"You a doc in a wheelchair?" the young man named James asked.

"I'm a doc in a wheelchair," Marc answered as their camaraderie started to grow.

"Well, I'll be damned," James said.

"That's what I said, only in stronger terms, when I found out I was going to be a paraplegic."

"War?"

Marc nodded. "Afghanistan. Got caught by flying shrapnel."

"Afghanistan for me, too. Land mine."

"Well, welcome to the club," Marc said, extending his hand to the man.

James accepted the handshake. "Yeah. And ain't that a bitch."

"We'll get you independent here. Won't be easy, and that's a promise, but you also have my word that when you leave here, things will be different. You'll be able to get a normal life back and do most of the things you used to do."

"How about you, Doc? How did that work for you?"

"I was a surgeon, which I can't do now because of my limitations, but I'm still a doctor practicing in a field that I like, a field I chose. I had some compromises to make, as you may well have to do, too. But it all works out. And you'll walk out of here ready to face the compromises when the time comes."

"It's awful hard to see it from my position right now, Doc."

"I know the feeling, and I had someone tell me the same things. I thought they didn't know what the hell they were talking about, but I was wrong."

"And you're independent, even in your condition?"

"Even in my condition." He smiled. "So do what they tell you, soldier, and we'll get you on the right track. That's a promise. And in the meantime, finish out your therapy session and I'll see what I can do about getting you in the weight room. You're going to need more strength until you're independent with your prosthesis." He showed off his finely defined biceps. "I work out every day to keep myself in shape, and since you're going to be fighting a lifelong problem, you need to get yourself into a routine that maximizes the rest of your body.

"Makes perfect sense since that's the life you've been given to live from now on. One of the reasons I took this job as head of physical rehab was that I've been there, and I know what the emotions are. I understand that some days you're raring to go while others you don't want to get out of bed. And I know what it's like to wonder what your life's going to be ten or twenty years down the line."

"Do you ever get over that, Doc?" the young man asked.

"To a certain extent, yes, you do. But I'd be lying if I said it will all go away, because it won't. You are different, so your life will be different. But it doesn't have to be a bad different."

"What about you?"

"For me the hardest part was overcoming the anger." He chuckled. "Not sure I've done that yet. Some days are better than others."

"Sometimes I get so damned mad I don't know what to do about it. I want to scream, or punch a hole in the wall. They want me to go into PTSD therapy, but I don't think I'm ready. I feel like I need to concentrate on one thing at a time."

"Well, we've got a great doc here who specializes in PTSD, so whenever you think you're ready to see her—"

"Another doc? What the hell does this one know about it?"

"More than you and me, James. A hell of a lot more than both of us put together."

James shrugged. "Maybe later…"

"Maybe later," Marc repeated, thinking of his own aversion to PTSD therapy. He was a good one to talk, refusing it in any form for himself, then having the audacity to prescribe it for his patients. But every case was different, and he handled the emotions just fine. He didn't need to talk to someone about it. Never had. Physician, heal thyself. Yeah, right. Attend to one's own defects rather than criticizing defects in others. Wasn't he just the hypocrite?

Anne stepped out of the doorway before Marc turned to exit the room. She'd heard every word he'd said and for the most part he was spot on. Amazingly, he had a skillful way of getting through to his patient that she hadn't seen before. Marc Rousseau was a good doctor, no matter in what field he was practicing, but he wasn't good when it came to himself. He recognized the merits of psychological counseling in PTSD for others, yet not for himself, and she couldn't explain that. Had no idea what he had bottled up inside him. But it was going to be huge when it exploded. And it would explode someday, somewhere.

"Were you eavesdropping?" he asked, catching up to her in the hall.

"Didn't mean to. I actually came down to make a patient referral. One of my patients sustained a head injury, and as a result his walking is very difficult. He ambulates with a walker and does OK, but I think he could be doing better. I thought maybe you'd work up an evaluation on him to see if there's any hope for getting him more independent."

"How are his emotional capabilities?"

"To be honest, he's volatile. Bad temper you don't see coming at you. Neurologically, he's had some damage, but the neurologist thinks he should be doing more than he is. Personally, I think he's angry at himself for not being able to get on with his life. I believe that if I can get him past some of his physical hurdles, he'll do a lot better emotionally. Oh, and he's married with children, and they're just about to the point of walking away from him because he's so unpredictable. His wife does love him, though, but she fears for her safety."

"How long's he been here?"

"Just a couple of days. His neurologist checked him in and his wife told him this is his last chance. So the man's motivated one minute, but he fights it the next."

"Sure, I'll have a look. Can you have his chart sent up to my office?"

"Already did. Along with one for a burn patient and another who had a crushed pelvis. Oh, and what you said to that young man on the mat table…very nice, Marc. You've got some finesse in you after all."

"Should I take that as a compliment?"

"Take it any way you wish, but personally I think there's more to you than meets the eye." And right now her eye was a little more than pleased by his scruffy look. And those shoulders… Oh, dear Lord, those shoulders.

Nope, she wasn't looking. It took everything she had to keep her life on track and the last thing she needed was to drag another man into it who had his own set of problems to deal with. So looking was allowed, but nothing else. Besides, there was his personality, which half the time wasn't nearly as pleasing as his good looks.

It was nearly ten by the time she was ready to leave, and from the parking lot she could see that Marc's office lights were still on. It was good to know she wasn't the only one who worked so late. Standing there, watching for a minute, she debated whether or not she should ask him out to grab a pizza or just leave well enough alone.

"You don't need this," she said as she fished her keys from her purse. Having a professional relationship was one thing, but carrying it beyond that…no way! She knew better. More than that, she knew how to resist it. But just as she was about to climb into the driver's seat, her cell phone rang.

"I was waiting for your call," he said. "The way you were hesitating and looking at my office window…I was sure you'd call."

"I might have, if I'd had anything to say," she said in a voice way more surly than she'd intended.

"How about we split a pizza?"

"I already ate," she lied, torn between going and not going. Part of her certainly wanted to, but part of her was afraid of what might come of it.

"It's just a pizza, Anne. Nothing more, I promise. Suit yourself, but I'll be out in five if you care to wait."

"How about we meet at Crazy Jack's for a burger? See you there."

Giving in felt right, and Anne clicked off her phone and studied the light in his office for the next few seconds until it went out, then she unlocked the car door. Once inside, she pulled out of her parking spot and was proceeding to the exit when all of a sudden another car pulled out of its spot and slammed directly into hers. There was an awful clash of tires squealing, cars hitting each other, horns honking. And the car that had hit hers actually pushed her car sideways into the bumpers of two other cars parked in the same row.

Anne's seat belt locked down so hard she thought she was going to die right there from a lack of breath.

Once her breathing returned to normal she assessed herself, as she would any patient. Pulse—rapid. Arms scraped and bloody from window glass. She knew she hadn't sustained internal damage, though, unless her ribs were broken, which she didn't think they were, in spite of the seat belt, but she was willing to bet she'd have a nice seat-belt bruise.

Finally regaining her wits, she looked outside to see if someone in the other car might need help and, much to her chagrin, she saw the driver had extricated the vehicle and was in the process of trying to drive off.

"Don't you dare," she choked out. But it was too late. Now all she could do was hope that the guard at the exit had heard the crash and could prevent the car from leaving. No such luck, though. She saw the car crash right through the wooden guard gate.

Anne was gathering up the items from her purse that had fallen out when, from the outside, she heard a familiar voice. "What the hell happened here? Anne, are you OK?"

"Someone hit my car and took off." Her nerves finally caught up with her as the lot guard came running up, and she smacked angrily at a tear running down her bloody cheek. "I can't believe he just drove away."

"I got his plate number, Doc, and I've already called it in to the police," the guard responded.

"Thanks, Gus," Anne said, still batting at tears.

Immediately, Marc tried to open the driver's-side door but it was too smashed in to budge. So, with cell phone in one hand and wheeling with the other, he went around to the passenger's side but was unable to get through between the other cars she'd been rammed into, so he went back to the driver's side and asked through the broken window, "Are you hurt, Anne?"

"Not too seriously," she called back out. "Bruising and abrasions mostly."

"Well, I've called emergency and help is on its way."

Within two minutes an ambulance from the next-door hospital arrived, and shortly after that the fire department emergency squad arrived and went to work to get Anne out of the car. That took only a minute or so, and when they lifted her out of the seat, she naturally insisted on walking to the hospital, but they put her in the back of the ambulance anyway.

All the while, Marc was pacing back and forth, around in circles, around the car. He felt helpless to do anything. But as they started to lift Anne into the ambulance, she held out her hand to him.

He took it. "I'm sorry I couldn't do more," he said.

"More? You helped me keep my sanity. It was awfully tight in there and you took my mind off being trapped."

He shrugged, then backed away and watched the ambulance span the two parking lots. Then he followed. Before he entered the ER doors, though, Marc called Jason, who was still at the hospital with Hannah. "She's OK, mostly shaken, but they'll do a full workup to make sure. Look, I'm on my way in there right now. How about I see her, then call you back with the details before you mention any of this to Hannah?"

"I'd appreciate that. She's doing fine—worried about the baby, of course. So I don't want to heap more onto that until we have some specifics."

The instant Marc clicked out of the conversation, he was wheeling through the emergency doors. Once inside, he went straight to the admitting desk.

"I'm looking for Anne Sebastian," he said impatiently.

"Sorry, sir, but the doctor is with her, then the police are waiting to question her, and she's not allowed other visitors."

"I'm not another visitor. I'm Dr. Marc Rousseau, her personal physician." He had no idea if that would work, but it was sure worth a try.

"Her physician?" The admittance clerk eyed his wheelchair suspiciously.

"Here's my ID," he said, tossing his rehab badge across the desk at her.

"Sorry, Doctor. I didn't realize—"

"That's fine," he said, pulling his ID back. "Just tell me where she is."

"Emergency four, down the hall, to your left."

Marc rolled with amazing speed until he came to the fourth room, where he knocked lightly, then pushed his way in.

"Who the hell are you?" the attending physician blurted out.

"A colleague. We work together at the rehab center. I'm Dr. Marc Rousseau, head of physical rehabilitative medicine. And you are?"

"Dr. Forester, third-year resident."

Marc gave him a cordial nod. Then wheeled past him. "How are you?" he asked, taking an assessment of her EKG and also the IV solution dripping into her arm.

"A little groggy. They're going to take me to X-Ray—"

"To do a CT scan to make sure she's not suffering any hidden internal injuries," Dr. Forester cut in, trying to take the authoritative position, which he'd so visibly lost. "Right now, it all seems pretty simple—"

"Easy for you to say," Anne snapped, then immediately apologized. "Sorry, but when a patient is in pain, the last thing they want to hear is how simple it is."

"You're a doctor, too, aren't you?" Forester asked.

"In charge of the post-traumatic stress disorder program," she said, her voice clearly weak.

Forester grimaced. "I just can't win."

Laughing, Marc took Anne's hand. "We've all had those days," he quipped as he studied the IV needle in the back of it. "And just as long as you get her taken care of, we've got no problems."

"Well, he's taken care of one thing, because I'm just about ready to..." With that, Anne nodded off. Which was just as well, as when she awoke she was going to have to deal with the way her face looked, which was a mess. And she'd had other abrasive pain and God only knew what else. But she was lucky to be alive, and that's all that mattered.

"Is she going to a room tonight, or are you going to keep her here?"

"We'll have her in a private room in about an hour. It might take her a couple days of recovery here before we send her home."

Marc nodded. "I'll go check and see what room, then meet her there." But his big concern was trying to keep her down, as the doctor had said she should be. Short of duct tape and a rope, she'd be up and about as soon as she woke up. Which wouldn't be good. So maybe he'd stay with her as much as he could and enforce doctor's orders.

Marc winced over that solution, then gave in to a smile. Never let it be said that he couldn't come out on top in the toughest of challenges. And Anne was one of the toughest he'd ever come face to face with.

CHAPTER SIX

"I'M SO SORE I don't know if I'm ever going to get out of bed again," Anne complained as she raised herself up in bed. Her head spun first, then the room spun around her.

She wasn't hungry, either, even though a snack tray had been brought to her since she'd missed her dinner. Turkey sandwich, tomato soup, all good in someone else's world tonight but not in her own. But the thought of hot tea was appealing, so she accepted that and pushed the rest of the bedside cart away. "You can have it if you're hungry," she told Marc.

Marc had spent the first part of the night in the room with her, pulling two chairs together and using them like a bed. "I think I'd rather have some nice hot coffee to keep me awake."

"You don't need to stay here and babysit me. I'm fine."

"Actually, I've been doing some dozing." Not true. He'd been watching her. Watching her breathing and everything else she did while she slept.

"I didn't mean to disturb you," she mumbled in her thick haze. "Why don't you go home where you can sleep in your bed?" Her heavy eyelids wanted to droop shut and it was taking everything she had in her to keep them open. "Before I doze off again, I need to call Jason and let him know—"

"I did, and he does. In fact, he was here for a while. Your sister wanted to come down, too, but that's been put on hold until tomorrow morning."

"She's good?"

"She's doing great. They'll probably release her tomorrow some time."

"You did such an amazing job…" Her eyelids finally fluttered shut. But somewhere in her deep haze she managed to remember something. "Need a car rental. Have to arrange that tomorrow."

"But you won't need it tomorrow. Probably not for a few days, with the meds they've got you on. So for now, concentrate on how lucky you are to be alive and relatively uninjured."

"Marc, were you able to feel the shrapnel from the IED?" she asked out of the blue.

"Why?"

"No reason. Mostly just curiosity. Because I felt the glass shards in my arm and they hurt."

"I had excruciating pain in places for a good long while. It was managed with pain meds, but as the pain went away, more damage surfaced." He shrugged. "And this is what I got. But I do feel pain in other areas, just not enough to stop me."

"So was physical rehab hard for you?"

"It was, and was the hardest thing I've ever had to do. And when I give up or slack off, it's difficult to regain what I lose, so I guess you could say I'm a slave to my rehab."

"Is that why you chose physical rehab medicine as a

specialty?" Her eyelids started to droop again, though she fought hard against the sleep that wanted to overtake her. But she didn't want to go to sleep, not yet. She was…afraid. Afraid of the dark, and the loss of control she'd have over herself and her surroundings when she slept. So she talked instead of giving in.

"Because I have experience, partly. Because I know how important it is on a regular basis, mostly."

"But do you like it?"

"Let's just say I don't hate it. It wasn't my first choice, but it was a field that was wide open to me and it's growing on me every day."

She sighed heavily. "So do you find it annoying when you hear someone like me complain because I'm in pain? Because I do complain."

"Yes, you do. And, no, I don't get upset. I mean, right now, when I look at your face and the way it's banged up, it makes me cringe to think about how much that must hurt."

"My face is that bad?" Her eyelids popped back open fully and she pulled the bedside tray over to her and flipped it open to the mirror inside. "Wow," she said, running her hands lightly over the cuts and scrapes. "That's pretty bad. I guess the painkiller has been numbing more than my pain."

"But it will heal."

"With scars," she said glumly. "Do you think I'll need plastic surgery?"

"Probably not. Facial lacerations tend to look worse than they are. And yours are more scrapes and bruises than anything else. Nothing that's going to mar your pretty face."

"But what if I do need it? I know it sounds trite after

what you've been through, but the thought of having surgery scares me to death."

He took hold of her hand and gave it a sympathetic squeeze.

"There nothing to it. You go to sleep, and you wake up later on." He smiled. "I've had seven surgeries and done hundreds, so I'm a bit of an expert here, on both sides of it."

"Seven?"

"Some were minor. Five were major. The worst part is the recovery room, where all you want to do is go back to your room and sleep, and they won't let you."

"Maybe I won't need surgery," she said hopefully as Marc straightened up, stretched, and transferred to his wheelchair.

"And maybe if you do, it won't be such a major trauma having someone there with you who's been through it all before."

"Meaning you?"

"Meaning I'm going to go grab a pair of scrubs from supply to sleep in and get myself cleaned up and ready for tomorrow. I'll be back in a few minutes."

True to his word, Marc returned with clean scrubs and went straight to the bathroom, shut the door and left Anne out in the room to wonder just how much function he had. In her mind, Anne saw Marc as having full function except for the use of his legs. Maybe that's the way it was or maybe that's the way she wanted him to be. Whatever the case, she could picture him in the shower, water running over his chest, his hair slicked back. And here she was, in rough shape, thinking about that! Shameful. Absolutely shameful. But as she lay back, the image refused to go away, and the only reason she could see for her condition was that her pain meds

were making her not only pain-free but delusional...
yes, that had to be it. She was...

By the time Marc emerged from the bathroom, Anne
was fast asleep. So before he made himself comfortable in his makeshift bed next to her, he bent over and
gave her a light kiss on the forehead. "Sweet dreams,"
he said, then prepared to sleep there for the night. No
reason not to, he told himself.

But as he looked at her, her skin so pale against the
white sheets, he knew he was treading on thin ice. Anne
was an intriguing, beautiful woman and he loved the
challenge of her. She probably wouldn't have been his
type before his accident, as those women had been fast
in and out his swinging door. But Anne would have
been the keeper. Except a man in his condition didn't
get to keep. There'd be no fairness in it; not for either
one of them.

He brushed the hair back from her face and recon-
ciled himself to a long, sleepless night and lots and lots
of thoughts about the woman he couldn't have, even if
she'd have him.

"Come on, Anne. Wake up. You've got to eat something
or they're going to force-feed you through a tube. A
great big one about the size of a garden hose."

She opened her eyes, expecting to find Marc there,
wet from his shower, but much to her surprise, all she
found was her sister in a chair, sitting next to her bed.

"I'm serious. They're going to stick in a feeding tube
if you refuse to eat your dinner."

"Dinner? Where did lunch go? And breakfast?"

"You slept through them. Moaned a couple of times,
but never really woke up."

"I was tired."

"You wanted Marc. His was the name you moaned."

"But he didn't hear me, did he?"

"Don't know. He left right after breakfast—had patients to see. Said he'd be back tonight. So unless you want him to see you with a feeding tube up your nose…" Hannah pushed the dinner tray in her sister's direction "…you'd better make an attempt."

It was meat loaf and mashed potatoes. "I'd rather have fruit."

"Quit complaining and eat," Hannah ordered.

"How about you eat it, then we'll say I did?" Anne tried to persuade her twin.

"How about you eat it and I'll report that you were a good girl?"

Anne huffed out an impatient sigh. "I'll eat, but I want to hear everything about the baby, like what did you finally name her?"

"Baby's doing well. Breathing on her own, eating like a little pig. Her blood sugar seems to be leveling and we named her Anne Miranda."

"What? You named her after me?" Anne Miranda Lewis.

"Yes, but we're calling her Annie."

"I don't know what to say except I'm flattered." Truly touched, she reached across and hugged her sister. "Why?"

"Because when we were little girls we always promised we'd name our babies after each other."

"But I never thought…"

"You know you're going to owe me one, don't you? But in the meantime…eat!" Hannah picked up a spoon and scooped up some mashed potatoes, then handed it to Anne.

"Not so bad," she said. "Not so good, either."

Hannah laughed. "Maybe I can come and cook for you after you get home."

"I want to go home. Tomorrow, if I can. Which is the only reason I'm eating this stuff. But let me warn you, I don't want your cooking." She wrinkled her nose in jest. "If I have anything to say about it, we'll order takeout."

"Even though you're insulting me and all I can do is sit here and take it, you're looking good, Anne. All things considered, you were very lucky." Hannah brushed back a tear sliding down her cheek. "Jason prepared me for the worst but…"

"After I heal, we may not be so identical anymore," Anne said.

"Or we may. Who knows? And who cares if you end up with a scar or two? I sure don't."

"Well, however I turn out, I can't wait to see Annie. As soon as they let me out of bed…"

"Which won't be until tomorrow," Marc said on his way in the door.

"I think I'll take this as my cue to leave. Besides, Annie's feeding time is coming up." Rather than walking out on her own, though, she called Jason, who appeared from out of nowhere to take his wife back to her room. "And I'll see if we can bring her down here this evening for a couple of minutes."

"I'd love that!" Anne cried. "Please, try."

"No promises."

"They're pretty close, aren't they?" Marc asked, surveying the empty food tray after Jason and Hannah had left.

"Soul mates."

"How does someone do that? You know, find a soul mate."

"Don't ask me," Anne quipped. "I tried and muffed it

pretty badly. A husband who cheated as much as mine did, let's just say that's a reflection on me, too. Meaning I'm not an expert."

"Your husband was a jackass."

"I'll have to agree with you on that. I was a pretty good wife for the time we had together, and if I'd had any inclination that going overseas would cause such a great divide between us…"

"You'd have gone anyway."

"He did marry an army doctor," she said, "and he knew what he was getting. I was honest with him about that, but what he wasn't honest about was his need for a long line of women outside our door the instant I was gone."

"Did I say jackass? I meant downright stupid."

She laughed. "Another point about which we can agree. But it's done, I got out, I'm a better woman for the experience. At least, that's what I keep telling myself."

"But did it make you stronger?"

She nodded.

"And wiser?"

She nodded again.

"Then I'd say it was a hard lesson to learn but a good one."

"I agree. But at least Hannah and Jason are getting it right. And he really stood by her through her bout with infertility and all the treatments she had to take in order to get pregnant. He was so…solid for her." The kind of solidity she wanted in a man next time. If it ever happened…

"Well, they're lucky to have each other. And it shows. So now, how about you swing your legs back up and rest for a while?"

"But I'm not tired."

"Be a good girl, follow doctor's orders and you might get sprung from this place by tomorrow afternoon."

"Is that a promise?"

"Not a promise. More like a bribe."

"I'm usually more alert, Marc. I was in the army, went through combat training, came through without a scratch, then to have this happen here…" She swiped back an angry tear. "I should have seen it coming at me."

"Well, the good news is they caught the culprit. A kid who had no call to be driving. He panicked when he hit you and the rest, shall we say, is going to get his driver's license suspended. Plus his parents are going to make him pay for the insurance claim." He grimaced. "It's hard to be so young, and showing off for your girlfriend."

"His girlfriend?"

Marc nodded. "She was in the car, too."

Anne cringed. "Oh, that's rough. But somebody could have been seriously injured or killed."

"Not as rough as a hit-and-run offense could have been if they'd treated him like an adult. He's lucky they're charging him with a juvenile offense because it could have gone the other way then he'd go to jail."

"Lucky," she said, as Marc reached over and ran a tender thumb across her scraped jaw.

"Boys with too much testosterone and not enough sense don't learn. Some of the things Nick and I used to do when we were younger would curl your hair." He smiled fondly. "We were always in trouble for one thing or another. Boy stuff mostly. Never anything harmful. Stuff like digging up Mrs. Wagner's garden one night. She'd just got it planted, and she'd actually used a map she'd drawn to lay out the colors and patterns. So Nick and I waited patiently until after she'd gone to bed and we…shall we say…replanted her entire garden so nothing matched the way she'd diagramed it."

"What did she do when she found it?"

"She left it to grow as we planted it, knew it was us, of course, and our parents volunteered us to help around her house, mowing the yard, weeding the garden, running errands. Our payback pretty much used up our entire summer school vacation. And while the look belonged in the jungle it was so mismatched, it really was pretty. Next year she paid Nick and me to plant her garden according to her diagram, I suppose because she assumed if we saw how difficult and time-consuming it was, we'd never mess with her garden again."

"Did you?"

"Hell, no! It took us three days to plant it the right way—she measured out each plant in each row with a ruler, and we weren't about to go back and redo it." He chuckled. "We lived an adventurous life, I guess you could say. Not bad kids but on the verge of it."

"You really miss him, don't you?"

"I do, but he made his choice. Oh, and don't get me wrong. Nick's not a bad guy. We just don't see things the same way."

She reached across and stroked his cheek. "I'm sorry for your loss," she said. "And for Nick's, too."

"Life happens," he said.

"You're very pragmatic."

"About some things. Stuff happens to the best of them," he said, smiling. "Look, I've got to get back to work if you're OK to stay here by yourself."

"I'm not that big a baby. Just a little shaken one, but I'll be fine. Go to work."

"Good, because I've got two more new patients to

evaluate today still, and more of that ton of paperwork to catch up on. So give me a call if they change their minds and spring you this afternoon and I'll come and get you."

"I can catch a cab just as easily."

"You afraid of my driving?"

"Not afraid. It's just that—"

"You assumed I didn't, or couldn't, and you're not flexible enough to allow yourself, even for a moment, to think that there are things I can do you never counted on."

"I didn't assume anything of the sort. And it's not always about you, Marc. The thing is, I didn't want to interrupt your day. I've already put you out enough and I didn't want one more incident on my mind."

"Yeah, I'll bet. Who in their right mind would want a paraplegic to drive them. Right?" With that, he spun and wheeled out of the room, leaving Anne to vow that even if he had the last car on earth, she wouldn't let him be the one to drive her home. Not with his attitude. No, she'd catch a taxi instead.

And she did. True to Marc's words, she was released the next day without fuss or muss, and went down to the pediatric ward to say goodbye to Hannah, who'd already been released and was back to visit Annie. Even as tired and sore as Anne was, she called a cab to take her home.

Once there, though, all the energy seemed to drain from her on her way up the sidewalk and she was forced to take a seat on the cement bench outside her door just to dig through her purse to find her key. It was like she couldn't move another inch, like her body had gone as far as it was going to take her. So she gave in to defeat and just sat there looking lost and forlorn.

At least, that's what Marc saw as he rolled up the sidewalk in her direction. And his heart did go out to her, seeing her defeated this way.

"You OK?" he asked gently.

"Just so tired."

"You should be. You've had a rough couple of days."

She swiped at tears of frustration and embarrassment running down her cheeks. "What are you doing here?"

"I heard you'd been released and since you didn't wait for me to take you, I thought I'd better come and see how you're doing. Which isn't so well, is it?"

She sniffled and shook her head. "I thought I could do this by myself but I was wrong."

He took her purse from her hands and fished the keys out for her. "Mind if I help you a little?"

"You don't need to waste your time on me."

"I've asked for help when I've needed to. Look, Anne, while I was recovering I had the gruffest therapist who had no compunction whatsoever about kicking me in the butt when I needed it. Physical therapist, not a clinical therapist for PTSD. Anyway, he wouldn't let up. Wouldn't let me rest. Wouldn't budge an inch from his position. It was the most grueling few months I've ever spent in my life and I'll admit I thought about quitting more than once."

"Why didn't you?"

"Because I needed somebody on my side. And he was, even though I couldn't see it very often." He chuckled. "I threatened to get a tattoo where he left his bootprint. But, seriously, you've just been through a major trauma and you need some help right now." He unlocked the door and helped Anne to her feet. "Sometimes, though, pride just gets in the way."

"Like today."

"It's good that you want to be so independent, but don't let it be to your detriment. Now, go inside, lie down on the sofa and I'll make you a pot of tea. No arguments."

"Not from me when it sounds like just what I need."

Within two minutes, Anne was reclining on her sofa while Marc puttered about in the kitchen, putting the water in the kettle to boil. It was a nice, cozy scene and she was glad he'd come in spite of her stubbornness.

By the time Marc delivered the tea, Anne was fast asleep. So he gathered some paperwork from his SUV and made himself comfortable across from her, in her recliner chair, and spent the rest of the evening keeping a watchful eye on her and enjoying the feeling of looking after her.

She wasn't helpless—not by a long shot. And she would have gained her strength back and gotten into the house without him, but it was nice knowing he had helped, and that he *could* help the most stubborn woman he'd ever met. Yes, it was very nice.

"You OK?" he asked two hours later, when she finally woke up.

She nodded and got out a strangled "Fine."

"Want me to stay for a little while?"

"No, you've done enough. And I think I want to go to bed."

"Are you sure?"

"I'm sure. And…thank you for everything you've done. I appreciate it, Marc. Even though we don't always get along, I really do appreciate it."

He cocked an odd smile. "I thought this *was* getting along."

"It's a reasonable facsimile. You're quite sympathetic when it comes to helping others, but you're brutal when it comes to helping yourself. Why is that? Why can't you treat yourself as well as you do your patients? Or even me. I mean, every soldier leaves something behind of himself on the battlefield and carries something extra home he doesn't need or want. And it's not like I'm telling you something you don't already know."

"So I do what? Take a session or two from you and make things all better? In case you've forgotten, there's nothing you or anyone can do to give me what I left behind or make up for what I brought home. Trust me, I don't need you counseling me in the open, on the sly, or any other way you can figure out."

Anne sighed with impatience. "You think I would do that?" she asked indignantly. "Sneak in some counseling somewhere? Counsel you without your consent? Or even counsel you at all, for that matter? You've got no right to accuse me of—of doing something I wouldn't do."

"But you're a counselor, and you know how often it happens. Someone decides one little piece of advice is all you need. One little piece gives way to another, then another. One is never enough. If I let you get your hooks in me, you're not going to let go without a fight."

"My *hooks*!" She folded her arms sharply across her chest. "You've got to be kidding. You actually think I want to get my hooks into you?" Why was he angry with her all of a sudden? She hadn't tried counseling him—at least, not to her knowledge. Wouldn't try. Yet he didn't trust her. And the thing that had her wondering most was why he had such an aversion to therapy. Maybe it was her. Maybe she was blurring the boundaries between personal and professional and hadn't even realized it.

She shut her eyes and drew in a ragged breath. So

what was she doing? Reliving Bill again? Trying to mold Marc into the image of who she'd want, if she wanted someone?

"Don't you?" he asked, interrupting her thoughts.

"I'd like to see you get some counseling, and I'll admit that. But that's because you've got a bad attitude stemming from low self-esteem."

"*Aha!* There it is. One little hook going in." He faked the gesture of removing a hook from his arm and holding it out for her to see. "I win, Doctor. You lose."

She shook her head, almost sadly. "I won once, Doctor. I had an emotional breakdown and came through it because I sought help—the kind of help you need to find."

"Because of your war experiences?" he asked, suddenly concerned.

"Because of my war experiences topped off by coming home to a life I didn't expect. We'd made this life plan, only he forgot to mention the part where I was pushed away and humiliated. But the thing is, I knew I was breaking down. The cause didn't matter. The condition did. To begin with, I can't even start to describe how much I didn't trust men after that. It was like they were all flawed in some way. So I checked into a clinic when I wanted to be strong again. When I wanted to trust again."

"Did it work for you?"

"Most of the way. I don't look at all men and see Bill. But I may come on a little strong personally just to compensate for what I lost, and if that's what I've been doing to you, I'm sorry."

"Look, I'm sorry about the hooks remark."

"You should be." Her lips curled up into a smile. "At best I have claws—tiny little claws."

"You don't take an apology well, do you?"

"Oh, I accept your apology. But at the risk of being accused of snagging you with another hook, let's just say that in my practice I've encountered worse than you."

"Worse than me? How so?"

"Broken nose once. He was the sweetest, most quiet little man… He'd been a clerk stateside and took tons of ridicule for his position. Anyway, he always sat there and smiled, then one day something triggered him and, wham, black eyes and a broken nose. I considered it progress, that he was finally coming out of his shell."

"I don't like fighting with you, Anne."

"Then prove it. Quit fighting."

"Just like that?" He snapped his fingers.

"Yep. Just like that." She snapped her own fingers. "Now, if you'll excuse me, I'm tired and I'm going to go to bed. Thank you for looking out for me, though. You're a good nurturer, though a real bastard sometimes."

He chuckled. "Call me if you need anything. And I mean it!" Then he retreated down the sidewalk to his SUV. Climbed with the skill of an athlete into the front seat and pulled the wheelchair into the passenger seat next to him. It all seemed too easy. In fact, everything he did physically seemed so easy, she could see why Jason had chosen him as head of physical rehab. There was a lot Marc could teach them. A lot he could teach her, as well. And she did so want to be taught. By Marc.

CHAPTER SEVEN

"I'M SURPRISED YOU'VE come back to work this soon," Marc said, catching up to Anne in the main hall of the rehab center. "It's only been a couple of days."

"Two days too long," she quipped. "I hate being side-lined."

"Are you OK?"

"Other than a headache and stiff muscles, I'm fine, and it's better being here, keeping myself occupied, than staying at home alone, dwelling on it." Getting grumpier every time it ran through her head, which was about a hundred times an hour.

"Good thinking. When I was injured I was infinitely better off being somewhere other than at home, by my-self. So when the time came for me to start functioning on my own, I was so...I guess you could say preoccu-pied with things that weren't helping me during my therapy—things like sleeping all the time or going on TV jags and watching for twenty-four hours straight—that I quit functioning altogether and ended up back in the rehab hospital." He shrugged. "There are a hell of a lot of ways to sabotage ourselves, I discovered. And I think I took a journey through each one of them. Until I started to swim and discovered an aptitude for that. It's what made the difference in my life, I think."

"But my injury is just a bump on the head and some abrasions. Your situation was so different."

"Different, or the same, it's all about feeling violated. Or angry because you were wronged."

"On different scales," she commented. As they approached the door to her office, she stopped. "Look, I don't remember whether or not I thanked you for all the help. But thank you, Marc. In your own unique way you were a great comfort to me." She bent and kissed him on the cheek. A kiss that was long overdue.

"I don't like gushy," he said evenly.

"I didn't figure that you did, but I had to thank you."

"So I'm thanked. Now, can we get off it?"

Anne laughed. "You certainly don't take praise very well, do you?"

"I don't need praise for doing what anybody would have done."

Like spending the night next to her in the hospital room? And the kiss? That had been way above and beyond the call of duty. But maybe he thought she didn't remember. Heaven knew, she wasn't about to bring it up as there was no way to know what would set him off.

"Anyway, it's good to be back to work, so…" She stepped through her office door and looked back at him. "In my time off I read a couple of articles on water therapy and I'm wondering if it could also help certain PTSD patients—especially now that I know you have all that great experience swimming."

"PTSD as in me?" he grumbled.

"Not you, per se. But it wouldn't hurt you. The thing is, I was referring to swim therapy in conjunction with my PTSD patients."

"Meaning me again? Get me in the pool and fix me?"

"That's not what I meant! I was just saying that some

of my PTSD patients could benefit from swimming. I just wanted you to supervise them or train them if they're not used to being in a pool." She sighed. "How many times do I have to tell you…it's not about you. Anyway, I usually have lunch about one in the doctors' dining room, if you're interested in joining me. Maybe we can go over some of the benefits of water therapy for people other than you. If not, I'll understand and maybe we can do it another time."

"Have a good day," he said. Nothing else. Then he wheeled off in the direction of the therapy room, and immediately regretted his outburst. Sure, he was a little overly sensitive on the subject, but did that mean he had to take everything she said personally? Truth was, he believed she was trying to be helpful to her patients by offering water therapy, and he'd practically laid himself out there on the sacrificial altar to help her, then taken offense when she'd asked. Damn it, anyway!

Anne sat down at her desk and closed her eyes. Well, so much for trying to be polite. It rolled right off him like water off a duck's back, apparently. But why? What kind of anger was he burying? Self-destructive—that's what. He was rolling headlong into a good case of self-destructive energy if for no other reason than that's where he wanted to be. The thing was, she was pretty sure he was self-aware, and even more sure that the fact she was a PTSD counselor didn't help the matter, as he was suspicious of her motives.

So be it, she thought. Let him be suspicious, if that's what he wanted. But it wasn't her intention to counsel him even if he asked…conflict of interest and all. Although she did admit that the more she knew him, and the fonder her feelings for him grew, the more difficult it became not to offer a suggestion here and there. And if that's what she was doing she'd have to watch herself more closely. Of course, maybe he was being overly sensitive, too.

What a pair they'd make! One on the offensive and one on the defensive all the time.

So why worry about it so much? Because she cared about him, that's why. She wasn't sure she knew why and she was positive she didn't want to find out. But somewhere, deep down, she felt an affection for the man, and whether or not he liked that, well, too bad. Too damned bad.

Marc kept his eyes on the clock, debating whether or not he wanted to go down and have lunch with Anne. It always seemed like she was pushing him toward PTSD therapy. Was that his own guilt feelings coming through because he knew he could use the help, or was she really pushing as hard as he accused her of? Whatever the case, now she wanted to do it in conjunction with his own therapy modalities. Maybe it was innocent, maybe she didn't mean anything by it, or maybe it was her stubborn belief that she could fix him.

However it played out, he didn't want to be fixed. He'd had enough of that—somebody always knowing what's best for him. Well, he already knew what was best and it wasn't droning on and on about his disability. He'd dealt with that already. Wasn't looking for a repeat, or in Anne's case, someone who meant well but just didn't get it.

In the end, the clock ticked right past the time and he stayed back in his therapy room, wondering if she really had expected him to join her or if her invitation had just been another way of pointing out the merits of a program she thought would benefit him. The hell of it was he was a big advocate of water therapy. He'd spent his fair share of time in the pool because it was good exercise. But when she'd suggested it for him, it had made him feel like a patient again. Put him at a disadvantage with Anne when all he wanted to be was a normal man. Wanted her to see him as a normal man rather than as a cause. Either way, it was a moot point. He hadn't gone, and that was that!

So he worked on through the day, and the day after that, totally avoiding her, even if she was on his mind more than he needed her to be. It had been two days since he'd talked to her other than a cordial greeting in passing, and he desperately wanted something to get his mind off her. Some good, hard physical work.

So after the day was over, and all his patients had been seen by either him or the various therapists who worked in the department, he decided to work it out with a swim. He almost laughed aloud over that one. The cause of their problem was her forcing him back to the water, yet that's exactly where he went anyway when he wanted to let off some steam.

The room containing the swimming pool was stark. It was long and narrow, just the perfect size to fit a lap pool, and one side was lined with wooden benches, while the other was lined with life jackets, various flotation devices and lifesaving equipment. The pool maxed out at six feet deep and there were no diving boards to fancy it up. It was a lap pool, pure and simple. Which was all he needed this evening.

Marc changed into a pair of black trunks, avoided looking at his useless legs, and lowered himself in, then pushed off the side and began to move his way through the water, not like a swimmer who kicked and splashed so much as a graceful fish. All the effort came from his upper body as he went from end to end, then back and forth another two times before he stopped to catch his breath.

"You have a lot of power in your upper body," she whispered in the dimly lit room.

Her presence there startled him, broke his stillness in the water, and he gasped. "What the hell are you doing in here?" he finally growled.

"Looking for you."

"Why?"

"I thought you might like to come over for dinner. It's the least I can do…"

"Not hungry," he grumbled.

"But you will be in due course, especially after the way you've been swimming, like you were running from the gates of hell."

"This is the gates of hell," he snapped. "In case you haven't noticed."

"But you swim so well."

"I swim like I'm disabled."

"If that's how you want to refer to it. But what I just witnessed was a man with a very skilled mastery of his sport—a sport I'd love for him to incorporate into my therapy plan. And if you do consent to it, it would have to be you doing the work because I'm not skilled enough."

"You just don't give up, do you?"

"Not when I think it's a good idea."

"But as you see, I swim. Your little plan isn't going to benefit me."

"Maybe start a swimming team, then. There are competitive teams for people with disabilities all over the country. Perhaps you could develop someone who's good enough to compete, or even compete yourself. Who knows?"

"Because I'm able to take a few laps?"

"Because I have an idea you're good at other sports, too. And one thing translates to another. Besides, you won't know if you don't try."

"That's assuming I want to try. Which I don't."

"So what you're telling me is that if some very gifted athlete ended up in your training program and you saw future potential in him, you wouldn't help him?"

Rather than answering, Marc pushed off the side and swam away from her. But that didn't dissuade her, as she walked along the side of the pool while he swam the length.

"You'd turn your back on him?"

No answer.

"Or better yet, have him transferred to another facility because you don't want to deal with him?"

Again, no answer.

"Why is that, Marc? A good rehab doc would love to find someone with that kind of skill level."

"Then maybe I'm not a good rehab doctor," he shouted. "Maybe I'm a damned lousy rehab doctor and I'm just here biding my time because I've got nothing else to do." He swam to the opposite side of the pool where his wheelchair was sitting and pulled himself out to the poolside. "All I wanted was a few minutes of peace and quiet where I could swim alone. That's not asking too much, is it?"

"Is there ever a time when you don't want to be alone?" she called into the hollow room.

"Is there ever a time when you do?" he responded as he dried himself off with a towel.

"I'll admit I'm social, and I'm not embarrassed by it."

"Well, I'm not and I'm not embarrassed by it, either."

"But don't you ever find yourself in the mood to be around people? And I don't mean your patients."

"Not really. I've chosen my life, and I'm fine with it."

"It chose you, Marc, and you never fought back. You let it consume you."

His side of the pool was quiet for a moment, then she heard the distinct sound of him transferring into his wheelchair. "I don't need your stinking therapy," he said as he wheeled toward the door to the dressing room.

"You need something," she yelled after him. But she was yelling into the dimness as he'd already gone in to change into his clothes. How could a man so independent in one way be so resistant to change in practically every other way? She understood his bitterness, but what she didn't understand was how he'd worked so hard to get himself to a certain point, then quit.

Determined to have the last word in this argument, she crashed through the men's dressing-room doors and stopped when she saw him sliding into his jeans. "You may not need my therapy, but what you do need is to get over yourself. You're self-centered and that leads to a miserable life."

"What if I am?"

"Is that how you really want to be…forever alone? Because I don't believe it, not for one little minute."

He slipped a gray T-shirt on over his perfect torso.

"So what are you proposing to do? Turn me into some Eliza Doolittle…the rain in Spain stays mainly on the plain?"

"No, I'm not proposing anything like that. I'm just saying that you might need help to get over the next hump."

"Provided there's a hump to get over."

Anne headed to the door to the hall. "Oh, there's a hump all right. You know it as well as I do."

"So why do you want to help me?"

"Because someone helped me along the way. Actually, several people did. And I want to pass that on."

"What if I don't want help?"

"What if you do?" she asked, as she entered the hall, leaving Marc all alone in the dressing room. Sure, she was overstepping, and her vow to leave him alone was already blown to bits. But people had overstepped to help her since she'd been as hard-headed as Marc. Once she'd given up the self-pity and all the things that went with it, she'd thought she was done with the whole mess, but that couldn't have been further from the truth.

She'd been moody, too, and bitter. She'd shunned people and been rude. Just like Marc. But a number of her friends had intervened and shown her what she was doing not only to herself but how she was destroying her friendships.

Marc needed that, but he didn't have any friends here. Which was why she'd taken that role upon herself. He needed someone. Besides, she actually liked him. In his less combative moments, when his barriers were down, he was a nice man. Under different circumstances she might have found herself falling for him, but that road was closed both ways. She didn't want it and he sure as heck didn't. Still, there was something about him…

She turned and went back into the dressing room, sitting down on the bench next to him. "Don't live a miserable life, Marc. It's so easy to do. I know because I was there."

"What I don't understand is why you've zeroed in on

me as your test subject. Do you always have a project going on and I'm the one for this month?"

"I didn't zero in. Maybe I feel a certain kinship— two doctors starting over in new fields. And in spite of yourself, I do like you. But you're not my project." She reached across and gave him a tender kiss on the lips. Brief, but sizzling. "See, my projects don't ever get that."

He smiled. "You're a confusing woman, Anne Sebastian."

"Not as confusing as you." She stood, went to the hallway door and pushed it open. "Definitely not as confusing as you." Although she did admit to herself she was pretty darned confused by everything about Marc, and that included her growing feelings for him. Love? Hate? Something in between, though admittedly the hands on the clock favored the love setting.

Damn, why did she have to be so confused?

Another evening alone, another bowl of cold cereal. Tonight it wasn't palatable. In fact, he was ready to pour it down the garbage disposal within minutes of fixing it.

"Damn," he said, choking down the first bite, then picking up the glass bowl and hurling it at the wall. Cereal and glass went everywhere, but he didn't care. Right at that moment he didn't care about anything except going to bed and hoping he could sleep until morning. Shortly after crawling in between the sheets, though, he was right back out of bed, in his chair, pacing the floor.

It wasn't like he wanted to spend his life alone. He'd had a girlfriend before he'd been injured. Nice girl. But he'd pushed her away along with everyone else, convinced he wasn't what she wanted anymore. Would she have stayed with him otherwise? Hell, he didn't know, didn't have a clue. He'd pushed too hard, then blamed it on her when she'd left. That had made things easier.

Now he was right back in the same pattern with Anne, pushing her away just as hard as he could. But for different reasons. Sure, he found her attractive. He even enjoyed being around her. But she was getting too close, hitting him in the places that hurt. Knowing him better than he wanted to be known. Hell, she knew things no one was ever supposed to see and all she had to do was guess and she got it right.

If there was ever someone with a proclivity for her job, it was Anne Sebastian. She was a neat little package of compassion and knowledge and intuition all rolled up into one. And that scared him, because her radar was out for him and he had no way of blocking it other than by waging a harder battle than she was. And he wasn't sure he could do that. Wasn't sure he had it in him. Or that he really wanted to. Then it occurred to him. Why not put her to the test? Would Anne leave him alone on the therapy front if he engaged more with her on the social front? Maybe it was worth a try to see just where this thing between them was headed.

With that plan in mind, he returned to bed, but that didn't do him any good, so he got back up, dressed and went back to work to tackle that mound of paperwork. But on his way in, he encountered Anne, who was also on her way back in.

"Patient in crisis," she said as she hurried past him and didn't even hang around long enough to hold the door open for him. When he got inside, though, he heard the crisis—someone down the front hall screaming his head off.

Curious, Marc went that way to see what was going

on and found a man standing at the ward clerk's station with a knife, threatening to kill himself. Several staff members surrounded him and Anne was at the front, trying to get everybody there to keep quiet. But to no avail. The buzz was loud, which was causing the patient more agitation.

"OK, clear the area," Marc said. "Everybody! Dr. Sebastian needs *everybody* to clear the area so she can work. So, please, exit this hall."

People began to back away until the only two left were he and Anne. A security guard and a nurse also stayed, but kept their distance.

Anne looked at Marc and gave him a silent thank-you, then turned her attention to her patient. "All right, Rick. Everybody's gone, so why don't you calm down and talk to me now?"

"I'm not talking to anybody. It's not worth the effort anymore. She told me tonight she was leaving me and there's nothing I can do to stop her. So what's the point?"

Very quietly and slowly, Marc rolled backward until he'd come to the nurse, and he ordered a syringe of sedative, a benzodiazepine, to have ready in the event they had a chance to use it. Once it was drawn, he went back to Anne, who was making no headway with her patient.

"He won't budge," she said quietly to Marc.

He pulled out his pocket and showed her the syringe. "Benzodiazepine," he whispered.

She nodded. "If we have the chance."

"We will," he assured her, then began to creep up behind Rick as Anne moved in closer.

"Look, Rick," she said, after she'd moved as close as she believed safe, "maybe I can talk to her to find out what this is about. I could get her on the phone right now."

"Too late," he said despondently. "She wants Rick Junior and Amber to be raised in a sane environment and she said I can't provide that for them. The hell of it is she's right. I can't. So why bother trying to get better when it's already a done deal? She's gone and I've got nothing to get better for."

"Your children are your reason," Anne said. "Even if you can't see them every day, when you get better the courts will work out a custody arrangement and you'll get to see them then. So how do you think they'd feel, knowing they were the reason their dad killed himself? They'd have to go through life with guilt and, trust me, it's something that would never go away. I think they'd understand a war injury such as you've got, but suicide?" She shook her head. "No child should ever have to live with that."

Rick Harper took a look at his knife and dropped it on the floor. Marc moved in to scoop it up before he had a chance to change his mind, while Anne held out her hand to help Rick away from the desk. Once he was out in the open, the nurse and security guard stepped forward and took him by the arms, but he resisted them, pulled back, shoved the nurse to the floor and would have shoved the guard down as well if not for Marc, who lunged from his chair and gave Rick the shot. Rick tried to fight back, but Marc's strength was far greater than Rick's, so he pinned him to the floor until another security guard rushed forward. But by that time either the sedative was kicking in or Rick had totally given up his will to fight, as he caused no resistance when the guard picked him up off the floor and escorted him back to his room.

"You OK?" Anne asked the nurse, who was in a hurry to get up and out of there. "I want you to go next door to the hospital's ER and get looked at. You, too, Marc," she said, her voice clearly showing her authority.

"Don't need to. It was just a scratch," he said, showing her the mark Rick had left on the underside of his right forearm.

It wasn't much, but it was a duty-related injury and there were protocols. "Sure you're fine. You always are. But just this once you're going to follow my order or you won't be coming back to work until you do."

"You're serious!"

"Damned serious," she said. "There was an incident here tonight and you got roughed up. Rehab policy. You get it looked at or you're not cleared to work, and I'm going to make this very clear to you. I won't allow you back to work if you don't follow my orders. I'll go to the board if that's what I have to do. Get it?" Besides that, she cared about him, probably more than she should, and even if he had been injured she doubted he'd tell anyone.

He huffed out an impatient sigh, more for effect than meaning it. "Got it."

"Good. Now, go next door."

He almost smiled as he turned his back to her. He liked her take-charge attitude. It was…sexy and she wore it well. And it was nice to know that she cared about him enough to enforce the rules. Even though it was a waste of time since he was fine, he was flattered by her attention. Still, Anne was clearly in charge, and who was he to dispute that?

Besides, maybe this could be the start of his new plan. Oblige her with the things that didn't involve therapy and maybe she'd forget about the things they fought about. Better yet, once he didn't prove to be such a challenge, maybe she'd forget about him and focus her attention elsewhere. That would be the best outcome, even though he did like having her around, liked seeing her from time to time. Liked her more than he would or should admit. And that was the hard part because he was afraid his feelings were well on their way past liking to something else he just couldn't deal with.

CHAPTER EIGHT

THREE DAYS LATER and all was normal. He was settling into his routine, establishing new departmental policies, establishing rapport with his patients and liking his job as much as any job he could like outside surgery.

All in all, things were going well enough and he was generally pleased. Pleased with his new place with Anne, too. Except for casual greetings, she was staying out of his way, mostly because he was fine as he didn't feel like the threat of PTSD counseling was always stalking him. Although in some odd way he did miss having her around. He especially missed the huskiness of her voice when she asserted herself. It always gave him sort of a tingle.

But this was the way things were meant to be, so he was going to have to get used to them, such as they were. Luckily, the board was allowing him to progress with some changes. They were reluctant, of course, since no one really knew him and he was not a proven expert in the field. But his preliminary ideas made sense. So phase one involved some construction, and a wall was being built to divide the main therapy room in two. That way, people with one form of injury wouldn't be discouraged by progress made by others with different injuries.

He remembered once during his rehab that one of the guys who was a quadriplegic became very belligerent and then inconsolable when a paraplegic who'd spent less time there had made significantly more progress. Of course, you couldn't compare the injuries, but to sit and watch one guy excelling over you, day in and day out…he'd really felt for the guy, which was why he'd set up this new arrangement as his first priority. His therapy was meant to help. Not hinder.

And there were so many more cases similar to that, cases where one patient's progress was actually impeded by another's through nobody's fault other than a lacking facility. The thing was, fighting the fight was hard enough, but watching other outcomes that might progress faster than yours…it could be heartbreaking. So now his therapy departments would have some distinctions in therapy levels. And later there would be private rooms for more individualized attention, or for people who suffered emotional distress. Yes, it was a good plan, and he was proud of it.

"It's coming along," Anne said, greeting him in the hallway.

"I hope we're ready in the next couple of weeks to set it up."

"How are you doing?"

"Is that a professional or a personal question?"

"Is that a professional or a personal comeback?"

Marc laughed. "You're always on guard, aren't you?"

"I was going to say it's the other way around. Look, Hannah is home now, and I'm going over there to fix dinner, so I'll talk to you later."

"Yes, I had an invitation."

"You did?"

"From Hannah herself. She called me about an hour ago and asked if I'd like to join you."

"And you said?"

"That I'd be delighted, of course."

"Of course," she replied.

"Is she up to company?" he asked.

"She's going crazy being home and not having her baby home yet. Having you there will distract her."

"What about you? Will it distract you?"

"No," she lied. "I barely even notice you."

"Now, that's what I call cordial." The corners of his lips turned up slightly, but it was the twinkle in his eyes that gave away his good mood.

Anne arched playful eyebrows and scurried away. It hadn't been her intention to invite Marc to dinner, but it seemed her matchmaking sister had outmaneuvered her. Well, damn it anyway. While she wouldn't exactly be distracted by Marc, she was going to have to be careful around him. Or else her sister and everybody else might get the wrong idea. And it was so, so wrong. Sure, he was handsome. Sure, she liked looking. But more than that? No way.

"Roast chicken, stuffing, whipped potatoes, green beans and cherry pie. Sure looks yummy," Hannah said. "Almost as yummy as Marc."

"Why did you do this?" Anne asked her out of earshot of the men.

"The way you two are off again, on again, someone had to," Hannah quipped as she tasted the potatoes.

"But why you?"

"It's time. You have a thing for him and unless I miss my guess, he has one for you."

"But there are too many fundamental problems in the way. First off, I'm not sure I'm ready."

"Because of Bill? Well, get over him. He was the

proverbial one bad seed and you've squished that into the ground."

"Then there's Marc's grumpiness…"

"Versus your stubbornness. Makes you a pretty good match, I'd say."

"And there's his need to be alone."

"Like you didn't go through that yourself? So is it really Marc's disability? Because if it is, get over it. He's one of the good ones who's temporarily going through a bad patch. We all have them, including you!"

Anne shook her head. "It's not his disability. It's more like I can't predict how he's going to be from moment to moment, and that scares me."

"Since when did you want predictability?"

"Since I had Bill."

"Do you have something going on with Marc?" Hannah asked bluntly.

"I don't know. I thought I knew what it should feel like with Bill, but look how that turned out."

"So it is Bill?"

"I'm not going to win with you, am I?"

Hannah smiled and shook her head. "And you don't really want to because you know I'm right about this. You're falling for Marc, even though you're fighting yourself over it."

"I should have stayed home," Anne grumbled, "and argued with myself. At least one side of me would have won."

"What? And miss an evening with Marc? I don't think you'd do that."

"I could walk out that door right now."

"Your loss, Anne, if you do."

"She's quite a cook," Jason commented as he took his second helping of beans. "Anne's the domestic one.

Hannah…not so much." He gave his wife's hand a squeeze. "But with a new baby, things might change for a while."

"Don't count on it," Hannah said as she nibbled on a chicken leg. "With a baby at home, I doubt if I'll even notice when you're here."

"I thought you were going to get help," Anne said.

"I don't know yet if I want somebody helping out with the baby or if I want to take a leave for a few years. Now that I've been separated from Annie for a few days, I'm not sure what I'll do. Maybe I'll decide after Mom and Dad are here. Oh, and Jason's parents are coming after ours leave, and his grandmother will be coming after that, so I've got a good two months to decide."

"Maybe Anne will hire out as a domestic," Marc teased. "Cooking, cleaning, that sort of thing."

"I had a husband once who expected that from me. He wanted me to work and he also wanted his meals on the table. It's hard to do when you're a military soldier. He cheated because he said he didn't get enough from me, that all my crazy hours, then going overseas, compromised the sacred estate of marriage."

"He called it 'the sacred estate'?" Marc asked.

Anne shrugged. "He did, which the judge found hypocritical, considering all the affairs he had while I was busy in the army."

"He didn't have much of a leg to stand on in the divorce proceedings," Hannah said, then immediately started blushing. "I'm sorry. I didn't mean…" Her voice trailed off as she scrambled for the right words.

"That's all right," Marc said. "I don't take offense that easily."

"He has a thick skull," Anne said.

"And you know me well enough to make that judgment?"

Anne straightened her shoulders. "You're like an open book, Marc. Very easy to read."

"You think so, do you?"

"I think so."

"Then give me an example," he said, grinning.

"Your new therapy rooms. Shows empathy. Lots of it, actually. You care for your patients' welfare, and while that might not be expressed in words, you show it in your actions."

"Or efficiency. It doesn't give me more space but it gives me a better use of what's there."

"*Empathy*, dividing your patient classifications. You can call it what you want, but anybody looking in can see it for what it is."

"Or a better way to spend their time in therapy where they don't have to envy someone who's making more progress or pity someone who's not." He smiled. "Shrinks work with emotions, rehab doctors and surgeons employ logic."

"Yeah, right," Anne said. "Empathy is only good for some."

"You said it."

She folded her arms across her chest, barely even noticing goodbyes from Hannah and Jason as they went off to the hospital for their nightly visit to see Annie.

"Why can't you take a compliment?" Anne asked Marc.

"What was a compliment?"

"What I said about what you're doing in your therapy rooms. That's where this all started and you misconstrued…" She looked around and suddenly realized that she and Marc were alone. "See, your arguing ran them off."

"Might have been your arguing."

"I was trying to pay you a compliment." His eyes just sparkled and he was so attractive. She'd admittedly married partially for good looks the first time and he stood in Marc's shadow, lookswise. In fact, Marc was a real head turner, rough edges and all.

"Compliment accepted, but I'm not accepting the blame for your sister running away. That's all on you."

Anne laughed. "I'll accept half the responsibility, not a percentage point more." She really enjoyed this banter and wondered how he'd been before his accident. A lot lighter than he was now, she decided. Damn war, with its casualties! There were too many on all sides. "But you have to accept half the responsibility for cleaning up because I'm pretty sure Hannah doesn't want to come back to it after she's said good-night to the baby."

"You wash, I'll dry. And you can put away since I don't know where anything goes, and I'll clean the table and counters. Deal?"

"Deal," she said. "But I'm wondering now how you're going to wiggle out of your end of the responsibility."

"Let's see…there are so many ways to do that. I could tell you I'm exhausted, or I've got a patient to see at the hospital, or maybe my muscles are cramping. Want some more?"

"That's plenty," she said, laughing. "And I'll admit you're pretty good at the excuses. I'm never quite that quick on my feet, and once I think of one, the moment has passed."

"You strike me as someone who's very quick on her feet. Like that patient who tried to kill himself the other night. What you said was brilliant."

"And what you did was brave." She filled the sink with sudsy water as Marc took the leftovers and put them in storage bags.

"Not brave. More like a response from my combat training. I've had to pull a guy off the ledge more than once while I was in the battlefield so I've had some practice."

"Why didn't you go into psychiatry?"

"Had no desire to get mixed up in someone else's mental health problems...*at the time*. Of course, things change."

"Just look at the two of us in our different fields."

"But you had a choice. I didn't."

"That's true," she said, as she handed him the first plate to dry. "But you could have landed somewhere in the surgical field if you'd wanted. As an administrator or teacher..."

"Except that wasn't me. I'm a hands-on kind of guy and I like to be closer to my patients than either of those jobs would have allowed me."

"Makes sense."

"So why did you change?" he asked.

"After I was a mess, I just lost heart for general practice. I became intrigued by the whole process of the emotional makeup that in many cases is related to a change in bodily function or perception. I'd come close to being a psychiatrist once before and had changed my mind, so I just changed it back with a little diversion.

"Psychiatry was one of my options, also radiology. I had choices, but radiology never interested me, and as for psychiatry, I don't come equipped with the kind of empathy you need to get involved on the level you do. I want to help, but not with someone's mental health because I've had my own days when I wondered if I was going insane or even going to make it."

"But look at me, Marc. I went down the wrong road and came back to work on that road."

"Because you've got a different emotional makeup than I have." He stacked the plates neatly, one by one, on the counter. "You implode, I explode. That makes a big difference."

Or a good combination, she thought as the last dish was washed, dried and put away. "So, your indentured servitude is over. You're free to go."

"How are you going to get home?"

She sighed intensely. "No car means I call a cab or beg a ride."

"What about a rental car?"

"My insurance should provide one, but so far they haven't. It's a little messed up, but I should get one soon."

"Then I can drive you."

"Sure you don't mind? Because I don't mind waiting here."

"It's late. You've got bags under your eyes. You look like you could use your sleep."

"Are you purposely trying to insult me, or does it come naturally?"

"Maybe a little of both." He hung up the dish towel and headed for the front door. "Or maybe I'm being honest."

"That I look like hell."

"You work too much. It shows on you. So, when was the last time you took a complete day off? One without any work at all?"

"It's hard to do when I have patients who might need me anytime."

"See, that's the thing. Devoted is one thing, but obsessed is another." Marc opened the front door for her, then followed her out. "And trust me when I tell you, I know obsessed."

"Because you are?"

"Because I used to be. Before I was injured. But being a para puts things in a different perspective."

"How so?"

"By necessity, it slows you down, to start with. Gives you a whole lot more time to think and reevaluate your life and what direction you want to go."

"But I'm not convinced you're going in the direction you want."

"It's better than the alternatives. I mean, can you see me teaching medicine to an eager class of first-year med students? It might work for some people but not for me."

"Because you're still too full of life to compromise?" she asked him.

"In my mind I am. And that's not to knock those who teach, because I admire the great teachers of the world past and present. More like it's admitting my weakness. As a teacher I'd never be great or even good. It's not in my makeup to do that and I'm smart enough to admit it."

He opened the car door for her, then rolled around to the driver's side, which was specially equipped for someone with his condition. "In my mind I'm still driving a sports car and I don't need something with hand controls that accommodates my wheelchair. But in my reality I've made the adjustment, and it's the best of all my choices." He shrugged. "And that's the way it is."

"It's a good choice," she said. "I'm already hearing good things about your work."

He chuckled. "But not about me?"

"You're not easy," she said as he put the car into gear

and they moved forward. "Not friendly, most of the time, not even cordial to your colleagues. Good with your patients, though, so I guess that's what counts."

"Being nice to everybody expends a lot of effort I don't want to waste. It's easier to ignore them."

"A smile or a simple nod of the head wastes effort? Aren't you grumpy!" She twisted to look out the window, wondering why she'd agreed to this ride in the first place. She understood that Marc had a gripe with the world, but he dwelt on it every minute of every day and that's what she didn't understand. Why would someone choose to make themselves miserable when help was available? Was he afraid of failure? That if he completely bombed out there was no place else left to go? Had he tried already and failed?

"I don't think that expressing my opinion makes me grumpy. It just makes me...opinionated."

"See, that's the thing. Your opinions are often grumpy."

"But when, exactly, am I grumpy to you? Point it out to me and I'll stop. In fact, spread the word to the staff. Tell them to call me out if I'm being grumpy to them."

"It's not grumpy so much as standoffish. And you're that way to darned near everybody but your patients."

As they pulled up in front of her house, she paused for a moment before she got out. "I'm the impatient one," she admitted, "and I'm sorry I attributed my attitude to you. But it's not easy seeing your own faults so clearly, is it?"

"It's not a fault. Just part of the personality trait that makes you who you are. Wouldn't want you to change."

"Yet that's what I'm trying to do to you."

"Running into a great big wall of resistance, though, aren't you?" he said, grinning.

"That's true," she said.

"How about we wave the white flag? You don't try to fix me and I won't point out all your own *insufferable* ways."

"I do have a few, don't I?"

"Just a few."

"Then truce it is." She reached out a hand to shake his, but somehow ended up in his arms. "Is this the way you always call a truce?" she asked him.

"I've never called a truce before and this seemed the right way to go about it."

"Maybe it is, but it scares me, Marc."

"Because I'm a para?"

"No. Because I'm not ready, and I don't know how to get myself ready."

"Do you want to?"

She shrugged. "I don't know… Maybe."

"Can't blame a man for trying," he said, gently pushing her away.

"Don't end it yet," she said. "Just give me more time."

"To find even more reasons to be uncertain? No, I don't think so."

She sighed heavily. "I made such a bad mistake once…"

"Which is in your past. Unless you're not completely over him."

"Believe me, I'm over him. But I haven't learned how to move on."

"With a paraplegic to boot."

"Don't make this about you, Marc. It's not!"

"In some way, it's always about me." He smiled regretfully. "I shouldn't have tried. I know better. Now, I think it's time for you to go in. Forgive me for not going in with you, but I'll watch you from here to make sure you get in safely."

She did. And quickly. And felt like kicking the door once she was inside.

The days dragged on one after another and not much changed except the interior factions of his physical therapy workrooms, and they made remarkable progress. He was pleased with their progress, and if things went according to plan, they would be completed within days.

The rehab center was planning on a small reception and dedication, neither of which he cared to be part of. But that went along with the job and maybe it would give him a chance to see Anne, who'd been conspicuously absent from his end of the world since that night in the car. What the hell had he been thinking? Actually, for a moment he'd been a normal man again. Nothing wrong or different about him. Same old urges and attractions. Same old responses. But he was no longer allowed to have these.

No, not him. Had fought honorably in his day. Been discharged honorably when it had been over for him. And been left with so little else to push him along the way. Oh, the help was there if he cared to go out and find it, but what was there to find that hadn't already been found, other than the pieces of pain and heartbreak he kept tucked away as a reminder? But the truth of it was that he'd left so much of himself behind. Until that moment with Anne. Until all the moments with Anne. But he wasn't entitled to those moments, was he? He'd paid his dues, yet that didn't give him back everything, especially the things most essential to life.

Well, she could stay away from him, damn her. Everyone else did, then wondered why he pushed so hard.

The answer was simple. It was easier to push than be pushed. For that one single instant he'd forgotten it, and he didn't blame Anne for her reaction. Wasn't even angry at her. It wasn't her fault. He'd inserted himself into her life in a place where he had no right, and had gotten what he deserved.

"I'm so glad she's home and things are finally settling down for you," Anne said to Hannah, who looked exhausted. Their parents were there, fussing over Hannah and the baby almost incessantly now, and Hannah was enjoying the pampering, happy to have her sister nearby to help when necessary. Or remind their parents they were doting a bit too much.

"There's no settling down with a newborn. Only brief moments of rest. Too brief, too few, and half the time I'm wrestling Mom or Dad for baby time."

"How's Jason handling it?"

"He's doing fine. Splitting the night shift with me and taking as much of it as he can when Mom and Dad will let him. But he needs his sleep, too."

"I can help, too," Anne volunteered. "I can come over some evening and watch her the entire night while you and Jason and Mom and Dad all go out to dinner, then get a good night's rest."

"Would you? I mean, you don't have to, but other than Jason's and our parents and grandparents you're the only one I'd trust with her."

"Just name the night."

"Friday," Hannah said without hesitation.

"Then Friday it is."

"Unless you have a date with that hunk Marc."

"Date? The man is…well, actually, so am I."

"What?"

"Reclusive. We almost had a moment, but we pulled back, and I'm not even sure which one of us did the pulling."

"So there's some attraction there?"

"Some, maybe. Or let's just say there could be. But…" She shook her head. "I don't even know what it is except that he quit just as we were about to get to the good stuff. So did I, though. It's like we've got the chemistry, but we're fighting it."

"Is it his chair?" Hannah asked.

"That's what I keep asking myself and I don't think it is. In fact, I don't even think of it. To me it's just the way he is."

"What chair, what hunk?" Anne's mother cut in. "Are you finally dating someone, dear?"

"No, Mom. Not dating. He doesn't date, and neither do I."

"Why not, especially if he's a hunk?" Joann Sebastian was petite, with glossy brown hair tied back from her attractive face. Without looking hard, she could have been mistaken for their older sister.

"So is it your baggage with your first marriage?" she asked her daughter.

"That's what I'm wondering. I mean, I picked a man who cheated on me, so what does that say about me?"

"It says you made a mistake. But someday you're going to have to get over it and move on. We all do stupid things, Anne. I almost flunked out of nursing school I was partying so hard, and how many times did I turn down your father before I finally went out with him? Probably a dozen." She pulled Anne into her arms and hugged her. "The best that can be said is that we're human and, coincidentally, that's the worst that can be said, too. We all have foibles."

"But some foibles seem bigger by comparison than others."

Hannah laughed. "Get over yourself. You're taking it all too seriously. If you care for the man, let him know and see how it works from there."

"I'm a coward."

"Who could miss out on the best thing ever," her mother retorted. "Too bad if you do, but don't come looking for sympathy from me if you don't even try."

"And that's what mothers are for," Anne said despondently as Annie woke up and started crying.

"So much for peace and quiet." Hannah pushed herself off the sofa to head up to take care of her daughter.

"Good thing Auntie Anne is more helpful than her sister," Anne said on her way up the stairs behind Hannah. "At least I can be called on to do something productive."

"Do something productive and call him," Joann called from downstairs. "Maybe he'll come over here Friday night and help you babysit."

"Quit nagging," Anne said at the top of the stairs. "It'll rub off on the baby."

"And stop moaning and start acting, or it'll become a habit," Hannah said.

The thing was, Hannah and their mom were right. Every word of it. But was she ready to change? That's the part she didn't know and didn't want to think about. Change was difficult. She'd done it once before and she wasn't sure she was up to it again. Wasn't sure at all.

CHAPTER NINE

THE WEEK WENT quickly and she'd had lunch dates with Marc a couple of times, conversations in the hall, even rides back and forth to work before her new car finally arrived.

But tonight she'd decided to do the babysitting alone rather than inviting Marc to join her. She didn't want him to think she was being too pushy, and that seemed pushy. Besides, she was looking forward to a little one-on-one time with her niece.

So Friday hopped up and, true to her word, she went off to babysit for the evening. But when she arrived, Marc's SUV was already there. "What's this about?" she whispered to Hannah. "What's he doing here?"

"Just having a meeting with Jason. He'll be gone in the next few minutes."

Anne's heart skipped a beat. Suddenly a night with Marc looked appealing, but that wasn't to be the case.

"And I'm afraid we're going to have to cancel. Annie has come down with a slight temperature, and we don't want to leave her. I did leave you a voicemail a couple times but I guess you're not listening to your messages."

"Busy day. Is there anything I can do?" The prospect of another Friday evening alone looked bleak. Nowhere to go but home, nothing to do but read. Her life was beginning to close in around her. Of course, that was her choice, wasn't it? She was the one who'd turned herself into a recluse. She was the one who hadn't looked outward for a life.

"Want to go for dinner?" Marc said from behind her. "Since you're not busy and neither am I, I thought maybe we could be not busy together."

"I could be persuaded," she said coyly. Coy? Why was she was suddenly sounding so coy? She was being silly, that's why. She'd wanted something to do and here it was, and she was acting like a schoolgirl out on her first date.

"There's a nice little Italian place over by the park. I've stopped in there a couple of times and it seems good. And it's easily accessible."

"I know the place. It's called Mama Maria's. Great pizza! Since I've finally got my rental car and you've got your SUV, how about I meet you there?"

"How about I drive you there like a real date and we can come back here later and pick up your car?"

"You sure you don't mind?"

"Unless you mind being seen with me."

"That's ridiculous."

"Glad you're going," Hannah said on her way back up the stairs, carrying Annie. "Now I feel better that you two are going on a date."

Anne gave her sister a frown, even though Hannah couldn't see it. "Just an impromptu meeting," Anne insisted.

"That would normally be called a date, except when Anne's involved," Marc replied, "since she makes it quite clear she doesn't date."

"She actually doesn't." Hannah jumped in to defend

her twin from the top of the stairs. "Even though we've tried to get her to."

"You know, I'm standing right here," Anne said. "Listening."

"We're not saying anything you don't already know," Hannah replied.

"The thing is, I won't defend myself because I don't want to. We all make our choices." Anne moved toward the door. "And on second thought, to make this seem less datelike, I'll drive myself. See you in ten, Marc."

"Well, have a nice nondate this evening," Hannah called to them.

"They have a nice brick pizza oven."

"I've seen the pizza, even smelled it, and it always seems delicious, but I've never been there," she said.

"Let me guess. You don't generally eat out alone, do you?"

"And you do?" she asked.

"I stop here for a take-out pizza every now and then."

"But you never stay here and eat alone."

"It's a lonely prospect," he admitted. "People look at you…"

"And pity you for being all alone. But the good thing is you vary your diet from cold cereal occasionally."

"Eating is just that. It sustains you. Doesn't matter what it is as long as it gets you by."

She studied him for a moment. "That's a sign of depression, you know."

He chuckled. "I knew you'd pick up on something like that. But the truth is I'm not depressed. I just don't prioritize my eating. Don't care about it one way or the other."

"Then why bother asking me out?"

"Because your plans changed and I was doing the polite thing."

"Then it is a pity meal."

"Maybe a little. But even though we've had lunch and a few hallway conversations, I've missed you this past week and I thought it would be a good way to catch up."

He'd missed her! That caused her heart to clutch. Because she'd missed him, too—those little barbs he was master of, that twinkle in his eyes when he didn't know she was observing him. But it had been easier to stay away than anticipate anything, because she had missed him, and that indicated to her that her feelings for Marc were growing, and shouldn't. And that's just the way it was because she could easily see herself falling for the guy. Or had already fallen.

"It's been a busy week," she replied, and that was no lie. She'd been in a time crunch almost every day, though this had also turned out to be a relief, keeping her away from her confusion over Marc. Not allowing her time to think. "I had four new patients admitted and a setback with one of my regulars. So busy I hardly had time to catch a breath. But I missed you, too."

"Want a personally guided tour of the new physical therapy facilities?" he asked after an hour of pleasantries about med school and childhood and other neutral territories.

"You can get in?"

His answer was to produce a bright, shiny silver key. "You think there's any way they're going to keep me out of there?"

She chuckled. "I suppose there's not."

"Then, that tour?"

"I'd love that tour! It reminds me of being a child and

sneaking around on Christmas morning to see where all the packages were hidden."

"Did you find them?"

"We usually found one or two. The rest were hidden in our parents' bedroom, which was strictly off-limits. It was so frustrating knowing they were on the other side of the castle wall yet having no way to get to them. The two of us tried year after year and we never defeated the keepers of the gate."

"My parents' strategy was different. They just put the gifts out and said, 'There, open them now and you'll have nothing to open on Christmas.'"

"Did you ever?"

Marc shook his head. "Nick opened his one year and spent a miserable Christmas morning without anything to open. He never did that again. But me, I always opted for the surprise."

"Except when it's a physical therapy annex and look who's sneaking in."

"I've got to make sure it's coming together correctly. The contractors won't let me in during the day."

"So you sneak in at night. How very...*Christmas* of you."

He laughed. "That *is* what it feels like."

"Then you've done this before?"

"Maybe a couple of times."

She faked a pout. "And I'm not your first accomplice?"

"Oh, you're my first. And if Security catches us I'm telling them you forced me to do it."

"Ah, the gentleman in you comes out." She laughed. "I'll tell them you told me there were Christmas presents in here for me."

"But it's nowhere near Christmas."

"Doesn't matter. He'll be so surprised by my reason I'll have time to escape, which leaves you sitting there holding the bag. Which I doubt has any Christmas presents in it."

"You'd actually let me take the fall for this?"

She nodded and laughed. Marc had it in him to be fun when his guard was down, and she liked that side of him. "So should we go see if we can get in without getting caught?"

The therapy rooms were pretty messy still, with tarps and carpentry scraps and tools everywhere, so they stayed at the doorway and looked in. "Right now it doesn't look half the size it used to be," she said.

"It's not going to be cramped when half the equipment is placed just right in here."

"Didn't you mention space for a couple of private rooms?"

He swallowed hard. "That's going to be a bit more difficult."

"Why?"

"The space I want is already occupied. I'd have to convince someone to move his or her office to another place in the building."

"Her meaning me?"

"It's all just on paper right now."

"You want me to move?" she gasped. "Seriously?"

"Not so much move as rearrange your work facilities."

"And when were you going to spring this on me?"

"When the board budgeted the money."

"Good, because I'll have something to say about that!" she said. "And it won't be in your defense." She smiled. "I'll win, Marc. Just you wait. I'm pretty good at waging battle." And besides, she liked working in his vicinity. It gave her a chance to take quick glances at him from time to time.

"My plan will make sense. You'll see. Your patients can meet anywhere but my patients…they need to stay in the same proximity because of the therapy equipment and the pool."

"So it's OK to inconvenience me and my staff?" She liked sparring with him, liked that connection, especially as neither of them took it personally.

"Not OK, but a better plan. But that's a long way down the road."

"It had better be, because I'm not going anywhere." She folded stubborn arms across her chest. "And I'm not changing my mind. Where I am suits me perfectly."

"In time you'll see the beauty of it, when I can figure out…"

"What? Where to put me?"

"Something like that. But it's not as drastic as it seems. Trust me."

Well, he had another think coming if he thought he could out-stubborn her into moving, because it wasn't going to happen. His warning gave her a chance to come up with her own defensive plan for when the time came. Suddenly, Anne was smiling. Nope, he didn't know how stubborn she could be.

"What's that about?" he asked.

"Only a plan of my own. You wait and see, Dr. Rousseau. You're not the only who can make plans around here."

"Well, I've got a plan."

"Should I trust you?"

"Of course not. But I'll tell you anyway. I'm going to go take a swim before I go home. Want to come take a swim with me?"

"I would, except I don't have a suit."

"No one's there at night. The pool's strictly off-limits. I can dim the lights, or do the gentlemanly thing and turn my head, even though I'm a doctor and I've seen naked bodies before."

"Ah, but this naked body isn't one of your patients."

"What happened to my brave little Christmas girl?"

"She was fully dressed when she was sneaking around, looking for gifts."

He shrugged. "Well, it's up to you. I'm going to get a swim in tonight, and you're welcome to bring your tired, achy muscles along and join me. Or watch me. Or neither."

He wheeled off toward the pool locker room and changed into trunks, while she stayed back in the hall, wondering if she should add a little adventure to her life. She was getting pretty stagnant, after all. She either worked or did something for her sister. That was it.

Anne thought of all the men and women she'd treated—the ones she'd helped, the ones she hadn't been able to help. Such bravery. And here she was, afraid to take a tiny step. Batting at the tears in her eyes, she pushed through the door to the pool, dimmed the lights, stripped down to her scant underwear and slipped in— they would dry quickly enough in the hand driers in the changing room.

"Change of heart?" Marc asked from the shadows.

But Anne didn't hear. She was swimming away her demons with one hard stroke after another. Covering the length of the pool with remarkable speed.

"You have a lot of grace in the water," he said, not even coming close to catching her.

"So do you, and strength, if you want to use it. But you'd rather waste your time, wouldn't you? Play like you're giving them something back rather than get really invested."

"You came in here to fight me about a swim team?"

"No, I came here to forget you, forget me, forget all of it." She swam up to the corner and huddled there awhile to catch her breath. And Marc allowed her all the space she needed.

"Look, I'm sorry," she said after a little while, when she could hear that he'd stopped swimming. "It's just that you've got so much potential and you're wasting it. So many people could benefit from your athleticism, but that's where you'd have to go beyond the call of duty and really put yourself out there."

"Didn't I already do that once?"

"And you want to stop living after that? See, what I don't get is the way you're wasting your potential, as well as the potential of others. You've got a long life ahead of you, Marc, and you act like your injury ended it then and there. But that's not the case."

"This is why I swim alone at night. So no one will bother me."

"Including your conscience?"

"My conscience is just fine, thank you very much!"

"Everything about you is fine except your conscience."

"Hey, I have an idea. Let's swim!"

Anne laughed. "Now I'll never know who won that round."

"Let's call it a draw." He swam up to her and splashed a little water in her face. "Race you to the end of the pool."

With that, she was in for the swim of her life, and discovered just how formidable he was in the pool as he outswam her by nearly half a length, then turned round and came back to meet her. She was laughing when he caught up to her…laughing and bobbing up and down in the water. "You're seriously good," she said, gasping for breath.

"Is that going to raise the old argument again?"

"Just sayin', Marc…"

"I'm good, I should coach."

"See. Even you know it."

"You don't give up, do you?"

"I do, but not easily."

He chuckled. "Well, neither do I."

"So I've noticed."

"Ready for another race to the end?"

"Knowing full well you'll beat me? I think I'd rather do this more leisurely while you swim circles around me."

She drifted close to him on her way to the edge of the pool…so close their bodies came into intimate contact, and the next thing she knew his arms were around her, hers were around him, and they were kissing, and it wasn't a friendly little peck on the cheek or lips like before but a full-out kiss where tongues probed and bodies tightened. If she'd ever had any doubt he could function as a man all the way, this kiss told her otherwise as the water pulsated, driving his pelvis into hers.

Had they not been in a public place, suits would have been shed quickly, but they weren't. As they were reminded when the full lights came on. "Who's there?" a voice boomed out.

Their heads popped up in the water and Marc moved quickly and protectively to block the guard's view of Anne, partially naked now, her remaining underwear having gone particularly transparent.

"Oh, Doc Rousseau, Doc Sebastian, I didn't know…

nobody told me." It was obvious that the security guard was quite flummoxed as he backed out of the pool room, his mind probably full of things that had never happened, but could have. Things both Anne and Marc wanted.

Anne was embarrassed, and swam straight for the corner of the pool for protection, while Marc had a good laugh as he went looking for her bra, which had somehow gone adrift in the heat of the moment. "Bet it will be rumored throughout the rehab center in five minutes. It'll probably take seven for it to get next door to the hospital."

"Five," she said, shaking. "Why so optimistic?"

"To cheer you up."

"I don't need cheering up. I need a towel."

Marc pulled one off a stack on the side of the pool and gave it to her. "Would we have?" he asked as he pulled himself up and out of the water.

"In that moment, maybe. But it was only that moment. Don't get it confused with any other moment because we got carried away and that's all it was." She climbed out of the pool, knowing full well she was on display in the glare of the overhead lights, but as she wrapped the towel around herself and stood up she noticed he was doing the courteous thing by not overtly staring. For which she was grateful and maybe even a little disappointed. "Give me ten minutes," she said, then grabbed up her clothes and scooted into the women's locker room.

When she got there, she simply stood with her back to the wall for a few minutes, wondering what had gotten into her. She'd certainly never done anything like that before and it horrified her to think she was capable of doing it with so little provocation.

Back in the men's locker room, Marc was smiling and whistling a peppy tune.

It had been two days since their encounter in the pool and while they'd exchanged quick glances and hurried hellos in the hall, that's as far as it had gone. Truth was, he'd gone too far and he wasn't happy with himself about it as Anne was clearly conflicted about what she wanted. So he shouldn't have pushed her. But what if they'd gone on to where they'd most certainly been headed? Then what? It would have been all or nothing, and Anne wasn't that kind of girl. She needed courting, slowly, deliberately. Anything else was below her. And here he'd probably come off looking like some randy beggar who was only looking for sex.

"Could have been worse, I suppose," Anne said, setting herself down next to Marc, who was taking some private time on the mats to do push-ups.

"We're talking now?"

"We never weren't talking. That was just your imagination."

"Were you processing what happened?"

"Over my embarrassment at being caught almost in the act? Absolutely, yes. But the strange thing is nobody's said a word to me. Or teased me. It's like nobody knows."

"I hope for your sake that's true, but I wouldn't count on it. I mean, what are they going to say? Done anyone in the pool lately, Anne?"

She laughed. "Maybe you're right. But I can still be embarrassed if I want to be."

"You did have a good time, didn't you?"

"Yes," she admitted. "Except for that whole public place situation, and I still can't believe I gave in to that."

"Well, you did. I was there."

"Sometimes you can't fight human nature, I guess."

"I've spent these past couple of days avoiding it," he said.

"By avoiding me. I know."

"I decided to let you have your space to work it out."

"And I appreciate that."

"So did you?"

"What? Get it worked out? It was simple. We got stopped from doing something we wanted in that moment. It's not a big deal."

"But it is to you, Anne. No matter what you say, I can sense that. Still see it in the blush in your cheeks."

"OK, it was. I've spent the last couple of days kicking myself. Then I let it go as much as I can. I'm good at that—letting go of the things that don't need to be hung onto. It's something I do in my counseling—teaching men and women to prioritize."

"So I've been worrying over something you dropped to the bottom of your priority list?"

"That about sums it up. What happened happened. End of story. Anyway, I'm going to a PTSD symposium down in downtown Chicago next weekend. I heard Jason's mandating you go as well. I thought you might like to come with me and sit in on some of the latest techniques, since the majority of your patients do suffer from it. Separate rooms. Hands-off policy!"

"Is this another attempt to get me to give in and get therapy?"

"Nope. It's something that will allow you to further your education on the subject. That's all. No hidden motives."

"Then thanks but, no, thanks."

"Even though Jason's requiring it?"

"Think I'll tell Jason I'm scheduled off all next weekend and he can't dictate my time off."

"What if I asked you to go as a favor?"

"Why?"

"Chicago for one is so…big. I don't like the idea of going alone, and since you have to go…"

"What good will I do you?" he asked, trying to avoid her gaze as she watched him exercise.

"You'll be company. I'll stop short of saying good company because I don't know if you will be, but I'm betting you can put on your good company face for a couple of days if you want to."

"So you know I might be bad company, yet you ask me?" Rather than annoying him, that made him laugh.

She shrugged, then laughed, too. "I think the odds are highly in my favor."

"You really want me to go, don't you?"

"It would be nice." She shifted backward to the edge of the mat as he rolled over and sat up.

"What do you want from me, Anne? Really? What do you want?"

"Do you like me?" she asked.

"What if I do?"

"Do you like me more than a little?"

"Why would I let myself go and do that?"

She shrugged. "Maybe because, in spite of your ways, I like you and I think you're worth the gamble."

"You consider me a gamble?" He scooted over to the edge of the mat table and transferred himself back into his chair.

"Well. You do have your moods."

"Which you attribute to PTSD!"

"Partially. But I think some of it's just plain discontent. You used to be more active and your limitations make you grumpy."

"If you mean I'd rather be operating, you're right. I would be."

"But that's not going to happen."

"I know that, but I don't have to like it."

"But you don't have to hate it, either."

He let out an exasperated breath. "So what do I get out of this weekend if I decide to go get some education I don't want."

"Time away. I could say with a charming companion, but I suppose charming is in the eye of the beholder and half the time I think I annoy you. Oh, and no repeat of the swimming-pool incident. That was then, now it's the aftermath of an incident." She blushed. "One not to be repeated."

"You're blowing things way out of proportion."

"And we went too far," she said awkwardly. "That pool's to be used for therapy, not for what we were doing."

"We didn't do anything, Anne."

She glanced up at him for a moment. "And we won't. So let's make this trip to the city as amicable as we can. OK?"

"Couldn't you have requested another doctor to go with you?"

"I could have, but Jason wanted you."

"And this is where I tell you I'm flattered?"

"Yes, actually, it is. Oh, then you accept, if not graciously, then fake a pleasantry."

"You're that sure of yourself, aren't you?"

"Yes, because we're still arguing about it and you haven't completely told me no."

He scowled at her for a moment, but the twinkle in

his eyes shone through. "Tell me, what are my perks, if I accept?"

"All expenses paid. Room with a view."

"Of what?"

"The skyline."

"Doesn't sound like that many perks to me."

"Best I can do. Maybe breakfast for one in bed— cold cereal."

"Well, I suppose it beats doing paperwork, doesn't it?"

Anne laughed. "You're not happy if you don't have something to complain about, are you? Looking at the trip as the lesser of two evils."

"One of the fundamental joys of my life."

"Anyway, we'll drive down Friday night and come home Sunday night. Pack casually, except for one suit for the reception on Saturday night."

"You're assuming I'm coming."

"I'm assuming you're coming. Now, I think I'm going to go get lunch. Care to join me?"

Marc declined, citing a patient appointment, then wheeled away, leaving her standing there watching him go. So what had convinced her to want him to come along? She wasn't sure except that the more she was around him, the more she liked him. His grouchiness or stubbornness or whatever you wanted to call it was a wall, and while she didn't know how she was going to do it, she was going to kick it down one way or another.

CHAPTER TEN

THE DRIVE INTO the heart of Chicago was blessedly short and quiet. They listened to music and, of course, they couldn't agree on what they wanted. She was in a classical mood, he was all up for blues and jazz. They stopped for dinner. He wanted tacos, she wanted Italian. So they agreed to disagree and finally found a compromise, talking about various patients.

It wasn't what he'd expected, but it was nice to get away. Not that he intended on attending much of the symposium with her. That would be an admission that she was right about him, that a little head-shrinking was all he needed. That's what this weekend was about and he knew it. Something to show him the error of his ways.

Well, she could show all she wanted, but he hadn't told her yet that he was going to spend at least half the time playing tourist. He'd decided to let that wait until the symposium actually started in the morning. Then he was going to Navy Pier while she sat in a stuffy room, listening to a stuffy lecture. Such was life…

The room was nice, and true to her promise, she gave him the one with the view of the skyline. Not that he was going to accept it, but he did like teasing her, liked goading her into decisions and actions she might not otherwise be drawn into. Such as being her plus one at the symposium. He'd been surprised when she'd asked him, but the more he'd argued against it, the harder she'd argued for it, and he liked that. Liked that drive in her.

And he hadn't really minded the compromise of Mozart on the drive since she'd been the one doing the driving. Personally, he'd only asked for tacos because she'd mentioned Italian first. Italian, or anything not cooked in the rehab's kitchen would have been fine. But she always expected an argument from him and he enjoyed giving it.

Of course, there was that incident in the pool, and that had twisted things up in his mind. Suppose it had been more for her? Suppose she was falling for him? Then what? How could he extricate himself from the situation without hurting her? Because he truly had no intention of hurting Anne. Fact was, if circumstances had been different he'd have been going after her as hard and as fast as he could. But those days were behind him now. He didn't get to go after the ladies because he couldn't discern what was genuine and what was pity.

With Anne, though, he didn't think he saw pity there. At least, if he did, he didn't recognize it as such. From the first day, she'd treated him like she did anybody else. No kid gloves. No tiptoeing around him. No guarding words. He liked that…liked it a lot. Still, there was nowhere this could go, no place where it could ever work out, because someone like Anne needed a man and not what was left of one. Forever alone. That was his motto now, and he had to live by it or else risk getting hurt.

"Nice view," he said, rolling in through the double doors.

"I'm across the hall with the view of the…roof and air-conditioning."

"I'll take that one since I'm not a gazer. It doesn't matter where I sleep."

"Doesn't matter where I sleep, either, so you get the view because I promised."

"But I insist."

"And I uninsist."

He chuckled. "So this is what our arguing boils down to? You say to-*may*-to, I say to-*mah*-to?"

"You're here, you stay."

"Or I can…" He wheeled out the door to the hall and crossed over to the other room. "Stay here."

"You're incorrigible, Marc! And I bet you don't intend on going to one of the lectures, do you?"

"I saw a couple on mind-body healing that might be good."

"Really? Because I'm sitting on one of the panels."

"Saw that, too." She was genuinely pleased he would attend her panel discussion. "Any other sessions?"

"Maybe one or two. No promises."

"But you'll escort me to the reception."

"I promised, and I don't break my promises." He smiled. "And I'm looking forward to it."

"Are you really?"

"I wish you trusted me more."

"It's hard to tell when you're serious and when you're…" She shrugged. "I just never know, Marc. And I know that's my fault as well as yours."

"Well, we've got a whole weekend ahead of us. Let's both try a little harder."

"Then I'll be the first to start off by taking the room with the view," she said, tossing her bag on the king-size bed.

The entire room was elegant, and even Marc noticed

that. Reproduction Victorian furniture, fresh flowers, a bottle of welcome champagne on ice.

"Do you drink?" he asked seriously.

"I'd never turn down a lovely glass of champagne. Care to pop the cork and do the pouring?"

Marc obliged, and as they clinked glasses he offered a toast. "Here's to a nice weekend with a friend."

"With a friend," she repeated, wondering if he really was a friend. She wanted him to be, even though it was difficult.

"So why champagne and not a beer?"

"Champagne's more elegant. I suppose a night in a nice room isn't beerworthy."

"It is among friends who are staying across the hall from each other."

"Then maybe there'll be beer in yours. At least, in the minifridge."

"What say we do this? Cork up the champagne, go find a pub and have a beer."

She smiled. "And that will make us both happy. I sure do like compromises."

"So what's going to happen to the essence of what's us, going from so opinionated to blending our opinions?" he asked. "If that's possible."

"Anything's possible. This is Chicago, after all. It's a city that's supposed to make you happy and fill you with possibilities. Just look at the view." She pulled back the curtains and exposed the most magnificent view of lights from buildings of all heights and sizes, as far as the eye could see. "Have you ever seen anything like it?"

"No, I haven't." He rolled up beside her to look, and for a moment he was tempted to take her hand. But he stopped himself by just brushing the back of her hand with his, then backed away. The last thing he needed was a romantic room with a romantic view. Now he wished to God he hadn't come, because this was going to be a lot tougher than he'd counted on, being so near her and yet so far away.

"I know this place. It's a little blues club about three blocks from here," she said. "Since you spent the whole trip listening to my classical music, would you like to go down there for an hour or so and see what's playing?"

"Can't," he said, stiffening as he backed away even more. This was almost too personal. "I need my rest."

"But I thought… I mean… It's still early, and I know you work longer shifts than this back home."

"The trip tired me out more than I thought it would and it's just now catching up with me." He saw that she looked perplexed, maybe even a little hurt, but there was nothing he could do to stop it. Getting any more involved with Anne was only going to lead to problems he couldn't control. Or fix.

"Want anything from room service?" she asked, the look on her face showing clear letdown.

"I'm fine."

"Was it something I said?" she asked.

"Nothing you said or did. It's just me, feeling tired, like I said." Lies, every word of it. She made him nervous. What he wanted from her made him more nervous and he just couldn't take it that far. Right now, his disability might not mean much to her, but what about years from now, or even months from now? Would it encumber her or hold her back? Could they even settle into a normal life, or would she end up resenting him? No, he just couldn't risk it.

"I just wanted you to enjoy the weekend," she said, backing away from the window and closing the curtains. "That's all this was supposed to be about. Why I suggested to Jason that he—"

"You suggested dragging me to the symposium in the hope that I'd learn something I'd recognize in myself? Which I already do." That he was a lousy liar.

"I didn't think for a minute you'd go to most of the symposium. Just to the reception tomorrow night. And, no, my intention isn't to parade you around like my pet puppy so people can ooh and aww me and tell me what a good girl I am for bringing the disabled man. I just didn't want to come alone. I get tired of always going alone, which is the way my life has been ever since I came back from Afghanistan. The thing is, Marc, I can be honest with myself. I've had a lot of practice and it works."

"Then if you're being so honest, are you attracted to me?" He hadn't meant to ask that question aloud, but it was out there now and he couldn't take it back.

"I am," she said, as heat rose in her cheeks.

"And do you expect me to be attracted in return?"

"Are you?" she asked.

"I need to know why," he asked.

"Are you?" she persisted.

"Tell me why, Anne. Why me? Is it because you want to be a martyr to a cause again? That you can't trust another man after what the first one did to you?" He slapped the wheels of his chair. "Don't you think this will get in the way eventually? After the novelty of dating the disabled man wears off?"

She stepped forward and slapped him. "You bastard," she hissed, then grabbed his bag and tossed it into the hall. "So much for calling a truce," she said as she stepped back.

"If there was ever a way to mess up a relationship,

that's it," he said to the bathroom mirror minutes later as he surveyed the red mark she'd left. And, yes, he'd deserved it because, damn it, he *was* attracted to her and those were words that should have been easy to say. All she'd wanted had been the truth and all he'd given her had been another brick in his ever-growing wall.

Talk about being a drama queen. She really wanted to go and apologize to Marc for slapping him, but half of her was convinced he'd deserved it. The other half thought he deserved it, too, but she was being over-reactionary about the whole situation. Either way, she wasn't ready to confront him yet. Didn't want to see him or talk to him. Didn't want to be anywhere near him. Of course, he'd made it quite clear he didn't return any type of feelings toward her. That was a mighty sore vein to open just after she'd finally admitted to herself, and to him, that she was attracted to him.

Well, now he knew and he could do anything with that information he wanted. In fact, now she wished he'd just go home and leave her to her weekend. It was going to be tough trying to glean any information from the workshops when all she could do was play out the last scene in her mind.

"Anne," he called as he knocked on the door. "I think we should talk."

Anne didn't answer for a minute, then finally replied, "I think we've said everything that needs to be said."

"I want to apologize."

"For being truthful? No apologies necessary."

"But I wasn't being truthful… There was no excuse for that."

"What you said was the truth. I don't trust men

because of what he did to me. And I'm not in the mood to discuss it."

"Would you be willing to talk if I told you that you're the most drop-dead gorgeous woman I've ever met?"

"Too little, too late. I don't need to be placated. Your first opinion, or shall we call it your lack of opinion, said it all. You don't get a do-over."

"Open the door."

"No! Now go away, leave me alone. I'm not in the mood to argue."

"You're only going to have to face me in the morning, or the day after that."

"I will when it's necessary."

"Are you sure—"

"Leave me alone, Marc," she said wearily. "Please, just leave me alone."

After that, not another word was spoken, and the frigid barrier between them remained up until daylight poked in through the gap in the curtains.

In her suite, Anne had barely slept. In his room, Marc was no better off. Sure, he was falling for her, and in his semi-dream state they'd met when he could still walk and their romance was epic. But when he cleared his head he knew that while he dreamed the dream, he lived the nightmare.

By the time he'd showered and shaved, and knocked on her door, Anne was gone. She did leave a note saying the reception was at six followed by the welcome banquet, but that he didn't have to attend either one if he didn't want to. She'd also left him a train schedule in case he wanted to go home early.

Talk about being blunt! He actually chuckled. That was one of the reasons he cared so much for her—her honesty. She was a straight shooter, unlike anyone he'd ever known. And he fully intended to go to that reception as her escort, whether or not she liked it. Then maybe somewhere in the evening they could talk, try to straighten things out.

The day rolled past pretty quickly for Anne as she went from lecture to lecture. Then at five she dashed up to her room to take a quick shower and get herself ready for the evening's festivities. She'd purposely kept Marc out of her mind until these past few minutes, when she'd wondered if she'd find him in his room or if he'd actually gone home as she'd hinted he do. As it turned out, he was waiting for her. Dressed in charcoal-gray slacks and a navy blazer, he was what writers referred to as breathtakingly handsome, and she did have to admit that even though he'd thoroughly embarrassed her, she still found him to be the most attractive man she'd ever set eyes on.

"So you're coming?" she asked as she rushed past him to the elevator.

"I was invited. Is the invitation still good?"

"Of course it is," she said, stopping at the door to wait, when what she really wanted to do was take the stairs to run away from him. "And about last night—"

"Last night was last night." Grinning, he rubbed his jaw. "Although I must say you pack quite a punch."

"I was angry."

"And what I said, or didn't say, was uncalled for. I'm sorry, Anne. I didn't mean to hurt you the way I did. I took a cheap shot, and I shouldn't have. Shouldn't have put you on the spot, either."

She shrugged. "No big deal."

"Except it was a big deal. And I was rude."

"Apology accepted."

"If you'd rather I don't go with you this evening, I'd understand."

"If you'd asked me earlier, I'd have said I prefer that you go home. But since you didn't, and since we've made up for now, I'm glad you stayed." She stepped into the elevator first, her face flushed, her hands shaking. This was a man to whom she'd admitted she had feelings, but nowhere in his apology had he admitted the same. Well, better to face her shame and get on with it rather than keep dwelling on it. Otherwise the rest of her trip was going to be miserable. Maybe even her job.

Nope, she'd made the admission freely and now it was time to get past it.

Their walk to the lobby where the reception was being held was a long, quiet one. Even in the elevator, where people were chatting, Anne and Marc were quiet. But once they got to the reception and introductions were made, conversation started to flow. In fact, Marc ran into a couple of old buddies, which made the evening even more pleasant for him.

By the time the dinner was over, he was ready to be out of his suit almost as much as Anne was ready to be out of her high heels. "Care to go for a walk?" he asked, once they were back in his room. "I thought that since it's still early we could go to the Willis Tower observation deck and spend a few minutes…observing."

"Can I change my clothes first, get into some jeans and walking shoes? These symposiums are fun, but there's nothing like relaxing at the end of the day."

"Sounds like a plan."

So ten minutes later they met at her door and went to the elevator. Got on and walked the three blocks to their destination, with Anne talking the whole time about various aspects of PTSD that had been discussed during that day's lectures. Luckily, the line to the observation deck was short, so the wait was only a few minutes. Once at the top, they found it to be a breezy splendor, being able to see miles and miles of lights in any direction.

"Can you believe that as many times as I've been to downtown Chicago, I've never once come up here," she said, perched at the edge of the enclosed bannister. "It's amazing."

"Well, this is my first time playing tourist in Chicago, too, and I'm enjoying it. I took in Navy Pier today, and tomorrow I might try to squeeze in the Aquarium or the Institute of Science and Industry *after* your panel discussion."

"It's boring stuff if you're not interested in PTSD."

"Nothing about you is boring," he admitted. "In fact, at the risk of another rumble I'd say you're pretty interesting."

"Me, interesting?"

"Well, I've already admitted you're beautiful. And that night in the pool showed how much I'm attracted to you."

"But those are all physical attributes. You never answered—"

"Yes. The answer is yes! But that's as far as it goes. I don't get involved."

"Well, this time I'm going to avert the argument and say there's so much to do here." She moved over to another side of the observation deck. "So many places to go, so many places to see." She looked down at Marc. "I'm glad you came along."

"More like you duct taped and dragged me."

She laughed. "That, too."

"But it was worth the fight."

Anne was doing her best to stifle a yawn but it did no good. She was exhausted from a long day, on top of a lack of sleep the night before. All she really wanted to do now was go back to her room and relax for a little while, then go to bed. "Do you mind if we call it an evening?" she asked, as another yawn overtook her. "I'm really tired and—"

"Want me to give you a lift?" he asked, his eyes twinkling.

"A lift?"

"In my chair?"

"Don't offer what you don't intend to go through with, because it sounds tempting. And as tired as I am..."

"I'm willing," he said.

"But I'm not. And how silly would that look anyway?"

"No sillier than you staggering into buildings because you're so tired."

"Thanks, but I'll walk."

"Offer stands."

"If you see me stagger into a building, just grab me, OK? I don't want to hurt any innocent buildings in my delirium."

As the two walked back to their rooms, a cool breeze blew from the buildings to the alleys and sent a shiver up Anne's spine. Without giving it a thought, Marc reached out and took hold of her hand, and they walked as any lovers would along the street, looking in windows, stopping to admire a sight that particularly interested them, or simply sky-gazing. It was beautiful early autumn, too, when the trees still clung ferociously to their leaves but the briskness swirled all around them.

Anne, who was acutely aware of Marc's calloused hand in hers, liked the strong feeling of it, and she was in no hurry to get back to the hotel. But three blocks was all she was allowed, and as they entered the lobby they dropped hands when greeted by a swarm of colleagues on their way out for some late-night carousing. Invitations were extended to join them, but Anne declined with a yawn and followed Marc to the elevator. Twenty-two floors later their evening was over. No more walking, no more holding hands. No more nothing. They entered their own little sanctuaries and that was it.

But it was a very nice way to end the evening. Except that ten minutes later, after she was in her grungy old nightshirt with her hair tied up and her face glopped with moisturizer, a knock on her door startled her.

"Who's there?" she called.

"Strangers bearing gifts."

Oh, no! She looked horrible. But there wasn't time to fix herself up, so, wiping off the face cream on her way to the door, she did open it a crack. And there he was with chocolate-covered strawberries and beer.

"It's lovely!" Anne exclaimed as she sank down into the soft cushions of the sofa in the living room and leaned her head back on the embroidered pillow. "But I apologize for the way I look."

"Quite the contrary. I owed you more than an apology," he said, taking his place next to her.

"We all make mistakes and say things we don't mean."

"You're too gracious," he said, bending forward to pick up a strawberry. Then he held it to her lips. "And I'm an ass."

"You are," she said, nibbling the first bite from between his finger and thumb. It was a beautiful red berry, all ripe and plump, dipped in chocolate and drizzled with white chocolate. And she really would have liked to take it from him much less gracefully, but Marc was making a sweet effort to put his rough edges behind him. So she took her bite and watched him devour the rest. They were like a couple who knew the subtle ins and outs of courting when, truth was, she'd never been wooed, never been courted in all her life. First marriage included.

"Why are you doing this?" she finally asked Marc after she'd shared another of the delicious strawberries. "And don't tell me it's an extension to your apology, because I'd already forgiven you."

"Maybe it's because I wanted to. It seemed like…like it was the right thing to do after all you've done for me."

"So it's payback?" Truthfully, she was a little hurt by that.

"Not payback. I'm really awkward in situations like this. Before my accident I wasn't a romantic. I've had plenty of girlfriends over the years, but they were merely situations. And while I didn't use them, per se, I never had any intention of getting involved, either. A long time ago, I promised myself I'd be a player until all my play ran out. So that's how I was living it. And, believe me, none of them ever warranted strawberries.

"But things changed. I changed when I went to Afghanistan and saw the conditions there. Some of the women…" He cringed. "They had to be so strong to survive. That's when I knew my life was headed in the wrong direction, that I had to change, and even before I was injured I vowed to do things differently once I was out of there. As luck would have it, the course my life would take became decided for me."

"But you're still at war with yourself."

"Over the loss. Over my lack of ability to change my life for myself. I never got the opportunity. Everything was taken away from me and I didn't have any control." He handed her a bottle of beer. "Here's to better times." He clinked his bottle to hers in a toast. "For both of us."

"Better times," she repeated, feeling so tired and yet so exhilarated. Her body wanted to snuggle into his arms and drift off, but her mind didn't want to miss a minute of his conversation. Didn't want to miss a minute of this closeness. "And just for the record, I am attracted to you. I meant it when I said it last night."

"You don't know what you're saying," he said, without pulling back from her.

"I always know what I'm saying, Marc. I see through your armored exterior and I like what's underneath. You're a good doctor, you care, and you're so darned romantic it's making my head swim. So, is this a seduction?"

He was taken aback by her straightforwardness. "It might have been at one time."

"But not now?" she coaxed, puckering her lips into a pout.

"Do you want to be seduced?"

"Do you want to seduce me?" she asked.

"Something tells me I'm the one who's being seduced."

"It's a beautiful night, we have strawberries, my bed is comfortable. So is the sofa, for what it's worth. So why not?"

"I haven't been with a woman since… I mean I tried once, but…" He shrugged.

She put her fingers to his lips to silence him. "Those

kinds of things don't matter and she must have been the wrong woman."

He bent his head low to her ear and whispered, "Just so you know, I can function as a man."

Her eyes twinkled. "I never had any doubt about that."

CHAPTER ELEVEN

SHE REALLY WANTED to linger in bed this morning, skip the first lecture or two and stay there with Marc until it was time for her panel, but the hospital was paying her way and she knew it was her obligation to attend the workshops. So, reluctantly, Anne dragged herself from the bed and barely made it to the bathroom she was so weak-kneed.

To say he was a skillful lover was underestimating it. Marc had been masterful in every way, and she desperately wished they could spend one more night there, but noon was checkout time and there was no disputing the fact that they were both scheduled to work tomorrow.

Too bad she couldn't have it both ways. But duty did call and she was nothing if not a slave to the things that had to be done.

Surely there would be another time, another place for Marc and her, though. She hoped so, anyway, because he'd made her feel like a…a princess. And normally one-night stands didn't get the kind of detail she'd gotten. At least she didn't think so as she'd never had a one-night stand before. In fact, the only man she'd ever had before Marc had been her husband, who hadn't been attentive, who hadn't cared about her pleasure, who'd done nothing with flair the way Marc had.

"It's time to get up," she whispered to Marc, after she'd showered and slipped into her black silk bra and panties. "You've got to check out for us in a few hours and I've got a couple of morning lectures to sit in on before my panel."

"Boring lectures," he said, patting the bed beside him.

"Mandatory lectures."

"Mandated by whom?"

"Well, not really mandated, but Jason didn't send me here to play. I'm supposed to—"

"To what? Ignore the man in your bed? The man who wants one more hour?"

"I can't," she protested.

"Who's to know? Nobody takes attendance at these seminars."

"I'll know."

"So what are you going to do? Go back and confess to Jason that you skipped a lecture because you decided to hang back and make love with me?"

"I'd like to hang back, but—"

"Be your own woman, Anne. Do what you want to do for a change, and not what someone else expects from you."

She looked down at him, studied the lines of him that were clearly visible beneath the sheet, then kicked herself for being tempted. But, God help her, she was. She wanted to feel his hands on her body again, exploring, bringing her to climax after climax. Knowing just when to start and stop, just where to touch, to kiss, to caress.

Mercy, was he good. So good she was sliding out of her bra before she even knew what she was doing and climbing back in the bed with him. One more time was what she promised herself, but with Marc there was never just one more time. And as she dipped her head below the sheets to give him the same pleasure he'd given her, she knew she was already spoiled for life. Marc had bared his all to her and an entire lifetime wouldn't be enough to take it all in.

"I really do have to catch the last lecture before my panel, then we have a luncheon and after that we can go to the museum, then it's back home," she said nearly an hour later as she slipped into the bathroom for a quick shower—and she didn't come back out until she was fully clothed this time. Totally satiated, yet on the verge of shedding her clothes and hopping right back into bed with him. He looked so sexy there, head propped up on one arm, chest muscles just rippling. So he was a paraplegic. No big deal, especially in the way he'd made love to her. And for a moment she wondered how many women he'd pleased the way he'd pleased her. "Well, I've really got to go now."

"You sure?"

She nodded. "I'm sure, so don't try and convince me to stay."

"Was I so good that now you're afraid of me?"

"You were," she answered directly. And that was the truth. He scared her because she was beginning to care too much. Even after all her vows not to do so, she was doing it, and she was too weak to resist him. "You make me feel things and do things I vow I won't, then you crook that little finger of yours and…" She shrugged. "Look what happens."

She buttoned her light pink blouse up to her throat and stepped into light gray shoes to match her suit. "I need time to think, Marc. When we get back I need time to think."

"You've got all the time in the world."

"But do I?"

"I'm not going anywhere, Anne." Truth was, he needed that same time to think.

"Enjoy it while you can," she whispered to herself as the elevator opened to her. Definitely, she would enjoy it while she could.

It had been a couple of days since they'd come back from the symposium, and while they had greeted each other coming and going in the hallway, Marc had been too busy to catch a breath, let alone pay any real attention to Anne. His new physical rehab room was getting ready to open, and he was busy attending to every last detail of it. The carpenters had made quick work of the construction and now it was up to Marc to take it from there.

So the hospital was humming with activity day and night, and for most of those hours, Anne worked, too. Taking her share of their agreed-upon time to think. She simply didn't know if she wanted to get any more involved with Marc than she was already. He was such a valiant man one moment, then the anger came out in him, and he wasn't willing to try to fix that. Maybe that's what scared her most.

Part of her wanted to be involved, though. In fact, most of her wanted to, but she was also afraid of where it could take her. The road certainly wasn't clear. Not for her, anyway, but she did so want to see around the next curve. See what was or wasn't there.

Perhaps that would happen, but so far there had been no indication it would. It was work as usual. Actually, harder than usual, as Marc was totally invested in getting his physical therapy area up and operational. So who was she to complain or feel neglected? As that's the way she herself was most of the time—business first. Now she was getting a dose of her own medicine, and finding that her mind was slipping back to the weekend far more often than it should.

"You seem preoccupied," Hannah said one evening when Anne stopped by to see the baby.

"Maybe I am a little."

"Nice weekend? We haven't really talked since then."

"It was a good seminar. Ran into several old friends, learned a lot."

"I understand Marc was with you." She gave her that look that told Anne her sister already knew something was going on.

"He was."

"And?"

"He didn't attend as much of the seminar as I'd hoped he would, but he did attend some."

"And?"

"And what?"

"Did you two, well…you know? I mean, I heard about the incident in the swimming pool, so I'm only assuming that…"

"What if we did?"

Hannah grabbed her sister and hugged her. "It's about time. I was so afraid you'd give up."

"Trust me, I haven't. Marc was…incredible. But he scares me. He can be so near, then so distant, and I don't need another relationship like that. Bill was distant and I didn't ever see it, so what does that say for me if I get involved with someone who's obviously distant?"

"So you're solving your problem with him by, what? Staying distant yourself? It doesn't work, Anne. You're at the point in your relationship now when you should be getting closer."

"I know I should, but I'm not even sure if there's a relationship."

"And you're too afraid to find out."

"What if it is?" Anne asked. "What if he expects something from me? Something I just can't give him?"

"Which would be what? Your complete trust?"

Anne nodded.

"Give him the benefit of the doubt before you toss him aside. He's not Bill and he doesn't come with a warning label that because he's a man he's destined to cheat. Real men don't cheat, Anne. That's a lesson you haven't learned yet."

"Why are you always so smart?" Anne asked.

"It's not that I'm so smart, so much as you're just wounded. Something bad happened to you once, but that's over now. You need to let go of it and look for something good. For Marc to get you so stirred up, I have to think that he's worth the effort."

Anne laughed, but sadly. "I could, but what happens once he's back in the swing of things…? He's a handsome man. Women look. Wheelchair or not, he could—"

"Don't say it, Anne. Because if you do, you doom yourself to not trusting any man ever again. Give Marc a chance to prove himself to you before you run so far away he can't catch you. Or any other man in the future if Marc doesn't turn out to be the one."

Anne gave her sister a kiss on the cheek. "The trouble with being a twin is that they know you so well."

"That's also the best part," Hannah reminded her. "So for now my sisterly advice is that you're the one he's looking at. Look back." Hannah smiled sympathetically. "And make it a good, long look. Now, how about some lemonade? Made fresh this afternoon."

"I'd love some," Anne replied. Although her mind wasn't on lemonade. It was on Marc and all the things she couldn't allow herself to have with him. Things that made her feel sad and melancholy. Things that hurt to the bone. Sure, it was easy enough for Hannah to see the problems and point them out, then give her encouragement. But seeing and acting were two different things. Hannah made perfect sense, but sense didn't always overcome fear.

"Mr. Ramsey is doing better," Marc commented to Anne after the weekly staff meeting. "He's not so depressed that it affects his therapy, which means he's making progress." Joe Ramsey had lost an arm to the war, which had been a devastating blow for an auto mechanic. "You've done a good job with him."

"Thank you," Anne said. She was genuinely pleased with his compliment. "After he's learned to use his prosthesis, I think he'll be a good candidate for vocational retraining."

"In a couple months, maybe," Marc responded.

"That long?" They were ambling along the corridor that passed Marc's new physical therapy area. Not touching or anything, but strolling close enough to each other that to an outsider they took on the appearance of intimacy.

"I want to make sure all the damage is repaired before we send him on down to start a new life completely. He's doing well with both of us. The prosthetics people teaching him how to use his new arm say he's getting more cooperative by the day, but the thing is, I don't want to push him out into the real world too prematurely. It's a scary place out there when you're forced to start over and, from what I can tell, he doesn't have much of a support system in place."

"Was it scary for you?"

"Horrifying. I'd practically pushed away all my support system and I felt so…vulnerable. I mean, I was working toward something new, but it still scared me. What if I failed? What would I have then?"

"How did you get over it?"

"The same way I get over everything—I apply myself even harder to my work. It's all I can count on."

"That's kind of sad in a way. There are lots of people out there who want to help you."

"But for how long? How long until my disability becomes a burden to them?"

"If they truly care, never." She laid a comforting hand on his shoulder. "But a lot of that's up to you, Marc, because you do the pushing first."

"I like your honesty," he said, then chuckled. "Most of the time. Anyway, about our patient…it won't hurt to keep him here a little longer than necessary so he won't have to deal with everything all at once."

Anne was impressed by his compassion and understanding of his patient. It was a side of Marc that didn't come out publicly. More than that, she was impressed by his honesty with her. It couldn't have been easy, admitting he'd been scared, maybe still was. But talking to others being treated by him, and judging from what she was learning, it was consistent. He had great empathy for wounded warriors.

She sighed and smiled, thinking about the way this awesome man kept himself hidden. "How's your physical therapy department coming along?" Anne asked Marc as they approached his door.

"I couldn't ask for a nicer setup. I've got my programs back up and running, got my rooms configured the way I want them, and things are working out well for my patients, especially now that I can separate them into like situations."

He was genuinely happy with everything. What perplexed him, though, was Anne. She'd been standoffish since they'd returned from the seminar over a week ago. She wouldn't meet his gaze when they encountered each other in the hall, had barely spoken until just now, and if he weren't mistaken, there'd been several times when he'd seen her turn and take another hall when she'd been coming toward him. What was up with that? Reluctance or embarrassment? He hoped the latter but feared the former.

Maybe this was her trying to make it up to him. Get things back to where they'd been before, which was a crazy mishmash of emotions. "Care to grab a cup of coffee?" he finally asked her before he entered his therapy room.

"I'm awfully busy today. Maybe after work?" she asked.

"After work," he agreed, hoping she meant it. *Really* hoping.

"He's a mild case, but it's affecting his progress in rehab. He'll regain his ability to walk again, maybe with some assistance for a while, but his emotions are keeping him from progressing and I thought maybe if you'd have a look at him…" Marc handed the chart over to Anne. "Then at your earliest convenience we could compare notes and see what we can come up with."

Anne took the notes and had a cursory glance at

them. "I'll read them over lunch and maybe by end of day I'll have a better idea of where he might fit into the program. Will that work for you?"

"No hurry. He's pretty cooperative and very quiet, so I wouldn't put him at the top of the emergency list. Maybe over that cup of coffee later today we talked about."

"I'll call you and let you know my time frame."

Which she did three hours later.

They met at a little coffee shop a block from the rehab center and took a seat by the front window. It was early, just after four, but the shop was practically deserted.

"So, did you look at the file?" Marc asked.

She nodded. "He's withdrawn, which is something I can deal with. But he needs a regular exercise regime for the stiffness in his back and shoulders."

"Percussive injury. He took a pretty bad beating when his transport truck overturned. And while his injury isn't long-term, we can work the stiffness out of him."

"In the swimming pool?" she asked, taking a sip of her mocha latte. "I still think you could utilize it more with your patients, and Mr. Westfall is a good example of that."

"So you're into diagnosing physical therapy now?" Marc asked.

She took sudden offense that another argument was about to ensue. "I'm an internal medicine specialist, so I have made referrals from time to time. So, yes, I'm into diagnosing now. Always have been."

"I don't need your physical therapy referrals," he said, his voice a little louder than it should be.

"I thought this was a two-way street, that we both make referrals as we see fit."

"That's all you've wanted from me from day one—to make a referral for my own treatment for PTSD. Admit it!"

"Do I think you need counseling? Yes, I do, and your hair-trigger temper is a good example of that. Get anywhere close to what you perceive as therapy for you and you go off, whether or not it was really meant to be about you. Which in this case it wasn't. So I do see classic signs in you. But I haven't made a referral that involves you and I won't because you're my colleague, not someone assigned to my care."

"Even though you want to!"

"You're wrong. My patients all *want* to be cured, they don't want to hang onto all the different symptoms of PTSD and use them as an excuse for not moving forward."

"So you're implying I do."

"What I'm implying is that you know yourself and your motivations better than I do. And here's the thing, Marc. You and you alone have to want to get through it before I'd even consider making a referral, and it would have to be you coming to me and asking."

"Now, let me ask you this! Is that why we were just a one-night stand?" he said in a voice much too loud in the small shop. "You're afraid of me? Maybe you don't want to be burdened by a man in a wheelchair? Is that it, Anne? Is that why you've been avoiding me?"

"I've been avoiding you because I've already had a man with his own kind of volatile nature. He yelled at me all the time and tore up my house when I confronted him about his affairs. He tried to make me the guilty party in the failure of our marriage and for a while I accepted that because I wasn't home enough. But he knew that going in, and he almost made it my fault. Almost. And I can't do that again, because it scares me. You scare me. You thinking that I'm covertly trying to give you therapy scares me. I do care about you, Marc. Deeply. Maybe I'm even falling in love with you, but you're up and down and I just can't handle that."

"Then that's why you want to treat me as one of your patients? So you can mold me into whatever you want in a man?"

"That's not fair. I haven't tried molding you into anything. And it's just like I said, you think I'm trying to turn you into one of my patients, but I'm not. I promise you, I'm not."

"Except when it comes to swimming."

"That's encouragement, and there's a huge difference between that and what you think I'm trying to do. You have natural grace and talent, which you underutilize. Or maybe it scares you that you can still be so good at something. I don't know which it is, but there's something holding you back, and I think it's you. Besides, it was only a suggestion that you're blowing way out of proportion."

"Get me in the pool, get another of my patients in the pool. Start a world-class swim team? That's what's being blown out of proportion."

"Because you'll succeed, or because you'll fail? Are you afraid of success?" she asked. "You take your steps grudgingly because you don't think you deserve anything more?"

Marc banged his fist so hard on the table it knocked over her cup of latte, spilling it all down the front of her white blouse. "I'm sorry, Anne," he said, his voice now more subdued. "I didn't mean to—"

"You need to get some help for that temper of yours, Marc." She stood and went to the counter to get some napkins to blot her blouse. Then she came back to the table to retrieve her purse. "You lost it today with me, and I understand the cause. But what if I were someone else? A patient, maybe another doctor? You'd lose your position at the rehab center and there's a good chance you'd also lose your license to practice medicine. So you wondered why I stayed away? It's because I knew this was inevitable. Problem is, there's more where that came from."

She reached down and squeezed his hand. "Oh, and just so you'll know in advance, you're not getting my space. You may scare me in a relationship but you don't scare me as a colleague. And I'm holding onto my office."

Stepping back, Anne headed to the door, leaving Marc sitting there alone. Her heart went out to him, but until he was convinced he was worth taking the risk for, she wasn't going to pursue anything more than a professional relationship with him. That's the only thing she could do. That, and hope.

Marc was up all night, thinking. Regretting. Rethinking. Somewhere in all that mess he'd made of things yesterday she'd said she might love him. But she was afraid of him. Which he deserved, because there were times he scared himself, like yesterday at the coffee shop. The way he'd behaved…there was no excuse for that. Anne had only been trying to help him, and he'd exploded, said terrible things, made horrid accusations. And deep down he knew that all she wanted to do was help him because she cared.

Well, he cared, too. But he didn't know what to do with it or about it. Maybe he was afraid of failure. Or, worse, of success. What would happen if he did succeed with her? Would he feel backed into a corner at some point and push her away, like he had everyone else? Actually, he was almost there. If Anne didn't have the patience of a saint, she would already have been long gone. And there was the failure she talked about. The one he brought on himself.

He truly was paralyzed, and it had nothing to do with his legs.

"Someone needs to kick me hard, Sarge," he told his cat. "She's reached out to me in so many ways and I keep pushing her back. And she's so vulnerable when it comes to relationships because of her ex." Sighing heavily, he picked up his cell phone to call her but he lacked the nerve to go through with it.

"She's right, you know," he said to his very unconcerned feline. "I do need help because I do have a pretty low tolerance point. And it's time for me to start moving in the right direction. If I get the girl in the bargain, life will be perfect. If I don't, at least I won't be spending the rest of my life like Sisyphus, always pushing that boulder up the hill."

Finally finding the courage, he punched in Anne's phone number, and when she said hello, he said two words and two words only. "You're right." Then he clicked off and waited for his new day to begin.

Anne paced up and down the hall, until Hannah finally made her take a seat in the doctors' lounge. "He's going to be fine, Anne. Give him time. This is only his first session, and Walt Anderson is a good doctor. He'll get to the bottom of what's bothering Marc."

She smiled, but impatiently. "I want it to help him, and I'm just afraid he's going to revert back to his belligerent self. But Marc's had a good hard look at himself now and he knows he's so close to the surface. I think it scares him." She stood up to pace again, but her sister pulled her back down. "The thing is, Hannah, I was so afraid I was going to lose him."

"As a patient or as the man you fell in love with?"

"Maybe both. We haven't gotten that far in our relationship yet to be able to sort it all out."

"Give it time, you will."

"I hope so because…well, you know why."

"Yes, I do know why, but do you?"

"Because I love him?" Anne said, her voice quiet and reverent. "Don't know why, don't know how, but he slipped in there."

"And it scares you?"

Anne nodded. "He's so broken."

"And you don't think the love of a good woman would go a long way in helping to fix him?"

"If he wants that love."

"He's seeking counseling because of that love. It might take a while, but he's taken the first step. Now it's time for you to do the same. Talk to him, Anne. Don't fight, don't diagnose. Just talk."

She sighed. "What if love isn't enough?"

"But what if it is?"

"You talking about me?" Marc said, pushing through the lounge door.

"And this is where I take my exit and go to my doctor's appointment," Hannah said, standing. She gave her sister a hug, then hurried out the door.

"How did it go?" Anne asked him.

"It was brutal."

Anne blanched but said nothing. Right now it was time to listen.

"But Walt says there's hope for me. He wants to see me three times a week privately."

"No group sessions?"

Marc shook his head. "Because I'm on staff here and he wants to maintain that line of separation. But he did say I could bring a guest."

"Are you going to?" she asked anxiously.

"Depends whether or not you want to come with me. As my support structure, though, not as my therapist."

"Why me?"

"Because I recognize we've got something, but we need to work through it to come out whole on the other end. I need you there, Anne, to hold me up. I'm still not sure how my real life's going to work as a disabled person, but if you want to be part of my life in spite of my disability…"

"I do," she whispered, batting back the tears threatening to spill. "I do so very much."

"Then you love me?" he asked.

Her smile for him melted. "I love you." And she sat down on his lap and put her arms around his neck. "But the question is…"

"Yes, I love you. Have from the start but I couldn't believe that someone like me would ever have a chance with someone like you. I think I'd given up on that aspect of my life."

"Oh, because of your temper?" she whispered as she bent so that her lips brushed his. "So now's as good a time as any to tell you I've had the architects evaluate *your* office for private exam rooms, and they're working on the preliminary drawings right now."

"And where would my office go?"

"There's a large janitorial closet at the end of the hall…" She laughed. "See, I told you you wouldn't beat me at this. I get what I want."

"And what else do you want?"

"You," she whispered. "Only you."

"Then kiss me, will you?"

"Gladly. Every day for the rest of our lives."

"Go!" Anne shouted from the stands as Marc traversed the length of the pool against five other competitors. Lately he'd been swimming competitively, sometimes coming in second, occasionally third, but most often first. He'd collected a few trophies and some ribbons and the local newspaper had even done a write-up about the paralyzed swimmer who was taking para-athletics by storm. Not only that, he'd started a small swim team at the rehab center and was getting them ready for their first meet. Life was great.

"You're going to do it!" she yelled over the voices of the other spectators. "Almost there. Give it one final push and… Yay!"

She ran down to the side of the pool and took his wheelchair along so he could climb out of the water, then gave him a great big kiss on the lips. "That's three firsts in a row!" she exclaimed breathlessly.

"Want to compete with me now?" he asked, chuckling as he dried off his hair.

"Oh, I've got some competition in mind, but that will keep for later."

Later… Marc loved that word because there was a

later in his life. One he'd never thought he'd have and one he would cherish every day of his life. Life didn't get better than that.

* * * * *

IT HAPPENED
IN VEGAS

BY
AMY RUTTAN

First published in Great Britain 2015
by Mills & Boon, an imprint of Harlequin (UK) Limited,
Eton House, 18-24 Paradise Road, Richmond, Surrey, TW9 1SR

© 2015 Amy Ruttan

ISBN: 978-0-263-24694-0

Harlequin (UK) Limited's policy is to use papers that are natural, renewable and recyclable products and made from wood grown in sustainable forests. The logging and manufacturing processes conform to the legal environmental regulations of the country of origin.

Printed and bound in Spain
by CPI, Barcelona

Dear Reader,

Thank you for picking up a copy of *It Happened in Vegas*.

I love writing about brothers—probably because I'm surrounded by them. My mother had three brothers, my dad was the youngest of eight, and there was only one sister right in the middle. I have a younger brother, and my own daughter has two younger brothers.

Brothers—I know them well. I know that the love they share, though not always evident to strangers, is there.

My hero Nick feels he's wronged his brother Marc, and for that he punishes himself—until both brothers learn to reach out and heal each other. Of course this is done with the help of a good woman by their sides.

Why did I set this story in Vegas? Simply because I love the desert and badlands—there's just something about the wide open spaces, the arid foothills and the landscape which seems so harsh. Nevada is a state that is on top of my bucket list. I hope I get to visit one day.

I hope you enjoy *It Happened in Vegas*.

I love hearing from readers, so please drop by my website, amyruttan.com, or give me a shout on Twitter @ruttanamy.

With warmest wishes

Amy Ruttan

This book is dedicated to all the brothers in my life
and my plethora of uncles, in particular two who are no
longer with us: Uncle Jim and Uncle Wavell.
And most especially to my brother Mike.
Sorry for duct taping you to the wall periodically
when we were younger.

Born and raised on the outskirts of Toronto, Ontario,
Amy Ruttan fled the big city to settle down with the
country boy of her dreams. When she's not furiously
typing away at her computer she's mom to three
wonderful children, who have given her another job as a
taxi driver.

A voracious reader, she was given her first romance
novel by her grandmother, who shared her penchant for
a hot romance. From that moment Amy was hooked by
the magical worlds, handsome heroes and sigh-worthy
romances contained in the pages, and she knew what she
wanted to be when she grew up.

Life got in the way, but after the birth of her second child
she decided to pursue her dream of becoming a romance
author.

Amy loves to hear from readers. It makes her day, in fact.
You can find out more about Amy at her website:
amyruttan.com

Books by Amy Ruttan

Dare She Date Again?
Pregnant with the Soldier's Son
Melting the Ice Queen's Heart
Safe in His Hands

**Visit the author profile page
at millsandboon.co.uk for more titles**

PROLOGUE

ANOTHER DINNER PARTY.

Jennifer plastered on another fake smile as she walked around the crowded reception hall in the Nevada State Capitol.

It's for a good cause. It's for a good cause.

And it was. She had nothing against a bill for soldier benefits. She just hated dinner parties like this, endless campaigns, looking good for the press. She knew her father; this wasn't just for the men and women who served their country. This was just because the elections were coming up in a few years and he was eyeing the White House.

It had nothing to do with soldiers.

Not a thing. It was all an image, another empty promise. She really hated politics. It brought out the worst in her father, a man she fondly remembered as being so different.

He hadn't always been this way. She remembered a different father, a loving, caring and *real* man. It was this political side of him she wasn't thrilled with.

Jennifer picked up a flute of champagne and tried to avoid the flash of cameras as reporters flocked around her father. Her perfect sister stood with her parents, smiling and chatting with the press, eating up the attention. The attention brought to her family made her nervous because she hadn't had the best relationship with them since her father had got into the political arena over a decade ago.

She was, after all, the black sheep, which meant the press were constantly dogging her heels. They'd backed off somewhat since she'd become a doctor. A doctor wasn't juicy enough for the paparazzi. Well, it was thrilling enough for her.

She'd rather be in the OR tonight, saving lives, but instead she was here and pretending to be part of the "perfect" family that her father wanted the world to believe they had.

Ha.

No family was perfect, but her father was ashamed of his roots. How he didn't come from a wealthy heritage.

He didn't want anyone to know that he was the illegitimate son of a congressman and an intern. That he'd worked with his hands to better their lives.

Her father only wanted his voters to see how he'd risen like a phoenix from the ashes.

Everything else burned away.

Jennifer swigged back the expensive champagne and then took another one, ignoring the waiter's eyebrow rising as she set her second empty flute back on the tray.

The waiter left before she could take a third.

It was probably for the best, but Jennifer just shook her head and meandered to a safe, dark corner where she could go unnoticed by everyone.

You'd think that accepting a trauma surgeon fellowship on the east coast would be something *most* parents would be proud of, and maybe her father would be, but her perfect sister, Pamela, had managed to become engaged to a high-society socialite from Manhattan and all Jennifer had managed to do was become a surgeon in a hospital.

It was like she had rabies or something.

No matter what she did, she couldn't shake off her past. She couldn't shake off the stigma of being the black sheep in the family.

The one who didn't want to rise from the humble beginnings of her life and mingle with the social elite. She wanted to help the poor and less fortunate.

She fumbled in her purse for the illicit pack of cigarettes, something which she'd been trying desperately to give up since her days as a hellion teen. She'd been off them for a while, but being around her family made her do crazy things.

"Why do you always do things to make me look bad?"

A shudder traveled down her spine as her father's voice whispered in her ear.

Jennifer pushed open the French doors and stepped out into the cool night air. The patio was mostly empty. Everyone was inside, enjoying the party.

There was one sad-looking cigarette in the package. Old and almost crumpled. She pulled it out and turned to toss it away, remembering why she'd quit when she'd started medical school.

It was being around her *perfect* family that made her go bonkers.

She didn't like the act. Couldn't they be real?

"That's not healthy for you, you know that?"

Jennifer spun around and saw that she wasn't alone on the patio. A soldier was half-hidden in the shadows, only three feet from her, sitting on a bench.

He leaned forward and she could see the hazel of his eyes reflected in the moonlight. His face was slim, long, but there was something enticing about it. When he smiled, it was a half-smile that ended in a deep dimple in his left cheek.

"I wasn't going to smoke it. I was going to get rid of it. I quit a long time ago," she said.

The soldier stood slowly and stepped out of the shadows. He was tall, lanky and devilishly appealing in his dress uniform. He whipped off the dress hat and held it under his arm, revealing a buzz cut.

"With all due respect, miss, it appeared that you were ready to devour that cancer stick."

Jennifer chuckled and glanced at the cigarette in her fingers. "Okay, I thought about it, but only for a moment."

He stepped closer and took the cigarette from her hand, snapped it in half and tossed it over the side of the patio into the bushes. "There, the temptation is gone."

"Hey, that's littering. You do realize that, don't you?"

He placed his hat back on his head and raised an ebony eyebrow. "Are you the litter police?"

"No, but you're a soldier. You should know better, hooah and all that."

This time he grinned and his white teeth gleamed in the darkness. "Hooah and all that?"

Jennifer laughed. "Sorry, I don't know. I'm on edge."

"And I just threw away your only means of escape?"

A blush tinged her cheeks. "Something like that."

"Well, my apologies, but I would hate to have you ruin your years of abstinence by lighting up tonight."

"I thank you for your concern, soldier. I do." She snapped her clutch closed. "Shouldn't you be getting back to the party?"

He shrugged. "It's not my thing, too many people. What about you?"

"What about me?" she asked.

He leaned in and a tingle zinged down her spine. "What're you escaping from?"

Don't let him get to you.

She was a sucker for men in uniform, men out of uniform and bad boys in general. All the types of men her parents didn't approve of.

Of course, the only men her parents approved of were from money, high society or a WASP. Also known as her sister's fiancé.

Jennifer cleared her throat and tucked an errant strand of hair behind her ear.

"Oh, I've made you uncomfortable."

"How do you know?"

"You're fidgeting. Admit it, you're nervous around me."

"A bit, but you're right. I'm escaping. I'm not really into shindigs like this."

"Want to get out of here?"

"Uh, you're a complete stranger."

"I'm a soldier, though. Doesn't that make me honorable or something?"

"Not really." She grinned. "I'm Jennifer." And she stuck out her hand.

He took her hand in his and the touch of his skin sent a jolt of heat through her blood.

"I'm Nick. I guess we're not strangers any longer?"

"Nope. We're not. What was that you were saying about getting out of here?"

He held out his arm. "I hope you don't mind riding a motorcycle."

"I don't mind in the least."

Nick turned to lead her back in through the party and

she pulled him back. "What's wrong? Are you having second thoughts?"

"No, I just don't want to go back in there." She didn't want some tabloid to snap a picture of her on the arm of a soldier. Not because it was bad, but because it was an invasion of her privacy, something she held dear because it was the only thing she could control.

He looked around. "Well, can you think of a better way out of here?"

"Hold this." She jammed her clutch into his hands and kicked off her heels.

"What're you doing?"

She smiled. "What, you've never jumped a fence, soldier?"

Jennifer picked up her shoes and tossed them out onto the dark lawn and then climbed the patio fence, dropping down three feet onto the grass below. "Are you coming?"

His answer was to drop her purse at her feet. She scrambled out of the way, retrieving her shoes as he dropped down beside her.

"How did you know to do that?" he asked.

Jennifer panicked. She didn't want him to know who she really was. If he knew she was a senator's daughter, he might not want to "escape" with her.

"It was obvious," she said, brushing it off like it was nothing. "Now, you have to provide the adventure."

He smiled again, that half-smile that brought out that delectable dimple. "Oh, I can provide the adventure. Like I said, my bike is parked down the street."

"Lead the way, soldier."

He took her hand and they ran across the lawn and out onto the street where his motorcycle was sitting. He opened up his pannier and tossed her a helmet as he put his hat safely away and then grabbed his own helmet.

"You carry two helmets? How fortuitous." She crammed it down over her head.

Nick took her purse from her hand and put it in the pannier next to his hat. "Well, I like to come prepared for adventure."

He shut the pannier and climbed on. She sat behind him, gripping him about the waist.

"You're being reckless. You're such an embarrassment."

The words had stung. Like a slap to her face. Her father had never spoken to her like that before, when he'd been a rancher.

Jennifer shook her father's words from her head as Nick started the engine, kicked the stand and took off, heading west out of Carson City.

She didn't know where they were going and she didn't care.

She knew that any rational female wouldn't go off with a man she'd just met, but something deep down inside her trusted him, probably when she shouldn't.

Jennifer didn't even freak when they left Carson City far behind them and headed into the state park.

After almost thirty minutes of driving, he pulled over at the Sand Harbor Overlook in Lake Tahoe State Park.

She let go of her hold on him and got off. Her legs felt a bit shaky, not used to riding on a motorcycle.

"What a great spot," she said as she took off the helmet, handing it back to him. He'd taken his off, too, and set the helmets on the seat.

"Yeah, I love it here. I was planning on coming here after the party. One last look, you could say." There was a hint of sadness in his voice.

"Are you heading overseas?"

Nick nodded. "My tour of duty is two years."

Disappointment gnawed at her.

Damn.

Not that she'd been expecting this to go anywhere, but she was disappointed that they would only have this time together, because once she finished her fellowship at the end of this summer, she could get a job anywhere. Or even stay in Boston. The possibilities were endless.

"See, now you feel all bad for me. Don't. I serve my country and I'm glad to do it. I also plan to be back to see this lake again."

Jennifer smiled. "Are you from around here originally?"

Nick shook his head. "No, but I've been stationed out this way for a year. Nevada grew on me. I don't think I want to be anywhere else."

He walked down toward the sandy beach through the tall pines, which sighed in the light summer breeze. It made her feel a little cold and she was regretting the sleeveless shift dress she'd chosen to wear.

The sky was bright, full of stars and a large moon was hovering over the lake. A large, bright moon that was reflected in the clear, calm water.

Nick stood on the beach, gazing up at the moon. He'd taken off his dress jacket and laid it on a large boulder. He was unbuttoning the shirt, his sleeves already rolled up to his elbows.

"You're not planning to swim, are you?" Jennifer teased.

He looked back at her over his shoulder and winked. "Maybe. Are you up for skinny-dipping?"

Jennifer chuckled. "Ah, no. It's cold. Especially here. That water can't be any more than fifty degrees."

Nick frowned and glanced at the water. "You think so?"

"I know so."

He looked at her. "So you're native to this area?"

"Yeah," she said, but with hardly any enthusiasm. It wasn't that she didn't like Nevada. As a child, she'd loved it. She'd loved northern Nevada, everything about it. The desert, the mountains and plains.

And she'd loved the Lake Tahoe area.

When she'd been younger, her father had had a ranch outside Carson City. They'd been so happy there, but then her father had sold it when she was ten. He'd told them he had bigger aspirations for all of them and he wasn't going to waste his life grubbing away on a ranch.

So, yeah, she loved Nevada.

It was just her father, the notoriety that went with being his daughter. She wanted to escape all that. In Boston, she wasn't the senator's daughter. She was Dr. Mills. Trauma fellow.

She didn't like being in the limelight. She didn't like being the black-sheep daughter, afraid to breathe the wrong way, worried that it would ruin her father's political career, seeing her face plastered on the local newspapers.

A splash and a shout distracted her from those thoughts.

Nick was wading in the shallow water. "Man, that is cold!"

Jennifer couldn't help but laugh. "I told you."

"Woo, so cold. Why don't you come and try it out?"

Jennifer shook her head, but couldn't stop laughing.

"You know, I never pegged you for a chicken." He was teasing her, egging her on. She knew it.

"I'm not chicken. I've been in Lake Tahoe before. I know *exactly* how cold it is."

Nick glanced down at his feet. "You know, it's not too bad. You get used to it."

Jennifer rolled her eyes and kicked off her heels. "It's probably because your body is succumbing to hypothermia."

Nick grinned. "Come on in. Just wade. I'm not brave enough to go swimming."

"I'm coming." She lifted her dress and undid the clasps on her garter belt to peel off her stockings, and when she glanced over at Nick, she could see his gaze transfixed on her legs. He was watching her roll down her stockings.

It caused her blood to heat, the thought of him watching her, knowing he was undressing her in his mind.

What am I doing?

Having fun, letting loose and living the way you used to live.

Living like everyone did.

Once she was free, she walked down to the water's edge and grimaced. "I can feel the chill from here."

"Come on in, you sissy." Nick bent down and sent a gentle splash in her direction. "People up north do this all the time."

"Yeah, well, people up north might be addled by the cold weather."

Nick chucked. "Think of it like a polar-bear dip."

She took a deep breath and waded into the water, which was frigid and bit at her skin like knives. "Oh, my God. You're insane."

Jennifer turned to leave, but he was over to her in a

flash, wrapping his arms around her waist and stopping her from leaving. They were so close she could smell his cologne. It was a clean scent, but there was something else she couldn't put her finger on. Whatever it was, it was making her feel faint.

His arms around her were so strong, steadying her.

She glanced up and his hazel eyes twinkled from the reflection of the water and the moonlight. He reached up and stroked her face, his thumb brushing against the apple of her cheek, and she turned her face into his touch instinctively.

"Can I ask you a boon?" he said, his voice deep and husky.

"A boon? Have I suddenly been transported back in time?" she teased.

Nick grinned. "A favor, then, for a soldier who's about to leave on a *long* tour of duty. I wouldn't normally ask this of a woman I'd just met, but this has always kind of been a fantasy of mine."

"What?" she asked, the butterflies in her stomach swirling around.

Nick leaned forward and whispered in her ear, "A kiss, in the moonlight."

A tingle raced down her spine. She didn't know what to expect, wasn't sure what she was willing to give him. A kiss seemed doable but, then, the way he was affecting her, the way she was feeling, being so free and standing in freezing-cold water with a stranger and wanting to do more than just kiss him…

He was going on a tour of duty and she was heading back to Boston to finish off her fellowship. Their paths would probably never cross again.

There were no expectations and when she looked back on this moment in the future, she could look on it with the fondness of something romantic she'd done, instead of looking on it with regret that she hadn't taken the chance, because something deep down inside her was telling her, screaming at her to take the chance.

"I think I can accommodate that request."

Nick smiled. "I'm so glad you said that."

She closed her eyes as he moved closer. She didn't know what to expect because kissing had never been her favorite aspect of physical contact.

Every time she'd been kissed before had been less than stellar.

When his lips brushed across hers, lightly, she knew that this was a kiss she'd been waiting for, she just hadn't known it. Until now.

His hands cradled her head gently, his fingers in her hair. He pulled her body closer so she was flush against him as his kiss deepened, making her weak in the knees.

Nick's hands moved from her face and down her back. The feeling of his hands on her, on the small bit of exposed flesh on her back, made her blood heat.

The kiss ended, much to her dismay, but Nick still held her and her arms were still around his neck as they stood in the shallow water of Lake Tahoe.

Jennifer took a deep breath. "I…I'd better get going."

Nick smiled at her. That lazy half-smile that made her heart flutter. "Really? You want to go."

Yes.

"No. No, I don't."

He bent down and scooped her up in his arms.

"Good." That was all he said as he carried her to shore.

CHAPTER ONE

Three years later

"I THINK YOU'LL be very happy here as our head of trauma."

Jennifer smiled politely at the chief of surgery, Dr. Ramsgate, as they walked the halls of the hospital.

"All Saints Hospital is one of the top hospitals in Las Vegas, and with our new trauma wing opening soon..." Dr. Ramsgate continued and Jennifer tuned him out, only because she knew all the benefits of All Saints Hospital—it's what had attracted her to this facility above all others in Nevada. The new trauma ward under construction would be the most modern in the country.

And her father was happy she'd returned to Nevada in time for his campaigning.

How good would it look if his surgeon daughter was working in her home state? Only Jennifer hadn't come home for her father.

She'd come home to lick her wounds after her cardiothoracic fiancé had jilted her and then stolen the research they'd worked on together, before marrying someone else. There was no way she was going to remain in the same hospital in Boston with him, let alone the same state.

She'd moved back to be near her family. To hide from the humiliation. To remember why she'd become a surgeon.

Even if it had meant turning down a job at a prestigious Minnesota clinic.

At least it's warmer in Las Vegas.

So that was a plus. She wouldn't miss the winters.

Jennifer had had to get back to her roots and, most important, she was going to keep away from men. Especially other male surgeons.

She wasn't going to make that mistake twice.

"And here's our current trauma department. It's not much, but it's served us well." Dr. Ramsgate was waiting for her to say something. "Of course, once the new wing is complete, this will close."

"It's wonderful. It's laid out well." It was a minor fib as she hadn't really even looked at it, but a quick scan told her she wasn't being totally false. It *was* laid out well. It was open and had lots of trauma rooms, with easy access to get gurneys in and out. Though the new trauma department would be better.

The ER was quiet for the moment, though she was sure that could change on a moment's notice, like so many trauma departments.

She was eager to get this walk-through over and done with so she could throw on some scrubs, a yellow isolation gown and get her hands dirty. Figuratively, of course.

Until then, she had to play nice with the chief of surgery.

"Come, I'll introduce you to the staff on duty before we head back upstairs to finish your paperwork." Dr. Ramsgate motioned to the charge desk, where a surgeon stood with his back to them. Jennifer's brow furrowed, because the surgeon leaning over the desk charting tugged at the foggy corners of her mind.

There was something familiar about his stance.

"Dr. Rousseau, this is Dr. Mills, the new head of trauma."

The surgeon standing at the desk turned to greet her and when she came face to face with him, the foggy memory that had been eluding her came rushing back, like a tsunami of the senses. It was an overload in her brain, the way it had happened.

Lake Tahoe, a brilliant moon, starry sky and a whispered request brushing against her ear that still made her body zing with anticipation even years later.

"A kiss, in the moonlight."

It had been three years and she wondered if he remembered her. He'd changed and so had she. His buzz cut had grown out, but his ebony hair was trimmed and well kept. There was stubble on his face, but it suited him. Even more than the clean-shaven face.

And a scar ran down his left cheek and she couldn't help but wonder if it came from his time overseas. There was no wedding ring on his finger, but that didn't mean anything. He might've come from surgery and taken it off.

His hazel eyes widened for just a moment, then he held out his hand. "It's a pleasure to meet you, Dr. Mills."

"The pleasure is all mine, Dr. Rousseau."

Dr. Ramsgate nodded, pleased. "Well, we'll let you get back to work, Dr. Rousseau. I have much more to show you, Dr. Mills."

Jennifer found it harder to breathe, her pulse was thundering in her ears like an out-of-control high-speed train and it was like she was going to derail right here in the emergency room.

Dr. Rousseau nodded, but didn't tear his gaze from hers until Dr. Ramsgate stepped between them, breaking the connection. If there even was one. Maybe she was losing her mind a bit.

What had happened between them had only been a fleeting moment.

"Dr. Mills, are you ready? I'd like to introduce you to some of the other staff members you'll be in charge of." Confusion was etched across Dr. Ramsgate's face at her absentmindedness.

"Yes, of course." She fell into step beside Dr. Ramsgate, though not without stealing a quick look over her shoulder at the charge desk, but Dr. Rousseau had disappeared; evaporated like he'd been nothing more than a figment of her imagination.

Only he wasn't.

He wasn't a foggy piece of a memory. One that she only allowed herself to think of from time to time. The one perfect romantic moment she'd had in her life. That soldier hadn't left her standing at an altar, hadn't stolen her work, and the kiss he'd given her still made her blood heat. Even after all this time.

This was going to be bad.

She had no inclination to allow her heart to open again, especially to another surgeon.

Jennifer knew she'd have to avoid Dr. Nick Rousseau and that wasn't going to be an easy thing. Especially now she was in charge of his department.

She was in serious trouble.

Nick put the chart back in the filing cabinet. He'd moved away from the charge desk when Dr. Ramsgate had stepped between them, breaking the connection between him and Jennifer. It had been the escape he'd needed.

He wasn't sure if Jennifer remembered him, from the look on her face. Maybe he just looked familiar to her, someone she couldn't place. Which was fine. It was good she didn't remember him, but he certainly remembered her.

There was no way he could forget that night.

Not when it was burned into his brain.

Not when every time he'd closed his eyes for the last three years he'd been able to feel the silky softness of her skin under his fingertips, inhale the fruity scent of her hair and taste the sweetness of her lips.

Though that's all that had happened.

Just a kiss.

Well, several kisses, but it had been all he'd needed to carry him through his long tour of duty. When he'd been working at the front line, patching up soldiers, saving lives and, yes, even when one thoughtless act of bravery had cost his own brother dearly.

Nick clenched his fist and shook those thoughts away.

No, he wouldn't think about Marc and he wouldn't think about his brother hating him right now, because he couldn't let those emotions out to air. When he thought of that moment, he hated himself. He'd let his anger get the better of him.

There was already talk circulating around the hospital about him, about his rages and about how he'd put his fist through a window once.

He was doing better. Or he thought he was.

Maybe it was seeing her again—whatever it was,

it shook him. He'd been surprised to learn she was a surgeon.

That night they'd spent on the beach, talking to each other, she'd never told him that she was a physician, in particular a trauma surgeon.

Then again, he'd never opened up about why he was going overseas on his tour of duty. He hadn't told her that he was an army medic.

She'd changed, but not so much that he hadn't recognized her. The long blond hair was gone. She sported a pixie cut, which still suited her. It gave him a better view of her long, slender neck and he knew that if he kissed that spot under her ear she sighed with pleasure.

Don't think about that.

Nick stifled a groan and left the charting area and headed toward the doctors' lounge to get a cup of coffee.

He didn't have time to date and had no interest in it.

After all, he was too irresponsible for any kind of settled life.

At least, that's what Marc had always said. And, frankly, Nick didn't deserve to be happy. Solitude was his penance for what he'd done.

After the accident that had paralyzed his brother and left him unscathed, he'd finished his tour of duty with an honorable discharge. Though there was nothing honorable in his mind.

If he hadn't tried to run out when the medic unit had been under fire to save his buddy, Marc never would've followed him.

And though he'd saved his friend and was deemed a hero, the IED had exploded, paralyzing Marc, leaving Nick without a brother.

Not that Marc had died, but he'd cut Nick out of his

life. It was like Marc was dead. Nick was definitely dead to Marc.

He was a ghost.

So Nick had left him alone, like Marc wanted. He hadn't returned home to Chicago. He'd settled in Nevada. In the place he'd last remembered being happy. With the vast, open desert plains and the mountains and foothills to the north, a man could get lost.

And he was lost. His parents didn't speak with him and neither did his sister. Marc needed them more anyway.

Here in Las Vegas, a man could be forgotten and maybe he'd be able to shake the ghosts of his past.

He just hadn't expected he'd run into one of them.

Jennifer had never told him she was a surgeon and he'd thought she was in Carson City, which was on the other side of the state, six hours away.

Then her name rang more bells.

Jennifer Mills.

She'd been at that state dinner thrown by Senator Mills. Was she his daughter? The one who'd been jilted? He didn't know much about it because he didn't really care about gossip columns. Heck, he didn't even have cable. Jennifer had her own cross to bear and he wouldn't pry.

Nick scrubbed his hand over his face. Dammit. She was off-limits for sure. Senator Mills had been the one to present him with his Medal of Honor for bravery. One that he kept hidden away under his socks because he didn't deserve it; especially after what had happened to Marc.

He was no hero.

He was irresponsible. Always getting into scrapes, and Marc had always been there to bail him out.

Now Marc wasn't there for him anymore.

Even though Nick's wanderlust and sense of adventure still ate away at him, he didn't feed the beast.

He just wanted to work. To be the best damn surgeon he could be. Maybe to show his brother he wasn't reckless and irresponsible.

Jennifer's appearance complicated things.

Nick poured himself a cup of coffee. The thought that she'd been involved with someone else made him feel a bit jealous.

Though he had no claim on her.

They'd only exchanged first names. They'd only shared a few passionate kisses under the stars.

He could work with her. Not that he had a choice, because in Las Vegas he was a nobody.

He wasn't a hero, he wasn't a soldier. He was just a face in the crowd and that's the way he liked it.

Nick slouched down in a chair, leaning his head against the low back to close his eyes for just a moment.

The door slammed and he sat up. Jennifer had entered, and pink tinged her cheeks when she saw him sitting there. He liked the way she blushed; she'd blushed like that against the sand when he'd kissed her.

"Sorry, Dr. Rousseau. I hope I didn't wake you."

"I wasn't asleep, Dr. Mills. I thought you were with Dr. Ramsgate?"

"He had a quick cardio consult and he told me I could get a cup of coffee in here." She nervously brushed at her hair, tucking the short strands behind her delicate ear, like she'd done when they'd first met. Only there were no more long strands.

She moved over to the coffeemaker and poured herself a cup, then proceeded to stand there, staring at the bulletin board, which was full of ads of stuff for sale and take-out menus. Just junk. She fidgeted with her hair again.

Nick could sense she felt uncomfortable. The tension was thick in the air. He knew the feeling of a standoff. The calm before the storm.

"You can have a seat. I don't bite and you should know that."

Jennifer spun around and frowned. "You do remember me, you dingbat."

Nick couldn't help but chuckle. "Dingbat?"

"I don't curse much. I try not to…"

"Dingbat isn't cursing. Now, the F word, that's cursing."

She winced. "Why did you act like you hadn't met me?"

Nick cocked an eyebrow. "You did the same thing!"

"I thought you were a soldier." She sat down in the chair across from him.

"I was. I was an army medic."

"You never told me that." A smile played around her kissable lips.

"Ah, we're going to play that game, eh? Well, you never exactly told me that you were a surgeon, or a senator's daughter, for that matter."

She blushed again. "Fine. You have me, but I would really appreciate it if you wouldn't spread around the fact I'm a senator's daughter."

"Is your father crooked?" he teased.

Jennifer's eyes narrowed. "Hardly. I just don't want the notoriety to follow me. I'm a damn good trauma surgeon. I don't want that to cloud my team's judgment of me. I *earned* my reputation."

Nick nodded. "Of course."

"Good." She bit her bottom lip. "Well, I'd better see

if Dr. Ramsgate is through. It's good to see you again, Dr. Rousseau. I'm glad no harm came to you overseas."

Nick didn't respond as she got up and left the doctors' lounge.

"I'm glad no harm came to you overseas."

Even though she'd truly meant it, it still stung.

He touched the scar on his face. The only injury he'd sustained when the IED had blown.

Could his brother say the same? His brother had been sent home a year early, had had to leave the service.

Nick got to finish out his tour of duty.

Nick could still walk, run and keep up with the fast pace of trauma.

Marc couldn't.

So, no, he hadn't come back home unharmed.

Nick crushed the empty coffee cup in his hand and tossed it into the trash. Crushing the cup in his hand sated his ire, but only just. There was only one thing he could do to control this—he was going to bury himself in his work.

He was going to forget that stolen moment on Lake Tahoe with Jennifer, because he didn't deserve that kind of happiness.

Nick was going to be the best surgeon he could be and maybe then his brother would think better of him and nothing, not even a woman, was going to distract him.

He couldn't let it.

CHAPTER TWO

JENNIFER WAS GLAD to get all the paperwork and HR stuff done in enough time to head down to the ER and actually practice some medicine. She hadn't had a chance to do any in a month, what with trying to find another job and moving across the country after her ex-fiancé had published the research they'd shared and been given a promotion at her old hospital in Boston.

She'd planned to stick it out. After all, he'd jilted her the previous year. She'd held her own and had faced him every day because she'd refused to be bullied out of the career she'd built, but then, when she'd let her guard down, he'd betrayed her.

The hospital board had backed him. After all, he'd been a surgical rock star, a god in their eyes, and he'd bring in lots of money.

Jennifer had been a nobody, as far as they were concerned. Just an easy, replaceable trauma surgeon.

So she'd given them the proverbial finger and left, leaving their trauma department to be run by a moron.

All Saints Hospital in Las Vegas had offered her everything to come and run their trauma department. And they were building a state-of-the-art facility better than that at Boston Mercy. So that was a plus. Even though it felt like she was returning home with her tail between her legs, she wasn't. No, she was going to make All Saints Hospital shine like a star, like a supernova.

She smiled to herself as she slipped on the disposable yellow isolation gown over her dark green scrubs. The dark green scrubs marked her as an attending, while the interns and residents ran around in orange.

Jennifer shuddered. It wasn't even a nice orange. Maybe she could have a talk with the chief about changing the color scheme of scrubs at the hospital.

Why the heck are you thinking about color schemes at a time like this?

She sighed. She didn't need to be having this weird internal dialogue with herself. Ever since David had jilted her, people hadn't treated her the same. They'd pitied her and she'd retreated a bit into her head.

That was another reason she'd had to get away. Though she knew the people at All Saints knew about her past. She could see it in their eyes, but she didn't care. She was going to hold her head high.

She was not some screwball, crazy, jilted-bride-type person. She was a surgeon. A fine one.

No. A damn good one.

A neutron star.

Okay, your obsession with astronomy really needs to stop now.

"Dr. Mills, the ambulance is seven minutes out!" a nurse shouted as Jennifer walked into the triage area.

"Thanks." She headed outside to the tarmac to await the arrival of the ambulance, craning her head, listening for the distant wail. It was a quirk of hers to know exactly how far away an ambulance was by the siren. Only with All Saints being right near the strip, Jennifer couldn't drown out the rest of the noise to hear anything.

"What do we have coming in?"

She spun around to see Dr. Rousseau in an isolation gown standing next to her.

Damn.

"I thought you were on a break, as in napping in the on-call room?"

"Disappointed that I'm not?"

Jennifer rolled her eyes. "Hardly, but I heard it's something minor. Something coming from one of the casinos. It's probably just a myocardial infarction. You know, too much excitement at the slots."

Nick cocked an eyebrow. "Oh, I think it's something a bit more than a minor myocardial infarction. Though I doubt you could call any myocardial infarction minor."

"You know something. Don't you?" she asked, scrutinizing him. "What do you know?"

"If you don't know, I'm not going to tell you. I want to see the look of surprise on your face when the ambulance comes in."

"That's unprofessional."

Nick grinned. "Hey, it's Vegas and what happens in Vegas…"

"Stays in Vegas. I know. I'm from Nevada." She crossed her arms and stared up at the sky. The buildings from the strip loomed from behind the back of a casino. You could see the top of the Eiffel Tower if you craned your head a certain way.

"It's priceless. Trust me. It's a great initiation."

"I'm the head of trauma. We're not supposed to be initiated or hazed."

Nick shrugged. "Come on. It's fun. Think of it as a morale booster."

Jennifer was going to say a few more choice words when the ambulance came roaring up. The paramedic jumped out and opened the back door.

"Jack Palmer, a twelve-year-old male who has a three-inch laceration to his forehead."

As the paramedics were bringing down the stretcher, Jennifer leaned over to Nick. "How is a three-inch lac supposed to be an initiation?"

Nick just grinned. "You'll see."

The little boy groaned as the stretcher was placed on the ground. His head was bandaged, there was blood coming through the gauze and the boy was hiccuping between groans. Jennifer stepped beside it and heard a tinny hum of "Happy Birthday."

"What's that noise?"

Jack hiccuped. "It's my birthday card."

"Where is it? I can hold your birthday card for you." Jennifer looked on the gurney, while a paramedic was stifling a chuckle and Nick was grinning from ear to ear like a Cheshire cat.

"No, you can't." Jack hiccuped again.

"Why not?"

Jack shook his head and his face flushed. Jennifer looked at the female paramedic. "What's going on?"

"The card is the reason he got the head injury. He swallowed the music player from the card."

Jennifer's eyes widened and she looked down at the patient. "What?"

Nick signed off on the patient and the paramedics mumbled "Good luck" before leaving. Jennifer and Nick wheeled the boy inside.

When they got Jack in a triage room with the door shut, he hiccuped again, playing that annoying tune. Jennifer turned away residents because it was just a simple head lac and as Jack was obviously embarrassed about his situation, she wanted to give him some privacy. For the time being, anyway. The news would get around the hospital and she would need to take a couple of residents in when she surgically removed it.

What happens in Vegas stays in Vegas.

"Jack, please tell me the paramedics are joking."

"Would I be here if they were?" Jack winced again, hiccuped another verse of "Happy Birthday." "Darn."

"How did this happen?" she asked.

"It was a dare. I swallowed it, choked and hit my head on the table."

"Order a CT scan. Stat," Jennifer said to Nick.

"I'm on it," Nick said, rushing out of the room.

"They're all going to laugh at me now. Aren't they?" Jack asked.

"No one is going to laugh at you, Jack. Not on my watch." Though it was very hard not to laugh just a little, but she kept it together. She peeled off the gauze and began to inspect the head wound, getting it ready to clean and stitch.

Nick had the feeling he was being watched. Intently. He had a sixth sense about when he was being watched. Actually, when he was being studied.

"More suction, please," Nick said to the intern who was working with him.

"Yes, Dr. Rousseau."

It was in that brief moment when the intern was suctioning that Nick snuck a glance up at the gallery. There was only one person in the gallery, watching his routine appendectomy, and that was Jennifer.

Not Jennifer. Don't call her by her first name. She's your boss.

She was Dr. Mills.

Only he couldn't think of her as Dr. Mills. She was Jennifer, and he watched her sitting in the gallery,

watching his surgery, her arms crossed in a very serious pose.

So different from when they'd been on the beach at
Lake Tahoe.

What he wouldn't give to be back there again. Right
now.

Then again, that was a dangerous thought.

One he didn't particularly want to think about because he couldn't indulge it, and he *so* wanted to indulge it, which was bad.

Nick tore his gaze away from her and focused back
on the appendectomy. He tried to ignore the fact she
was in the gallery. He'd known there was someone in
there, watching him. Other surgeons and interns had
watched him before. It didn't faze him, but the moment
he'd glanced up into that gallery and seen it was her,
it was different.

And it irked him.

Why was she affecting him so much?

Maybe he shouldn't have flirted with her, but he
couldn't help himself when he was around her. It was
like he lost all control.

And control was important.

Control meant that he wouldn't act before he thought.

That behavior in the past had been disastrous for
him. He just had to look at Marc to remind himself of
that daily.

"Don't go out there. Are you crazy?"

"I have to, he's my friend. I'll be okay." Nick ignored
his brother's arguments and ran out into the fray. Bul-
lets whizzed past him, his brother screaming his name
behind him.

Nick forced himself to focus as he pulled on the

purse strings and inverted the stump into the cecum. He couldn't think about that right now.

"Your recklessness cost you your brother." Those had been the last words his father had said to him.

When he thought of that moment, he became angry. He lost control.

So he couldn't let Jennifer into his head.

When he did, he lost the control that he fought so hard to maintain. He was a respected surgeon. He did his job well.

His anger wouldn't get the better of him.

No one's life was in danger and the window-smashing had been a one-off. He rolled his shoulders, tension creeping up his spine. He had to get out of there.

"Why don't you close, Dr. Murphy?" Nick said to his resident as he stepped away from the patient.

Dr. Murphy handed his clamp to a nurse and moved around to finish off the appendectomy as Nick walked toward the scrub room, with one last look up at the gallery.

Jennifer wasn't there anymore. She'd left.

He was going to have to try to avoid her. It was for the best.

Of course, he'd said that to himself before, and what had he done? He'd thrown her an interesting case, to watch her reaction. The patient had probably been one of the first of the interesting cases she'd see, working in the trauma department of All Saints Hospital.

He could've taken that case instead of surprising her with it.

Once he'd realized how much he'd been enjoying the banter with her, he'd left the room. Left her to deal with the patient on her own and found his own case.

An emergency appendectomy.

He pulled off his soiled gown, tossed it in the laundry bin and threw the gloves in the waste receptacle before heading to the sink.

"Thank you for that."

Nick glanced over his shoulder and stepped on the bar under the sink, turning on the water so he could scrub.

"For what?" he asked, feigning innocence, though he was anything but. He knew exactly what she was talking about.

"You know very well."

Nick shook the excess water into the sink and grabbed a towel. "I thought you deserved an interesting case on your first day."

Jennifer raised an eyebrow. "Swallowing part of a birthday card isn't very interesting."

"How can you say that? He serenaded you with every hiccup."

She pinched the bridge of her nose. "It was an annoying song."

"How many of those have you seen?"

"None."

Nick shrugged. "Then I don't really see the argument. You got an interesting case."

"Which I promptly passed on to a resident to retrieve through an endoscope."

"You gave it up?" Nick gasped.

Jennifer just rolled her eyes and walked away from him.

Just let her go.

Only he couldn't. He followed her. "I can't believe you gave it to your resident."

"It was easy for my resident to do."

"I gave you an interesting surgery. You could've had

my appendectomy instead." He fell into step beside her. "I could've kept it."

Jennifer snorted. "I wish you had. As it is, Dr. Fallon is an excellent surgical resident and I'm sure I left the patient in capable hands."

"I'm sure you did."

Jennifer stopped and turned to face him. "You did well in there. I mean, I didn't have a good view way up in the gallery, but you have a good touch with your interns and residents in the OR."

Her admiration, her praise pleased him. A lot of people had avoided him since his mishap when he'd first arrived. It's why he was known as a lone wolf, though he wasn't. Not really.

Nick nodded. "Thank you for your professional appraisal. Is that why you came to the gallery?"

She hesitated and tucked a wisp of hair behind her ear. "Of course. Why else would I come?"

Nick didn't believe her for one second. He didn't know her well, but he knew when someone was lying. It was a sort of superpower of his, and she was lying.

"I thought you wanted to call me out on the carpet for a swallowed birthday card."

Her brow furrowed and a flicker of a smile played across her pink, kissable lips.

Get a hold on yourself. Stop thinking about them as kissable.

"It did keep playing the music over and over. I hope his birthday wasn't totally ruined. However, my appearance in the gallery was because I'm evaluating all my trauma surgeons."

"Should I be worried?"

She smiled slyly. "Is there a reason why you should be worried?"

Nick chuckled. *Run. Turn and run.*

Tension hovered between them and he longed to kiss her again. All he had to do was reach out and touch her. Put his arm around her and bring her close to him, pull her against his body and—

His pager went off before he even had a chance to do anything. *Saved by the bell.*

"Let's go, Dr. Rousseau." Jennifer held up her pager. "Large trauma coming in."

She pushed past him and ran down the hall.

Avoiding her was harder than he thought.

He was doomed.

Jennifer watched him work across the ER. A large pileup on the interstate had flooded the hospital with crash victims. Thankfully, there were no *interesting* cases. Just regular trauma—not that it was good, but at least she could scrub in instead of having residents fish music makers out of kids' stomachs.

She'd gone to the gallery to call him out, but then she'd watched him do the appendectomy. Had seen how he'd taught his residents and interns. He'd been so calm and the fluid motion of his hands as he'd inverted the stump had been pure poetry.

Her ex-fiancé wouldn't have lowered himself to do an appendectomy. Even though he was a cardiothoracic surgeon, an appendectomy was beneath him. Best left to the general surgeons and residents.

Appendectomies were easy. What he'd wanted had been the high-profile cases. The cases that would get him the press coverage, would give him the glory.

When she'd first met David, she'd admired his drive and she'd swooned when he'd paid her attention. He'd made her feel like a princess, but all she had been was a trophy, and when he'd found something brighter, something shinier, she'd been dropped.

David had got what he'd wanted from her. The publicity, the research and her heart.

Nick seemed to revel in simplicity. Or at least that's what she got from watching his surgery, his easygoing attitude, but he was guarded.

There was a wall there, one he used flirting to hide, but he was keeping people out. In her brief time talking to other staff members, they'd said he was a bit of a loner. Kept to himself, ate his lunch alone and not many people knew much about him.

The only conversations he engaged in were medical. Case files, papers. The only other thing the staff knew about him was that he had served in the military and been decorated. Something about bravery, but no one knew for sure.

There was also an incident about him getting angry with another surgeon and smashing a window in the doctors' lounge. Anger issues, which had been swept under the rug. It had happened so soon after his return from overseas that people had given him the benefit of the doubt, but for the most part the staff stayed away from him.

Jennifer would've never pegged him to have anger issues.

Everything about him was a mystery.

And she couldn't help but wonder why.

Don't wonder. Just keep away.

It was for the best. She was here to work. To be a surgeon. She didn't need or want love.

When the hubbub of the ER died down and she was scrubbing out of surgery, she saw Nick again. He was rushing down the hall, his surgical gown billowing out behind him as he pushed a gurney to Recovery.

He was a mystery man and she had a thing for mystery men.

Damn.

She glanced at the clock. She still had six hours left on her shift and it was now after midnight. She really needed to get some sleep.

Jennifer headed to the nearest on-call room and collapsed on a cot. As she lay down, she glanced at the nightstand and saw a medical journal.

"Oh, you've got to be kidding me." She picked up the magazine and stared at the grinning face of the man who'd left her standing in a white puffy dress while the press had snapped thousands of pictures of the disgraced, heartbroken and jilted senator's daughter.

The journal was touting Dr. David Morgan's medical breakthrough and how he was up for an award for excellence.

With a *tsk* of disgust and rage, she tossed it at the door just as it was opening, thus beaning Nick in the head, right between the eyes.

She held her breath, hoping he wouldn't get angry with her. Instead, he rubbed his forehead and bent to pick up the magazine.

"Uh, is this your way of telling me you want me to read more medical journals?" He glanced down at the cover. "Ah, I've been meaning to read this one. I'm eager to read all about the Morgan method for aortic dissections."

Jennifer kept her snort to herself and rolled over in the cot. "If you don't mind, I'd like to catch about thirty minutes of sleep before I'm paged again."

The door shut and the room went dark, but she knew

she wasn't alone as she heard him move across the room and the mattress creak across the way.

The room was silent, and even though she was dog tired, she couldn't sleep knowing that he was across the room. Lying there, all mysterious and handsome, and she knew he was a good kisser. She'd experienced it firsthand.

Damn.

"Are there any private on-call rooms in this hospital?" she asked.

"Nope." Nick yawned. "Is my presence disturbing you?"

"No, I just don't know if you're a snorer or not. I'm a light sleeper."

"I don't snore. Now, if you don't mind, I've been up for twelve hours." The mattress creaked again as he moved.

"Good." She rolled back over and closed her eyes, trying to will herself to fall asleep, but it wasn't working.

"You know, of all the ways I imagined us sleeping together, this wasn't how I envisioned it."

Jennifer's cheeks heated. "Excuse me?"

There was a chuckle in the darkness.

"What's so funny?" Jennifer asked.

"I get under your skin, don't I?"

"No, you don't."

"I do."

Jennifer cursed under her breath and sat up. "I'm going to sleep on a gurney down in an abandoned hall."

"No, no. I'll let you sleep." The bed shifted again and then the room filled with light. "Have a good sleep, Dr. Mills."

The door shut and Jennifer lay back against the pillow. She didn't think she was going to fall asleep after her run-in with Dr. Rousseau, but once she closed her eyes again, sleep came easily.

The pager vibrated in her hand and she woke with a start. She flicked on the bedside lamp and saw it was coming from the ER.

It was her first twenty-four-hour shift, and even then she wouldn't go home after her shift was done. She had something to prove here and she would stay here as long as it took.

This was going to become her second home. Besides, her condo was sparse and empty. If she went home, there would be messages from her father. Invitations for her to go out campaigning with him, to show the voters she wasn't a pathetic loser like they all believed she was.

She just wanted to escape the stigma of it all.

She wasn't any of those things. She was a surgeon, for heaven's sake.

Only the more you listened to the naysayers, those creeping doubt weasels, the more you started to believe it.

And she hated that loss of control.

She hated that her confidence was all shot to heck.

Jennifer clipped her pager back to the waist of her scrubs and headed down to the ER. When she got there, it was relatively quiet.

"Who paged me?" she asked the charge nurse.

"Dr. Rousseau. He's in Room Three, needs a consult on a patient."

Jennifer groaned inwardly. "Thank you."

What patient had he dug up now?

Did this one have a tiger coming out of his chest?

Tassels glued to the forehead? Cards embedded in the abdomen?

"Dr. Rousseau, you paged me?"

Nick glanced at her briefly. "Yes, the patient is adamant that they're seen by the head of trauma."

Jennifer approached the bed and then froze when she saw her father was on the gurney. "Dad, what happened?"

"Ah, there she is." Her father grinned. "I had a fainting spell during a speech at the convention center and they brought me here. Or rather I asked them to bring me here. I said I would be in good hands with my daughter."

Nick's eyebrows rose.

Jennifer pinched the bridge of her nose. "Dad, that's all well and good, but as I've told you before on numerous occasions, I can't assess you."

Her father looked shocked. "Why not?"

"Because you're my father. I can't treat family." She sighed. "You're in good hands with Dr. Rousseau."

Her father looked confused. "Why can't you do it?"

"I don't have time for this, Dad." She turned to Nick. "Please keep me informed, Dr. Rousseau."

"Will do, Dr. Mills."

Jennifer turned and left the trauma exam room, but Dr. Rousseau was close on her heels.

"Can I speak to you for a moment?"

Jennifer paused and crossed her arms. "Sure."

"I'm sorry I paged you. He was making such a fuss. I thought discretion would be the best bet. There's lots of reporters out there."

Jennifer's stomach clenched. The press. She hated the press. The damage they did, looking for sensationalist stories, but then again she was biased.

"It's okay, Dr. Rousseau."

Nick cocked his head to the side. "I don't think it is."

"No, it really is. Just…just don't spread it around that my father's here."

"Okay. I'll keep it to myself."

"Thank you. He doesn't need any more attention drawn to his campaign." She turned to walk away and then stopped. "When is your shift over?"

Nick grinned, his hazel eyes twinkling. "Are you asking me out?"

She blushed. "No. I just wanted to implement some changes to the schedule."

"Oh." She noticed he looked a bit disappointed, but then he shrugged. "As soon as I take care of your father, I'll be going home. I won't be in for another shift until Wednesday."

Jennifer nodded. "Thank you."

Nick nodded curtly and headed back to the exam room.

CHAPTER THREE

"DRAG RACES? YOU dragged me to a drag race in the middle of the desert?" Jennifer shook her head as her best friend Ginny grinned and handed her a bottle of water. "We could've stayed at brunch in the air-conditioned bistro or gone shopping."

She needed groceries desperately and her condo was full of boxes. She'd been working for a week and still hadn't had time to sort through her stuff or make her condo a home.

"Chillax. This is fun!"

Jennifer rolled her eyes. "Yeah, because this is how I wanted to spend my day off, sitting on a hard bench watching motorcycles race across the desert."

"Yeah, but look how hot those guys are."

Yeah, she remembered that. Clearly.

Jennifer chuckled and couldn't disagree with her friend. Not that she could see any of the riders' faces. They had nice bodies clad in leather, and she was always a sucker for motorcycles.

Nick rides a motorcycle.

Her heart beat a bit faster as she thought about that moment she'd thrown caution to the wind and climbed on the back of Nick's bike. He had been a stranger, a man leaving on a long tour of duty, but she hadn't cared.

That had been when she'd still been carefree. Before the press had got hold of her and David had publicly humiliated her. Though she was more annoyed by the stolen research than the jilting.

The lack of accreditation of her in his paper had made her look like a fool in front of her colleagues. It had been like they'd all known David would screw her over.

David had broken her heart, but she could never regain her research. All the countless hours she and David had spent together, working on repairing an aortic dissection by trying a surgical grafting procedure with artificial veins, and he hadn't credited her.

Now the surgical procedure was being deemed innovative and the grant money he'd got for a medical trial he'd received, well, he had it made in the shade.

Whereas right now she would kill for some shade. It was too damn hot in the desert. She'd spent too long up north in Boston.

Even though she was wearing a big straw hat, it wasn't protecting her from the hot sun.

Ginny was whistling as her boyfriend, Jacob, climbed on his bike. Ginny waved at him, blowing kisses.

"So, once his race is over, we can head for a nice air-conditioned bistro or something on the strip?" Jennifer asked, grinning.

Ginny laughed. "If he wins, he keeps going until he's eliminated."

"Or wins it all?" Jennifer offered.

Ginny tapped her nose. "You've got it. Seriously, though, Jenn, thanks for coming with me."

"Of course. I'm sorry for griping. Not used to the heat. The North made me too soft."

"I still don't know how you survived all those bitter cold winters."

"Layers. Lots of layers." Jennifer winked.

Ginny chuckled. "Oh, they're starting!"

Jennifer turned to the race track. Two motorcycles sat there, revving their engines as the lights flashed from red to green.

In a split second it went from revving engines to a cloud of dust as the bikes raced across the desert plain in less than a minute.

Jennifer couldn't keep up with the fast pace and the screams deafened her. When the dust finally settled, there were two bikes at the end of the track.

"He won!" Ginny leaped up. "Come on, let's go down there. I promised him a kiss if he won."

"And if he didn't?"

Ginny grinned. "You don't want to know."

Jennifer laughed and followed Ginny down off the bleachers toward the track. Jacob and his opponent were riding their bikes back slowly up the side to where all the other competitors were waiting.

As they approached Jacob, he was shaking hands with the biker he'd just trounced and Jennifer had a nagging suspicion that she knew him.

Ginny ran ahead and threw herself in Jacob's arms while Jennifer lingered behind. As Ginny gave Jacob his reward, the competitor turned and Jennifer groaned inwardly.

"Dr. Mills," Nick said in surprise, running his hands through his hair.

"Dr. Rousseau." Jennifer took her large hat off. "I didn't expect to see you here."

"I could say the same thing."

Jennifer looked at Ginny, but she was still involved with Jacob and she was stuck here with Nick.

"I didn't know you raced bikes on your free time." Jennifer played with the brim of her hat, picking at some loose thread.

"Yeah, it's something I do to unwind."

"This helps you unwind?"

Nick smiled. "You knew I rode a motorcycle."

"Yes, but I wasn't aware that you raced it."

Nick shrugged. "Like I said, it's something I do to unwind."

"Most people read a book."

"I'm not most people."

Jennifer chuckled. "Sorry you lost."

"It's no big deal. Not really a professional at this. Believe it or not, I have another job."

"Really?" They both laughed together.

Stop flirting. Stop flirting.

"Sorry for interrupting." Ginny had that goofy grin on her face like she always did when she was being mischievous. "Jennifer, I'm going to stay with Jacob in the tent. He can give me a ride home and you can take my car if you want to leave."

"I can take her home," Nick said.

Ginny grinned again. "You two know each other?"

Jennifer groaned inwardly. "We work together. Dr. Rousseau is a surgeon at All Saints and works in Trauma with me."

"She's my boss." Nick winked.

Jennifer sighed. *Great.* At least Ginny didn't work at the hospital. At least that rumor wasn't going to be started. Nick hadn't told anyone else about treating her father for heatstroke and dehydration.

No one was any the wiser and Mills was a common name.

"Sorry, Dr. Mills, would you like a ride home?"

"Not on your bike. Not today."

"You've been on my bike before."

Ginny's head whipped round. "You have? This is news."

Jennifer glared at Nick. "It was nothing. It was a long time ago, so you can wipe that smirk off your face."

Ginny threw up her arms. "Fine, fine. So, are you going to take Dr. Rousseau up on his offer, or do you need my keys?"

Before Jennifer could answer, Nick stepped between them. "I'll take her home."

"Well, that answers that. I'll call you later, Jenn."

Before Jennifer could stop Ginny from leaving, she took off and Jennifer was left alone with Nick. Again.

It had been a bit of a godsend that he'd been off duty for a couple of days and the day he'd returned, Wednesday, had been her day off.

She'd managed to avoid him at the hospital. It had become easier to forget about him. To not think about him, but now, standing here in the middle of the desert, beside his bike, well, this was exactly where she didn't want to be. This situation was absolutely and utterly dangerous.

"Maybe I'll just catch a cab back home."

"Why?" he asked.

"Your panniers won't hold my hat." It was a feeble excuse, but she was grasping at any straw to get out of this situation.

"I drove my car."

"Why? How are you going to get your bike home?"

"It isn't my bike. I don't have mine anymore." There

was a hint of sadness in his voice. "I was racing a buddy's bike today."

There was really no escape.

"Okay. I would love a ride home."

Nick grinned. "See, now, was that so hard?"

She couldn't help but laugh then. "It was, actually."

"Let me just take the keys back to my buddy and we'll hit the road."

Jennifer nodded as he turned toward the competitors' tent. She watched him walk away from her. The dark leather molded his broad shoulders and the dark jeans were tight, giving her a good view of his butt.

He looked hot. Both in the sense that the heat of the desert was stifling and the fact she could picture her hands on his backside, squeezing the cheeks.

Don't look at it.

Jennifer turned away and watched as another drag race started and finished. She didn't know where Ginny had got to, but she was with Jacob. They'd spent the morning together. She knew she should head for home so she could get some unpacking done before she had to return to her duties tomorrow.

Nick returned, twirling a set of keys around his finger. "You ready to go?"

"Sure, if you are."

"I am. Won a couple races and lost." Nick shrugged. "It is what it is."

They walked in silence toward the parking lot, moving through the crowds. It was hard to talk over the roar of the motorcycle engines.

When they got to the parking lot, Nick stopped and pulled off his leather jacket. Underneath, he was wearing an indigo-colored V-neck shirt. The blue suited him, given the dark color of his hair, and she saw tattoos up and down his forearms, like sleeves. She hadn't known he had tattoos. They suited him, too.

He was such a stereotypical bad boy on the outside, but when he was in the hospital, he was so put together. So professional. Sure, he was a loner, that's what the nurses and other surgeons said, but he didn't look like the tattooed easy rider he was portraying now.

And she had a hard time thinking he had anger issues. He was so laid back.

He was an interesting character. So black and white, or was he? She had a feeling there was more to him.

"Whew, that's better. It was fine when I was out there on the bike, racing, but walking to the car, it's a little hot."

"Yeah, hanging out in the desert isn't my idea of a fun time," Jennifer said.

"What is your idea of a fun time?"

She grinned. "Air-conditioning."

Nick chuckled. "Come on, you were complaining about the cold temperature of Lake Tahoe. I believe you said something about people from the North having addled brains."

"What I said was that people up north are addled by the cold weather. I should know, I've spent the last several years in Boston."

"Boston?"

"Yes. I did my fellowship there."

"Yet I met you in Carson City."

"I was there to support my father."

"Ah, yes," Nick said. "The senator."

Jennifer groaned. "Don't remind me."

"Not a fan of politics?"

"No, not really. I mean I vote, it's just… It's a long story."

"I have time."

Jennifer shook her head. "I don't really want to talk about it today."

"Fair enough. Here's my ride." Nick unlocked the vehicle remotely. He drove an SUV. A black SUV, and it suited him, having been a soldier and everything. "Sorry, my car doesn't have air-conditioning, but we can get a nice breeze."

"It's great and it's exactly the kind of car I pegged you for. Though it's not really a car, is it?"

Nick opened the door for her. "You pictured me in an SUV? Are you stereotyping me?"

Jennifer slid in and he walked around and climbed in the driver's side. "No. I'm not."

"Sure you are." He winked at her and she rolled her eyes.

"Well, when you said you didn't ride a motorcycle anymore, the SUV seemed like a natural transition."

"Never really thought of that before." He started the engine and they pulled out of the parking lot, heading out to the highway. You could see the strip in the distance and in the rearview mirror were the mountains.

"I may complain about the heat and hanging out in the desert, but I do love this place." Jennifer sighed, letting her guard down.

"So why did you choose Boston?"

She shrugged. "Good surgical program."

"And you just decided to stay there?"

"You're asking a lot of personal questions."

Nick grinned and glanced at her quickly. "I'm just trying to figure you out. I like figuring people out."

"Why do I have to answer all these questions? Why can't I get some answers from you?"

"You haven't asked any questions."

Jennifer cocked an eyebrow. "Haven't I?"

"Nope."

"Okay," she said. "I have one. Why did you leave the army?"

Nick's demeanor changed in an instant. "I was honorably discharged. I didn't leave."

"Honorable discharge usually means that you weren't going to stay in after your tour of duty. Why did you leave?"

Nick's brow furrowed. "I was discharged. No big secret."

Only she didn't believe him. There was something going on there and she didn't know why he didn't want to talk about it. Then again, she didn't want discuss why she'd left Boston, why she hated the sight or any mention of David. Also, she was hiding the fact she was a senator's daughter from everyone.

As they approached the city, she saw a big billboard was up, plastered with a picture of her father asking for votes.

Jennifer groaned inwardly.

"So, why don't you want anyone knowing that you're the senator's daughter?"

"I told you, it's complicated and a long story."

Nick nodded. "Complicated I get, but people know."

"I know, but I like to pretend they don't. Helps me focus on my work."

"I get it, wanting to forget."

She was glad he didn't want to poke and prod any more. She wouldn't question him about his time in the army and he wouldn't bother her about her father.

"I don't want to go back into the city." She hadn't meant to say that out loud. It had just slipped out.

"Want to go to Lake Tahoe?"

Jennifer laughed. "No, that's, like, six hours away and I'm working tomorrow."

"Okay." Nick turned on his indicator and took an exit away from Las Vegas and the strip. They were heading east toward Arizona.

"Where are we going?" she asked.

"Hoover Dam."

Her eyes widened. "The Hoover Dam?"

"You sound nervous."

"I am! I hate heights."

He glanced at her. "Really?"

"Yeah, really."

"Oh, come on, it's wide and stable. We can walk around the top. You won't fall off. What do you say?"

"Okay, I guess. I've never seen it."

"Aren't you native to Nevada?"

Jennifer shrugged. "So? Have you seen all the touristy places in your home state?"

"No, I haven't."

"Where are you from? Am I allowed to ask that question or is that forbidden?"

"Illinois. I'm one of those people who have been addled by the cold weather."

Jennifer laughed. It was easy to laugh with him and she couldn't remember the last time she'd laughed like this.

She couldn't recall if she'd even laughed like this with David. They'd laughed, they'd shared good times, but she couldn't remember if it was the same. Which made her think it wasn't.

Which was sad, as she barely knew Nick.

What am I doing?
She was weak.
So weak.

Nick knew he shouldn't have offered to take her home and he definitely shouldn't be taking her to the Hoover Dam. At least, that's what he was telling himself over and over again in his head, but when he'd seen that it was her there at the drag races, he hadn't been able to help himself.

He'd gravitated toward her.

At first, all he'd seen had been a gorgeous, tall woman in plaid clam diggers, wedge sandals, a white eyelet blouse and a ridiculous straw hat. Her look was very rockabilly. So different from the classic Jackie O type of look she'd had going on when he'd first met her.

She intrigued him.

Still, he should've kept away. He should've walked away, and he was annoyed that now someone from work knew what he did in his spare time.

Only he couldn't keep away from her. He lost all control and he hated himself for it, but not totally, because now that he had her up here, he was glad he'd brought her.

Especially since she was standing in the middle of the Hoover Dam, her arms straight out on both sides, crouched over like the dam was actually rocking back and forth and she was going to plummet off the side.

It was hilarious.

"Shut up, shut up, shut up," she cussed at him. "It's not funny. I told you I was afraid of heights."

There was a definite hint of panic in her voice.

"I'm sorry." Only he wasn't. This was fun.

"I told you but, oh, no, you didn't listen to me."

He laughed. He couldn't help himself.

"I'm sorry, but if you could see yourself now."

Her eyes narrowed and she stuck out her tongue. She stood up a bit straighter and lowered her arms slightly, especially now that people were walking past and shooting her strange glances. One thing he'd figured out about Dr. Jennifer Mills was that she didn't like the limelight. She didn't like attention.

And he got it because being a senator's daughter probably didn't help.

Maybe that's why she'd become a surgeon. To hide away in an operating room rather than get involved in her father's politics.

Not that he blamed her for not following a career like politics. Politics bored the heck out of him.

Of course, he didn't know much. He'd followed his brother into medical school. He'd spent his whole life following Marc's lead, for the most part.

Except now.

Now he couldn't follow his brother's lead and the only set of wheels his brother was driving these days was a wheelchair, and it was his fault. His brother had followed him out there, to save him again, like he always had, only this time Marc had suffered for it.

When Nick had been discharged from the army, he'd decided to live differently. He'd sold his motorcycle, though it had killed him to do it.

It eased the guilt. At least, that's what he tried to tell himself, because really it didn't.

He'd settled into a good, respectable job instead of driving across the country and living in the back of an RV, experiencing North America.

When Marc had been injured, he'd sworn to himself he wouldn't be reckless anymore. Maybe if he showed his brother that he was trying to pull his life together, well, maybe then Marc would forgive him.

How can Marc forgive you if you can't forgive yourself? He shoved that unwelcome thought away, his fists tightening.

Get control. Control.

"There," Jennifer shouted. "I think I'm okay. I think."

Nick glanced over at her. Jennifer was standing ramrod straight, but at least she wasn't bracing herself not to topple over the side of the dam.

"Good, now why don't you come over to the edge and look out the viewfinder?" He wandered over to the viewfinder in question, expecting Jennifer to follow him, only she didn't. She stared at him like he had cats bursting from his ears.

"What?" he asked.

"You're crazy!"

Nick leaned over the edge, looking down at the Colorado River.

"Don't do that!" Jennifer shrieked.

"What?"

"You'll plummet to your death that way."

Nick chuckled. "Oh, come on."

Jennifer just shook her head. "No way."

Only he wasn't going to take no for an answer. He walked over to her and took her hand. "Come on. Where's your sense of adventure?"

"On solid ground."

He grinned. "First you didn't want to wade in Lake Tahoe and now you don't want to come and see the splendor of the mighty, tamed Colorado River."

Jennifer rolled her eyes. "What's with you and bodies of water?"

"Come on. Indulge me and I'll never bother you again."

"Fine, but I'm holding you to that."

Nick laughed. "I'm sure you will."

He managed to get her over to the side, but her eyes were closed. Tight. Nick placed her hand on the side of the dam.

"See, you're safe. A high wall protects you. It's made of cement. Nothing is going to happen. Just open your eyes."

Jennifer let out a shaky breath and opened her eyes. "Oh. My. God."

He snorted. "It's fine. You're fine."

She took some deep breaths and glanced down. He watched her and couldn't help but smile. Being around her was like a breath of fresh air and the urge to kiss her again, to taste her lips, washed over him.

Nick clenched his fists and fought the urge to pull her into his arms. Like he fought every time he saw her, and every time it was getting harder not to give in.

She represented a moment in his life when he'd been carefree, when he'd been happy and sure of the direction of his life.

Nick cleared his throat and moved away from her. His hand was still on top of hers.

Get a grip on yourself.

"Well, why don't we head back to Las Vegas?" he asked, clearing his throat again.

"Sounds good. I've tested my fear of heights long enough." Jennifer moved away from the edge and quickly started walking toward the exit.

He smiled as he watched her, but then the smile disappeared when he realized again that he couldn't have a future with her.

Why did he always have to meet her when he couldn't have her? It was unfair but, then, life wasn't fair.

He couldn't have a future with her.

He didn't deserve a future with her.

Nick was unusually silent as they drove back to Las Vegas. It was a bit unsettling, because it was an awkward silence.

Jennifer hated awkward silences. They drove her batty.

"Knock, knock."

Nick shot her a questioning glance. "Are you telling me a knock-knock joke?"

"I'm trying."

He grinned. "You're trying? Do you have knock-knock joke learning disorder?"

"Well, they only work if the other party plays along," she said. "Now, knock-knock."

Nick shook his head. "I don't do knock-knock jokes."

"How can you not?"

He shrugged. "I just don't."

"Party pooper."

He sighed. "Okay, fine. I'll play along, but it had better be hilarious. I don't want to be let down by a mediocre knock-knock joke."

"Oh, the pressure is on."

"Do you fold under pressure?" he teased.

"Oh, no, I rise to the challenge."

He chuckled. "Fine. Lay it on me."

"Knock-knock."

"Who's there?" he asked petulantly.

"You're ruining it!" Jennifer screeched, punching him in the arm.

He gave her a strange look, like she was insane, and maybe she was. "How am I ruining it?"

"Let's try it again, shall we? Knock-knock."

"Who's there?" He batted his eyelashes.

"Better."

"Better who?"

Jennifer chuckled. "Sorry, I meant it was better."

Nick groaned. "Oh, please. This is why I don't participate in knock-knock jokes. You're making this painful!"

"Sorry. Let's take it from the top."

He groaned again. "No, let's not. This is the longest knock-knock joke ever!"

"I promise it's worth the wait." She smiled sweetly at him. "Please? I mean, I did go on top of the Hoover Dam for you. You can humor me."

"You're…" He trailed off, chuckling. "Fine, but this is the last time."

Jennifer grinned. She was enjoying herself; she liked torturing him. "Knock-knock."

"Who's there?"

"Howie."

"Howie who?"

"Howie gonna hide this dead body?"

There was silence.

"That was the most *pathetic* knock-knock joke I've ever heard," he said, mocking her before bursting out laughing.

Jennifer started laughing. "I know it's stupid, but you're laughing."

Nick shook his head. "I hate you a little bit right now."

"This is my street," Jennifer said. "Make a right."

Nick flicked on his blinker and turned into her quiet cul-du-sac where a row of townhomes stood at the edge of a new development. "Nice neighborhood."

"Thanks. It's quiet. Mine's the one on the end. Number twenty-four."

"Okay." Nick pulled up in front of her place and put his SUV in "park." The awkward silence descended between them again, only it wasn't so much awkward as something more.

Like the night they'd met.

It was heady and made her pulse race, her body heat. It made her feel nervous and excited.

It was dangerous.

"Thanks for the ride." Jennifer hoped her voice didn't shake.

"Hold on." Nick slipped out of the driver's side and ran around to open the door for her. No other man had done that for her.

"You didn't have to do that," she said.

"Any man of honor would." There was a twinkle in his eyes and he walked her toward her steps. "I had a good time today, Jennifer."

"Me, too." Her cheeks heated. They were so close, all she had to do was reach out and pull him closer. She wondered if he tasted the same or if she'd get the same rush if she kissed him.

Nick cleared his throat and stepped away, breaking the connection. "I'll see you around at work." He looked away and then glanced at her quickly. It was like he was fighting himself, his body and movements agitated. "Good night, Dr. Mills."

Jennifer watched him hurry away. She was disappointed, but angry at herself for letting it get that far.

They were colleagues. Nothing more.

Only for a moment she forgot all about that. She forgot about everything and it was nice.

"Good night, Dr. Rousseau," she whispered to herself as she watched him drive away toward the strip.

Even though she liked spending time with him, she just couldn't.

It was dangerous to get close to another man.

Especially the likes of Dr. Nick Rousseau.

CHAPTER FOUR

IT HAD BEEN two weeks since Jennifer had gone to the Hoover Dam with Nick. The night she'd almost kissed him.

She'd thought nothing of it, because they hadn't kissed. They'd parted on good terms. Or at least she'd thought they had until work. It was like Nick was avoiding her. At first, she'd thought she was seeing things when she would see him coming toward her and he would turn and walk in the opposite direction.

When it had first happened, she'd explained it all away, but for two weeks she'd barely seen Nick, who was one of her surgeons. She was head of trauma and one of her surgeons was avoiding her, and it damn well annoyed her.

And she knew people were talking about it.

There was something up and it was undermining her precarious authority. Which she'd been trying to build since her arrival.

She had yet to earn the respect of all her trauma surgeons.

Jennifer needed that respect if she was going to do her job well, and she *was* going to do her job well. She had something to prove, and even though all those who pitied her, who looked down on her, were over a thousand miles away in Boston, she didn't care because she'd sworn she would never be pitied again.

"Where is Dr. Rousseau?" she asked the charge nurse at the desk.

"He's in surgery. He's running a bowel for someone apprehended by the police. A suspected drug runner with balloons full of cocaine."

Jennifer winced. "How long has he been in surgery?"

The charge nurse looked at her watch. "He should be out soon."

"Can you have him come to my office when he's done?"

"Of course, Dr. Mills."

Jennifer nodded and headed toward the OR floor. It was then she ran smack into the man in question. He looked startled to see her and then glanced around, looking for an escape route. Only there wasn't one.

"Dr. Rousseau, I understand you were running a suspect's bowel for drug-filled balloons."

"Yes, I recovered three balloons and they are currently in the hands of police. The suspect is handcuffed in the recovery room and is expected to make a full recovery."

"Glad to hear it."

Nick nodded. "Is that everything, Dr. Mills?"

"No. It's not. I'd like to speak with you."

"About what?"

"About the trauma department and some procedures I want implemented. You see, I had a meeting about a week ago and you weren't in attendance."

"Someone had to be on the trauma floor."

Jennifer nodded. "I understand, but now you have to be informed and kept up to date. After you give your report to the police, come and see me in my office."

She turned on her heel and walked away from him, not giving him the chance to argue with her or make an excuse to get out of it.

He was beside her in an instant, his arm slipping through hers and dragging her into a supply closet.

"What're you doing?" she asked, or rather demanded.

Nick locked the door behind him, leaning against it. "Why do you really want to meet with me?"

"What are you talking about?"

"I was informed about the trauma changes last week when you sent out that memo."

"So, it doesn't mean I can't touch base with all my trauma attending on staff, does it?"

"It's because I've been avoiding you. Isn't it?"

Jennifer glared at him. "It has nothing to do with ignoring me. I'm trying to run an efficient and functional trauma department."

Nick took a step closer to her, his arms crossed. Suddenly she felt a bit like a deer caught in headlights. He was the oncoming car and she was stuck on the highway.

"I have a superpower. I can tell when someone is lying to me." He stepped closer again. "And you're lying."

"How am I lying?"

"You didn't really want to talk to me about the efficiency of the trauma department."

Jennifer stared him down. "Fine. I did want to talk about the fact you're avoiding me. We're trauma surgeons and I can almost guarantee you that we'll be working together again, so this avoidance thing, whatever it is, has to stop. I won't have this kind of behavior in my department. If you have a problem with me, tell me to my face."

He frowned. "Fine."

And that was all he said. She was expecting more, but there wasn't any more.

"Thank you, Dr. Rousseau." She moved past him to get out of the supply closet. She didn't really need to know why he was avoiding her, but at least it wouldn't happen anymore.

When she tried to open the door again, he stopped her.

"Dr. Rousseau, what are you doing?"

"I was avoiding you because…it's for the best."

Her heart skipped a beat. "For the best?"

"Yes, because when I'm around you, I'm fighting the urge to kiss you."

Her pulse began to race. "P-pardon?"

"You heard me." He moved closer to her and she re-treated against the door, trying to keep her heart from beating out of her chest. She fought her own urge to reach out and kiss him, too. It was hard, especially since she knew what those kisses tasted like.

"Dr. Rousseau, I think—"

"We have to keep this professional, Dr. Mills. I know that. My avoiding you was childish, I know, but it's the only way I've been able to keep control."

"Okay, Dr. Rousseau, but we have to work together." Part of her was screaming to run. To turn and flee, but another part of her needed to know why he wanted to avoid her.

"Yes. I understand." Nick took a step back. "It won't happen again."

"Good."

This time she listened to her instincts and managed to get the door to the supply closet open and leave.

Nick watched Jennifer power walk away from the closet. She was running away from him. He was glad she was leaving.

He'd tried to keep his distance from her, but she was right—they worked together. They couldn't logically keep apart.

They had to work together.

Plus, she was technically his boss.

Which made her even more out of bounds.

Jennifer was trouble. Only she was the kind of trouble he craved desperately. The kind of trouble he missed.

Why the hell did trouble always follow him? Why was he so attracted to trouble?

Because it felt so damn good.

It had taken every ounce of his strength that night when he'd dropped her off not to kiss her. As they'd stood out in front of her place, there had been expectation in the air and he'd wanted to give in. He'd wanted to take her in his arms and drown himself in her.

Only he hadn't been able to.

His pager went off.

Damn.

Well, he didn't have any time to think about his own personal problems. Not now, with a massive trauma coming in.

He tossed his surgical gown and cap into the soiled-laundry receptacle and grabbed a fresh scrub cap off the shelf before running off to Trauma.

When he got to the emergency department it was in absolute chaos. Jennifer was across the department in an isolation gown, directing traffic and clearing a path.

"What happened?" he asked a resident as he grabbed an isolation gown.

"There was a plane crash."

"A plane crash?"

"A private plane went down after a failed takeoff." The resident turned and ran to meet the ambulances, and Nick was close on his heels.

Everything else was going to be put aside. Right now he was a trauma surgeon. Trauma was something he was good at.

Even after the stupid screwups he'd made in his past, all the reckless choices, he'd never failed in surgery. He loved what he did, and while he was in the operating theater, he forgot everything else.

He forgot his time overseas. He forgot the IED explosion. He forgot the look on his brother's face when Marc had told him that he was paralyzed, the look of blame on his face, the disappointment in his parents' voices. The guilt ate away at him.

Everything was gone when he was trying to save a life.

As the first patient came in off the ambulance, he let all of it go and focused on the patient. The rest of the world was just background noise. He could be anywhere and nothing would faze him.

It was how he'd survived on his tour of duty.

When the sound of war and chaos had been around him, he'd had to learn to drown it all out and focus on the soldier lying on the table in front of him. The brave man or woman who'd fought for their country and now needed him to save their life.

It was a survival instinct for him.

"Charge to fifty."

Nick looked up to see that Jennifer was working across from him. They were in the OR and he couldn't recall how they'd got here, but he was here now.

"Clear."

He moved his hands away as Jennifer shocked the heart, but the monitor still didn't move.

"Assystiline," the scrub nurse shouted.

"Charge the paddles again. Clear." Jennifer shocked

the heart once more and the monitor began to show a heartbeat again.

"We have a sinus rhythm," the nurse said.

He looked at Jennifer across the patient. Their gazes locked, then they continued trying to repair the damage done to the man's spleen.

Nick hadn't had a chance to do a surgery with Jennifer, but the way they were working together almost seamlessly was something of a miracle. It was like they'd been working together for a long time.

"Dr. Murphy, hold the retractor, and can I have some more suction?" Nick cauterized and threw stitches as fast as he could.

"I think this spleen is beyond salvageable," Jennifer remarked. "I think we're going to have to do a splenectomy."

"Agreed."

Their eyes met across the table again. It was a moment that they understood each other, that they knew what needed to be done.

And together they would save this life.

"You did a good job in there, Dr. Rousseau." Jennifer scrubbed her hands.

"Why, thank you, Dr. Mills." Nick grinned at her.

"I've only had a chance to observe you from a distance; this was my first time working with you and I hope it won't be the last."

She watched his face, but he just nodded.

"I'm sure it won't be the last."

Jennifer rolled her shoulders. "I have got to get a coffee."

"I need to get some sleep."

"Sleep would be good, too."

Nick shook his hands. "I've been here for forty-eight hours. I need to crash like yesterday."

"Well, at least tomorrow you can sleep."

"Sure."

"Why, what're you going to do on your day off?"

"Drag racing. For my friend."

Jennifer grabbed a towel and dried her hands. "Why are you racing your friend's motorcycle?"

"He fractured his femur and can't, but he makes the bulk of his livelihood from racing and I'm doing what I can for him."

"You miss it, don't you?"

Nick frowned. "What?"

"Well, you had a motorcycle with two helmets in the pannier. You seemed to love riding it, yet you gave it up, and I'm just trying to figure out why."

He shrugged. "Does it matter?"

"Yeah. Unlike you, I don't have superpowers."

She saw that half-smile again that made her feel a bit weak in the knees. It made her think of his body pressed against hers, his hand in her hair, holding her so close. He made her swoon.

"Well, I have nothing to hide."

"I think you do," she said. "We all have something to hide."

"Do you?" he asked.

If you only knew.

Only she didn't say anything and he was waiting for an answer. "No. Nothing to hide."

Liar.

He grinned, one that was a bit evil, and crossed his arms. "Nothing to hide, eh?"

"You know my only secret." She was a terrible liar. She always had been. "I'm a senator's daughter. That's it."

"And a former smoker." He winked and she groaned.

"Right. I forgot about that. I forgot you took my last cigarette and tossed it out into the bushes."

"I saved your life. Smoking is no good and you should know, you're a surgeon."

"Ha, ha, ha. I've been good. I haven't lit one up in a long time."

"Good." His hazel eyes were twinkling again. "Well, I'm going to get some sleep."

Jennifer nodded. "I'm going for that coffee. I still have another twelve hours and some paperwork I have to do before I can go home."

Nick nodded. "Good work today, Dr. Mills."

"You too, Dr. Rousseau."

CHAPTER FIVE

JENNIFER DECIDED TO have lunch outside in the courtyard off the cafeteria. She'd been stuck in the OR most of the morning and she needed a dose of vitamin D. Of course, the minute she stepped outside for a moment of peace, she ran smack-dab into Nick, who was sitting at a table under a tree and having some lunch.

Alone.

He had a book and a sandwich. All the other surgeons were sitting at tables, talking. Only Nick wasn't. He was alone.

There's a reason he wants to be alone.

She knew this. He didn't open up much.

Or perhaps the others had been avoiding him since that window incident, which was still whispered among the staff members when they talked about Dr. Rousseau.

She didn't know much about him. All she knew was that he was from Chicago, hated knock-knock jokes and competed in drag races for his friend who had a broken femur.

Oh, and drove an SUV.

Just let him be. You don't need to get to know him.

That was what the rational side of her said.

The side that protected her from opening up to another man or another surgeon, because she'd sworn she'd never get involved with another coworker again. It could only lead to heartache and betrayal.

Still, she couldn't help herself. She walked out into the courtyard with her own meager light lunch and gravitated toward him.

"I thought you didn't read?" she asked.

Nick smiled, but didn't look up. "Someone suggested reading as a way to unwind. So I'm doing that."

"Feeling stressed?" she asked cautiously.

"Not particularly," he said casually. "I just thought I'd give it a whirl."

"What're you reading?"

Nick glanced up at her, surprise etching his face, but only briefly, as he glanced down at his book. "*The Fellowship of the Ring* by Tolkien. Thought it was about time I caught up on some of my old English assignments."

"A little late to turn them in now."

Nick grinned. "Yeah, but I figured why not."

"Do you mind if I join you?"

There was a brief moment she thought he was going to turn her away. Like he was searching for an excuse to say no to her in that pause that seemed to stretch for several agonizing minutes.

"Of course."

Jennifer sat down across from him on the picnic table, setting down her salad and her bottle of water.

"So, have you read Tolkien? Want to start a book club?" He waggled his eyebrows, teasing her.

"No, sorry, I can't say that I've had the pleasure of reading Tolkien. I tried once or twice, but I got distracted with other things."

Nick grinned. "Yeah, life has a habit of getting in the way sometimes." He put the book aside.

"So why do you eat out here?"

"Why not? It's beautiful out here. Nice shady spot, it's quiet and very conducive to reading."

"The nurses and some of the other surgeons tell me you're a bit of a lone wolf."

Nick snorted. "Really? A lone wolf. Is that all they're saying?"

"Yes."

"They told you about my temper and the window."

Jennifer fidgeted. "Do you want to talk about it?"

"What's there to say? I got angry at some pompous surgeon and took it out on a window instead of his face." Nick sighed. "I was fresh from the front. I haven't had an outburst since, if that's what you're worried about."

"I know. I've been told."

He nodded. "I really wish it had been his face. He was such a jerk."

Jennifer chuckled. "Well, it might've been best it was a window."

He grinned. "So you came out here because you feel bad for the poor old wolf?"

Jennifer chuckled. "Hey, I told you before, I'm just trying to figure you out."

"You seem so determined to categorize me. Have you done the same for the other surgeons in the trauma department?"

"I have."

He crossed his arms. "Is that a fact?"

"I can read people, usually. Maybe it's the one thing I inherited from my politician father. He seems to be able to read people and get around them."

"Reading people is my superpower, too." He winked at her.

"I thought you said your superpower was telling if someone was lying."

He leaned over the table. "I have so many hidden depths. Besides, I thought you didn't have a super-power?"

Jennifer shrugged. "I lied. Guess your superpower failed you there."

Nick chuckled and she couldn't help but laugh with him.

"Seriously, though, why are you so antisocial? Are you afraid someone else will tick you off?"

"No, I'm just a private person. Besides, it's so noisy and chaotic in the ER that when I have a moment to myself, I like to have peace and quiet. A chance to de-compress. When I was overseas there wasn't much op-portunity to get a quiet moment. Working in a mobile hospital unit, you're constantly on the go."

"I bet," she said. "Where were you stationed?"

"Kandahar. I worked with surgeons from several countries, but mostly with the Canadian contingency that were running the hospital unit I was working with. My brother worked…" He trailed off and then cleared his throat, ending the conversation.

"You have a brother who's a soldier?"

"He was," Nick said quickly.

"I'm so sorry. Did he die in service?"

"No, he's not dead. He's in Chicago. Still practicing." There was a hint of sadness to his voice she couldn't quite understand, but she got the distinct feeling in the change of demeanor that the topic of his brother was completely off-limits at the moment and, even though she wanted to know why, she wasn't going to press it.

She was only his colleague. His boss.

That was it.

She didn't have the right to know.

She knew that, but she still wanted to know and that was a dangerous thing.

Get up and walk away.

"Well, I have to check on my patients." She stood up. "It was nice talking to you, Dr. Rousseau."

"Nick."

"Pardon?"

Nick smiled. "You can call me Nick. My friends call me Nick, remember? I think we agreed to be friends, or at least on friendlier terms."

Her heart skipped a beat.

"We're not friends, Dr. Rousseau. We're colleagues." She regretted the words, but they didn't seem to affect him at all. He was still smiling at her, that devastating one that had attracted her to him in the first place.

Dammit.

"Colleagues call each other by their first names. Besides, I don't understand why we can't be both."

"From what I hear, Dr. Rousseau, you don't have many, if any, colleagues who are friends."

"Ooh, harsh. Did you come over here today to insult me?" He winked.

It was annoying.

"Dr. Rousseau…"

"Nick."

Jennifer took a deep breath. "Fine. I'll call you Nick. Look, I'm just concerned about your loner attitude and the running of my trauma department."

He tilted his head to one side. "Is my lone-wolf status detrimental to my performance? Because I think you'll find that it isn't. The other day when we were working together in the OR, we worked seamlessly, and according to you, we aren't friends. We barely know each other. All we've shared is…"

"A kiss." Jennifer's cheeks flushed with blood and she gazed into his hazel eyes.

"Yes, a kiss. We've had intimacy."

She was well aware they'd had intimacy, and having that level of interaction with men never ended up good for her. She was a sucker for punishment, that's what she told herself as she sat back down.

"Why don't you have any friends?" she asked. It was blunt, but she had to change the subject, and fast.

Nick sighed and looked at her like she was crazy. "I have a friend. The guy I was racing for."

"I mean here at the hospital. Your place of employment. You've been here a year. I thought in the army you all were a tight-knit community."

"We were, and I can't tell you how many friends I've lost because of war. It makes me a bit wary to invest emotionally in someone I could lose."

"But you're not at war here."

Nick sighed. "It's a different kind of war I fight now."

Jennifer reached out and touched his hand, and his eyes widened in shock. Even she was surprised by it.

What are you doing?

She didn't know.

"Do you want to tell me about it?"

Nick pushed her hand away and stood, collecting the remainder of his lunch. "No. I don't."

"Why?"

"We're not friends, remember? You just said so yourself."

Jennifer sighed. "You're right. We're colleagues."

"Then what do you want from me, Jennifer?"

"No more avoiding me. If you have a problem with me, come speak to me, but don't avoid me."

"Fine," Nick said tersely.

Jennifer watched him walk away. She wanted to run after him, but she let him go. She didn't know what she was doing. Caring about Nick was not high on her priority list. Or at least she shouldn't let it be, it couldn't be. It wasn't her job. The only thing she had to worry about when it came to Nick was his ability as a trauma surgeon.

He may be a lone wolf, but he was a team player at least.

Jennifer didn't want the world knowing about her senator father or her ex-fiancé, so she got why Nick didn't want to share his experiences.

They say war changed a man, and even though she hadn't known Nick well enough before to determine if he'd changed or not, she could understand it if he had.

It wasn't her business to care. The only thing she had to concern herself with was his ability to practice medicine.

Only she did care.

She cared a lot.

Nick usually lingered around the hospital when his shift was over because really he had nothing to go home to. Work got him through the loneliness. Only, after his awkward lunch discussion with Jennifer, he had to get out of there when his shift ended three hours later.

He had to get away from her fast. When he was around her, he wanted to bare his soul. Let all the emotions he kept carefully bottled away pour out of him.

It was too easy to open up to her.

Only he couldn't let her in. If he let her in, then his

guard would come down and he'd lose control. He'd become that careless and reckless person his brother believed him to be.

Nick had planned to return to Chicago when his time in the army was over.

Only plans changed. He'd taken his honorable discharge sooner than he'd ever intended and he couldn't go to Chicago. That's where Marc had gone and his brother had been adamant that he wanted nothing to do with Nick.

So Nick gave Marc his space.

He'd returned to Nevada, to the place where a beautiful woman had granted him a boon and kissed him in the moonlight at Lake Tahoe.

Damn.

He didn't want a romantic entanglement. Especially with a coworker. He'd hurt enough people in his life, hadn't he?

He left the hospital, instead of working an extra shift, to avoid further temptation. He knew Jennifer was working there until at least seven and he just needed to get away. So he got into his SUV and headed over to Ty's garage. Maybe he could borrow the motorcycle for a while and just hit the open road. Let the world take care of itself and just forget about it all.

He parked in front of Ty's body shop. The garage door was open and Ty, cast and all, was sitting beside a sweet-looking black 1968 Ford Mustang GT-390. It had just been waxed and it shone as it caught the last few rays of the Las Vegas sun.

Nick whistled as he approached to let Ty know he was there so Ty wouldn't mess up the airbrushing detail he was currently doing.

"Sweet ride."

Ty looked up. "Hey, I didn't expect to see you today. Aren't you usually at the hospital?"

"I was," Nick said. "My shift is over."

"And you left the hospital on time? Dude, that's unbelievable."

"No, what's unbelievable is you're working with a broken femur. You're supposed to be on bed rest."

Ty snorted. "What're you, my doctor or something? Besides, I'm not standing. I'm sitting. I'm resting it."

Nick chuckled and pulled up a swivel stool to sit next to Ty. "Ha, ha. Very funny."

"I swear I'm getting rest, but I'm self-employed. I don't have the luxury of taking medical leave. It's bad enough I'm not out there racing and racking up business for my detailing."

"I get it. I'm sorry I can't race for you this weekend. Double shift."

"Nah, man. It's okay. You're a trauma surgeon. You have lives to save." Ty set down his airbrush and stretched. "So what can I do for you?"

"Wondering if I can borrow your bike for a ride?"

"Of course. You know where the keys are."

"Thanks." Nick stood and took the keys off the hook on the wall.

"So, you need to clear your head?" Ty asked.

"Yeah."

"Who is she?"

Nick tried to suppress his shock. "What?"

"It's a woman. It has to be. So, who is she?"

"Why does it *have* to be a woman?" Nick asked.

Ty chuckled to himself. "In my experience, it's *always* a woman."

Nick grinned. "Well, it's not."

Liar.

He knew his friend totally didn't believe him, but Ty wasn't one to pry. "Well, enjoy the ride. I can't tell you how I'm itching to go on a bike ride again."

"I hear you, but, seriously, get yourself back to bed or that leg will never heal. Do you know what kind of break it takes to fracture a femur?"

Ty rolled his eyes and flicked on his air compressor. "Yeah, yeah. Get out of here before I change my mind again."

"You'd better be in bed by the time I get back." Nick left Ty's garage and headed out back to where the motorcycle was waiting for him. It was calling to him. Riding the bike under a dusk sky on an open road into the desert was heaven.

He'd missed it when he'd been serving overseas.

When he'd needed to clear his head over there, he'd learned to seek solitude instead of a ride, but it hadn't been the same.

The solitude felt good, but some real miles between him and the ghosts of his past, or in this case Jennifer, was what he really needed.

He put on his helmet and threw his leg over the seat before popping the key in the ignition. The distinctive purr of the bike revving to life under him made him smile as he headed out of the city onto the highway.

When he was on the road he forgot everything.

Or at least he usually did, but not her. Not Jennifer. Instead, he was recalling every vivid detail of when Jennifer had ridden with him that one time. Her long, slender arms wrapped around his body, holding him close. Her breasts pressed against his back, her legs open.

Get a grip. You don't need an erection at this moment.

Nick turned the bike back toward Las Vegas. Back to the strip and back to the hospital.

He didn't exactly know what he was doing. All he knew was that he wasn't acting rationally at all. He had to see Jennifer.

When he pulled into his parking spot in the hospital lot, she was heading to her car. A briefcase in her hand and a coffee in the other. She didn't see him, he could leave. Only he couldn't.

"You know coffee late at night is not the best thing."

She turned and was visibly surprised to see him. "Dr. Rousseau, I thought you left at four?"

"It's Nick, remember?"

"My apologies, Nick. Aren't you supposed to be at home, sleeping?"

"I should be, after a night shift, but I'm wide awake. Must've been the coffee I had."

She smiled briefly, tucking her hair behind her ear. "Well, you've already clocked your maximum amount of overtime."

"I'm not here to work."

Don't. Do it.

She frowned. "Then why are you here?"

"I gave a lot of thought about what you said."

"What did I say?"

"About not having many friends at work. I don't let many people in."

She smirked. "You came all the way back here to tell me that I was right?"

"No."

"No, it's okay. I'm not complaining. I like being right." She grinned.

"I came back to see if you wanted to go have a drink?" That wiped the smirk off her face pretty fast.

It surprised him, too. Women and asking women on dates usually didn't make him feel so anxious.

"Right now?" she asked.

"No. How about in an hour? I'll meet you at the Petrossian Lounge at the Bellagio. Does that sound good?"

"More than good."

"So it's a date?"

"How about two hours? I would really like to shower after that nasty surgery I just got out of."

Nick laughed. "Do I want to know?"

"No, you don't." She smiled at him, her blue eyes sparkling. "I'll meet you at the Petrossian at nine."

"Sounds good, Jennifer."

She blushed and walked swiftly to her car. Nick started up the bike, put on his helmet and headed back to Ty's to get his SUV so he could go home and shower.

What have I done?

Sealed his own doom, of that he was certain.

CHAPTER SIX

"YOU LOOK *GOOD*."

Jennifer bit her lip and turned to examine her butt in the full-length mirror again. She wasn't so sure about Ginny's assessment of her. It'd been a long time since she'd gone out with a man for the first time.

Even though she told herself over and over again that she had nothing to be worried about, that they were going out just as friends.

Did he actually say just as friends?

Jennifer *tsked* under her breath and ran her hands over her ivory lace cocktail dress, which was covered in sequins. It was the dress she'd bought on a whim a couple of months ago because it had been on sale and had had a designer label.

One that she'd kept trying to justify to herself over and over again.

See, now it's paying off.

"Would you stop fidgeting?" Ginny got up from where she was lying on Jennifer's bed and stood beside her. "You look hot."

Jennifer rolled her eyes. "Hot is not the look I'm going for."

Ginny grinned, in that mischievous, annoying way she had. "Why not?"

Jennifer couldn't help but crack a smile at Ginny. "Because he's a coworker."

"He's the guy from the drag races, isn't he?"

"Yes," Jennifer said.

"Come on, *he's* hot."

Jennifer just shook her head. "Hot isn't everything. Trust me. I know."

David had been good-looking. Devilishly good-looking. All the women at the hospital, even patients, had swooned over him. He was broody, powerful, confident and brilliant, and it was all an act. Jennifer had found out the hard way. The outer version of David was confident, but inside he was insecure and needy, and she'd been so blinded by love she'd given him everything he'd wanted.

She'd learned her lesson.

"It's just a drink between coworkers. That's it. Nothing more."

Ginny cocked an eyebrow. "Who are you trying to convince, because a casual drink between coworkers could happen at the local watering hole, but, no, he suggested taking you to the Petrossian during cocktail hour. That's something more."

Don't go.

A wave of sheer panic overtook her. Ginny was right. This was a date.

"I have to call it off." Jennifer turned around and made a grab for her phone, but Ginny was quicker, snatching it from her.

"No way."

"Ginny, give me the phone."

Ginny shook her head. "No way. You're not going to call and cancel. Even if this is more than just a drink between coworkers, which I *so* think it is, you're going to go and meet him."

"What nonsense are you spouting?"

"You've been working like a crazy woman since you arrived in Las Vegas. You barely go out and it was the same in Boston. I'm not an idiot. I know David hurt you, but you don't have to live like a nun, because he certainly didn't. Did he?"

Jennifer winced, reminded of how fast David had moved on when he'd left her rotting in her wedding dress, exposing her to the paparazzi who'd had a field day with it. They'd taken her down like a lion taking down a gazelle.

She'd gone into hiding until the heat had died down.

David had moved on with a vapid woman who praised him from the sidelines. Jennifer wasn't going to let her career slide to prop up someone else's.

At least, that's what she told herself when she'd donated the wedding dress to a secondhand store and focused on her career.

Of course, that left no time for anything else.

Or anybody else.

She stopped grabbing for the phone and Ginny grinned. "You know that I'm right."

"I hate it that you are." Jennifer sighed. "What am I doing?"

Ginny shrugged. "A date? Why are you so worried, does the hospital have a policy against staff members dating?"

"No, but I'm technically his boss. I'm head of the department."

And wouldn't the press have a field day with that.

Ginny shrugged. "So?"

They had a bit of a stare down and Jennifer sighed. "I won't call it off. It'll be fine."

"Of course it will be. Have fun. Let loose. You're so uptight and no one will be taking pictures of you. It's not going to be like that."

"Right."

Ginny handed her back the phone. "It'll be fine. Come on, I'll drive you to the Bellagio."

"Thanks," Jennifer said, hoping her voice didn't shake. Ginny left the room and Jennifer glanced at herself one more time in the mirror.

Even if this was a date, and she wasn't entirely convinced that it was, it was a one-time thing. Nothing bad was going to happen because she went out with Nick.

He was an unknown trauma surgeon.

Much like you.

And that was fine by her.

Ginny drove her to the front door of the Bellagio. A valet rushed forward and opened the door for her, and after the door was shut, Ginny powered down her window and leaned over.

"Hey, smile, and good luck."

Jennifer waved at her and took a deep breath as she headed into the Bellagio.

Why am I so nervous?

She'd been out with Nick before. Granted, it had been three years ago, so she had no reason to be so nervous, like the preteen wallflower she'd been in high school. When her father had only been Mayor of Carson City, and even though he had been well-to-do, Jennifer had still been socially awkward, klutzy and unpopular.

The woman at the front desk pointed her in the direction of the lounge.

You can do this.

Jennifer held her head up high and moved toward the bar. The casino floor was a hive of activity, but she moved through the crowds quickly and into the bar.

The sound of a piano drowned out the noise of the gamblers as she headed inside the elegant bar. A few heads turned when she walked past a group of well-dressed men, and that gave her the confidence she needed in that moment.

She smiled to herself and walked toward the other end of the bar, looking for Nick. She didn't know exactly what she was looking for; she supposed she was looking for the same leather-clad guy she was used to seeing, or the surgeon in the scrubs and the white lab coat.

When the designer-suited, dark-haired guy at the bar turned around, he almost took her breath away.

The sight of him in that impeccably tailored black suit was an assault on her senses. Her body suddenly didn't belong to her at that moment; it belonged to her hormones, which were sitting up and taking notice of the devilishly handsome man in front of her. He grinned at her and moved toward her. That damn smile that made her insides a bit gooey.

Get a grip on yourself. You're a surgeon. A respectable one.

And then she wondered what being a surgeon had to do with anything. Surgeons, contrary to popular belief, were humans, too, with needs, wants and desires.

She plastered on her best smile, but she probably resembled something akin to a frozen mannequin, her heart thundering in her ears and her stomach dragging at the bottom of her feet.

Don't forget to blink and breathe.

Jennifer suddenly felt like a real mannequin, badly posed and wooden.

Nick stopped in front of her and she let out the breath she'd obviously been holding, but wasn't aware until it escaped past her lips.

"Hey" was all he said.

"Hey" was all she could formulate in her brain at that moment.

"You look fantastic." Then he took her hand, brought it to his lips and pressed a light kiss against her knuckles. That simple touch caused a shiver of delight to run down her spine and her knees to shake, just slightly.

Jennifer pulled her hand away and cleared her throat. "An interesting choice for a couple of coworkers to have a drink, don't you think?"

Nick didn't respond, just smiled. "Let's find somewhere private to speak."

Her heart was hammering and she was worried it was going to burst out of her chest, but she followed him past the main bar to a small alcove, where a velvet couch was located.

She sat down on the low couch. They were completely hidden by a large white column, but she had a great view of the pianist on the grand piano.

"I'll get the first round—what would you like?" he asked.

"Um, surprise me."

"Really?"

"Should I be worried?"

He didn't answer, just winked and walked away. Jennifer leaned over to watch him walk, and as if he knew she was watching him, he glanced over his shoulder and smiled at her. A smoldering smile of promise.

I have got to get out of here.

Jennifer sat up straight and glanced around the bar. She'd never been to the Bellagio before; she'd seen it countless times but had never set foot inside.

The stained glass over the bar was beautiful, the piano music set the tone for a comfortable, elegant, but relaxed atmosphere. If she wasn't careful, she could get used to this. She could sink back into this couch and fall asleep.

"Don't doze off on me."

She glanced up to see Nick with two cocktails in his hands. He set the glass down in front of her. It was dark, almost red, with ice and a twist of lemon.

"What is it?" she asked, sniffing it. There was gin, definitely gin.

"A Negroni. Try it."

She took a sip and was pleasantly surprised by the oaky taste, which wasn't usually her thing, but this was good.

"Well?" Nick asked.

"I like it. What's in it? I taste gin."

"Vermouth rosso and Campari bitters." Nick leaned back. "Enjoy your drink before we head out."

She paused in mid-sip. "Head out?"

"We're not spending the whole evening in a bar, plus you look way too good to hide away here in the corner."

"Dr. Rousseau…"

"Nick." His gaze locked with hers and his hazel eyes had that twinkle again, like they had years before.

"Nick, you said to meet you for a drink. I'm doing that."

His gaze narrowed. "You're quite…unbending, aren't you?"

"Well, that's a nice way to put it. So I'll take it."

He chuckled. "Yeah, you can say that. I have to wonder why, though. You certainly weren't like this when we first met."

No. She hadn't been, and look where that had got her. David had flashed her a smile, several compliments and the next thing she knew, they'd been in bed together. She was much more reserved now.

Even with Nick, though their time together hadn't resulted in sex. It had just been a hot and heavy make-out session on the beach.

She'd been too careless in her youth.

"Good Lord, Jennifer. You're only thirty-four."

Jennifer tried not to snort as Ginny's voice infiltrated her thoughts.

"No, I guess I wasn't like that. I was a little bit more carefree, wasn't I?"

"A bit. As I recall, you were almost about to light up and then tossed your shoes over the fence you climbed to escape your father's event. Though at the time I didn't know that Senator Mills was your father."

"Shh," she hushed him. "I don't want anyone to know."

Nick looked around. "You think there are paparazzi hanging around here?"

"There always seems to be, but they're like ninjas." Jennifer smiled. "A lot has changed in three years. A lot."

Nick nodded, his expression a bit more serious as his lips formed a thin line. "Yes. A lot has changed."

"You gave up your bike. That surprised me."

Nick shrugged. "Death trap."

Jennifer cocked her head to one side. "I find that hard to believe since you race your friend's."

He took a sip of his drink. "Like you said, things changed. It was no longer…feasible to keep it."

He was lying or hiding something, but then again she was hiding so much, too, so who was she to judge?

It was hard not to break down and confess his deep, dark secrets to her. Hell, it was torture not to pull that drink from her hand, pull her roughly into his arms and kiss her. Maybe more.

He'd known she was going to dress up, he just hadn't expected how utterly fantastic she'd look. Nick had known she'd look good, but he was so used to seeing her in business attire, scrubs or even a shift dress. Like the hot pink shift dress she'd worn the night they'd met.

He had not expected the ivory beaded dress that clung to her curves, and when she'd moved in front of him to sit down, he'd noticed the back was cut away, exposing an expanse of her glowing skin.

It was all he could do not to reach out and touch her just so he could feel the silky softness of her flesh.

He'd only planned to spend the evening in the bar, getting to know her or at least making an attempt so she wouldn't nag at him that he didn't have friends or try to. He hadn't been expecting this.

Nick's gaze was transfixed by her long, shapely legs as she crossed them, and the memory of their night on the beach flashed through his mind. Her lying out on the sand, their lips locked and his hand moving up her thigh, under her dress.

He cleared his throat and took a drink.

"So why did you sell the bike? Besides it being a 'death trap'?"

He laughed and swirled the liquid around his tumbler. "I had planned to be gone longer than three years. So I sold it rather than see it rot in a garage."

Liar.

He'd sold it and sent the money to Marc.

"You okay?" she asked, her voice gentle, full of concern.

"Of course. Why would you ask?"

"I don't know, you seemed to get so sad. Sorry if I brought up a touchy subject."

Nick smiled. "You didn't."

"So why didn't you stay over there? You said you planned to be gone longer. What happened?"

"An accident." Nick touched his face. "This scar is one of a couple I received when an IED exploded."

"Oh, my God. Well, I'm glad you're okay. Was anyone killed?"

"No," Nick said quickly. "No."

No, but his brother had been paralyzed and the man who'd been severely injured, the man he'd saved, had ended up taking his own life. He hadn't been able to live with the memories.

So his act of valor had all been for nothing.

Marc's injury. For nothing.

Just nothing.

"Well, that's a relief."

"Yeah, it is." There was a lump in Nick's throat and it was harder to breathe. He set his drink down. "Can we change the subject? I don't like to talk about my time over there."

"Sure," she said gently. "Of course. I don't mean to pry. I really don't."

"It's okay. Really, but I'd rather talk about something more upbeat, like this surgery you told me not to ask you about."

Jennifer groaned and laughed. "Really, you don't

want to know about an abscess bursting during a bowel repair."

"Ugh."

"I warned you."

Nick chuckled. "That you did."

An awkward silence settled between them and Jennifer was fidgeting again, playing with wisps of her short blonde hair.

"So, where did you go after Lake Tahoe?" he asked, breaking the silence.

"Boston, remember? It's where I did my fellowship in trauma."

"Right. You did tell me. What hospital again?"

Now she looked uncomfortable. "Uh, Boston Mercy."

"Is that where Dr. David Morgan did his groundbreaking research?"

Something changed quickly in Jennifer's demeanor. Her expression became pinched and he knew he'd hit a nerve.

"Yes, as a matter of fact it is."

"Do you hold a grudge against Dr. Morgan or something?"

Her eyes flashed with annoyance. "Why would you ask that?"

"I've heard the gossip about you and Dr. Morgan."

Jennifer rolled her eyes, but then relaxed. "Yes, I worked with Dr. Morgan, but I don't want to talk about him."

Now Nick couldn't help but wonder why Dr. Morgan was off-limits for discussion. Had Dr. Morgan and Jennifer been involved?

That simple thought made him jealous and that flash of jealousy made him worried. *Who cares who she dated before?* Only he did.

Just the thought of that smug, smiling bastard on the front of that prestigious medical journal made him cringe inwardly, because he didn't want to think about anyone else's hands on Jennifer. Only his hands.

"Well, we seem to be getting off to a good start." Jennifer set down the empty glass. "All we seem to be able to discuss at any length is topics we don't want to talk about."

"Yeah, it seems that way."

End the night. You tried. It didn't work.

Only he didn't want to end it and that thought scared him.

"Do you want to go dancing?"

Her eyes widened in shock. "What?"

"Dancing? Do you want to go dancing?"

"You mean like to a nightclub?"

"Yes, but not one of those bass-infused places. I'm talking about somewhere classy, given how we're dressed, well, it might be a bit of a fast-moving place."

Jennifer looked unsure. So he held out his hand.

"Come on, Jennifer. Live a little, like you used to do before Boston's cold winters hardened your heart." He winked and she laughed, taking his hand. He helped her to her feet. She was slightly taller than him in those platform stilettos, but he didn't care.

"Lead the way, then."

"With pleasure. It's not far." Then he put his arm around her, his hand resting lightly on the small of her back, touching her soft skin as he ushered her out of the Petrossian toward The Bank nightclub in the Bellagio.

They crossed the busy casino floor out toward the north entrance, up the escalator to the nightclub.

He paid the entrance fee and kept his arm around her

as they entered the dark club, decked out in gold and glass. The place was swarming with glitterati and celebrities. Cameras were flashing like weird strobe lights.

Jennifer froze. "I have to leave."

"Why?" he asked.

"Photographers are all over this place." There was a hint of panic to her voice. How horrible it was not to have any privacy. He could hide at least.

"Just one dance with me. Besides, the photographers will be more concerned with the celebrities that are here. They're totally going to ignore two trauma surgeons dancing on their night off."

Jennifer smiled and nodded. "You're right." Though he wasn't convinced by her tone. It was like she didn't believe him.

Nick led her out onto the dance floor, which was a bit of a crush, and pulled her close to dance. His hands on her hips, her body moving with his.

What are you doing?

Yeah, he didn't know. He'd lost all sense and purpose. He couldn't think with having her so close.

Her lips were moist and red. The rest of the world was drowned out to him; all he saw was her. All he felt was her.

It scared him, but before he could stop himself, he leaned in and she sighed—not in annoyance or resignation but in anticipation as pink flushed her cheeks.

She wanted it, too, and, God help him, there was no going back.

"Oh, my God, Michael!" a woman screamed, shattering the moment. Nick looked around to see a young woman screeching, her companion passed out on the dance floor, his body twitching.

"Help! I think he's having a heart attack. Is there a doctor in the house?"

Jennifer and Nick glanced at each other.

"Me!" they shouted simultaneously and descended on the man on the dance floor.

CHAPTER SEVEN

"His radial pulse is weak." Jennifer shook her head. "Mr. Brannigan, can you hear me?"

The man just moaned.

"It might've been a CVA. Look at his face." Nick pointed to where the left side of the man's face was drooping. Mr. Brannigan looked to be no more than forty.

The music had ended and a lot of useless people were surrounding them. "Did anyone call an ambulance?" Jennifer snapped.

"Paramedics just pulled up at the north entrance," someone shouted.

"Thank God," Jennifer mumbled under her breath.

"We have to get him back to the hospital." Nick rolled the man on his side to make sure he wouldn't choke.

"The CVA could be caused by a clot, an aortic dissection... Anything could've thrown the clot." Jennifer glanced over her shoulder at the distressed woman. "Did he say anything before he collapsed?"

"Uh, no. I mean, he said he had some pain and then his speech slurred."

Nick frowned. It was then the paramedics showed up.

"Possible CVA. You need to start a large-bore IV and take him to All Saints."

The paramedic regarded him. "And you are?"

"Trauma surgeon at All Saints."

Working with the paramedics, they got Mr. Brannigan up on a gurney, out of the Bellagio and into the waiting ambulance.

Nick helped Jennifer up into the ambulance, much to the paramedic's chagrin. Then Mr. Brannigan's wife was in the back as well.

"Are you coming?" Jennifer asked Nick.

"I'll follow in my car."

The paramedic shrugged. "Might as well hop in, Doctor. It's all hands on deck."

Nick climbed into the back and the paramedic shut the door. Within a minute, the ambulance was racing along the strip to All Saints. It was a short ride.

The back of the ambulance opened and Jennifer was right beside the gurney with Nick as they wheeled it into the trauma department.

A nurse steered Mrs. Brannigan to the sidelines as Jennifer and Nick wheeled the patient into a waiting trauma pod.

"Could someone get my shoes from my office?" Jennifer shouted as she grabbed a disposable isolation gown from the wall, and gloves.

Nick had removed his suit jacket and placed it on the hook where he'd grabbed his gown from.

"I need to do a transesophageal echocardiogram. Make it happen and set up a CT scan, stat!" Jennifer shouted, sending residents and interns running in all directions. "I also need a neurology consult fast. Someone page the neurologist on call."

"What a way to end the evening."

Jennifer glanced up at Nick. He was grinning as he took the man's blood pressure.

"Yeah, it was." Jennifer moved to check Mr. Brannigan's radial pulses. "The left is weaker than the right. Could be a CVA or could be an aortic dissection. We won't know until we get him into CT."

"Well, let's get him down to CT." Nick turned to address an intern who was securing the IV pole on the patient. "Tell the neurologist that we'll meet him down in CT."

Jennifer cocked her eyebrows. "We? Is this a two-man job, Dr. Rousseau?"

Nick shrugged. "We hadn't quite finished our date, Dr. Mills."

She rolled her eyes and together they pushed the gurney out of the trauma pod. She kicked off her ridiculous stilettos when she saw the resident she'd sent off bring her sensible and comfortable slip-on sneakers.

Once she had them on, they pushed the gurney at a run to the elevator.

"Get out of the way!" Jennifer shouted. It was as she was pushing through the buzz of a bustling ER that a flash went off. Dread coursed down her spine and she looked back to see a photographer scurry through the ER. Though she wasn't a hundred percent sure that's what she saw. It could all be in her mind.

It's nothing.

And even if it was something, it didn't matter at the moment. The only thing that mattered was saving the patient's life.

Everything else could wait.

It was morning when Jennifer, stilettos in hand, walked out of the hospital for a breath of fresh air. Mr. Brannigan's aorta had been dissecting and they'd discovered he had Ehlers-Danlos syndrome, a disease that affected the connective tissues. Mr. Brannigan suffered from frequent bruises and tears. High blood pressure from smoking had caused the lining in his aorta to weaken and dissect.

And since it was a type A and their cardiothoracic surgeon was busy doing a heart-transplant recovery, Jennifer and Nick had worked over Mr. Brannigan. Nick had done dissection repairs in the field, and before she'd chosen to work solely in trauma, she'd helped David on cardiothoracic patients. It was part of their research.

Mr. Brannigan was lucky that he'd had two trauma surgeons who knew what they were doing when it came to delicate aortic dissections.

Her shift started in an hour, but she was going to go home first and change. She didn't want her designer dress to get ruined or lost or crumpled up in her locker. As she stood there, she got some odd looks from patients.

She knew the sneakers and the designer dress didn't exactly go together, but her feet were a bit swollen from standing for so long, trying to save a man's life.

Nick stumbled out of the ER, stifling a yawn, his coat hooked over his shoulder. Dark stubble on his face, the sleeves of his white dress shirt rolled up to reveal the tattoos. They made quite a pair.

"Good job in there, Dr. Mills." He winked.

"You too, Dr. Rousseau." She sighed. "I'm going to head home to change into some comfortable clothes, maybe have a shower."

"Is that an invite?"

Jennifer gasped and then laughed. "You are bold, sir."

An older woman shuffled passed them, giving them a strange look, and Nick just chuckled.

"What's so funny? I've been getting strange looks since I stepped outside."

"They probably think you're a high-class call girl." Nick waggled his eyebrows and Jennifer couldn't help but laugh.

"Are you serious?"

Nick shrugged. "This is Vegas after all."

Jennifer rolled her eyes. "How are you getting home?"

"I could ask the same thing of you. I can walk to the Bellagio, no problem. It's only a block from here. Is your car parked there?"

"No, my friend dropped me off. I'll probably call a cab."

Nick shook his head. "I'll drive you home. It's the proper way to end the date anyway. Come on." He held out his hand and, though she shouldn't have, she took it and they walked away from the hospital, down the street to the Bellagio.

Was she dreaming, because weird, surreal stuff like this didn't happen when she was awake. The only tell-tale sign was that her feet ached from standing in surgery for several hours. Add that to having a night out on the town after having just finished a shift at the hospital, she was surprised she was still standing.

They passed the Bellagio fountains up to the main entrance, where Nick handed over his valet ticket.

"You paid for valet parking. Nice."

"It's easiest. Besides, I planned on impressing you after the nightclub when I took you back to my place to seduce you."

Heat flushed in her cheeks, until she realized he was grinning like a fool with a sparkle of devilment in his eyes. She punched him on the arm.

"You're a pain, you know that?"

Nick shrugged, not fazed. "So I've been told."

"Who told you that?" she asked.

"My parents, sister, old girlfriends and my bro…" He trailed off and his easy demeanor vanished.

"Your brother?"

"Yeah."

"You miss him, don't you?"

Nick nodded. "I do."

"So why don't you call him or go visit him?"

He shook his head. "It's not that easy. It's complicated."

"Ah, no need to say any more." She understood complications, living with her parents, watching her sister put up with an adulterous bastard all to save face. Her sister rarely talked to her anymore since Jennifer had pointed out that she should do something about Gregory and his lying ways.

Since then, she and her sister hadn't been on the best terms.

"You have a sister, don't you?" he asked.

"I do and we don't talk much, either, so like I said, I get it. She's a little miffed at me for suggesting her husband is a bit of a douche."

Nick grinned. "Is he? I mean, is that justified?"

"Oh, it's justified. He's cheated on her numerous times. My niece was born last year and he was at his mistress's house while my sister gave birth in the hospital on her own."

Nick frowned. "That's terrible. Gives the rest of the male population a bad name. Why doesn't she leave him?"

"That's the crux of our arguments. She's too afraid

to leave him. She loves him and is blinded to his faults. She's not very confident."

"And you are?"

"I wouldn't put up with a cheat." *Again.* It was hard for Jennifer to judge anyone; it's why she wasn't angry at her sister. Jennifer knew that David had had a couple of one-night stands, but still she'd stayed with him.

She'd been an idiot. She'd been in love, she'd been blinded by it, and David had taken advantage of that fact. Made excuses. Oh, yeah, she'd been in her sister's shoes. She was the last person to judge.

The valet pulled up in Nick's SUV. The valet opened the door for her and she climbed into the passenger seat.

Nick got behind the wheel and they drove away from the Bellagio.

"It's seven in the morning and the strip is still hopping," Nick remarked. "That's what I love about this city."

Jennifer shrugged. "It's a city. I prefer the country."

Nick raised a brow. "I find that funny."

"Why? My father was a rancher before he was a politician. He had this great ranch up in the foothills north of Carson City." Jennifer sighed. "Some of the best years of my childhood. There was no need for keeping up appearances."

"You needed to keep up appearances?"

Jennifer chuckled. "Oh, yes. I was a bit of a rebel in my teenage years. It's where I picked up the nasty habit of smoking."

Nick nodded. "I was a bit of a rebel, too."

Jennifer leaned her head back against the seat and smiled at him. "So you said. Something about a pain in the ass."

"I didn't say pain in the ass. I said I've been told I was a pain." He winked at her.

"You're splitting hairs now."

He laughed, his smile so bright. She loved the dimples, even if they were covered by ebony-colored stubble.

She could so see the bad boy in him. The bike, the tattoos, the leather and the mystery he hid deep inside him. He may not admit to some deep, dark secret, but something was there and she wanted to find out what that was.

"So you were a bit of a rebel when you were a teenager."

"Oh, yeah. I was always getting into scrapes and Marc *always* bailed me out." He frowned, but only for a moment. "He always did warn me that one day he wouldn't be there."

"I'm sorry," she said.

"It is what it is."

"And how about now? Are you a bad boy now?"

He glanced at her briefly and grinned, his eyes dark with promise. "Would you like to find out?"

She blushed and cleared her throat. "Nick, you know that's not a good idea."

"Why not? We could always finish what we started on the beach three years ago."

"No, we couldn't." Though honestly she'd thought about that moment. Thought about how things might've been different if she'd allowed him to make love to her.

You couldn't change the past and she couldn't use hers as a crutch to keep her from the present and the future.

"Here's your place." Nick put the SUV into "park." "I guess I'll see you at the hospital in a couple of hours."

Jennifer nodded. "Yes, you will. No excuse. If I have to do it, you do, too."

Nick nodded. "Well, for what it's worth, before the aortic dissection and all, I had a good time with you."

"Me, too." It wasn't a lie. She had. It had been a long time since she'd allowed herself to let loose a bit. To get dressed up and go for a night out on the town.

"We'll have to do it again some time. Finish what we started, because I'm tired of having all these half-dates with you."

Her heart skipped a bit. She opened the door and slipped out. "Thanks for the ride home. I'll see you in a while."

She shut the door and jogged up the steps of her condo. Nick drove off and she watched him disappear around the bend, her pulse still racing as she toyed with the notion of going out with him again.

Why not?

For the first time in a long time, she couldn't come up with an excuse as to why not. There was a paper on her front step and the headline about a doctor caught her attention. She picked it up and the blood drained from her face.

Presidential hopeful's physician daughter moves on from famous former fiancé and parties with handsome ex-armed forces surgeon.

The paper was plastered with pictures of Nick and her at the Petrossian, The Bank and then running through the ER as they were working on Mr. Brannigan.

Jennifer swallowed the lump that had formed in her throat.

This was exactly what she didn't want. She didn't

want this notoriety following her and, staring at the paper in her hand, all she could see was the picture of her running from the church, tears streaming down her face.

Senator Mills' daughter jilted!
Left at the altar. Senator Mills' daughter disgraced!
Dr. David Morgan: successful surgeon, break-through research and new woman in his life.
Dr. Mills' bitter heartache.

She couldn't go out with Nick again.
There was just no way.

CHAPTER EIGHT

SHE COULDN'T GET away from him now.

Nick had his sights set on Jennifer. She was in the scrub room alone, having just completed a surgery. He was going to get some answers.

She'd been avoiding him, and though that should be a relief to him—because if she was absent, he wasn't so tempted by the thought of being with her—it irked him to no end and he wanted to know why.

He barged into the scrub room. Jennifer jumped, then quickly glanced around her, looking for a way to escape. Only there wasn't one.

"Well, long time no see, Dr. Mills."

She regained her composure. "What're you talking about, Nick?"

"Oh, so it's still Nick, then?"

Jennifer frowned. "What has gotten into you?"

"Well, seeing how a couple of weeks ago you were angry at me because I was avoiding you, I think the answer is pretty self-explanatory."

"I'm not avoiding you." She stepped on the bar under the sink and began to scrub her hands, vigorously. "I was in surgery."

Nick leaned against the doorjamb. "Oh, really? That's a long surgery."

"What're you talking about?" she asked.

"A surgery that lasted two weeks. Impressive. Do tell me about it."

Jennifer rolled her eyes and shook the excess water off her hands before grabbing a paper towel. "I've been busy. I haven't been avoiding you."

"I think you're lying."

Her eyes narrowed. "I'm not lying." She tried to push past him, but he put his arm across her escape route.

"I just want to know," he said. "Much like you pestered me when I was avoiding you."

"Ha!" She shot him a triumphant look. "Vindication. You were avoiding me."

"And you're avoiding me."

"I'm not, actually. I've been busy."

"Look, I saw the paper. I know you hate the limelight, but there's no reason to avoid me."

"Not avoiding. I am *head* of the trauma department."

"I get wanting to hide. Trust me."

"Do you want to talk about why you're hiding?" she asked.

"No."

"Well, then, now can you let me pass? You can't really hold me captive in a scrub room."

"Why not?" He grinned and leaned forward. "It's kind of exciting to have your attention like this."

Her eyes widened and she gave him the scariest stare; it looked a bit deranged as she moved closer to him.

"What're you doing?" Nick asked.

"I'm staring you down so you'll move," Jennifer said.

"It's freaky."

"It's not supposed to be freaky. It's intimidating."

Nick laughed. "It's anything but. The only way that stare is intimidating is because of its freakiness."

Jennifer stopped the stare. "I know Krav Maga."

Nick shook his head and stepped to the side as she walked past him, but he fell into step beside her. He wasn't going to let her get off so easy.

She *tsked* under her breath when she saw him beside her. "Didn't my Krav Maga threat scare you off?"

"No, because, you see, I was in the army for quite a while. I know how to fend off Krav Maga."

"You're a pest." She tried to say it in a serious tone, but her voice broke with a chuckle. "Usually my threats with Krav Maga and the stare down work."

"You don't really know Krav Maga, do you?"

Jennifer chuckled. "You got me. Seriously, though, when do I have time?"

"So what happens when someone, for instance me, calls you on the Krav Maga?"

Jennifer stopped and turned to face him. "What do you mean?"

He grinned. "I mean show me your moves. Come on, show me how you'd scare away a would-be pest."

She smiled, her eyes twinkling, and held up her hands like she was trying to complete the crane move from *The Karate Kid*.

"Whoa, hold up there, Ralph Macchio. Don't be trying to sweep my leg or something."

Jennifer put her hands down. "Who? What are you talking about?"

"Have you never seen *The Karate Kid*?"

"No, I'm afraid I haven't. I grew up on a ranch and in my early childhood we didn't have television. No way to watch movies."

"We'll have to watch it together. Maybe you can pick up some more helpful moves in case someone else challenges you over your slick, nonexistent Krav Maga moves."

Then her easy, fun demeanor melted away. "Uh... sure."

Nick cursed under his breath. "Sorry, look, I just want to be friends." He was hoping that would smooth things over, but it didn't. Her cheeks flamed, as if that wasn't acceptable, either, and he became a bit frustrated. Women were so frustrating to him. Especially stubborn women like Jennifer. This was why he didn't get involved with women, yet she drew him in and it drove him crazy. He didn't know why, but it was a pain in the butt.

"I have to go, Nick." She turned to leave, but he grabbed her arm and dragged her into the empty on-call room they'd stopped beside.

He moved in front of the door and flicked on the light.

"What're you doing?" she asked, her voice rising. "I have patients to see."

"No, you don't. I know for a fact you're coming off your shift."

"Are you stalking me?"

"No," he said. "I just want you to extend the same courtesy that I did. No avoiding. I thought we had a good time together a couple of weeks ago, yet something happened when I dropped you off the morning after. I don't know what and honestly I don't need to know, but no avoiding. I just want a peaceful work environment. I can't handle drama."

Her expression softened. "Fair enough. Friends, we can be friends." Though there was something in her tone that made him think that's not what she wanted, but it was how it was going to be and maybe that was for the best.

"Good." Nick opened the door and they walked out into the hall together. "I'm just starting a twelve-hour shift."

"I know. Who do you think made the schedule?" The mischievous twinkle was back in her eyes. He liked this version of her best.

It reminded him of the woman he'd left behind three years ago.

Before everything had got so messed up.

"I don't mind. You can give me a twenty-four-hour shift from time to time. I don't mind the long hours. Nothing else to do."

"No friends or family?" she asked.

"I think we've had this discussion before. Besides, I *tried* to go out once…"

"Say no more. I'll make note. I try to do long shifts on rotation to keep everyone fresh and on their feet. I've been taking the bulk of them, but I can certainly pass some on to you. I have things to do in my free time."

"Like making placards for your father's campaign?"

Jennifer laughed out loud. "Oh, he wishes. No, I keep out of politics and out of the spotlight as much as possible."

"Dr. Rousseau and Dr. Mills, I'm glad I found you."

Nick and Jennifer turned at the same time to see Dr. Ramsgate walking quickly toward them.

"Oh, Lord," Jennifer whispered under her breath, which made Nick chuckle.

"I'm so glad I found you both." Dr. Ramsgate stopped in front of them. "Most of my senior staff know, except you two, and I wanted to tell you in person. Dr. David Morgan from Boston Mercy is coming to All Saints for three months to present his research to our cardio-thoracic doctors."

"That's good for the hospital. I read about his re-search in the medical journals." Nick glanced at Jennifer to gauge her reaction, but she'd gone quite pale. Her lips were pressed together in a thin line and her arms were wrapped around herself, like she was hold-ing herself up.

"I'm sure you two will make sure Dr. Morgan feels welcome." Dr. Ramsgate glanced at Jennifer apprehen-sively.

"Of course," she said, but there was tension laced in her words.

Dr. Ramsgate grinned, obviously relieved but also completely oblivious. "He's hoping to get his hands dirty in the trauma department while he's here and pos-sibly finding emergent candidates for his clinical trial."

"Of course," Jennifer said quickly. "If you'll excuse me, I have to get back to the trauma department."

Jennifer turned on her heel and ran away. Nick watched her flee, because that's what it was. He knew it had to do with Dr. Morgan.

"Is Dr. Mills quite all right?" Dr. Ramsgate asked. "I thought she'd be okay with it."

"I'm sure Dr. Mills is fine," Nick said, though he was lying through his teeth. He knew that. "She just got out of surgery. If you'll excuse me, Dr. Ramsgate, I have to get back to the trauma floor."

Even though he should probably leave Jennifer alone, he couldn't help himself. Something about Dr. Morgan irked her and he was going to find out what.

Only by the time he managed to get out of Dr. Rams-gate's clutches and head in the direction she'd disappeared, a large trauma was on its way in and Nick had to let it lie. Only he couldn't. She was hurting.

Who cares? You want to keep your distance from her.

Only he wasn't sure if he did.

Friends can care.

His conscience was right, but when it came to Jennifer, he couldn't quite help himself and that scared him.

He's coming. *He's actually coming here.*

Jennifer's stomach twisted in a sharp pang as what Dr. Ramsgate had said sank in. Again. She was nauseated and was trying very hard not to hurl, which ticked her off. She was angry at herself for allowing the memory of David to affect her.

She'd come here for a fresh start and she was better than this.

When did I become so weak?

Jennifer sank down on the cot in the on-call room. She knew the others knew. It's just she preferred it when they kept it to themselves.

And now that David was coming, that wasn't going to happen.

She cringed inwardly, thinking of the stares, the whispers.

The pity.

I need to go home.

Her shift had ended hours ago, but she didn't want to go home. It was lonely there and she knew if she ended up there, she would think about David. Couldn't she escape the ghosts of her past?

Where did she have to run to? Alaska?

No more running.

That's what she'd told herself when she'd left Boston.

She'd held her head up high the best she could, but there was only so much she could take.

She had stuck it out as long as she could in Boston, but when David had won the Godwin award for all his research and then married that new woman, all within a year of breaking her heart, well, she'd run.

Run back home to escape the ghosts of her past, and those ghosts had found her.

"Oh, I didn't know… Jennifer, what're you still doing here?"

Jennifer glanced up to see Nick. He was in his scrubs and looked bone tired. "What time is it?"

"Three in the morning. I'm taking my first break. Trying to get some shut-eye before something else happens."

Damn.

"I didn't realize what time it was."

Nick shut the door to the on-call room. "I thought you left five hours ago when your shift ended."

"I meant to, but I…I lost track of time and I guess I dozed off."

Liar.

She hadn't realized she'd been sitting frozen in this position for so long. Which made her feel even that much more pathetic.

Since she'd come to Las Vegas, she'd had big plans to get her life back together. Sure, the presence of Nick had kind of thrown her for a loop, but it wasn't a big deal.

"I have to get out of here." She stood up and tried to push past Nick, but he grabbed her. "Let me go."

If he didn't, she was going to lose it. She was overtired, emotional. She couldn't cry in front of Nick. She couldn't.

If she did, she'd appear weak. She looked at him

and couldn't help it, she couldn't keep the emotions bottled up.

"Jennifer," he whispered. "What's wrong?"

"Dr. Morgan was my fiancé. He broke my heart."

"I know." There was a hint of confusion in his voice. "Is that the only reason?"

Jennifer sighed and sat down on a cot. "I met him in the final year of my fellowship. Three years ago. After we…" She could feel the blush spreading up her cheeks.

Telling Nick about David felt like she was almost betraying him. Even though, after their night on the beach, which had been nothing more than a make-out session, there had been no commitment. Heck, she hadn't even known Nick's last name, but still the guilt gnawed at her. The embarrassment of admitting to Nick there had been someone else, and that was foolish.

"Go on," he urged. He hadn't even seemed to react to her admission about the two of them together.

"David and I worked at the hospital together." Jennifer sighed. "He was already an attending and I was a bit starstruck. He has a very big personality. It ended badly."

"Why did it end?"

Jennifer bit her lip. She didn't want to tell him why it had ended. She didn't want to share her humiliation.

It was bad enough that it would be forever floating around in archives and internet caches. Anyone who wanted to do an internet search of her could find the headlines, the photos of her with a tear-streaked face, running from the church, and her father's pathetic speech saying that the family hadn't been disgraced by the unfortunate incident and that his party would still fund Dr. Morgan's research.

Most of all, she was worried Nick would think less of her for being weak. For being such a pathetic failure.

She glanced up at him. His hazel eyes were warm, full of concern, and she fought the urge to throw herself into his arms, to ask him to comfort her.

"Jennifer, you can tell me."

No. No, I can't.

Only she didn't verbalize the words, the words she fought so hard to say. She was very careful with her personal life.

And then the headline and the pictures of her and Nick racing that patient out of The Bank nightclub and photos of the two of them dancing, enjoying drinks and working in the ER flashed through her mind.

She couldn't have a private or personal life, thanks to her father and his presidential aspirations.

There was a page and Nick glanced at his phone. "Damn," he cursed under his breath.

"What is it?" Jennifer asked, thankful for the distraction.

"A major trauma coming in. ETA ten minutes. I have to get back to the ER."

"I'll come with you."

"You don't have to, you're supposed to be off duty."

Jennifer shook her head. "I'm here. I'm head of this department and I'm going to save lives. Let's go."

Nick nodded and they left the on-call room together, running side by side down the hallways toward the ER.

She'd managed to evade the answer to the question she didn't want to answer.

For now, but she was sure it wouldn't be the last of it.

And she knew she'd have to gird herself against the onslaught of press, against the presence of David working in her department again, because even though her flight instinct had taken over, she wasn't going to run from this particular ghost again.

She was going to hold her ground.

Which was easier said than done.

CHAPTER NINE

It was a full day before the trauma from a multi-vehicle pileup had ended and Jennifer was flagging.

At least working on people, doing surgeries and saving lives drowned out her self-deprecating thoughts. She didn't think about David once.

She knew one thing: she needed to get home and get some rest. She could barely keep her eyes open since the adrenaline had worn off. It was so bad that not even coffee was working to keep her awake. She'd had enough espresso to give her the ability to see through time.

"You look beat."

Jennifer glanced at Nick. He was in his street clothes, a backpack slung over his shoulder. He was dressed like he was about to climb on his bike, clad in dark denim, leather and biker boots. He was such a contradiction. Inside the hospital he was smart and professional. Outside he was rough, rockabilly. He was the stereotypical bad boy. She almost expected him to pick up a guitar and get up on stage.

I'm really tired.

She scrubbed her hand over her face. "I'm exhausted, but also hungry. I've missed a few meals and a granola bar just doesn't cut it."

Nick nodded. "Well, you're in no state to drive. I'll take you out for a burger and fries."

Though she wanted to say no, her stomach growled happily in response. "Okay."

She propelled herself off the wall and followed him across the parking lot. She felt like she'd been scraped off the floor of a movie theatre. She felt sticky, gross and she didn't know what else.

Nick reached out and slipped his arm around her, effectively waking her up.

"What're you doing?"

He cocked an eyebrow. "Keeping you upright. You're lurching across the parking lot like some kind of drunkard."

Jennifer chuckled. "You're right. I'm exhausted."

"I'm not surprised." Nick opened the passenger side of his SUV. "Get in before you do damage to yourself or become a speed bump."

She laughed. "The way I'm feeling right now, I could *so* become a speed bump. I think that's a great profession."

Nick grinned, his eyes twinkling. He shut her door and then climbed into the driver's side. "I don't think you should take up the career of professional speed bump."

"Oh, why's that?"

Nick revved his engine and waggled his eyebrows before pulling out of the parking lot. "Such a waste of a beautiful woman."

Jennifer's cheeks flushed and she leaned her head against the side of the door. "So where are you taking me? It had better be a good place to get burgers. I'm a bit of a burger connoisseur."

"Is that a fact?"

"I love hamburgers, but I rarely indulge."

"There's a place on the outskirts of town, off the interstate west of here. It looks like a bit of a dive, but it's the best place I've found since moving here. I'm not a fan of burger chains."

"Me neither." Jennifer smiled at him. "It sounds great. I love little diners. Though if the burgers suck, I'm never, ever going to trust your judgment again."

He chuckled. "Deal."

She fought sleep, but it was hard when the rhythmic movement of the SUV was lulling her to sleep.

"Hey, sleepyhead." Nick shook her and she glanced up to see him leaning over her.

"How long have I been out?" she asked, hoping she hadn't been drooling or snoring. She'd been known to do that if she was overtired. Of course, that was according to Ginny and sometimes Ginny couldn't be trusted.

"About an hour."

She sat up straighter then. "You drove an hour out of town for a burger?"

Nick shrugged. "You told me it had to be good or you wouldn't trust my judgment again. I had to make this stop count."

Jennifer climbed out of the SUV. They were certainly in the middle of nowhere. To the east and west there were mountains, but they were on a flat plain of scrub brush and desert off a highway.

In the distance, she could see an outline of a town.

"Where the heck are we?" she asked.

"Are you complaining?" he asked, teasing her.

"No, just curious. This reminds me of home a bit, I mean with the mountains."

Nick smiled. "We're on the outskirts of Pahrump,

Nevada and This Little Burger Shack has the best burger and fries I've ever had."

Jennifer saw the neon sign and indeed the place was called This Little Burger Shack and it was just that. A shack off the highway. It was not a restaurant, more like a double-wide trailer. People were ordering their food from a window and then sitting down under a metal awning to try and get some shade from the sun.

Although it was dusk and there was a chill in the air.

"Go grab us a table in the little bit of sun that's left and I'll order."

"How do you know what I want?" she teased.

"I think I know what *you* want." He turned and headed to the line, while Jennifer tried to hide the blush that was threatening to creep up into her cheeks.

She claimed the last table in the sun, but there was still a chill in the air coming down off the mountains. She reached into her bag and pulled out her dark blue fleece hoodie. It was ratty, but it was comfortable and she needed respite from the wind.

Being overtired and hungry certainly didn't help matters. She slipped on her hoodie and sat down on the top of the picnic table. The table had been painted neon yellow, but now the paint was chipped, and as she glanced down at the seat where her feet were resting, she saw there were initials carved into the wood. From the looks of it, some had been there for decades.

She couldn't help but wonder about those people.

Where were they now?

Those who had carved their initials in a heart with someone else's, were they still together? She secretly hoped so.

"Here you go." Nick set a cardboard box down beside her, which was overflowing with fries and one giant burger.

"I'm never going to eat all that."

"I just got a burger, we can share the fries." He sat down beside her, resting his feet on the seat.

He unwrapped his burger from its paper and took a bite, chewing it and making exaggerated moaning sounds. "Heaven. I've missed these."

Jennifer shook her head and took a bite. It was good. Meaty, juicy and with a hint of garlic and something else. She loved garlic. "Holy, that's good."

Nick shot her an *I told you so* look and continued to eat.

They ate in silence, watching the cars traveling up and down Highway 160. The sun was setting behind them and to the east the first few stars were coming out in the blue sky. The moon was only a quarter full, which was good. It seemed to be on the full-moon nights that the ER would be packed with weird cases.

She crumpled up the wrapper of her burger. "That was good. You were right."

"I'm always right."

Jennifer snorted. "Sure. I hope I don't get food poisoning from eating a random burger on the side of a highway cooked in a trailer."

"I promise you, you won't. I missed having a good old-fashioned hamburger when I was overseas." He cleared his throat. "Anyway, glad you enjoyed it."

Nick changed the subject quickly, like he always did when he mentioned his time overseas. She knew she wasn't the only one with ghosts. Maybe that's another reason she was so drawn to him. She wanted to know what he was hiding from, but she also didn't want to push him. The last thing she needed was more drama in her life.

Right now she just wanted to enjoy this moment.

"I'm exhausted. I just need to get home and crash."

Nick nodded. "I'll take you home."

"Well, I certainly hope so," she teased, and he laughed. The uneasiness that had descended between them had melted away.

It was so easy with Nick, but also difficult because he was the type of guy she wanted to be with. She just wasn't sure she could open her heart again.

She wasn't sure if she was ready.

Or if she wanted to be.

Nick pulled up in front of Jennifer's place. They'd chatted for a bit on the hour's ride home, but then she'd dozed off again and he couldn't blame her. But when he pulled up in front of her place, she was absolutely dead to the world.

To be honest, he didn't try overly hard to wake her. She looked so peaceful.

So instead he drove her to his place. He lived in a modular home at the north end of Las Vegas.

It was dark by the time he got home. He opened the door and made sure that Rufus, his black Labrador, was secure. Rufus was old; he just raised his head in question and wagged his tail politely. It was as if he knew that Nick wanted him to be quiet at the moment.

"Be right back, pal."

Rufus just let out a huff and went back to sleep.

Nick headed back out to the SUV, leaving the door to his home open, and reached in, picking up Jennifer in his arms. She huffed a bit, similar to Rufus, but didn't wake up.

He kicked the door shut with his foot. He'd come back later and get her bag and make sure it was locked.

He carried her inside.

Rufus looked up, wagging his tail, interested in what Nick was bringing inside, but he didn't get up.

The door to his bedroom was open and that's where he took her. He laid her down gently in his bed and then tucked her in. He watched her for a moment, curled up on her side. So peaceful, so beautiful. He had to get out of there before he did something he'd regret, like getting into bed with her and taking her in his arms.

Only he couldn't move. He was frozen to the spot.

Why had he brought her here? He should've just woken her up and got her into her place.

He'd doomed himself. He reached out to touch her cheek, but she rolled over on her side and proceeded to snore. Nick pulled himself away.

He tried not to laugh as he backed out of the room, shutting the door. Rufus held his head up, cocking it to the side, listening to Jennifer's snores.

"Yeah, I know, pal. I had no idea, either."

Rufus wagged his tail, stood up and trotted toward him. Nick clipped on his leash to his collar and took him outside and then clipped the leash to the peg in his small yard so Rufus could sniff around and do his business.

Nick got his bag and Jennifer's out of the SUV and then waited until Rufus finished. His modular home sat up on a hill at the end of the community and from this vantage point, he could see the strip to the south.

He missed the stars.

The lights of the city drowned everything out.

The first time he'd seen stars had been when his dad had taken him and Marc out of the city. Out of Chicago to the Wisconsin Dells. They'd camped in a tent, their mother complaining bitterly, but it had been the stars that night which had drawn Nick in.

Brilliant.

The inky blackness had been filled with a million pinpricks of light. He'd stared at them until he'd fallen asleep.

I miss my family.

Chicago didn't offer the same view of the celestial heavens and he was learning that Las Vegas didn't, either. Too much light pollution.

Kandahar, however, offered the stars.

Often after a long shift, when there'd been a lull in casualties, he would step out of the tent for a breath of fresh air and watch the skies, looking for falling stars. It had calmed him. It had been the only time during the blood, the wounded and the dead when he'd felt truly at peace.

Rufus let out a soft bark to let him know he was ready to go back in.

"Be right there, pal. Keep it down, though, we have a guest."

Rufus just pawed the ground and wagged his tail.

Nick dropped the bags inside on the kitchen table and then brought Rufus inside. Rufus trotted to his doggy bed on the floor, turned around three times and collapsed in a heap, letting out a huff as he settled for the night.

"Well, at least you're comfortable."

Nick glanced at his old rickety couch. He'd bought the home semi-furnished. It was a ridiculously large double-wide trailer with five bedrooms and a bunch of other rooms. It was a family home. He couldn't remember why he'd bought it other than he'd liked the location and it had been in his price range, but it meant that most of the rooms were empty, including all the bedrooms besides his. There was a kitchen and living room, which held the most uncomfortable couch on the planet and his television.

There was some work to do on this home. It had outdated décor and needed some things replaced. Nick had plans to flip it, but of course working at All Saints in the trauma department didn't leave him much time to work with his hands.

Nick ran a hand through his hair. He didn't relish curling up on the couch, which was too short for his length. He glanced at the bedroom where Jennifer was sleeping.

He could just curl up beside her.

Nothing was going to happen. His bed was a king-size bed. He could just keep on the other side of the bed and sleep comfortably.

He'd stay on top of the covers.

Don't do it.

Only his body told him differently. He headed straight for bed.

Jennifer was still curled up on her side, facing his bedroom window. Nick carefully kicked off his boots and pulled off his shirt and pants. He pulled on a pair of track pants instead of sleeping in his heavy denim.

Jennifer continued to snore.

He sank onto the far side, facing away from her. His body was quite aware that she was close, his blood heated and it took all of his willpower not reach out and wrap her up in his arms. He just wanted to keep her safe, but how could he keep her safe when he hadn't even been able to keep his brother out of the line of fire?

They were better off being friends.

Friends was safe.
Friends was easy.
Or so he kept trying to delude himself into believing.

CHAPTER TEN

JENNIFER DIDN'T KNOW what she was dreaming, but the most god-awful smell stirred her from her sleep, and as her body woke her up, she became aware of a panting sound. Really heavy breathing, which was mingled with the horrible breath.

She cracked open one eye and was met with a big wet maw, black with sharp teeth, a long, slobbery pink tongue and a wet nose.

"What the *hell*?" Jennifer shrieked, and jumped up to see a large black Lab sitting on the floor, staring at her with interest. At her shriek, the dog started barking. As she glanced around the room, she realized she wasn't at home.

The dog was a dead giveaway.

Jennifer calmed down and took stock. The dog was sitting on the floor, head to one side, totally interested in her.

"So, where the heck am I?" she asked the dog.

The dog panted and cocked its head the other way, as if to say, *I know where I am.*

"You're a big help."

The dog let out a friendly bark and then got up and trotted from the room.

She climbed down from the bed and cautiously

headed to the door. The last thing she remembered was being in Nick's SUV and heading for home, so she assumed this was Nick's residence, but maybe not. Maybe he'd sold her off or slipped something in her burger. She wouldn't put it past him—he had, after all, given her a child who'd swallowed part of a birthday card for her first patient on her first day.

The absurdity of the thought made her chuckle.

She headed out into the main living area, which was open concept. There wasn't much furniture and there was no sign of Nick.

She caught sight of her bag on the kitchen table.

The dog who had given her her disgusting wake-up call was curled up on a ginormous dog bed and watching her with that forlorn look that most labs had.

"Don't look at me like that," Jennifer said. "Your master is a bit of a dingbat."

The dog wagged its tail.

She headed toward the bathroom. The door was partially open and she really needed to go. Maybe Nick was outside, getting the paper or something. She ran across the trailer and opened the bathroom door. She turned around quickly and ran smack dab into a wall of wet, muscular man flesh.

Blood heated her cheeks as she slowly looked up and saw she was currently pressed against a very naked Nick who had obviously just got out of the shower.

"Good morning to you, too." He grinned in that way that was hard for her to resist.

Run.

"Dang." Jennifer tried to disentangle herself but ended up hitting Nick in a spot she would rather not have. He doubled over and cursed in pain.

"Sorry!" she cried, as she fled the bathroom and

tried to hold in her laughter. Her body was shaking from shock, embarrassment and humor.

Nick flung open the door. A towel was around his waist, but the rest of him was quite naked. His chest was hard and sculpted with muscles, including that V-cut muscle that made her knees feel a bit weak.

"Sorry to have given you a fright," he said calmly, but his eyes were still twinkling.

"You didn't, your dog did."

Nick glanced at the dog, which raised its head in question. "Rufus woke you up?"

Then it was a he. Well, that explained a lot.

"Yes, panting in my face. He has a charming aroma first thing."

Nick chuckled. "Sorry, he's quite venerable and doesn't usually get up to inspect guests."

A pang of jealousy shot through her. Guests? There had been other women here? "You often have guests in your bedroom?"

Nick grinned again, that devious one. "No." And that was all he said as he meandered over to the kitchen, opened the fridge and pulled out a carton of orange juice.

"Want some?" he offered.

"No, thanks." She ran her hands through her hair, which was standing up on end. A hazard of short hair.

"Suit yourself."

"Why am I here?" she asked.

"You fell asleep and I couldn't rouse you worth anything last night. So I brought you here to sleep it off." Nick poured himself a glass of orange juice. "Come on, nothing happened. You slept and snored most of the night."

Oh, God.

"I snored?"

"Like a lumberjack." He winked.

Jennifer groaned. "Sorry. I guess I took your bed. Where did you sleep?"

The question caught him off guard because he choked on the orange juice he was drinking and set it down.

"I don't like the sound of that." She crossed her arms and attempted the stare again. "Nick, where did you sleep?"

"With you."

"What?" She advanced on him and he held up his hands.

"No, it's not like that. There was nowhere else to sleep. I slept on top of the covers on the far side of the bed. Away from you."

"I ought to slug you." Then she sighed. "Well, thanks for taking care of me, but I should get home."

"Why?"

"What do you mean, why? Do you want me to spend the entire day with you or something? Haven't we seen enough of each other recently?"

"It's my day off and your day off. And tomorrow is a day off. Let's go for a drive." He smiled. "Come on, you know you want to."

She did. She really did. If there was one thing Jennifer loved, it was going for car rides, and she liked being with Nick.

Friends could go for car rides, right?

"Okay, you talked me into it. Can I at least use your shower?"

"Of course. There are towels in the top drawer of my dresser."

"I hope the door locks." She shot him a look, grabbed

her bag from the kitchen table and headed into the safety of the bathroom.

Then she remembered she needed a towel. She opened the top drawer, which held socks, but there was a glint of metal and she pushed aside the socks to see a Medal of Honor resting there. Hidden.

Why was Nick hiding this? Most men would proudly display their medals, but his was at the bottom of his sock drawer.

Maybe he doesn't have a place to put it?

Which could be a real possibility. Nick didn't have much.

"Did you find the towels?" Nick asked through the closed door.

"Uh, yeah." She closed his sock drawer and found a towel in another drawer. "Thanks!"

She shouldn't be digging through his things. That was his business. Just like certain things she kept from him.

Though she shouldn't spend the day with Nick, she didn't want to be alone.

Today she wanted to forget that David was walking back into her life.

Today she just wanted to be free of all that, even if only for a little while.

They'd been driving for some time and it wasn't until they got on Highway 6, which meandered through Death Valley National Park, that she realized they were headed to Lake Tahoe. Not that she minded in the least.

It was one of her favorite spots in the world and she hadn't been back there for a long time.

She was going to be exhausted the next day, but it didn't matter as she had tomorrow off, too.

"Why Lake Tahoe?" she asked, though she wasn't really complaining about it since she was enjoying the drive so much.

Nick shrugged. "Why not?"

"No reason. It's a great place, but isn't it a little far for a drive? I mean, who's going to take care of Rufus?"

"My neighbor's teenager. I pay him to do dog walking when I'm doing long shifts at the hospital. He is a dog walker for several dogs in the neighborhood."

"Oh, good, that's good to hear. I would hate to think that Rufus was locked up all day by himself."

"What kind of character do you take me for?"

They laughed together at that. "How long have you had Rufus? You said he was venerable."

"A year. He's a rescue dog. When I got back from Afghanistan, I found him in a Vegas shelter and I don't know...we were made for each other."

Her heart melted a little bit. She had a soft spot for dogs, and especially for men who had dogs and treated them kindly.

Dammit.

"You've gone quiet. Are you a dog person, Jennifer?"

"Yes, of course. If I wasn't, I wouldn't have been as calm as I was with your dog's drooly mouth in my face this morning."

"Well, I promise to make it up to you, because I have a cabin at Lake Tahoe."

"How the heck did you afford that?"

"I have hidden depths. Though my cabin isn't much. It's basically a shack."

Jennifer chuckled. "You have a thing for shacks."

"Are you calling my home a shack?"

"No, but the burger joint and now this. Your home, from what I've seen of it, is nice. Empty, but nice."

Nick grinned. "Well, I spent all my money on my shack, so I couldn't really afford to furnish my sprawling modular home."

"I have one suggestion, though," she said.

"What's that?" he asked.

"Get another bed."

"You don't like sharing a bed with me?"

The blush was creeping up her neck again. She both loved and hated the way he affected her.

"You're not answering me," he teased. "You're evading my question."

"What was the question?" she asked, playing dumb.

"Sharing a bed with me and whether or not you liked it, which I personally think you did."

Jennifer snorted. "Is that a fact?"

"Oh, I know it is."

She laughed. "Well, since I don't really recall it, I can't comment otherwise."

Nick feigned horror, but she could tell it was all in jest. "To be honest, I don't really recall it either. I do remember having to put in some ear plugs so I could actually get some sleep."

Jennifer slugged him in the shoulder.

She couldn't remember the last time she'd felt so free, so alive. This was what it was supposed to be like with someone, and she couldn't ever recall joking and laughing like this with David. When she'd snored, he'd woken her up and sent her to another room, because he was a big cardiothoracic god of a surgeon who needed his rest.

In retrospect, she should've seen the signs a lot sooner, but she hadn't because she'd thought she'd been in love with David. Now she knew she hadn't been.

"You went quiet. Is everything okay?"

"Everything is fine."

And it was, for the moment, but she didn't know how long it could or would stay that way. She couldn't get involved with someone she worked with again—she couldn't because if something went wrong, she wasn't going to turn tail and run.

Only she could be with someone like Nick.

She'd always had a thing for bad boys and the only man she'd ever thought she'd loved, the man her parents had approved of, had been worse than any bad boy she'd gone out with.

The seven-hour drive flew by, surprisingly. They stopped to grab a bite to eat and take some pictures.

It was suppertime when they turned off the main road and headed down a densely forested laneway. Now she understood why Nick preferred an SUV, because there were so many ruts in the hard-packed dirt and gravel.

Soon they were at a clearing where a small A-frame cabin stood on the edge of a cliff that overlooked Lake Tahoe.

Nick parked out front. "Like I said, it's a shack and it's not on the beach, but I have a fantastic view. You can hike down to the lake from here, it's about twenty minutes."

"It's gorgeous." Jennifer climbed out of the passenger side and wandered over to the back of the A-frame.

"Actually, if you come inside, my deck has a nice view."

"Sure." Jennifer followed him in through the front door. The cabin was small. It was all open concept with a small kitchen and living-room combo. The back wall was entirely windows to enjoy the view and a large stone fireplace took up one side.

There was a mudroom with a washer and dryer and a bathroom on the other side of the entrance.

"Where do you sleep?"

"The loft."

Jennifer walked into the living room and looked up. Sure enough, there was a stairwell with a loft.

"From up there, you can see the lake. I also have skylights up there."

"More light?" she asked.

Nick shook his head. "I like sleeping under the stars."

Jennifer's heart skipped a beat at the thought of that and the night they'd lain on the beach together, under the moon and stars. She suddenly longed for that stolen moment again.

It had been before she'd had her heart broken. Before she'd been damaged and he'd been damaged by war.

They'd been so innocent back then.

"Want a glass of wine?" Nick asked, intruding on her thoughts.

"I'd love one."

"Head out on the deck and I'll bring you one."

Jennifer nodded and headed toward the wall of windows. There was a patio door and she slid it open, breathing in the fresh air of Lake Tahoe.

It'd been three years since she'd been back. She'd never brought David here. She'd kept meaning to and there had been plans to spend part of their honeymoon here. When things had ended, she'd been sad at first they'd never got to share this place together, but now she was glad that the memory of David hadn't tainted this place.

The only one she'd shared it with was Nick, and for that she was glad.

"Here you go." Nick walked out onto the deck, holding two filled wineglasses.

"Thank you, but you have to stop this."

"Stop what?"

"Choosing my drinks."

"What do you mean?" he asked.

"First the Negroni, now the wine."

He winked. "I can always take it back."

"I'm not complaining." She grinned and took the glass from him.

"And I haven't been wrong in any of my choices, have I?"

Jennifer shrugged. "That remains to be seen." She took a sip. It was a good wine and she wasn't a wine connoisseur by any means. Most of her history of alcohol involved long-necked bottles or lime and salt. She wasn't surprised it was a good wine. He did have an excellent taste in things, but she wasn't going to let him know that.

"Well?" he asked, leaning on the railing. "Was I right? It is a good choice?"

She leaned back against the railing beside him. "Yes, it's a good choice."

"Glad to hear it."

They gazed at the lake, with the sun setting behind the mountains. It was beautiful, as beautiful and calm as that night they'd first visited, and she wished they could stay here forever. Just like she wished that night, the first night they'd met, could've lasted forever.

"It looks like it'll be a clear night tonight," she said.

"Good," Nick said with a sigh. "It's why I bought this place, so I could see the stars."

"You like stargazing?"

"I do." He set his wineglass on the railing. "Growing

up in Chicago, in the city, I didn't get to see the stars often. But after that, no matter what the strain or stress, the stars were a constant, they were peaceful and uncomplicated. It calmed me."

"Did it work when you were overseas?"

Nick nodded. "Always."

"Was it horrible over there?" she asked, though she doubted she'd get a response. Every time she tried to get him to open up, he closed up again, building a wall back up, and she was no better.

"I know you don't like talking about it…"

"No, it's okay." Nick ran his hand through his hair. "Yeah, it was. It was war and war is horrible, but my job, my service to my country, that was why I joined the army."

Jennifer smiled. "You were passionate about being a medic?"

"I was." There was a bitter tone to his voice.

"Why did you leave?"

"I was discharged."

"So you've said, but from your tone I can tell it wasn't your choice."

"It was." Nick picked up his wineglass and finished the contents. Even though he'd said it had been his choice to leave, she didn't believe him.

"Why didn't you stay?"

"Why didn't you stay in Boston?" he asked, turning the question around on her.

"I told you."

"Ah, right, you were engaged to Dr. Morgan and he broke your heart."

Jennifer nodded. "Essentially."

"I think there's more."

She cocked an eyebrow. "You're turning the question around."

"How?"

"There's more to your story, as well."

Nick cleared his throat and straightened. "How about another glass?"

He reached out and tried to take her glass, but she pulled it back.

"My fiancé jilted me. He jilted me, and as a senator's daughter, I was publicly humiliated."

Nick's expression softened. "I'm sorry."

"Don't be sorry. I don't want pity. Pity was why I left Boston. Pity was why I ran." She was trembling, her hand was shaking so badly because she'd sworn to herself she would never let anyone else know what happened to her. She'd planned to hide, but she didn't want to hide from Nick.

Not here.

Not now.

"I don't pity you. I get why you ran. We all have ghosts we run from." He took her empty glass and set it down beside his.

"And what ghosts are you running from?" she asked.

He moved closer to her, making her heart race with anticipation. Nick reached out and touched her face, his thumb running across her cheek.

"I'm running from someone I hurt. Someone I cared for deeply, but who wants nothing to do with me anymore."

A surge of jealousy rose in her, thinking about Nick with another woman. "Oh, yes?"

"My brother Marc."

Thank. God.

"What happened to your brother?"

"He was injured in an IED explosion. Paralyzed."

"I'm so sorry, but I don't understand how it involves you."

Nick moved away from her. "My impulsiveness. I tried to be a hero and he got caught in the crossfire. We had a falling out. So, instead of returning home to Chicago, I came here."

"Your brother is in Chicago?"

Nick nodded. "Yeah, and I'm giving him his space."

Jennifer moved closer to him, placing her hand over his. "Nevada is a place you can get lost, I suppose, for both of us."

Nick's eyes darkened with something, a look she'd seen before when they'd been standing in the lake. That look had taken her breath away three years ago and it was doing the same thing now. She turned away from him to get some space because if she stood here a moment longer, she wouldn't be able to control herself.

She wouldn't be able to stop what was coming.

Maybe I don't want to.

It was going against everything she'd promised herself when she'd come out to Nevada. She'd sworn she'd never get involved with someone she worked with again, but Nick was different. He wasn't like David. He would never humiliate her. Never hurt her.

How can you be so sure?

She wasn't, but right now she needed this.

"Jennifer, I'm so glad you came back to Nevada."

"Me, too." She bit her lip, her body thrumming with anticipation. His breath was hot on her neck, his lips so close she was sure he could feel her pulse racing as his fingers caressed her neck.

"Nick," she whispered.

He pulled away. "Do you want me to stop?"

Run. Save yourself.

"No. No, I don't want you to stop."

CHAPTER ELEVEN

NICK WASN'T SURE if he'd heard her correctly. They'd come so close to this moment, but each time it was interrupted, the connection broken and the magic lost. He almost wondered if he was asleep and dreaming this. If it was a dream, it was one hell of one.

She looked so beautiful standing in the sunset on his deck. The red and orange light of the sun setting made her skin glow, and when she smiled at him, truly smiled, it made his blood fire up and the need to possess her was too strong in him to fight.

Dr. Morgan had been an idiot to walk away from her, but he was glad he had, because if he hadn't, they wouldn't be here together in this moment. Again.

"Don't stop, Nick."

He pressed his forehead against hers, his body tensing as he held himself back from pressing against her. He wanted to take this slowly, he wanted to savor this moment so if it was merely a dream or a one-off moment in time, he could have it always. Relive it in his mind and cherish it.

"You're sure? I didn't ask you for a boon this time."

She sighed, her voice shaking as she reached out and ran her fingers through his hair, making his body tremble with desire. He wanted her so badly.

"I want this, Nick. I can't fight it anymore."

And that was all he needed to pull her tight and kiss her, drinking in the taste of her.

Vanilla. It was the same. He remembered these lips. He'd dreamed about these lips for so long.

Jennifer relaxed in his arms, her mouth opening, and their kiss deepened. When they broke apart, he didn't let her go. He couldn't, as he stared at her, eyes sparkling and her lips swollen. He wanted to kiss her again.

"I think we should move this inside," she said, blushing slightly.

"What?"

Jennifer took his hand and led him inside and up the stairs to the loft. The only thing up there was his bed.

"We don't have to do this, Jennifer." Though he wanted to do it, badly.

Red stained her creamy-white cheeks, but only for a moment. "Yes, we do." And as if to drive her point home, she pulled her T-shirt over her head, kicked off her flip-flops and undid her jeans, pulling them down until she was standing there in a matching pink lace bra and panties set.

Even if he'd wanted to say no, he couldn't.

His pulse was pounding in his ears, his body singing with want and lust. She sauntered over to him, confident and sure of herself. So like the woman he'd first noticed, the woman he was attracted to.

The woman he wanted.

She wrapped her arms around his neck.

"Are you going to turn me down, or are we going to finish what we started?"

In reply, Nick scooped her up in his arms and carried her to the bed, pressing her against the mattress. This was what he'd pictured for so long, having Jennifer beneath him again. This time it wasn't the beach; she was in a bed. His bed, and there wasn't as much clothing separating them as there had been before.

He ran his hand over her body, trailing his fingers over her flesh, leaving a trail of goose bumps in their wake. It was too much to take in; his senses were overwhelmed.

"I want you, Jennifer. I've dreamed about this moment for so long, wondering what if." He pressed a kiss against her neck, making her tremble under his touch.

"Me, too, Nick. I want you so much."

He hesitated. He didn't know what he was waiting for, and maybe he was just trying to savor the moment. "I can't resist you and I tried so hard." His lips captured hers in a kiss, his tongue entwining with hers. Jennifer pulled him down onto the bed until he was on top of her. He took a deep breath, trying to regain control as she ran her hands over his body.

Reaching for him, she dragged him into another kiss. His hands slipped down her back, the heat of her skin driving him wild. He found the clasp of her bra and undid it painstakingly slowly, before he slid the straps off her shoulders.

The sharp intake of breath from her made his blood heat and when his gaze alighted on her state of half-undress, a zing of desire raced through his veins. He kissed her again, his hands moving to cup her breasts, kneading them. Jennifer closed her eyes and a moan escaped as he caressed her sensitive flesh.

She untucked his shirt from his pants before attacking the buttons and then peeling it off. It got tossed over her shoulder. She stroked his smooth, bare chest before letting her fingers trail down to the waistband of his jeans. He grabbed her wrists and held her there, before roughly pushing her down on the bed, pinning her as he leaned over her. He released her hands and pressed his body against hers, kissing her fervently, as though he would never be able to kiss her again. Even if this was just one moment between them, he was going to make sure Jennifer remembered it. She snaked her arms around his neck, letting his tongue plunder her mouth, his body coming alive as if it had been in a deep sleep.

He broke the kiss and removed her underwear, his fingers tracing over her calves. Each time his fingers skimmed her flesh, she let out a moan of pleasure, and when his thumbs slid under the sides of her panties to tug them down, she went up in flames. Now she was totally naked and vulnerable to him.

He moved his lips over the softness of her breast, laving her nipple with his hot tongue. She arched her back, wanting more.

"You want me, don't you?" Nick asked huskily.

"I do. So bad," she whispered.

His hand moved down her body, between her legs. He began to stroke her.

All Jennifer could think about was him replacing his hand with his mouth. The thought of where he was, what he was going to do made her moan. As if reading her mind, Nick ran his tongue over her body, kissing and nipping over her stomach and hips to where he'd just been caressing. His breath against her inner thigh made her smolder and when his tongue licked between the folds of her sex, she cried out.

Instinctively, she began to grind her hips upward; her fingers slid into his hair, holding him in place. She didn't want him to stop. Warmth spread through her body like she'd imbibed too much wine, her body taut as ecstasy enveloped her in a warm cocoon.

She was so close to the edge, but she didn't want to topple over. When she came she wanted him to be buried inside her.

Nick shifted position and the tip of his shaft pressed against her folds. She wanted him to take her, to be his and his alone.

Even if only for this stolen moment.

She'd never wanted someone so badly. She was driven by an insatiable need, one that only Nick could fill. Jennifer wanted him to chase away the ghosts of the past. Make her forget it all.

He thrust quickly, filling her completely. There was a small sputtering of pain, just like the first time. She clutched his shoulders as he held still, stretching her. He was buried so deep inside her.

"I'm sorry," he moaned, his eyes closed. "I've just pictured this moment a thousand times." He surged forward, bracing his weight on one arm, while his other hand held her hip. She met every one of his sure thrusts.

"A thousand times," he murmured again.

Nick moved harder, faster. A coil of heat unfurled deep within her and pleasure overtook her, the muscles of her sheath tightening around him as she came. Nick stiffened, spilling his seed.

He slipped out of her, falling beside her on the bed and collecting her up against him. She let him, and laid her head against his damp chest, listening to his rapid breathing.

What am I doing? What have I done?

She knew exactly what she'd done. Jennifer had broken the one cardinal rule she'd set out for herself since she'd left Boston and come to make a fresh start. She was angry at herself for being weak, but it felt so right. So good, and that scared her.

You don't have to be alone. You don't have to harden your heart.

It was time to move on. It was time to live her life, even if it was a scary prospect.

When she woke up, the sun was streaming through the skylights. She rolled over and Nick was lying on his back, a strategically placed pillow the only thing covering his body. His black hair was mussed and there was a thick growth of stubble on his face.

She grinned and moved closer. Now she could see the tattoos closely. Not that she knew what the designs meant, or the roman numerals wrapped up in the intricate designs, but the tattoo sleeves suited him.

There weren't many physicians she was aware of who had them, but, then, they probably stemmed from his time in the army.

She ran her fingers through her hair and realized it was standing straight up on end. Moving as quietly as she could, she wrapped a sheet around her and tried to tiptoe to the bathroom, but her klutzy nature took over and she stubbed her toe against the end of the bed and let out a string of curses.

"Good morning," Nick said, before yawning. He sat up. "There's nothing like waking up to someone cussing like a sailor."

"Ha, ha. I stubbed my toe. I was trying to be discreet."

Nick grinned. "Well, at least I know I have you trapped up here. There's no running away and disappearing."

"I wasn't running away. I was going to the bathroom."

"What's with the sheet?"

She blushed and held her head up higher. "Discretion."

"You're a bit of a prude. I like that." He moved and tossed the pillow to the side, coming toward her across the bed.

Jennifer averted her eyes and took a step back. "You need to keep to your side of the bed, sir."

"Sir, now?" He grabbed hold of her sheet and tugged her forward. "I prefer Dr. Rousseau to sir."

"Stop! I'm trying to exit this room with dignity." Only she was trying so hard not to break out in a fit of giggles.

He stopped pulling. "Dignity? I've seen you naked." There was a twinkle in his eyes and he pulled her down on the bed again, pinning her down with his body.

"Nick, what're you doing? It's a seven-hour drive back to Las Vegas. We have work tomorrow."

Nick groaned and rolled off of her. "You're right. We do have to hit the road." He climbed out of bed and started pulling on his clothes.

"I'll go freshen up in the bathroom and then we'll head for home." She shot him a warning glance as she readjusted her sheet and headed down the stairs to the bathroom to make herself presentable.

When she'd managed to wash up the best she could in the very old-fashioned bathroom in Nick's cabin, she wrapped her sheet around her again and headed back to the loft. Nick was in the kitchen, washing the wine-glasses and making coffee.

"That smells good," she said, her stomach rumbling.

Nick turned around. "It's just instant, I'm afraid. I haven't stocked the cupboard for the summer. There's a lot of work still to do. I don't have much time to do it."

Jennifer shrugged. "Instant is fine. We can pick up

a muffin on the way back to Vegas. Provided it's not some random muffin from a shack."

Nick chuckled. "I swear. We'll hit a reputable chain."

Jennifer ran up the stairs and dressed quickly, in case she was ambushed again, and when she went downstairs, her cup of coffee was waiting for her on the counter.

Nick was outside on the deck. She was glad last night had happened, though she'd sworn it never would, but at least now maybe she could work with him without all the sexual tension in the air. She didn't know where it was going or if anything would come from it, but at least sex was no longer hanging in the air. It was like a huge weight had been lifted from her shoulders.

She picked up her coffee and walked outside to join him. The air was crisp coming down off the mountains and there were some whitecaps on the aquamarine lake. She wished they could spend longer here, but it was a long drive back home. He looked over his shoulder as she approached.

"I didn't thank you for last night." She could feel the blush rising in her cheeks again, like she was some virginal young woman.

"You don't need to thank me," Nick said. "Last night was amazing, but what happens now?"

"Yeah, I was wondering the same thing."

Nick nodded, his face serious. "We can take it slowly. I know you came out of something bad and I…" He trailed off and she wondered what he'd been going to say, but she didn't want to press him. She didn't want to pry and ruin this moment.

"We can take it slowly." She wrapped her hand around the cup, savoring the warmth. "I don't want things to become weird between us and I do want to see where this goes."

"Yeah, me too. I can take it slowly. You're worth taking it slowly."

Her heart skipped a beat. "Thanks."

He smiled, making her heart melt a bit as he reached out and brushed his knuckles across her cheek. "No thanks needed for the truth."

"Truth. I'm hoping that we can tell each other the truth, that we don't hide anything from each other."

Nick's brow furrowed. "It's hard for me, but I'll try. For you I'll try."

"Good, and I will, too." She leaned over and kissed him, one that started as a peck and was quickly becoming something more. She pushed him away. "We have work tomorrow."

Nick grumbled. "You're right. Just promise me one thing."

"Of course."

"No more lame knock-knock jokes."

She laughed. "Finish your coffee so we can get out of here already."

"Okay, okay."

They finished their coffee, washed the cups and packed up the garbage, throwing it in the Dumpster at the end of the property, and headed back to Vegas. Only this time, they didn't take the scenic route, which was a shame, but it was after ten in the morning and they had to get back to Vegas in a decent time.

As they pulled out onto the interstate, Jennifer was bombarded every fifty miles or so with large billboards of her father and she groaned inwardly.

"Your father's campaign is starting to pick up," Nick remarked.

"I can see that. I was wondering why I've been getting a few calls from him."

"He's been calling you?"

"And I've been avoiding his calls. I don't have time to talk to him. Too busy at work."

Nick frowned. "Maybe it's not about the campaign. Maybe you should return one of his calls. I know if Marc called I'd answer."

"That's different."

Nick shrugged. "Not really. It's family."

"At least your brother doesn't want to use you to win votes." At least that's how it felt when her father called her out of the blue. He'd never given two figs about her when she'd been mending her broken heart. He'd claimed to be busy with his work.

Now he was eyeing a bigger prize, he was calling her constantly.

She still couldn't believe he'd ended up coming to the hospital on her first day of work.

"Even if he did, I would take his call." There was a hint of sadness in Nick's voice and Jennifer felt guilty for griping about her family. They might be bothersome, but at least they were reaching out.

"How long has it been since you talked to him?"

"Too long. He got injured and had to end his tour of duty, whereas I finished out mine."

"I'm sorry."

Nick shrugged. "It is what it is. I just hope he finds happiness."

Jennifer sighed. "I'll call my father when we get back, but I promise you it's stuff about the campaign and I want nothing to do with that."

"Why?"

"The press. I don't want to be in the limelight, unless it's for my research." Her stomach twisted. "Only I don't have much time for research like I used to, working in Trauma."

"Yes, but I couldn't see myself working anywhere else." Nick shot her a sidelong glance. "It's a rush, saving lives when every second counts."

She smiled at him. His passion for his work was evident and she admired it. It was refreshing. To be a surgeon, you had to be all in and enjoy your job, but there was something deeper in Nick, the lone wolf of All Saints, and for the first time she really saw him.

And she hoped she could get back just an inkling of that passion again.

For so long she'd been moving like she was a zombie through a series of routines, hiding all her emotions, protecting herself so she wasn't vulnerable or exposed.

It made her nervous that he got to her that way.

For the rest of the journey they chatted about work and other things. It was an enjoyable drive. He talked about how he wanted to fix up his cabin and rent it out to skiers in the winter and rent it out in the summer when he wasn't going to use it.

He also mentioned he'd love to take a couple weeks off and just get lost in the wilds up there. Just him and Rufus. Jennifer was envious. She'd love to lose herself for a while. It'd been so long since she'd done that.

Tomorrow, when David showed up, she'd hold her head up high. She'd face him and deal with it. She had no reason to fear him, and being with Nick lessened the pain.

You don't need a man to prove your worth.

That was what her grandmother had always taught her and it was true.

So she'd face David tomorrow and show him she was strong. Show him she didn't mourn his loss one bit.

She was still the same surgeon she always had been.

CHAPTER TWELVE

JENNIFER STOOD IN the attendings' bathroom and checked on her makeup and outfit. The black pumps were killing her, but she wanted to look her best. She'd even put on pantyhose, which were bothering her.

Her white lab coat was starched and pressed.

She took a deep breath and blew it out and then made sure her red lipstick hadn't smudged her teeth.

You can do this.

The announcement was being made in the new trauma wing, which had still been under construction when she'd first arrived. The attendings from the trauma department would be there as Dr. Ramsgate unveiled it and introduced David to the team.

His research was about detecting dissecting aortic aneurysms before they dissected. The research she'd assisted on because she'd been in the ER and had seen them happen when they first came in and he was just the cardiothoracic surgeon who repaired them.

Don't think about it. Be gracious. The press will be there.

And that's what made her most nervous about this whole situation. The press. She just prayed that none of the press involved knew about her shared past with David. That it stayed in Boston, that all the questions today were about the new trauma wing and Dr. Morgan's work.

She opened the door to the bathroom and Nick was waiting in the lounge. He was wearing his white lab coat, but under that was tailored pants, a blue dress shirt and a royal-blue tie. He was clean-shaven and looked as starched and pressed as she was.

"What're you doing here?" she asked. "I thought you would've gone down with the other surgeons."

"You look beautiful," he said, looking at her from head to toe, which gave her a secret thrill.

"You're not answering my question."

Nick grinned. "I thought you'd want some moral support on the way down there."

"You're right." She ran her hands over her skirt again. "Ginny picked out my outfit."

"Ginny has good taste." Nick cleared his throat. "Everyone is waiting down there."

Jennifer nodded and took a deep breath, jamming her hands in the pockets of her lab coat. "Lots of press?"

Nick nodded and fell into step beside her as they left the attendings' lounge. "You're going to be okay."

"I have to be."

Nick nodded. "You can do this."

They didn't say anything else as they walked side by side to the new trauma department. When she walked over to the podium, there were some murmurs. Dr. Ramsgate, who had his back to her, turned when she entered the room, and as he turned she saw him. She saw David again and she felt like she was going to hurl.

He had a smug smile plastered across his face, one she wanted to wipe off with her fists.

Keep calm.

So she smiled, but one she was sure didn't reach her

eyes, as she approached the podium. There were a few flashes as she approached and she had a sinking feeling that her story, her history with David, had preceded her.

I can do this.

"Ah, Dr. Mills, now that you're here, we can proceed. I'm sure you've met Dr. Morgan before." Dr. Ramsgate shifted to the side so that David could step forward.

The room went quiet as he moved toward her, his hand outstretched and that insidious grin on his face.

"Jennifer, it's so good to see you again."

"It's Dr. Mills, if you don't mind, and I'm glad you chose our fine facility for your *research*." It was hard to keep censure out of her tone, but David was unfazed and ignored it, like he usually did.

"Why don't you introduce me to your team?" David said, nodding at her six trauma attending standing in a row with their backs to the curtained wall.

"Of course, but I think we should get started. The press is getting restless."

David's eyes narrowed. "You would know all about the press, now, wouldn't you?"

She clenched her fist and counted to ten in her head.

Dr. Ramsgate got to the podium and welcomed the press. Jennifer stood next to David and tried to keep herself calm, like she was unaffected by his presence and didn't want to reach out and wring his neck.

She glanced over at Nick, who was standing at the far end, expressionless until their eyes met and then he gave her a quick smile and nod.

Jennifer returned them and then faced the crowd, trying to focus on the moment she'd unveil the new trauma wing with Dr. Ramsgate.

David leaned over. "I see you've moved on."

"You moved on as well." And she glanced at his hand. "Or is that over, too?"

David didn't answer her.

"And now our head of trauma, Dr. Jennifer Mills, will unveil our new state-of-the-art trauma facility that will serve the residents of Las Vegas and will save many, many lives."

There was applause and Jennifer walked past David and stood with Dr. Ramsgate. They pulled the cord together and the sheet dropped away to reveal glass, polished chrome and the beautiful fluid lines of a state-of-the-art trauma facility.

It took her breath away. It was beautiful.

She stepped in front of the doors, which opened with a hiss, and there was applause. "I would like to welcome everyone to All Saints Trauma. We have a dedicated team of surgeons, residents, interns and nurses to serve the greater Las Vegas area. One of our attendings would be happy to guide small groups through the department and explain the layout." She smiled as the press applauded and began to filter into the new trauma department.

Jennifer searched the crowd for Nick, but he'd been cornered by the press and was taking them through the facility.

"Impressive facility," David remarked, sidling closer to her.

"It is." Jennifer didn't want to engage in any social pleasantries, but he knew she didn't like to make a scene. He knew that she didn't like the limelight, which made his rejection of her all the worse, because he knew how to strike at her, to make it sting.

"You look lovely, by the way."

Jennifer didn't respond. She crossed her arms and

stared at the trauma department, watching the press move through it.

"Oh, come on, you're not going to say anything to me? I'm here for at least a month minimum. You're not going to ignore me the entire time, are you?"

"Perhaps." She smiled to herself.

"Don't be so childish, Jennifer," David snapped.

"You don't want to start something with me here. You're goading me because the press is around."

David snorted. "Hardly."

"If you'll excuse me, Dr. Morgan, I have a tour to give." She left him, hopefully stewing in his own juices. She just didn't have time to put up with him, but at least now she knew she could handle him.

She wouldn't let him get inside her head.

She wouldn't let him control her ever again.

It took all of his strength not to go over and punch Dr. Morgan squarely in the face when he saw him all over Jennifer and Nick heard the comments he was making. Dr. Morgan was trying to bring her down. He was looking for power over her.

David was a bully. Plain and simple.

Nick detested bullies.

Maybe that's why he'd got into so many fights as a kid. Fights in which Marc had had to intervene and usually then they'd both come out of it bloodied, but they'd never lost.

Nick chuckled to himself at that thought and it dissipated some of the rage that was bubbling up inside him.

A month ago, he would've gone over to Dr. Morgan and clocked him one, or put his fist through another window. Something had changed, and the only thing it could be was Jennifer's presence in his life.

He didn't feel like such a ghost of his former self. For the first time in a while, he felt alive.

And he knew why, though he didn't deserve it.

He lost sight of Jennifer when he gave a couple of groups of press their tours around the trauma wing, but he was sure she was fine. She was a strong, capable woman.

So he made his excuse to Dr. Ramsgate and headed back to the old trauma wing, which would be shutting down tomorrow when the doors to the new wing opened up. Right now, he needed to be doing what he was here to do.

He'd been in the pit for a few hours when Jennifer came wandering in with signs notifying patients that the change to the new department would be at midnight. She was stopping and talking to people in the waiting area.

She may claim that she didn't want much to do with people or the limelight, but as Nick stood at the charge desk, doing his charts, he could see that people gravitated toward her. She had a way with people, and when she was in a room, their attention shifted.

He gravitated toward her. When she was around he couldn't help himself. Try as he might, he couldn't help himself.

And he didn't deserve her.

Yes. I do.

He'd taken it further than he'd intended to with Jennifer, and though he hadn't planned on it, he was happy that she was in his life.

He wanted to be with her and the thought of having happiness made him feel a bit guilty, when he had no reason to be.

He glanced back over his shoulder. She was taping

up the signs on the doors, and as if she knew someone was looking at her, she turned and smiled at him.

Nick nodded and turned back to his charting, but soon the scent of her perfume tickled his senses and he knew she was standing behind him.

"Have the press left?" he asked, as she set extra signs down on the charge desk.

"Yes, for the most part. Dr. Morgan is eating up the spotlight."

Nick snickered. "He seems to enjoy the limelight."

"That should've been a dead giveaway when we were together."

"Has Dispatch been informed that as of midnight they're to bring the ambulances around to the other side of the hospital?"

Jennifer nodded. "Yes. It should be a smooth transition. We'll leave everyone who is already in this trauma department here until they're discharged or moved off this floor. All newcomers will go to the new wing. Thanks for taking the midnight shift down here while I'm up there, making sure all the bugs are worked out in the new wing."

Nick shrugged. "I like this trauma department."

"You'll like the new one, too."

"Change for change's sake."

A phone rang and she pulled her cell phone out of her pocket and frowned. "It's my father. Again. I'd better take this or I won't get any peace."

"Do you think he saw the unveiling?"

"Oh, yes, he's probably wondering why he didn't get an invite."

Jennifer walked away and Nick let out a heavy sigh. He needed to distance himself from her, but he couldn't.

She was like air. He needed her, only he was certain if he stayed with her he'd be her downfall. He'd ruin her like he'd ruined everything in his life.

CHAPTER THIRTEEN

"Well, finally you've decided to return one of my calls," her father said petulantly over the phone.

Jennifer rolled her eyes. "I've been busy. I'm a trauma surgeon, Dad. The ER can get a bit chaotic."

"I don't think you've been that busy." There was something in the tone of his voice that made her stomach sink and skin crawl. He knew about the trauma wing and he was angry she hadn't told him about it, but she hadn't wanted the opening of the new wing of the hospital to be overshadowed by her father's campaign.

Besides, she didn't want her father and David in the same room. Not after her father had taken David's side when she'd been jilted.

"Look, today was a small gathering of press and surgeons. I couldn't make room for your campaign to be there."

"What're you talking about?" he asked, thoroughly confused.

"The press conference today that was televised. The hospital opened a new trauma department." She deliberately glossed over the fact that David was there.

"Well...I can't say that I'm not disappointed you didn't include me or my campaign in that venture. You know how much I support hospitals and healthcare equality."

"I know, I know. I'm sorry, Dad. Next time." She crossed her fingers and hoped he didn't know she was lying through her teeth.

"That's not the publicity I'm calling about, Jennifer."

"What publicity are you calling about, then?"

He sighed. "Have you looked at today's paper?"

"No." It was harder to breathe and she ran into the attendings' lounge, which thankfully was devoid of any surgeons. She searched through the pile of papers on the coffee table and the moment she found it she dropped to her knees and tried not to faint.

"Oh, my God," she whispered.

"You see. It's all over the place and I know Dr. Morgan is in Las Vegas. There's no denying it. This, coupled with this new *friend* of yours… Well, I think it's best to keep a low profile."

It was a warning—she didn't mistake his words or his tone.

"It doesn't matter who he is."

"Jennifer, the pictures show you spending a weekend with him, both in a trailer and a cabin at Lake Tahoe."

A headache began to form right behind her eyes. "I can see the pictures, Dad."

"Then you should know that you have to be more aware that the press is following you. You are a senator's daughter, a daughter of someone who is trying to become a candidate to run for president. You have to be more discreet."

"I have to go, Dad."

"Promise me this won't happen again."

"Goodbye, Dad." Jennifer hung up the phone, even though she could still hear him protesting on the line.

No matter what she did, she couldn't be discreet enough for her father's liking. What was she supposed to do, remain celibate? Never find love or happiness?

Yes. That's it exactly.

That's exactly what she'd set out to do and then she'd ended up in the same hospital as Nick. She glanced at the headlines.

Senator Mills' daughter's wild weekend with fellow surgeon.
Love nest at Lake Tahoe.

There was a picture of Nick carrying her into his home, but more horrifying was the blurry picture of the two of them in bed, in his cabin, the morning after. They'd followed them to Nick's property and invaded their privacy.

Nick was a private man.

He was going to be so mad when he saw the pictures, the headlines. He'd never want to see her again.

This is why I should've never gotten involved with someone at work.

She'd brought this on herself and she would face whatever came her way. Even if it meant that another man she loved walked out of her life.

Love? Did she love Nick?

The realization hit her like a ton of bricks. She loved him. When they were together, it was so easy and she forgot about everything else.

I have to get out of here.

Only she couldn't escape quite yet. Her shift didn't end until after midnight. Right now, she had to get her head together and finish her work. She wasn't going to run away from the headlines, she wasn't going to run away from David and she certainly wasn't going to run away from Nick.

She picked herself up and slammed the paper back down on the table.

"You know, I caught the headlines this morning."

Jennifer spun around and saw David standing in the doorway, that smug smile on his face. How had she ever fallen for him? Sure, he was handsome, but now she could see how shallow he was. Hindsight was twenty-twenty and she couldn't change the past.

"I'm glad to hear you can read."

"You were always bad at jokes, Jennifer." He moved toward her, picking up the paper she'd discarded. "Isn't this the surgeon currently working on the old trauma floor?"

"Dr. Rousseau? Yes, it is, he's a friend of mine."

David raised his eyebrows. "Just a friend?"

Jennifer crossed her arms. "What's it to you?"

"Just looking out for your best interest. You know I care about you." And then he reached out, trying to touch her, but Jennifer stepped away.

"Don't touch me."

"Come on, Jenny. Can't I apologize for what I did to you? Can't we make up?"

"My name is Jennifer and you call this making up?" She shook her head.

"What're you talking about? I always called you Jenny."

"I didn't like it then and I don't like it now." She pushed past him, but he grabbed her arm and pulled her back. "Let go of me."

"I just want to talk," he snapped. "What's wrong with that?"

"Let go of me. This is your final warning!"

"Or you'll do what? Come on, Jenny, you don't—"

Jennifer stamped her heeled foot onto the top of his foot hard, making him curse in pain as he reached down to cradle his foot and his newly scuffed leather shoes.

She smiled at her handiwork before leaving the attendings' lounge to get away from him. She wanted nothing to do with him.

Right now, she needed to get back to work. Everything else could wait until later.

There was a knock on her door at three in the morning. She should just ignore it, but it was incessant and she didn't want whoever it was to wake her neighbors. If it was David, she was going to do more than just step on his foot, she was going to take him by the... Well, she was going to hurt him.

The knocking started again as she peeked through the peephole. It was Nick, standing on her doorstep, in his leather jacket and holding the paper.

Jennifer groaned inwardly and opened the door.

"Hey," Nick said, but there was no hint of humor, no smile.

"What're you doing here?"

"Can I come in?"

Jennifer nodded and let him inside. She shut the door. "I see you saw the headlines."

Nick glanced at the paper in his hand. "What, this?"

"Yeah, that." Jennifer moved past him and toward the kitchen, and she heard him following her. She flicked on her kettle. "Want some coffee?"

"No, I think I'm going to turn it down. I just got off my shift and need to sleep."

Jennifer nodded. "Well, I'm not sleeping anyway."

"Because of this?" Nick slapped the paper down on the counter.

"Yes, well, that's one of the reasons."

Nick cocked an eyebrow. "Is that the reason your father called you?"

Jennifer nodded. "He wanted me to be more discreet with my new *friend*."

Nick grinned. "Friend, huh?"

"When I was a teen I rebelled quite a bit. I was a bit of an embarrassment to my family. So I try to avoid the limelight and now this…"

Nick wrapped his arms around her. "This is nothing. Those pictures are an invasion of privacy."

"You're not mad?"

"No, why would I be mad?"

"I'm confused. Why are you here, then?"

"I was worried about you. You just disappeared after your shift. I thought we were going to do something or at least talk, but you were gone."

"I had to get out of there." Jennifer switched off the kettle, which had begun to wail. "I thought you would be mad about the photographs."

"I'm not thrilled, but really, there's nothing I can do, nothing we can do. You can't stop living your life because of it."

Jennifer pushed out of his arms. "I don't like to be humiliated. I don't like the attention."

"So you've said."

"Maybe that makes me a bit of a lone wolf, too."

Nick chuckled. "It's not a bad thing. Why did you run today? Was it because of David? What did he say to you on the podium?"

"He irks me and it's not just the jilting." She took a

deep breath. She hadn't told Nick about the research, because it was a secret shame she carried. How she'd been duped by the man she'd loved, how hours of her life researching dissecting aortic aneurysms had all been for naught because it had been claimed by Dr. Morgan.

"David and I worked together on his breakthrough research. He stole my work after he publicly humiliated me."

Nick frowned. "There was no way to sue him?"

Jennifer shook her head. "No, because we were supposed to be getting married. I…I thought we'd share it and then we didn't get married, but by then it was too late."

"Bastard." Nick smiled at her. "Look, I understand about running away from problems, I do. But don't let him get to you. You're better than him."

Jennifer nodded. "I know. Honestly, I thought you'd never want to be around me again because of those pictures. They were taken on your property at Lake Tahoe, Nick."

"That's not your fault. You didn't know. If you knew and they were in cahoots with you, yeah, I might be a little ticked, but you didn't know. It's not your fault."

"What if they find out about your past?"

Nick's smile disappeared. "Ah…well, that's a bit different."

"See, you're better off without me." She turned away, but he spun her around, his eyes intense and locked on her.

"I decide who's good for me or not." And as if to prove something to her, he pulled her against his body and kissed her for all he was worth. The kiss was even better than the first two times they'd kissed.

It was urgent, passionate. Like he was staking his claim.

When it ended, she leaned her head against his shoulder, his arms around her. "I can't get hurt again. I can't let anyone humiliate me again."

"I won't ever do that to you."

Jennifer's heart skipped a beat. She wanted to believe him, but David had shattered her trust in all men completely. She just didn't know what to believe anymore.

All she knew, all she wanted was to feel.

She wanted Nick to make her forget this day. She didn't want to think about the headlines or using discretion. With him, she felt like her old self. Carefree.

Nick helped her forget.

She didn't want to pretend to be this perfect person anymore. She didn't want to hide. All she wanted right here and right now was Nick.

Jennifer took his hand and pulled him toward the stairs.

"Jennifer, are you sure?" he asked.

"More than sure." She kissed him again, running her fingers through his hair and down his neck. "Just one more night."

She just wanted one more night with Nick. Even if their relationship didn't work out in the long run, she needed him at this moment. Nick was stable, he was a constant, someone she could cling to. Someone who saw her and understood her.

"Please, make love to me, Nick."

"Jennifer," he whispered, stroking her face.

"Please."

Nick scooped her up in his arms. Her arms came

around his neck, tangling in the hair at the nape of his neck. He carried her to her room, to her bed.

No words were needed as he moved up the steps. He set her down on her feet in front of him.

"You're so beautiful," he murmured as he cupped her face with his hands. He pressed his lips against her and she melted into him.

The last time they'd been together it had been fast, hot and heavy. This time she wanted to take things slowly with him.

Nick let his hands drift from her cheeks down to her shoulders and where her simple white cotton nightgown was held up by two ties. He pushed her satin housecoat off and then pulled on the ties of her nightgown.

She let out a moan and bit her lip, thinking about what would come next, about him possessing her. Nick made her burn, in the best way possible.

"What's wrong?" he asked.

"Nothing, I just… Nick, I can't get enough of you."

Nick's eyes sparkled in the darkness and she kissed him again, holding her soft body against his, trying to meld the two of them together.

He undid her nightgown and it fell to the floor. He trailed his mouth down her neck, the flutter of her pulse heating his blood further, and when his kiss traveled down over her breasts, she gasped.

"Did I hurt you?" he murmured against her ear, drinking in the scent of her.

"No." Jennifer moved and sat down on her bed, taking his hand and pulling him closer. "Never."

She reached out and undid his jeans, tugging them down so he was naked. He kicked them off as she reached into a drawer for protection. Ginny had given them to her as a housewarming gag gift when she moved to Las Vegas. At first she'd been scandalized by the prospect, but now she was glad for them. She opened the packet and reached out to touch him.

"Oh, God," he moaned. His body trembled as her hands stroked his abdomen.

He let her pull him down on the bed beside her. They lay down together and he ran his hands over her body slowly. It was torture.

And when he slid her underwear off, she bit her lip. He kissed her again, her legs opening up to welcome his weight. He kept the connection as he entered her. She cried out as he stretched her, filled her completely.

He began to move, her body stretched out beneath him, and he stroked her long, slender neck.

Her nails raked across his back as he increased his speed.

The only sound was their breathing as they moved together as one. Nothing between them. There was no going back for her.

Jennifer groaned as she tightened around his erection, her body releasing as her orgasm moved through her. It didn't take him long before he followed her. He threw back his head, his hands on her hips, holding her tight against him as he came.

She never wanted to let Nick go.

She didn't want to walk away from him again, but she was scared to try. So scared.

"I think...I think I'm falling in love with you."

His body stiffened. "What?"

Jennifer propped herself up on one elbow. "I think I'm falling for you."

Nick sighed. "I thought that's what you said."

She waited for something from him, but he didn't

say anything. He just stroked her face. "I don't think you know who you're falling for."

"I know who you were, Nick."

He sat up. "Do you?"

"I know you're a surgeon. I know you're a caring, strong man and were a soldier. One who earned the Medal of Honor—"

"How do you know that?" he asked, agitation in his voice.

"What?"

"How do you know about my medal?"

"I saw it in your drawer the night I stayed over."

Nick cursed under his breath. "You went snooping through my things?"

"I was looking for a towel. I opened the wrong drawer. Why are you hiding it? You should be proud of it."

He snorted. "Proud? I'm not proud of it. It just reminds me of… I'm not proud of it."

"What does it remind you of?"

Nick shook his head. "I have to go." He got up and started pulling on his clothes.

"Don't go."

He paused and sat back down on her bed. "I got that medal for saving Marc's and another man's lives. The army honored me when I didn't deserve it. Marc is paralyzed because of me."

"He's not paralyzed because of you! He's paralyzed because of an IED explosion." Jennifer pulled him closer. "He didn't have to go after you."

"He's my brother. He's always protected me, always gotten me out of stupid jams that I got myself into."

"And he's an adult. He didn't have to follow you. You have to stop blaming yourself."

"I should go," he mumbled.

"No, I'm sorry. Just stay. Stay with me."

Nick nodded and they lay back down together. She curled up against him, listening to his heartbeat.

She was falling hard and fast for him, but she also felt like one wrong move and he might just bolt.

Nick stayed only until she fell asleep. It was still dark out, but dawn would be coming soon. He put on his clothes and left her home. He was hoping no paparazzi were out there, lurking, but only for her sake.

Jennifer put on this brave front, but she was scared of being hurt again. She was just as scared as he was. He was terrified of hurting someone he loved again, of driving a wedge between himself and that person, of having yet another person in his life not talking to him.

And he didn't want Jennifer not talking to him. He didn't want that wedge between them. For the first time in a long time he'd felt like himself again. Not a zombie, not someone living and going through the motions.

He wasn't alone anymore. Yeah, he thought of himself as a lone wolf, but that's not what he wanted.

He missed the camaraderie of the other medics. He missed his brother.

He missed being able to pick up a phone and talk to Marc about anything. Marc would always have the answer; he'd always know what to say to put him at ease.

The silence between them had been going on too long for him. Yet he'd sworn to Marc that he would keep his distance, that he wouldn't interfere in his life. It's why he'd left Chicago, left all his friends behind to come to Nevada.

He was in exile, in self-imposed solitary confinement, and he certainly didn't deserve Jennifer, but he was so glad she was there.

The moment he'd realized she'd left the hospital he'd known why. He'd seen the headlines, just like he'd seen them the night they'd saved that man's life at The Bank nightclub. It must be horrible to live under such a microscope.

Even though her father rode her hard about being a black sheep or whatever, at least her family hadn't cut her off, like his had.

She could be your family if you wanted her to be.

Only he wasn't sure that he deserved that. Though he longed for it.

He'd bought the cabin up at Lake Tahoe to be an income property, but the more time he spent there, the more he pictured kids and a wife and, yeah, even Rufus running around and enjoying the great outdoors.

He had the double-wide trailer and numerous bedrooms and though he'd sworn to himself that he would flip it, he couldn't help but picture the same scenarios in his head as he walked through each and every empty room.

Now those fantasies included Jennifer and a life with her because, try as he might, he couldn't deny it. He loved her.

Of course, those were all just fantasies he'd had, but now it could be so easy to have everything he'd ever wanted with her, but he was too afraid to try.

CHAPTER FOURTEEN

"Excellent work, Dr. Harvey," Nick said as he began to close the incision site made by the All Saints cardiothoracic attending on call. He'd been working another long shift in the ER when a dissecting aortic aneurysm had been brought in.

"Thank you, Dr. Rousseau. I'm surprised you called me, though, I thought all these cases were to be taken care of by Dr. Morgan." There was a hint of censure in Dr. Harvey's voice and Nick couldn't blame him.

In the two weeks Dr. Morgan had been here, he'd been prancing around the hospital and barking at the trauma staff like he owned the place. Nick didn't understand how someone like Jennifer could've fallen for a creep like David Morgan, but that was just his opinion and he was a bit biased.

"Well, I have a feeling Dr. Morgan isn't an on-call specialist."

Dr. Harvey snickered behind his mask. "Doesn't Dr. Morgan know that most of the dissections I've seen in my career in Las Vegas happen at night? People think it's a bad case of heartburn; they ignore it all day until at night when it gets unbearable. You'd think a cardiothoracic surgeon, especially one studying dissecting aortic aneurysms, would know that."

"I saw the same thing overseas during my service. Nighttime was when soldiers would be brought in." Usually it was uncontrolled blood pressure in a high-stress environment that would bring it about. He hadn't seen many, but he'd seen enough.

"Ah, yes, you served overseas as a medic. Stress-induced, I suppose?" Dr. Harvey asked.

"Yes, because every soldier gets a physical before heading overseas."

"Maybe you should be conducting his trial." Dr. Harvey laughed, but Nick didn't join in. He was just a simple meatballer. He didn't have aspirations of medical trials or surgical breakthroughs.

Why not?

"Good job to you as well, Dr. Rousseau. Can I leave you to finish up?" Dr. Harvey asked.

"Of course. Thank you for your help."

Dr. Harvey nodded and stepped away from the surgical field, heading toward the scrub room. Nick finished closing the patient, and when he was done, he left it to the nurses to get the patient up to the ICU because the man had a rough recovery ahead. He peeled off the surgical gown and tossed it in the hamper and disposed of the gloves and mask.

The door to the scrub room opened as he washed his hands, but Nick didn't look up. He was too tired to care who it was.

"I heard you repaired a dissection in here."

"Yes, Dr. Morgan. Dr. Harvey and I repaired a dissection."

David shut the scrub-room door. "Why wasn't I paged?"

"You were," Nick said. "You were at dinner, or so you told the charge desk."

David's eyes narrowed. "She didn't tell me it was a type-A dissection."

"When she called you, we were still doing the scans." Nick picked up the bar of soap. "Time is of the essence in cases like this."

"I'm well aware of the histology in cases like this," David snapped.

"Then you should've raced over here instead of finishing your steak." Nick rinsed his hands and then toweled them off.

"How dare you?"

Nick snorted. "What? Save a man's life?"

"This is my *field*. I'm the one to be consulted."

"As I said, you were called. Perhaps you should set up camp here in the hospital for the remainder of your time here—that way you can get to the dissections as they come in." Nick didn't have time to waste on this arrogant moron.

A bully. That's what he was.

"Here's the patient's chart, Dr. Rousseau." The scrub nurse was looking at them, surprised.

"Thank you, Nurse Smith." Nick took the chart and tucked it under his arm. "If you'll excuse me, I have a surgical report to prepare and a family to speak to."

Nick tried to walk by, but David stood in his way.

"Next time, you will wait for me."

"And let someone die while you take your time getting to the hospital? I'm sorry, but that's not how I practice medicine." Nick pushed him out of the way and left the scrub room, hoping that would be the end of it, but he wasn't so sure.

David didn't seem like the type of guy who gave up. He was the type of guy who was catered to and schmoozed. People did what he wanted, when he wanted. David was a real snake in the grass and Nick was sure, because he'd stood up to him, that David wasn't finished with him. Not by a long shot. But he didn't care.

He headed for the trauma floor to finish his charting and do his report in one of the new offices designated for just that purpose, since he didn't have his own office, and just as he'd feared, he heard quick footsteps behind him.

Nick didn't acknowledge David as he fell into step beside him.

"I don't think we'd finished our conversation back there, Dr. Rousseau."

Nick feigned surprise. "Really? Because I was certain we had."

Watch your temper. The temper was what always drove him to take out a bully. Usually he was pretty easygoing, but if someone rubbed him the wrong way and pushed him too far, he'd snap, and he didn't really want to punch David out in the hospital and humiliate Jennifer further.

She'd made it clear the other night how she felt about it.

They'd managed to evade the press and act more discreetly.

It was better this way. He could take it slowly with her. No one would get hurt.

"Oh, we're not done, Rousseau. Not by a long shot," David hissed in his ear, before grabbing him aggressively and pushing him back.

"What is your problem?" Nick snapped. "You were called, you didn't respond and the man will live. I say that's win-win, wouldn't you, Doctor?"

David's eyes narrowed. "Oh, don't give me that. I should have you fired for not having me priority paged."

"What do you want from me, Dr. Morgan? Do you want an apology? If that's the case, one will not be forthcoming."

David sneered. "Is that so? Well, I think in your case some apologies are in order."

"What the hell are you talking about?"

David leaned closer. "I know all about your brother and his *accident*. I also know you have a bit of a temper. Are you going to smash any more windows, Dr. Rousseau? That would *really* embarrass your girlfriend."

Nick counted to ten in his head.

"I have no idea what you're talking about." Nick really wanted to tell him where to go, but he'd promised Jennifer he'd behave. He'd promised her that he wouldn't embarrass her ever.

"Oh, come, Dr. Rousseau. Your act of valor was well publicized, but others don't speak so highly of you. Your brother, for instance, called you reckless."

"You've talked to my brother?"

David smirked. "Once. He mentioned he had a reckless, thoughtless and careless brother. Isn't that why Dr. Marc Rousseau is in a chair, because your impulsiveness got the better of you and your brother ran in to clean up the mess?"

It was like a knife to the gut. David was baiting him. He wanted a fight and Nick knew then without a shadow of a doubt it had nothing to do with dissections or saving a man's life. Hell, it didn't even have anything to do with his *precious* research. It was Jennifer. Plain and simple.

David was jealous that he'd been with Jennifer, or, even more perturbing, David wanted Jennifer back, and if that was the case, there was no way in hell Nick was going to stand aside and allow that.

Nick froze and stared at David, his pulse thundering in his ears and anger threatening to overtake him. "Tread carefully."

"Is that a threat?"

"Take it how you want." Nick watched him and counted in his head, trying to keep himself in check, but the urge to knock the guy out was a battle he was losing.

"I'll have you fired for noncompliance."

"You think the board will fire me for saving a man's life? Because I don't think that will happen. I'm a damn good trauma surgeon and I'm done bandying words with you. If you know what's good for you, you'll stay out of my way, Dr. Morgan."

"Oh, of course you think your *precious* position here is safe. It's because you're sleeping with the head of trauma. Tell me, Rousseau, does it make you feel good about yourself and your failed career in the army to be doing your boss? Does it make you feel like a bigger man?"

Nick pulled back his fist and plowed it into David's face, knocking the surgeon out cold in the middle of the new trauma department.

It had been all he could do to contain his anger, but the man had kept pushing him. It had been bad enough the bastard had talked bad about his brother, but to say things about Jennifer... It had driven him over the edge. He'd managed to keep that reckless, unpredictable side of himself hidden and locked away for so long, but it was just like when he'd run out to save his friend from the IED explosion and when he'd smashed his hand into the window. He'd acted before he'd thought.

"Dammit," he cursed under his breath, shaking his hand, which stung, and then he realized everyone in the trauma department had stopped what they were doing. Everyone was looking at them, and as he turned around, he saw Jennifer standing there and behind her was a group of reporters, who were furiously taking pictures.

"Nick, how could you?" Jennifer wasn't blushing, but he could tell she felt mortified. She walked past him and knelt down beside David. "Someone get a stretcher."

Seeing her on the floor, tending to her ex, caused a pang of jealousy to flood through him and he didn't like feeling this way. He didn't like becoming this irresponsible person again.

"Jennifer, I—"

She held up her hand. "I don't want to hear it."

Two other doctors helped Dr. Morgan to his feet and got him on a stretcher, where he was moaning. Nick stood there, trying to get his anger in check.

"Take him to a private trauma room," Jennifer whispered to the other attendings.

"Jennifer, I can explain."

"Not now, Nick. Not now, and I think it's best you go home for the night." She couldn't look him in the eye as she moved past him and tried to usher the press out of the area.

Nick cursed under his breath and picked up the discarded chart, handing it to a nurse. "Have Dr. Harvey finish the operative report and inform the family of Mr. Berlin's progress."

"Yes, Dr. Rousseau." Even the nurse couldn't look him in the eyes as she took the chart. Nick glanced down at his fist. His knuckles were bloody and bruised, but that wasn't what hurt most.

He was ashamed he'd hurt Jennifer. Embarrassed

her and ruined something good. He ruined everything good in his life.

He was bad news and he had to get out of the hospital before he embarrassed her further. How could he expect to have any kind of life with Jennifer when every personal relationship he had was strained? When the people he loved ostracized him?

And he wanted Jennifer.

He loved her.

Nick was tired of being alone, but the only way he could face the future was to face the ghosts of his past, and he wasn't sure he was ready to do that, but he was going to try.

First, though, he had to make a phone call.

"Jennifer?" It was a pitiful moan.

Jennifer tried not to roll her eyes as David came to. There was a secret satisfaction seeing his face with a big red mark across his cheek. There were a few times she'd wanted to slug him; she just hadn't had the guts.

"Yes."

He smiled and reached out for her, but she didn't take his outstretched hand. She stepped back from him and crossed her arms.

"What's wrong?"

"I don't know why you're looking to me for comfort," Jennifer said. "Last time I checked, you'd married Rita after leaving me at the altar."

David sighed loudly. "Are you still on that? That was two years ago. Can you live and let live?"

"Do you want me to call your wife to come and comfort you?" She cocked her head. "Although I see you're not wearing your wedding ring."

His face turned red. "I took it off while I was doing surgery."

She didn't believe him. Not one bit. "Right."

"Fine, my marriage is over. It didn't last."

"That doesn't surprise me."

David sat up. "I was a fool to leave you. That's why I chose All Saints in Las Vegas. I've come to see if there's a chance for us."

When her heart had first been broken, Jennifer had often thought of this moment happening, but now she didn't want this. She didn't want David anymore. Maybe she never had.

All she wanted was Nick.

She'd told him the other night that she thought she was falling for him, but really she'd already fallen. She was in love with him.

"There isn't a chance for us, David. And I realize now how painfully we're not suited to each other. I'm sorry you chose All Saints on the foolish notion that I would fall back into your arms again, but I'm not interested. I'm here to do my job."

"It's because of that Dr. Rousseau fellow, isn't it?"

"Dr. Rousseau has nothing to do with my decision not to give us another chance."

David's lip curled. "Doesn't it? I saw the headlines. You romping around Las Vegas with him like some kind of tramp."

Jennifer took a deep breath. Now she was beginning to get an inkling of why Nick had clobbered him. "Going on a date doesn't make me a tramp. Cheating on a wife or a fiancée makes you a tramp and, David, you're a big one."

He rolled his eyes. "Did you just call me a whore?"

Jennifer grinned. "I believe I did."

"I made a mistake, coming here." David shook his head.

"You sure did. Now I want you to tell me what the heck happened. Why did Nick feel the need to punch you out in the middle of my trauma department?"

David sat up slowly, rubbing the side of his jaw. "He instigated it."

"I highly doubt it."

"Come on, Jennifer. If you only knew what kind of person he was—"

She held up her hand. "I don't care what kind of person he was before. Dr. Morgan, I'm going to recommend your program be removed from my trauma department."

"Dr. Ramsgate won't go for that. Do you know how much prestige I bring with me? I'm a cardiothoracic god."

Jennifer took a step closer and gave him the stare down, and from the wide-eyed expression on his face, she could tell it wasn't amusing him like it had amused Nick. It was having the desired effect.

"You're going to leave my hospital. You're going to do it peacefully and quietly. I don't care what *damn* excuse you use, but you're going to leave."

"Is that a threat?"

"Damn straight. I have papers proving how much I assisted in your 'solo' breakthrough research. I held off trying to put my name on it because I was hurt and embarrassed, but now I don't care anymore. I'm not embarrassed. I don't care how it'll affect my father's presidential campaign. If you don't want me raising a stink about stolen work, I suggest you find another place to continue your trial."

David paled. The threat had worked. She'd never in a million years do such a thing normally, but she would if it meant getting David out of her hospital. She didn't want to see him again. She was over him, way over, and she wasn't going to be ashamed about her past any longer.

"That's blackmail."

"Take it as you will." She smiled at him. "You have forty-eight hours to get out of my face."

She turned and left the room, shutting the door and drowning out the sounds of his curses. It would work, and if he went to the press or the board, she had the paperwork, the proof that she should be credited, and if there was one thing about David that she knew, he didn't like sharing the spotlight.

Jennifer knew her father wouldn't be pleased with her, or about the scene caused today, but she didn't care. His election wouldn't be hurt by it. Far from it, and maybe for once it would show Dr. Morgan in a bad light.

Yeah, the fight had mortified her, until she'd realized what it was about. Nick had been standing up for her honor and she'd dismissed him. The hurt on his face made her heart ache.

She never wanted to hurt Nick.

As soon as her shift was over she was going to make things right by him. She was going to tell him how she felt.

She was going to tell him she loved him.

She was going to open her heart one more time and take a risk, a chance on love. Even if it meant her heart would be broken again.

Living without love wasn't something she wanted.

She wanted so much more.

She wanted Nick.

Now she just had to break it to her father that there

would be some headlines about her and two surgeons fighting over her.

Jennifer smiled as she pulled out her phone and dialed.

Rufus just wagged his tail politely as Nick slammed the door behind him.

"Sorry, pal." Nick set his keys down next to the phone.

Call him.

Sweat broke across his brow as he thought of Marc. Of his family.

Call him.

He wanted to. He wanted to apologize and make things right, even if it fell on deaf ears.

He had to do this if he wanted to move on.

Talking to Marc would probably never ease the guilt, but it would give him closure and maybe then he could move on.

He picked up the phone and switched it on. The dial tone sounded loud. Too loud. He switched it off, cursing under his breath.

I can't do this.

Marc was better off without him. His family was better off without him. Jennifer was better off. And when he thought of Jennifer living without him, it tore at his heart.

That's not what he wanted.

If she could face David, he could face his own demons. Nick switched on the phone and, as if on autopilot, dialed the eleven digits he knew so well.

It rang twice and his pulse thundered in his ears.

"Hello?" the familiar voice answered. One he'd missed. Nick didn't say anything. He couldn't.

"Hello?" Marc sounded annoyed. "Who's there?"

It was now or never, and if he didn't do this, how could he ever be with Jennifer?

Quite simply, he couldn't.

"Who's there? I can hear you breathing."

"Marc, it's me. Nick."

There was silence on the other end and Nick couldn't help but wonder if he'd made a horrible mistake. Maybe their father had been right. Perhaps he should've kept away.

"Nick?" Marc didn't ask this question in anger, more like in shock with a hint of hope. "Is that really you?"

"Yeah," Nick said. "It's been a long time."

"I'll say. Where the heck have you been?"

"Nevada."

"Nevada? Why are you there? I thought you were going to come back to Chicago when your tour of duty was done."

"I wanted to give you space. I know that you blamed me for what happened to you."

There was silence again and muttered curses under his breath. "Who told you that?"

"Dad."

Now the cursing was louder. "I'm not mad at you, Nick."

Nick didn't believe him. How could he not be mad at him? "Marc, I paralyzed you."

"You didn't paralyze me, Nick. An IED explosion did."

"But it was my fault. I was reckless and my running out there to save someone cost you."

Marc sighed. "I know. I was ticked you lived life so recklessly. I won't deny that. I thought about it over and over again when I realized I'd never walk again, but I didn't have to run after you. That was me. Not you."

A surge of emotions washed through Nick and he scrubbed a hand over his face. "So you're really not mad?"

"No, you idiot," Marc said, with a slight laugh. "I just didn't know where you went after your tour of duty ended and was working through stuff of my own."

Nick chuckled. "I've been a fool."

"Yeah, we both have been."

Nick didn't say anything else, but his heart was very full. For the first time in a long time he felt whole again. He could finally move forward. There were countless roads of opportunity.

"So," Marc said, breaking the silence. "You're in Vegas?"

"I am."

"Seen any good shows?"

Nick laughed and launched into an easy conversation with his brother, as if they'd never been parted. All that time when he'd thought he'd never see his brother again, when he'd felt less than worthless was washed away. He'd been given a clean slate, a second chance. At everything.

And this time he wasn't going to blow it.

CHAPTER FIFTEEN

JENNIFER STOOD IN the middle of the new trauma department. She hadn't seen Nick in two days. After he'd gone home, he'd taken personal leave for a few days. She'd gone by his place, but no one had been home. Even Rufus was gone and she knew he'd retreated up to Lake Tahoe.

He'd needed space.

She just hoped she hadn't blown her chances with him.

When he was gone, she missed him.

She missed the joking, the stolen looks and the understanding. He got her like no one had ever done.

He even let her tell him stupid knock-knock jokes.

David had left the hospital, claiming that a new position had come up at Boston Mercy and he'd accepted. Dr. Ramsgate had been disappointed, and even though the press had splashed the quarrel across the front pages, Jennifer had smoothed it over.

Dr. Harvey and she had explained the reason for the fight and the board was on Nick's side. He'd done all that was required of him and Dr. Morgan hadn't been available to do the surgery. The utmost importance was the patient's life.

The transition to the new trauma department had

gone smoothly and the old trauma wing was being turned into a walk-in clinic with a hefty pro-bono grant from Senator Mills.

Everything was falling into place. Except Nick.

She sighed and started to walk over to the old trauma department, where she was overseeing plans to turn it into the walk-in clinic, and as she walked down the once bustling hallway she was surprised to see a man in dark denim and leather leaning against the wall.

It took her a moment to realize she was staring at Nick in his street clothes.

"Do you have a moment?" he asked.

"Of course."

"Good, let's go outside." Nick turned and walked to the old ER doors, pushing them open, and Jennifer followed him outside, squinting as her eyes adjusted to the bright sunshine.

"Working a night shift?" he asked.

"Yes," she said, and then chuckled. "I've been pulling a lot of all-nighters the last couple of days."

Nick nodded and they took a seat on a park bench overlooking the strip. "Look, I wanted to say I'm sorry about what happened. I didn't mean to humiliate you in front of the press like that."

"There's no need to apologize—"

"No, let me finish."

She nodded. "Okay."

Nick scrubbed his hands over his face. "I didn't ever want to hurt you. My whole life I've seemed to screw up relationships with the people I care about and you walked back into my life and…"

Jennifer reached out and touched his leg. "I get it."

Nick nodded. "You do. You do get me. You see me."

"I do," she whispered. "Just like you see me."

He shook his head. "Only I don't. You asked me not to humiliate you, you told me how terrified you were of the press, and then I punch out that…well, and I punched out David."

"I know." She smiled.

Nick winced. "Right, you were there."

"I was and it doesn't matter."

"It does, because I said I would never humiliate you and I did just that."

"You didn't humiliate me. You gave me freedom."

Nick smiled. "I love you, Jennifer."

Her heart leapt, hearing the words. It was hard to believe and if it wasn't for the fact the sun was beating down on her and making her sweat, she might've believed she was dreaming. This was the last thing she'd been expecting from him. "You love me?"

Nick nodded. "I didn't think I could ever love someone as much as I love you. I didn't think I deserved to love someone. Not when I couldn't even forgive or love myself."

"Oh, Nick. You didn't paralyze Marc. An IED did."

"I did. He ran after me. Everyone told me not to go out there and rescue my comrade but I did anyway and Marc…he was coming to my rescue like always and paid the price I should've paid."

Jennifer slid closer to him. "It wasn't your fault. You did a heroic thing, don't blame yourself."

"I couldn't forgive myself until I had Marc's forgiveness and I was trying to give him distance. Trying to fade from his life, but that wasn't right. So I called him."

"And what did he say?"

"He reamed me out for not calling him sooner." Nick smiled. "We worked it out. I think, in time, I'll have my brother back. It's going to take some healing, but...yeah."

Jennifer squeezed his knee. "I'm so happy for you."

"As for David, I'll try to work with him. I swear there will be no more fights in the trauma department."

"Don't worry about Dr. Morgan. He's gone."

Nick was confused. "How?"

"I blackmailed him." She laughed when she saw his wide-eyed expression.

"What do you mean, you blackmailed him? You? Blackmailed him?"

"Is that so hard to believe?" she teased.

"It is, actually. That's kind of scary. How?"

"I threatened to sue him for stealing my part of his precious research if he didn't leave the hospital, and he wasn't to tell anyone that I coerced him into leaving or that it was your fault. I have all the paperwork to prove the theft. Well, I did. He took it, just to make sure I didn't go back on my word."

Nick chuckled. "I can't believe you did that. That's... Wow."

"Changing your mind about me?" She winked.

"Never. So why did he come here?"

"He didn't come here for research. He came here to try and get back together with me."

"I thought so." Nick went very quiet.

"I turned him down. I don't want to get back together with David. I was blind last time. I thought I was in love, but it wasn't love. I've never loved him. The man I love is you, Nick."

"What...what did you say?"

"I said I love you, too. I'm not just falling for you. I already fell for you. Long ago, probably when you put up with my stupid joke."

He beamed, but then the smile disappeared. "What about your father? I'm not exactly his idea of a good choice."

"I don't care. He never approved of anyone except David, and look how that turned out." Jennifer snorted. "My dad is not the best judge of men."

"And you are?" Nick teased.

She smiled and moved toward him, her heart racing. "I'd like to think so."

An answering smile spread across his face. "Really?"

"I do. I came here to escape my ghosts and swore that I would never ever get involved with another surgeon, but then you were here and… I held onto the memory of you for so long. That one perfect night. I didn't think it could get any better and I was scared to try, but you worked your way in and I'm so glad you did."

Nick reached out and pulled her against him, kissing her, and she wished they weren't sitting on a park bench out in front of a hospital. She wanted to seal the deal skin on skin, in his bed or her bed. She didn't care which.

All she wanted was Nick, and she was willing to risk her heart again to have that.

"I love you, Jennifer. I do." Nick ran his thumbs over her cheeks, his hazel eyes twinkling. "I love you so much."

Jennifer stroked his cheek. "I'm willing to try again, Nick, and I'm willing to try with you. Just don't break my heart or I'll slug you."

Nick grinned. "Deal." He pulled her back into a kiss that melted her into a pile of goo and she didn't give a damn that someone might be lurking in the bushes, taking pictures.

She'd found love. Real love, and this time there would be no running away.

This time, she was never going to let him go.

EPILOGUE

One year later

JENNIFER WANDERED OUT of Nick's cabin, which had been updated to include a more modern bathroom. As she walked across the deck, Rufus raised his head and wagged his tail at her approach. She reached down and gave him a pet.

The sun was setting over the lake and it reminded her of her first night here.

Except now they didn't have to rush home the next day—they had the week off, and this time she had a toothbrush and a change of clothes.

Her father's campaign had been unsuccessful and he'd finally taken it as a sign to retire from the world of politics. He'd bought a ranch again, just as a hobby farm, outside Carson City, where they raised horses this time instead of dust bunnies and failed crops.

Though there was talk her father was going to run for mayor of Carson City again, but, then, who knew with him? Her father liked the limelight.

She took a sip of wine and sighed happily. She loved Tahoe and she loved it that this was just her and Nick's spot. No one else came up here, well, except Rufus.

She just wished Nick would get back here so they

could enjoy this sunset together. He'd gone to town over two hours ago and he hadn't told her why.

"He's a dead man, you know that, right?" she said to Rufus. Rufus responded with a happy pant and then got up and trotted across the deck. "Where are you go…?" She trailed off when she realized Nick was standing in the doorway, wearing his old uniform.

"Did you reenlist or something?"

"No, I just thought that I would do what I'm about to do right. I thought I'd wear what I was wearing that first night I saw you."

Jennifer paused. "Wait. What?"

Nick chuckled and walked over to meet her. He looked so damn fine in that uniform. She'd forgotten how good he looked. And then he got down on one knee and her own knees buckled.

"What're you doing?"

Nick smiled, his hazel eyes twinkling. "I think it's pretty obvious. Jennifer, will you marry me?" And then he held out a ring.

She didn't even have to think. She knew. "Yes."

He grinned and stood up, slipping the ring on her finger and then pulling her close. "Good. I didn't want to have to lock you up here until you agreed."

"You're a dingbat." She glanced down at her hand. "You know my father will want to plan the wedding. Some big lavish affair."

Nick shrugged. "If that's what you want."

"No, I don't. How about we get married today?"

"What?"

"We're in Tahoe. In Nevada. Let's do it."

Nick shook his head. "My brother will say it's irresponsible."

"I doubt that."

Jennifer grinned at the look of shock on Nick's face when he turned round to see his brother Marc wheeling himself onto the deck. His girlfriend, Anne, followed him, both of them grinning.

"What are you doing here?" Nick asked in disbelief, walking over to his brother to take his hand.

"Your…well, I guess your fiancée flew us down from Chicago as a surprise." Marc winked at Jennifer.

Nick turned back. "You flew them down?"

Jennifer shrugged. "You two talk on the phone, but you know doctors and their work schedules—everyone is too busy all the time. So I arranged it."

Nick kissed her quickly. "Thank you."

"You've got quite a woman there. Don't screw this up," Marc teased.

Nick laughed. "I won't. I swear."

"So? Do we go get married now or wait until the morning?" Jennifer said.

"You're serious? I thought you were kidding."

Nick kissed her, passionately, just like he had that first time, and it made her forget everything, except taking him upstairs to their bed, but they couldn't do that with their guests there.

Suddenly getting married right at this moment didn't seem like such a good idea. The only thought she had in her mind now was getting to know her new family. The wedding chapel would be there tomorrow.

"No, we'll wait until tomorrow. That's the responsible thing," Jennifer conceded. "How about we all have a nice dinner and some wine?"

"Sounds good to me!" Anne said. "Come on, Marc, let's finish unpacking."

Marc and Anne headed back into the cabin.

"I can't believe you brought him here," Nick said in disbelief.

"Think of it as an engagement gift." She kissed him again. "I love you and if you ever hurt me, I'll fire you!"

Nick laughed and then picked her up. "You're the boss."

* * * * *

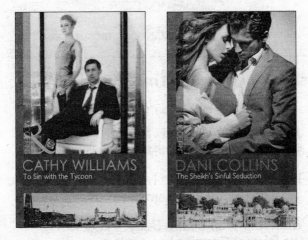

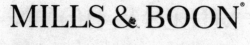

MILLS & BOON®

MEDICAL
ROMANCE™

THE ULTIMATE IN ROMANTIC MEDICAL DRAMA

A sneak peek at next month's titles…

In stores from 3rd April 2015:

- **Just One Night?** – Carol Marinelli
  and **Meant-To-Be Family** – Marion Lennox

- **The Soldier She Could Never Forget** – Tina Beckett
  and **The Doctor's Redemption** – Susan Carlisle

- **Wanted: Parents for a Baby!** – Laura Iding
- **His Perfect Bride?** – Louisa Heaton

Available at WHSmith, Tesco, Asda, Eason, Amazon and Apple

Just can't wait?
Buy our books online a month before they hit the shops!
visit www.millsandboon.co.uk

These books are also available in eBook format!